Hereville

How Mirka Got Her Sword

Barry Deutsch

Colors by Jake Richmond

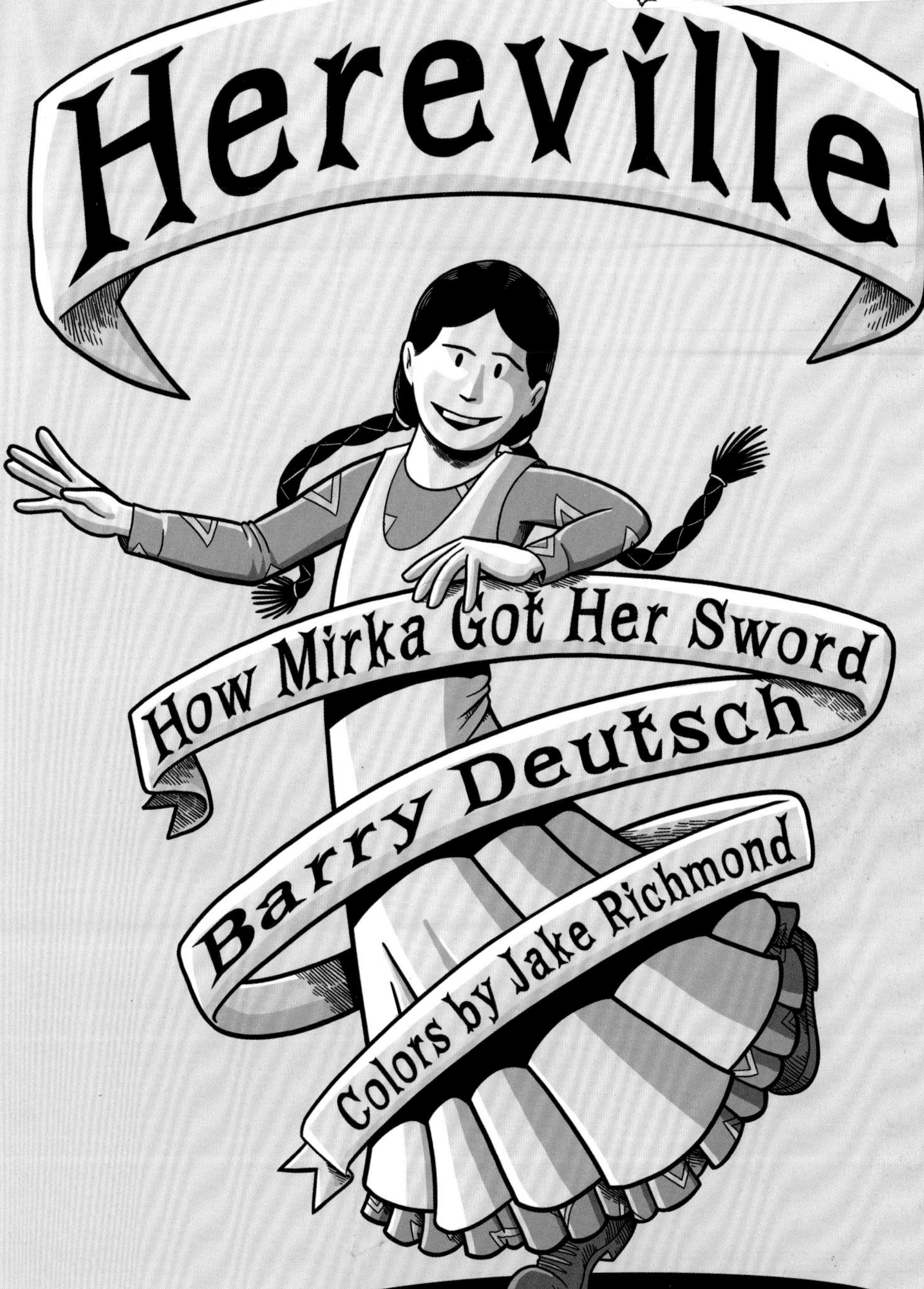

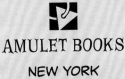

AMULET BOOKS

NEW YORK

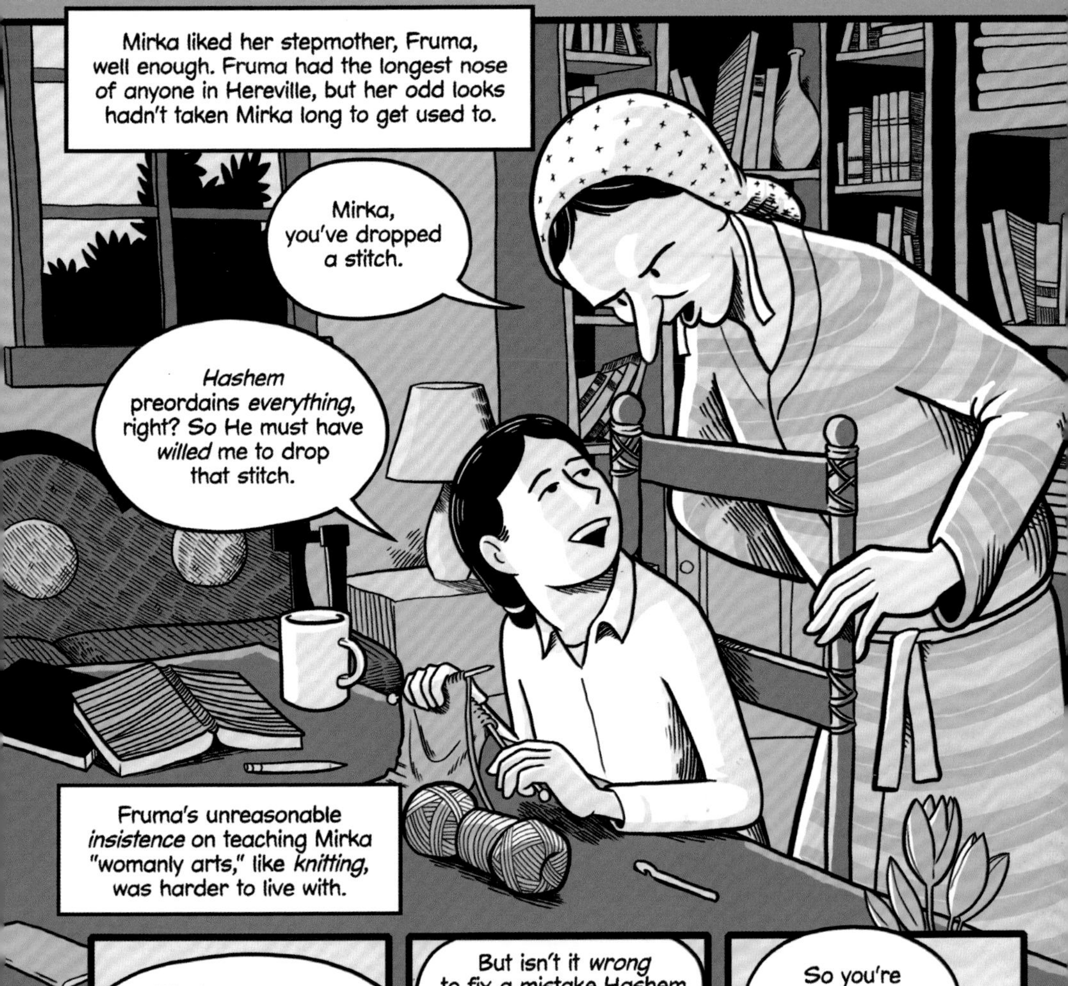
Mirka liked her stepmother, Fruma, well enough. Fruma had the longest nose of anyone in Hereville, but her odd looks hadn't taken Mirka long to get used to.
Mirka, you've dropped a stitch.
Hashem preordains *everything*, right? So He must have *willed* me to drop that stitch.
Fruma's unreasonable *insistence* on teaching Mirka "womanly arts," like *knitting*, was harder to live with.
Whatever you say. Don't *keep* knitting — use the crochet hook and *fix* it.
But isn't it *wrong* to fix a mistake Hashem preordained?
Maybe Hashem also preordained you *fixing* it.
So you're saying Hashem can't make up His mind?

Hashem: God

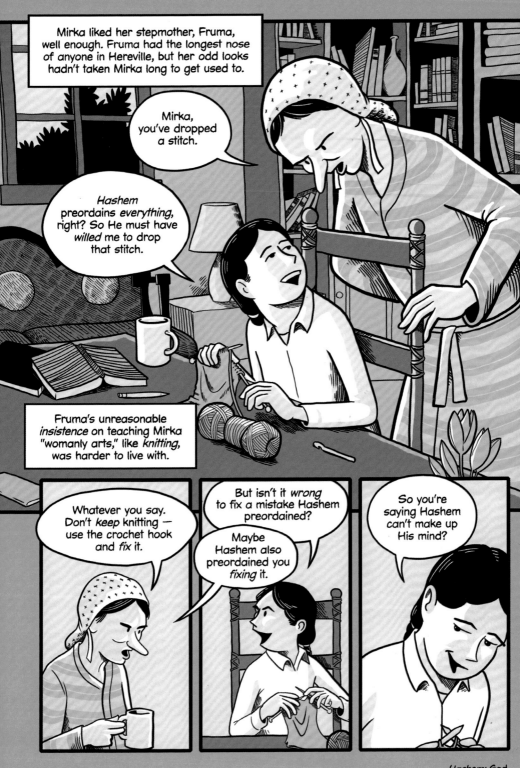

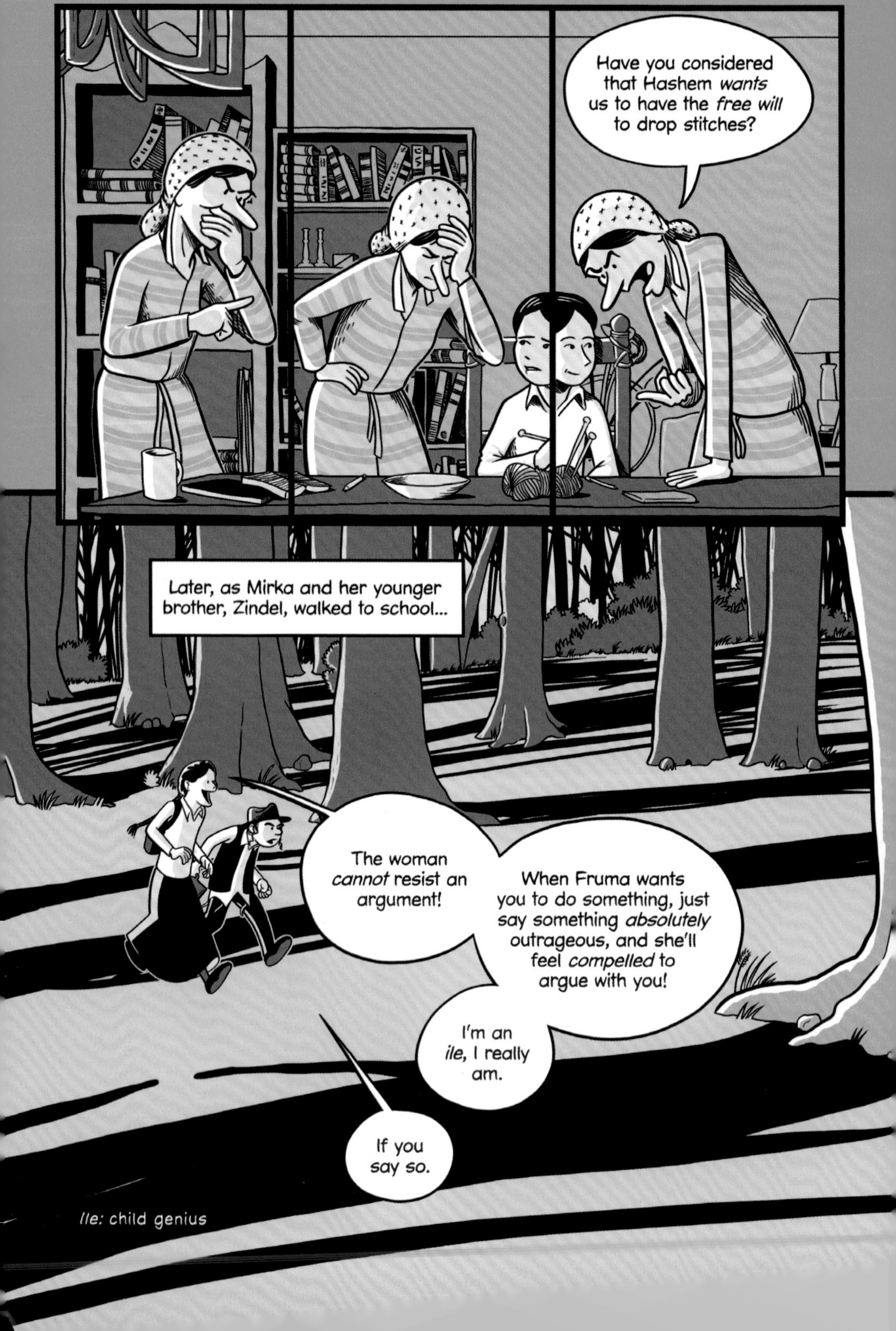
Have you considered that Hashem *wants* us to have the *free will* to drop stitches?
Later, as Mirka and her younger brother, Zindel, walked to school...
The woman *cannot* resist an argument!
When Fruma wants you to do something, just say something *absolutely* outrageous, and she'll feel *compelled* to argue with you!
I'm an *ile*, I really am.
If you say so.
Ile: child genius

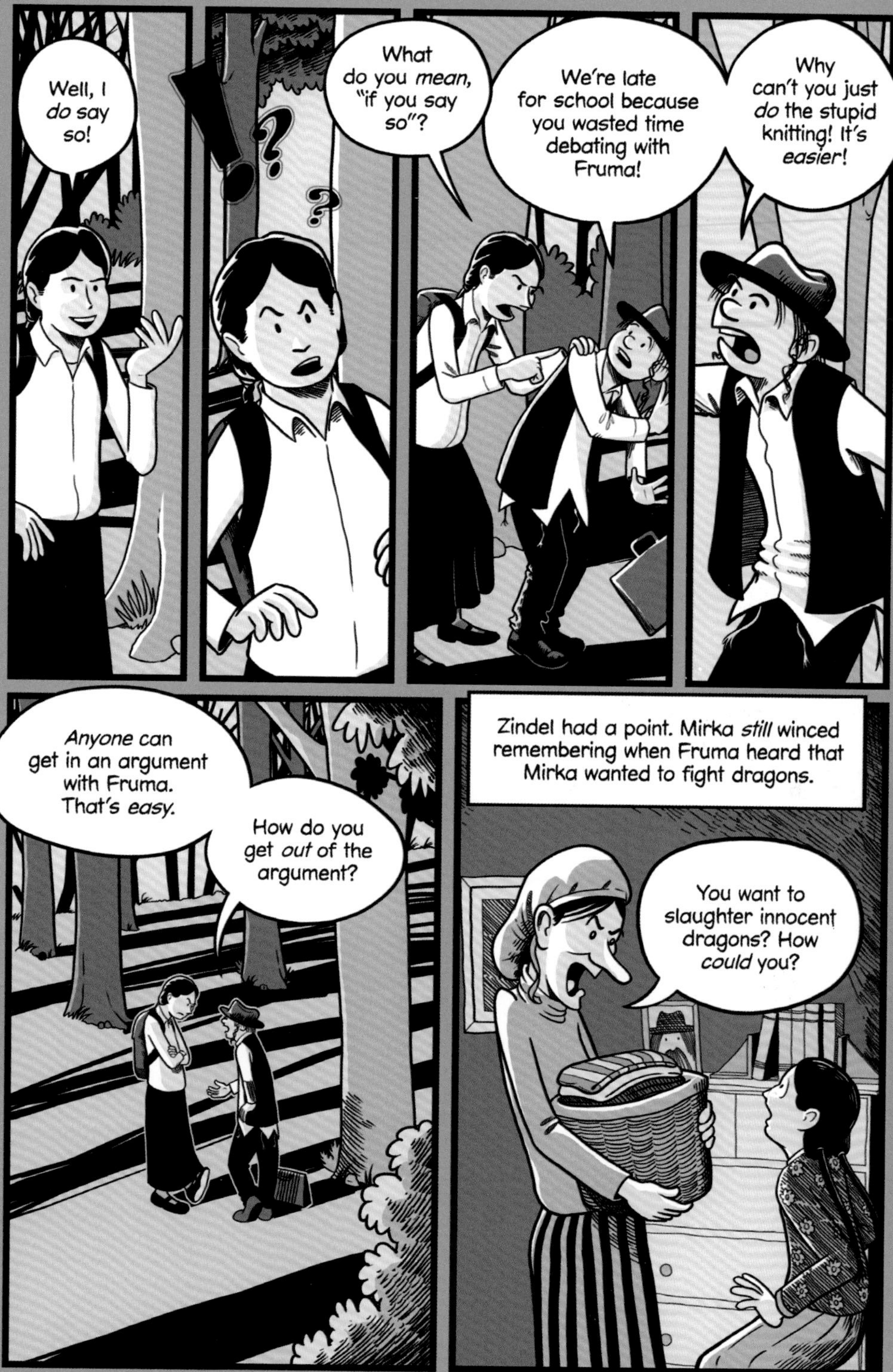
Well, I *do* say so!
What do you *mean,* "if you say so"?
We're late for school because you wasted time debating with Fruma!
Why can't you just *do* the stupid knitting! It's *easier*!
Anyone can get in an argument with Fruma. That's *easy.*
How do you get *out* of the argument?
Zindel had a point. Mirka *still* winced remembering when Fruma heard that Mirka wanted to fight dragons.
You want to slaughter innocent dragons? How *could* you?

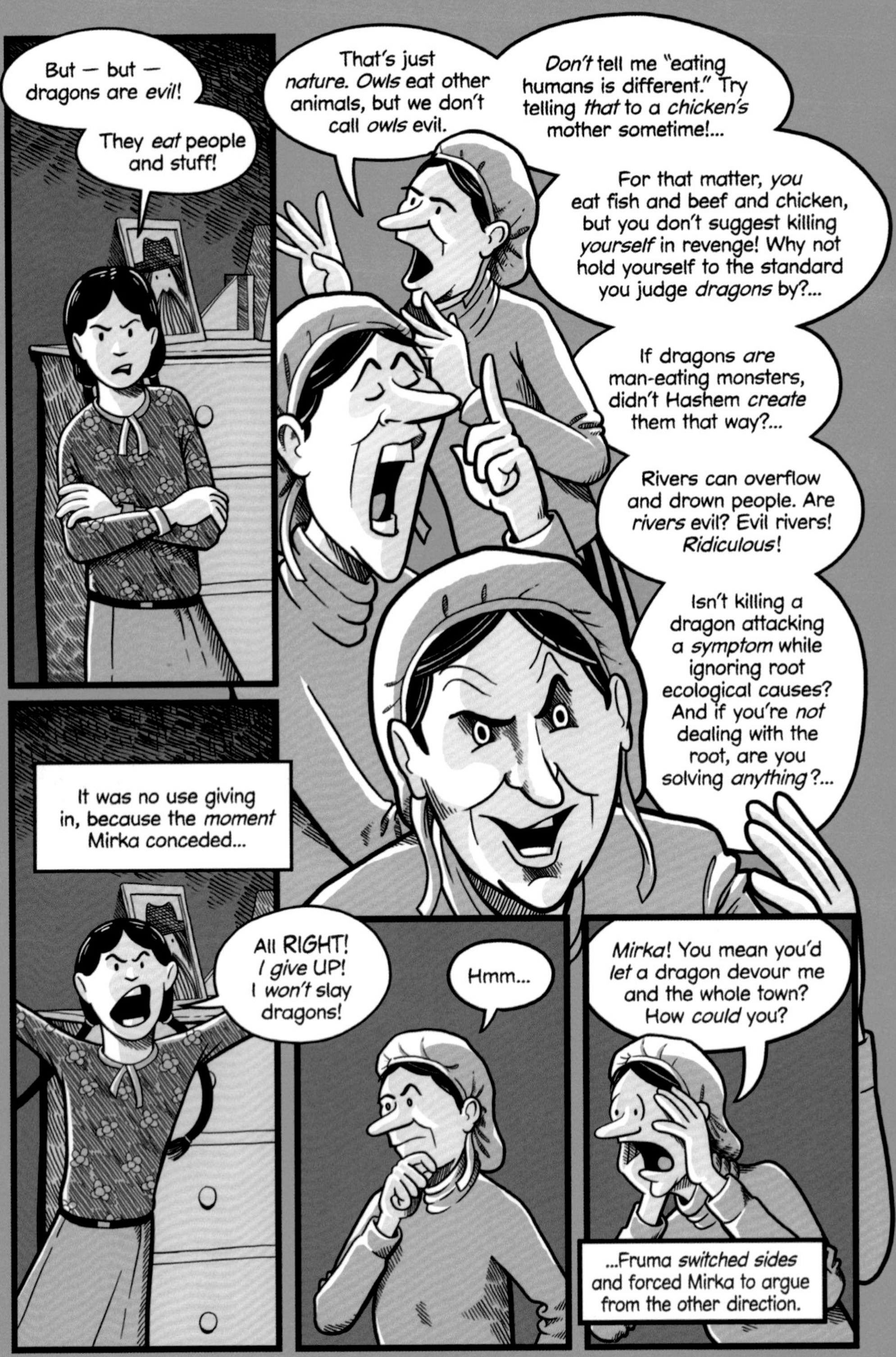
But — but — dragons are *evil*!
They *eat* people and stuff!
That's just *nature. Owls* eat other animals, but we don't call *owls* evil.
Don't tell me "eating humans is different." Try telling *that* to a *chicken's* mother sometime!...
For that matter, *you* eat fish and beef and chicken, but you don't suggest killing *yourself* in revenge! Why not hold yourself to the standard you judge *dragons* by?...
If dragons *are* man-eating monsters, didn't Hashem *create* them that way?...
Rivers can overflow and drown people. Are *rivers* evil? Evil rivers! *Ridiculous*!
Isn't killing a dragon attacking a *symptom* while ignoring root ecological causes? And if you're *not* dealing with the root, are you solving *anything*?...
It was no use giving in, because the *moment* Mirka conceded...
All RIGHT! *I give* UP! I *won't* slay dragons!
Hmm...
Mirka! You mean you'd *let* a dragon devour me and the whole town? How *could* you?
...Fruma *switched sides* and forced Mirka to argue from the other direction.

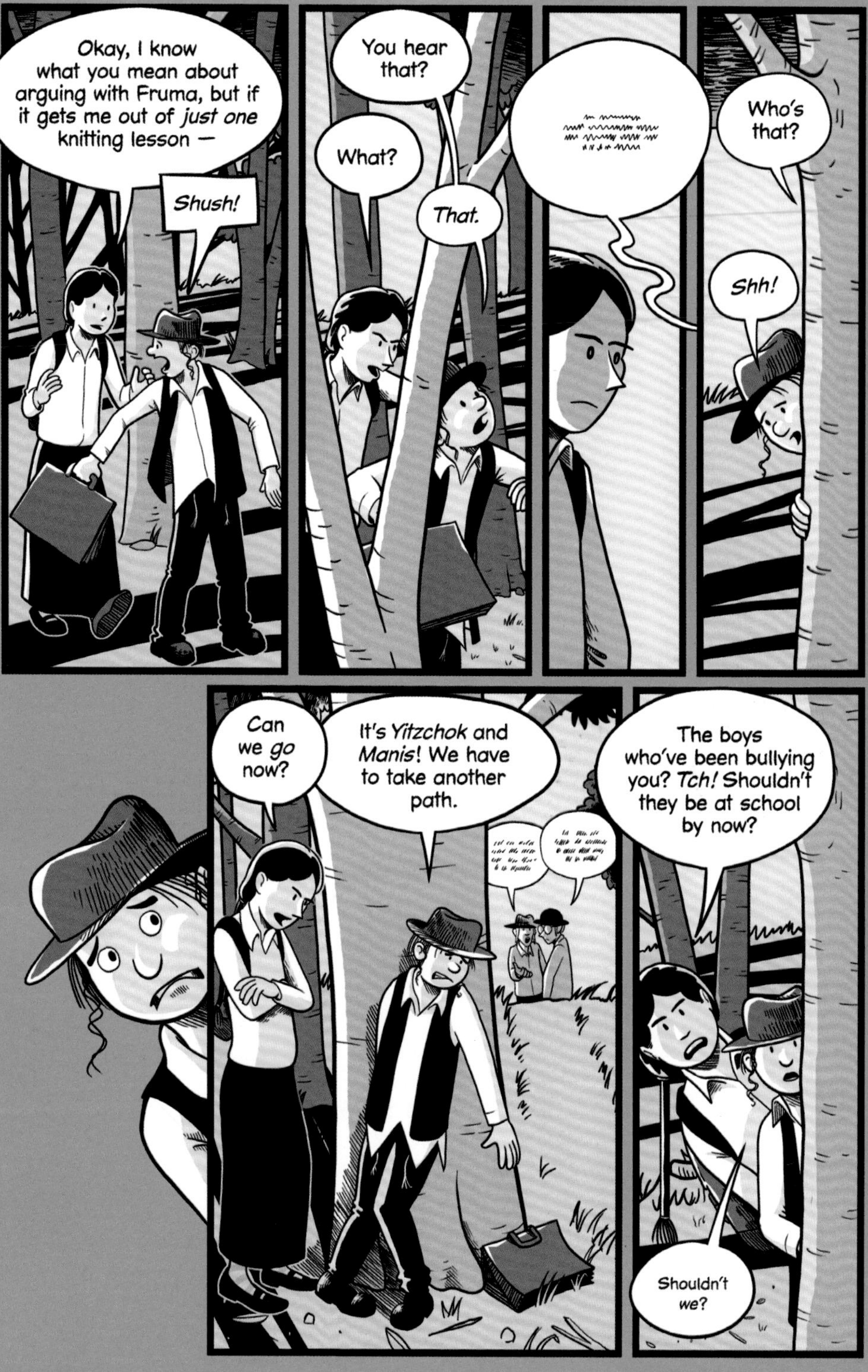
Okay, I know what you mean about arguing with Fruma, but if it gets me out of *just one* knitting lesson —
Shush!
You hear that?
What?
That.
Who's that?
Shh!
Can we *go* now?
It's *Yitzchok* and *Manis*! We have to take another path.
The boys who've been bullying you? *Tch!* Shouldn't they be at school by now?
Shouldn't we?

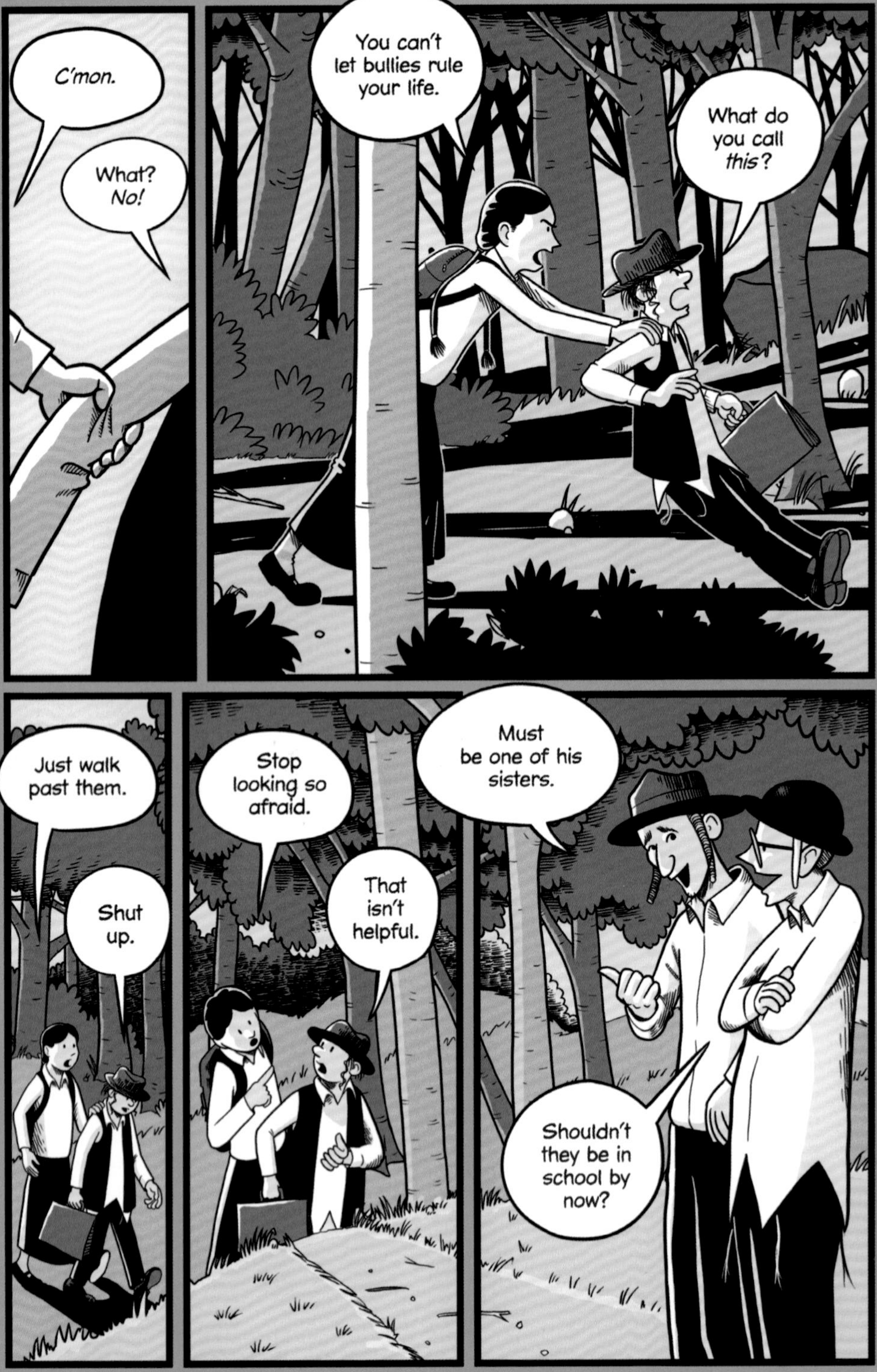
C'mon.
What? *No!*
You can't let bullies rule your life.
What do you call *this*?
Just walk past them.
Shut up.
Stop looking so afraid.
That isn't helpful.
Must be one of his sisters.
Shouldn't they be in school by now?

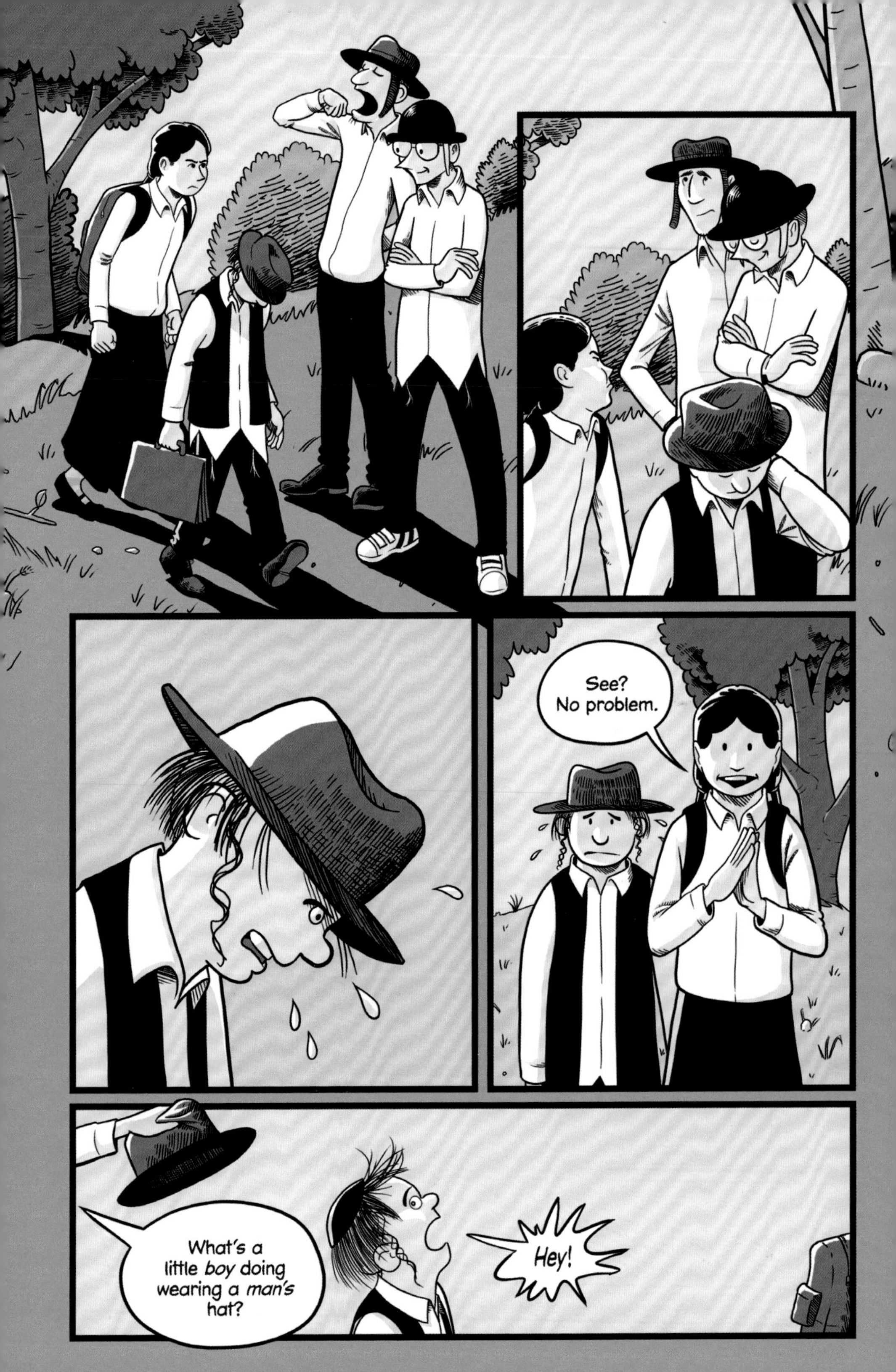
See?
No problem.
What's a little *boy* doing wearing a *man's* hat?
Hey!

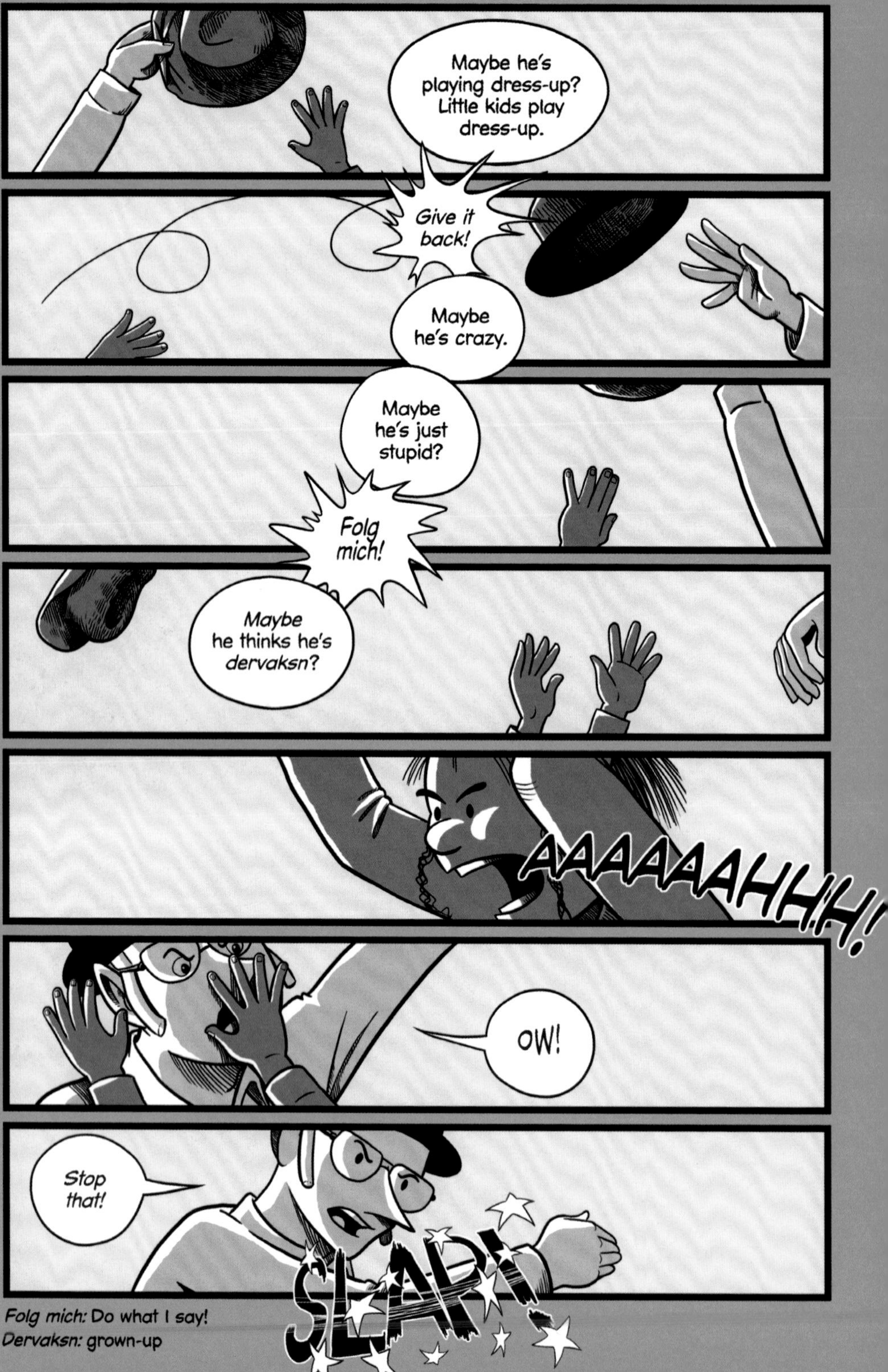
Maybe he's playing dress-up? Little kids play dress-up.
Give it back!
Maybe he's crazy.
Maybe he's just stupid?
Folg mich!
Maybe he thinks he's *dervaksn*?
AAAAAAHHHH!
OW!
Stop that!
SLAP!

Folg mich: Do what I say!
Dervaksn: grown-up

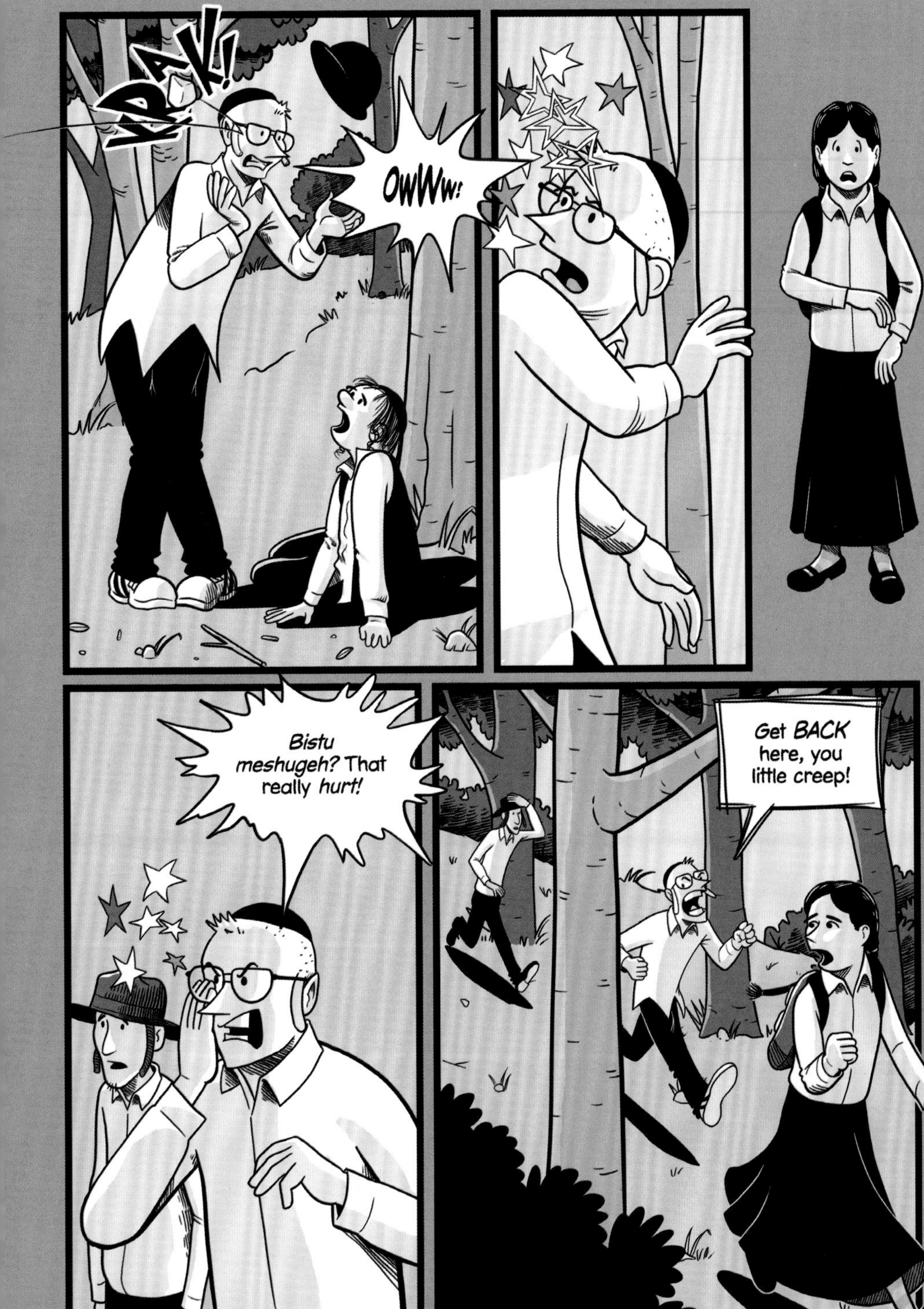
KRAK!
OWWW!
Bistu meshugeh? That really hurt!
Get BACK here, you little creep!

Bistu meshugeh: Are you crazy?

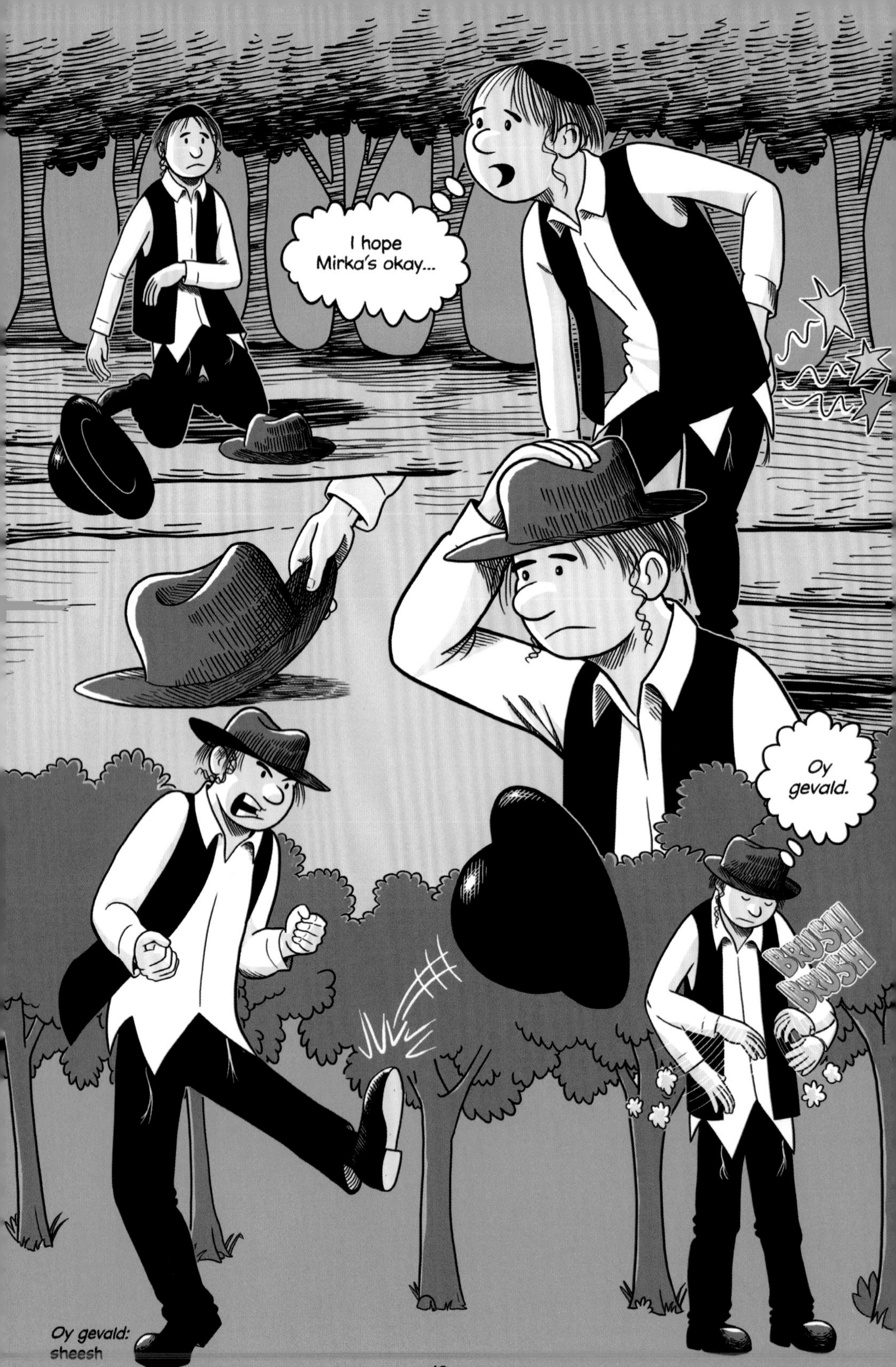

I hope Mirka's okay...
Oy gevald.
BRUSH
BRUSH

Oy gevald: sheesh

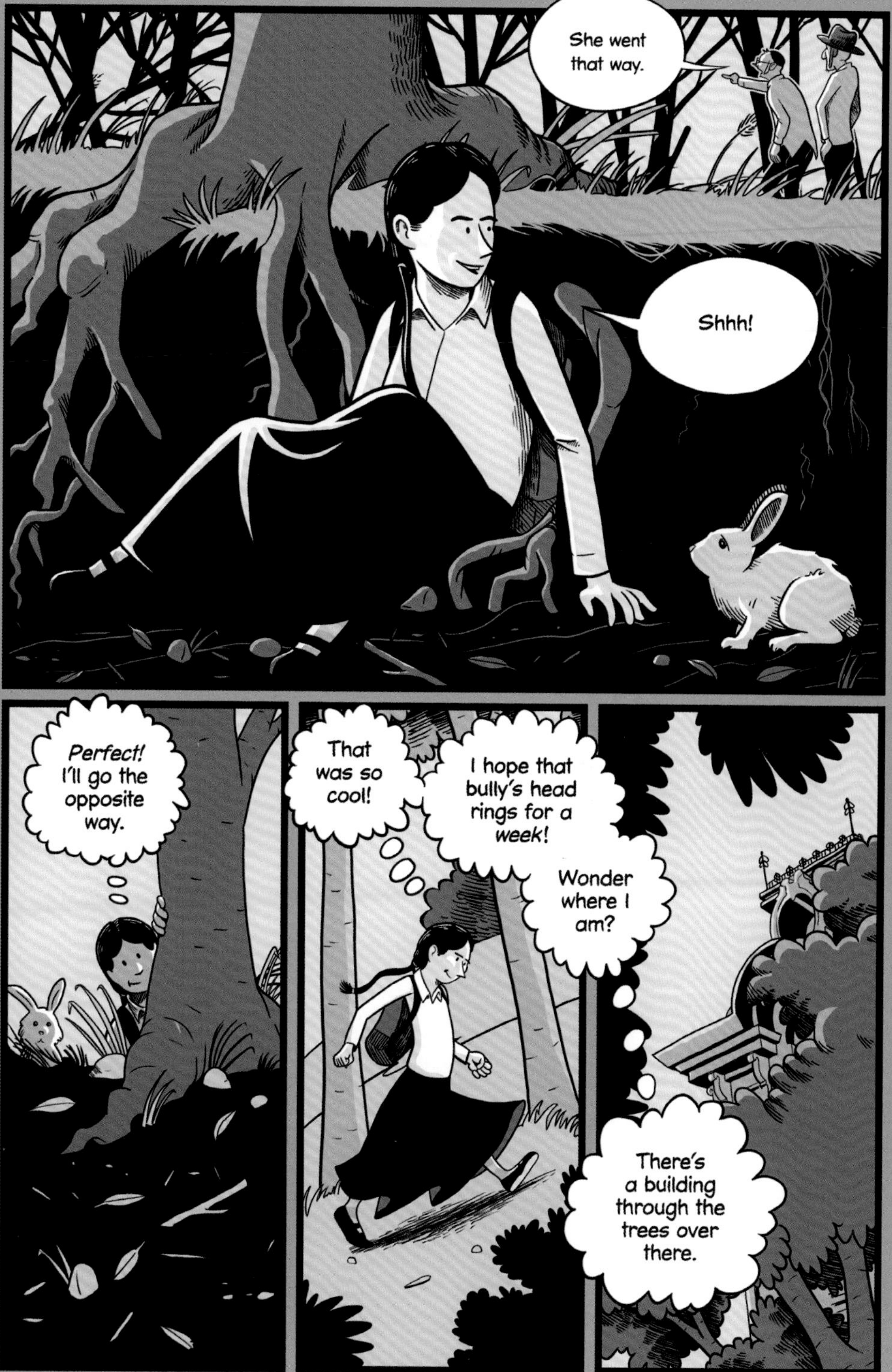
She went that way.
Shhh!
Perfect! I'll go the opposite way.
That was so cool!
I hope that bully's head rings for a *week*!
Wonder where I am?
There's a building through the trees over there.

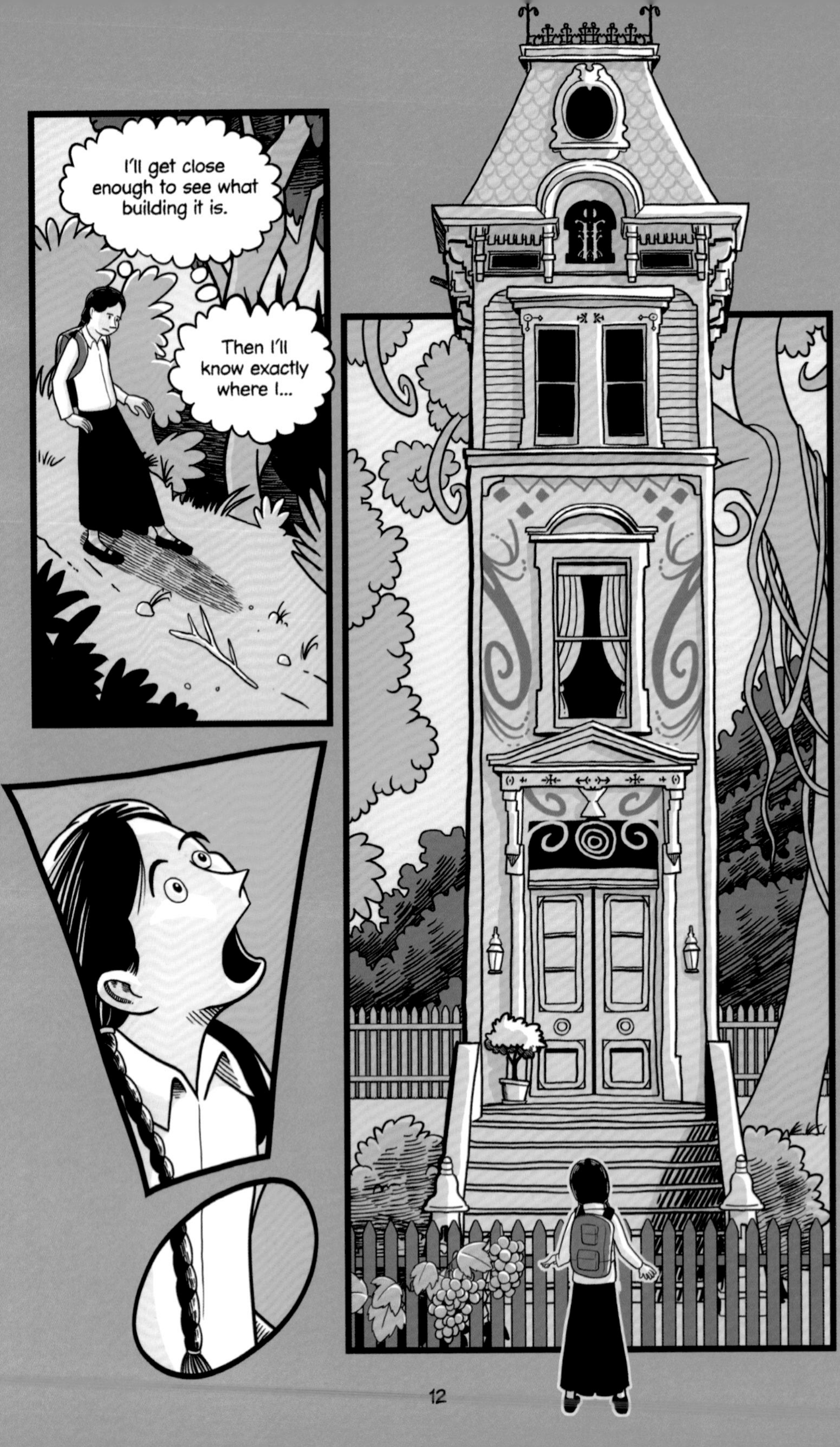
I'll get close enough to see what building it is.
Then I'll know exactly where I...

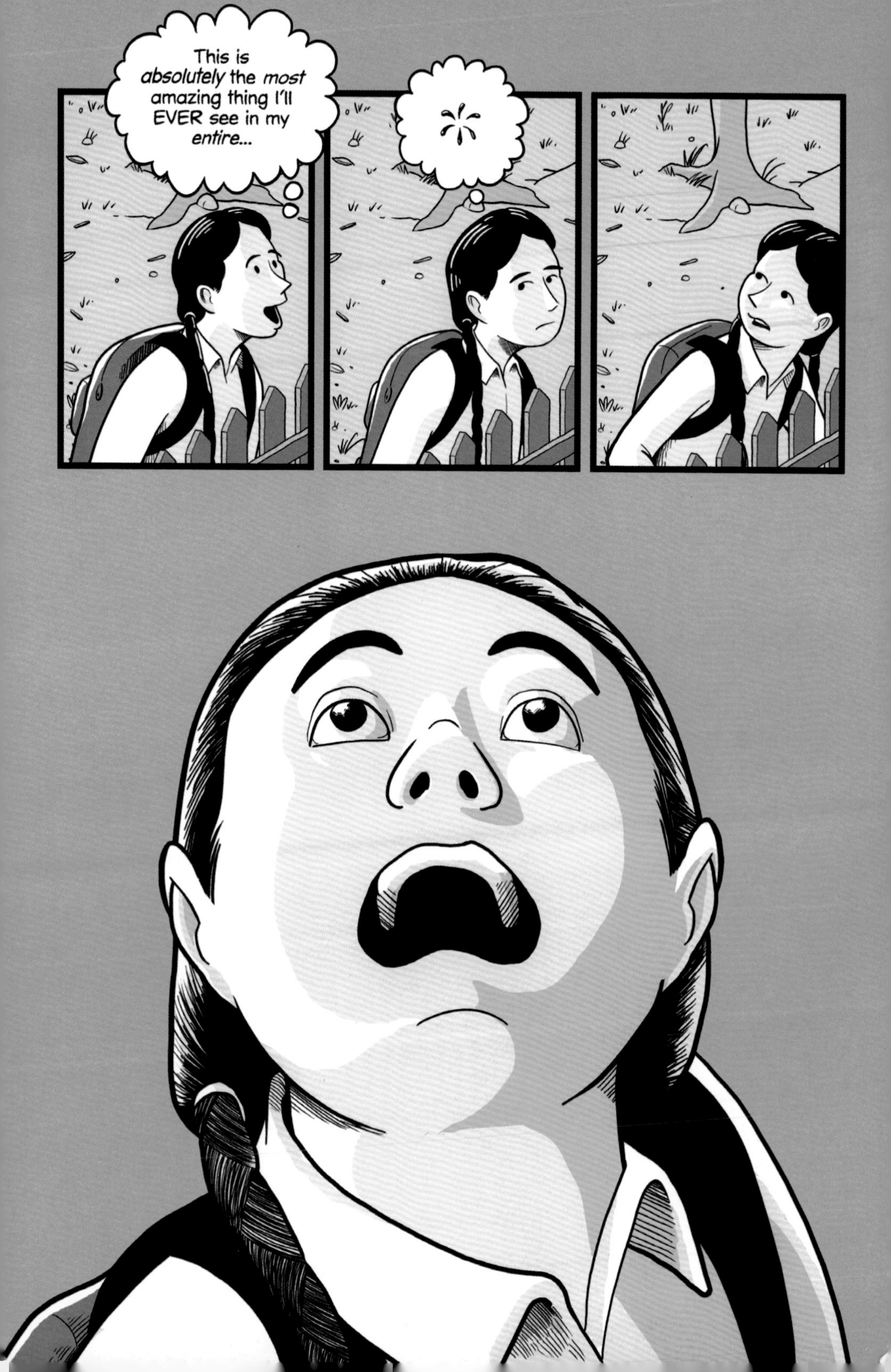
This is absolutely the most amazing thing I'll EVER see in my entire...

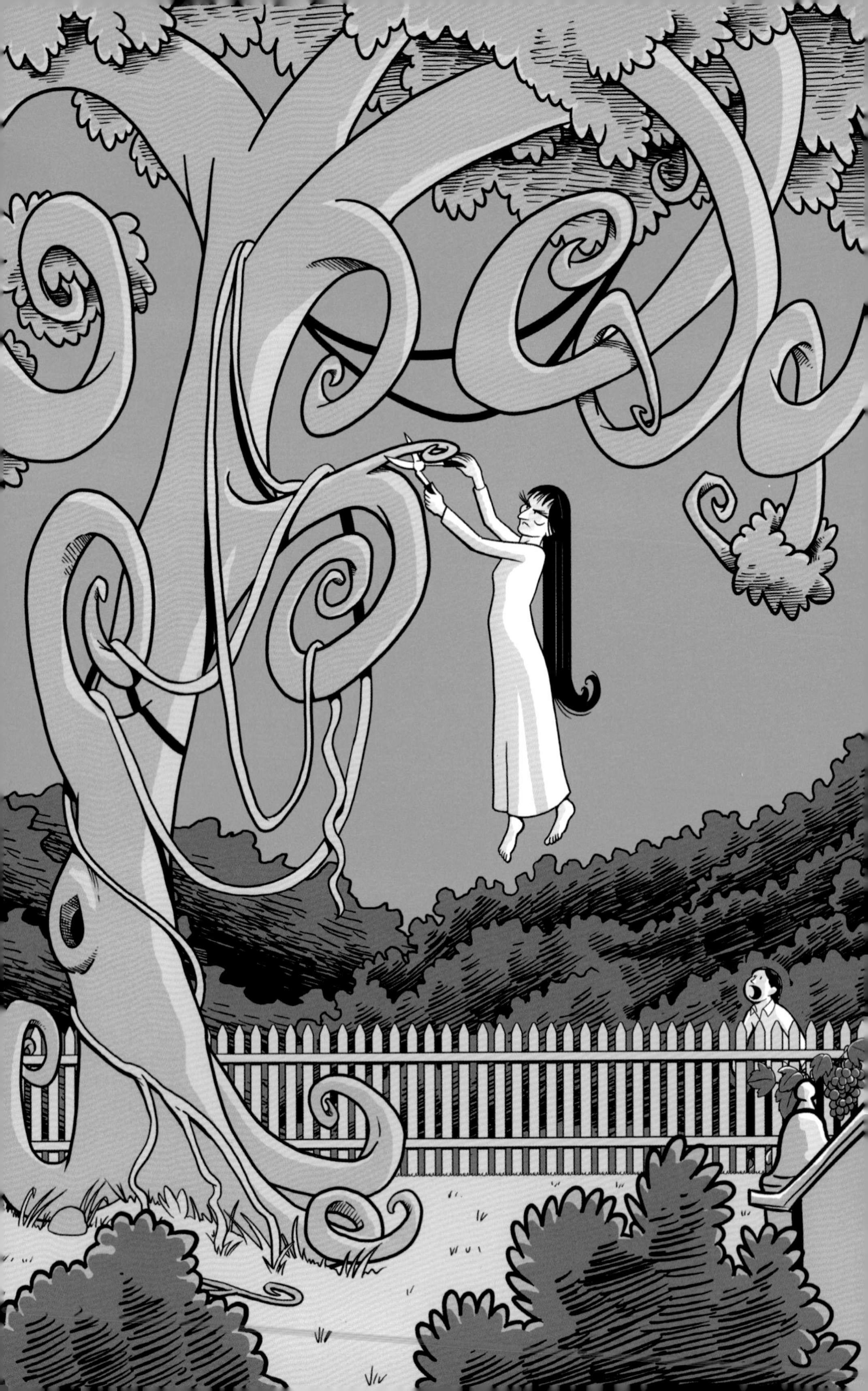

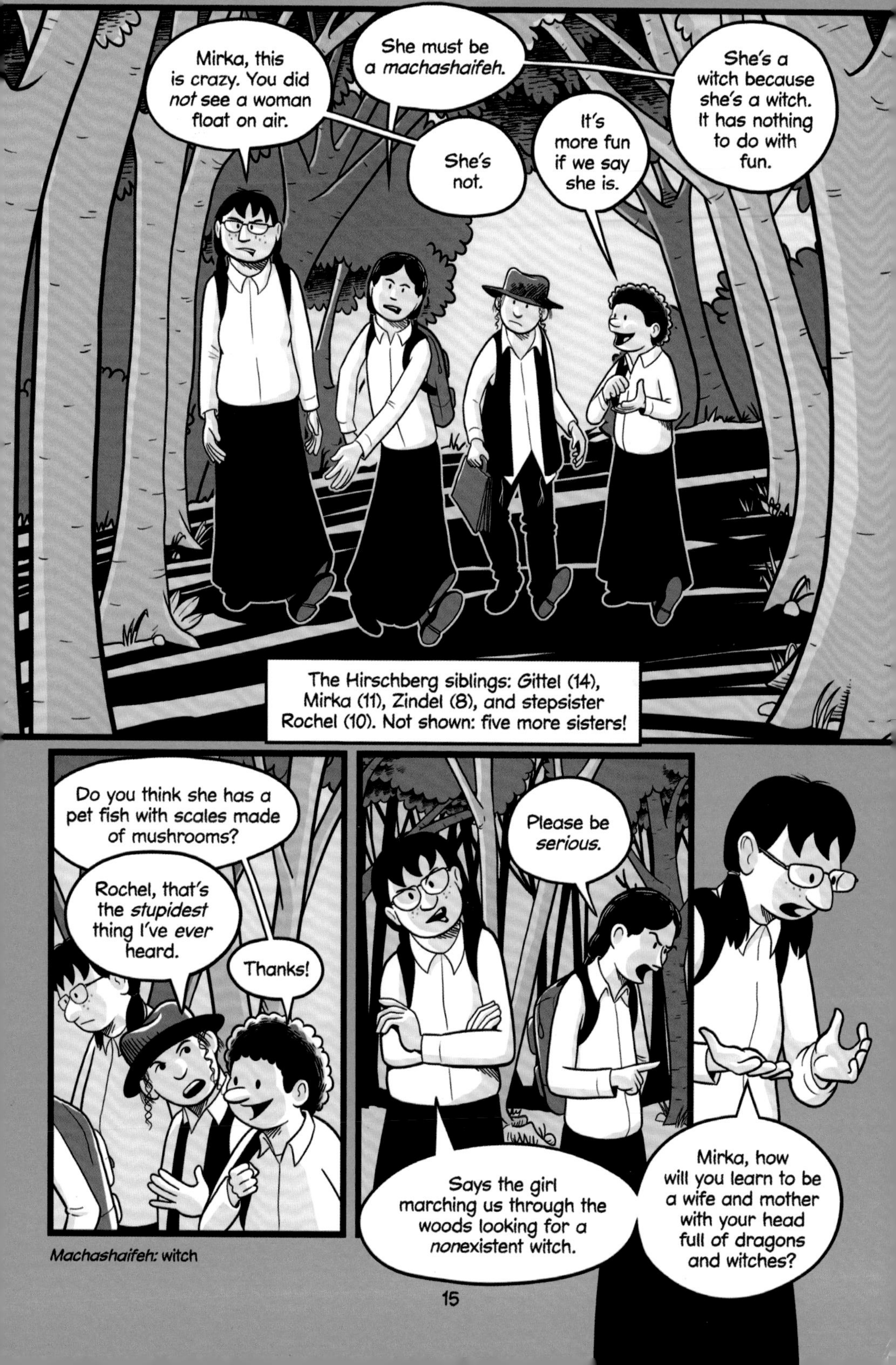

Mirka, this is crazy. You did *not* see a woman float on air.
She must be a *machashaifeh.*
She's not.
It's more fun if we say she is.
She's a witch because she's a witch. It has nothing to do with fun.
The Hirschberg siblings: Gittel (14), Mirka (11), Zindel (8), and stepsister Rochel (10). Not shown: five more sisters!
Do you think she has a pet fish with scales made of mushrooms?
Rochel, that's the *stupidest* thing I've *ever* heard.
Thanks!
Please be *serious.*
Says the girl marching us through the woods looking for a *non*existent witch.
Mirka, how will you learn to be a wife and mother with your head full of dragons and witches?

Machashaifeh: witch

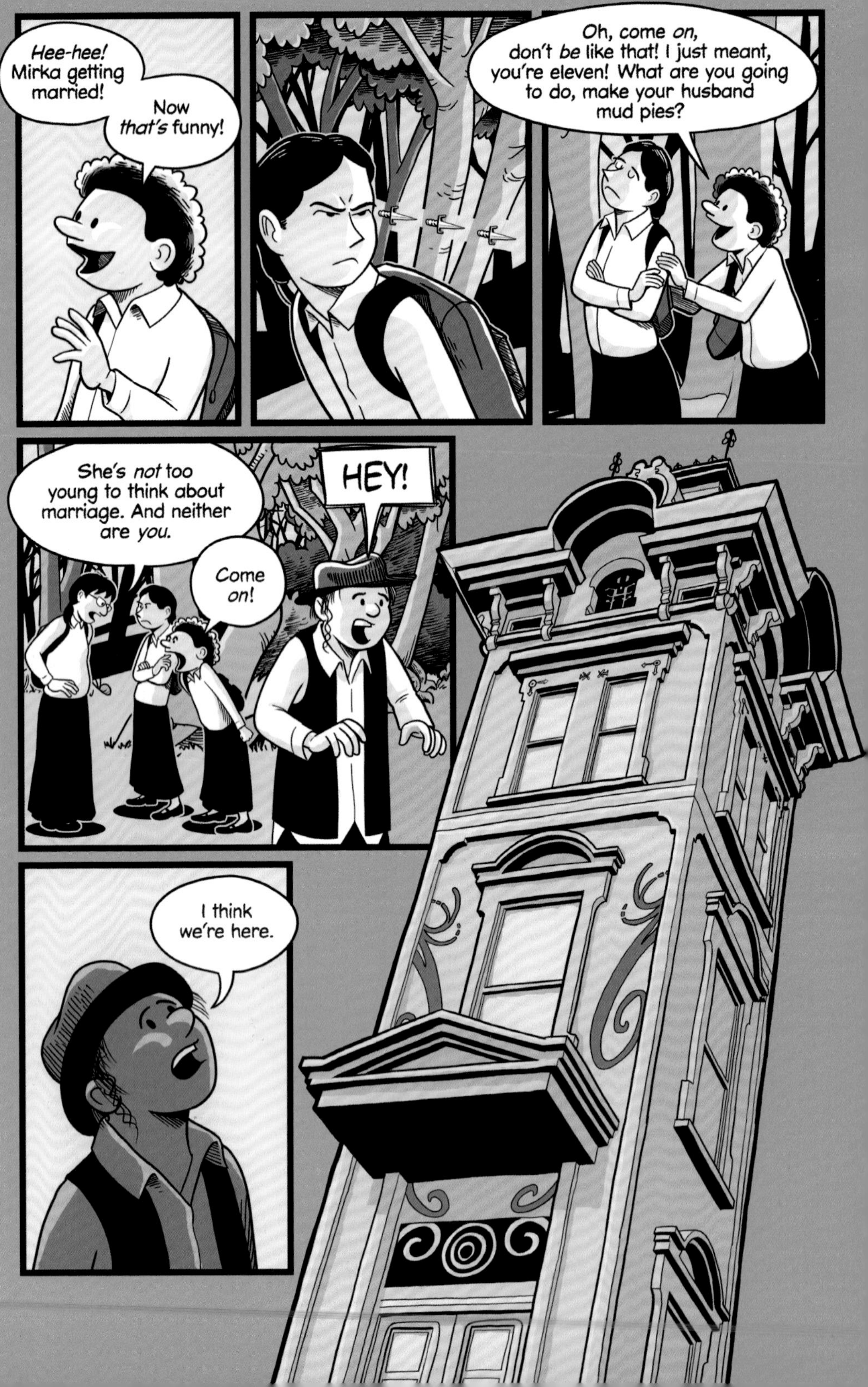
Hee-hee! Mirka getting married!
Now that's funny!
Oh, come on, don't be like that! I just meant, you're eleven! What are you going to do, make your husband mud pies?
She's not too young to think about marriage. And neither are you.
HEY!
Come on!
I think we're here.

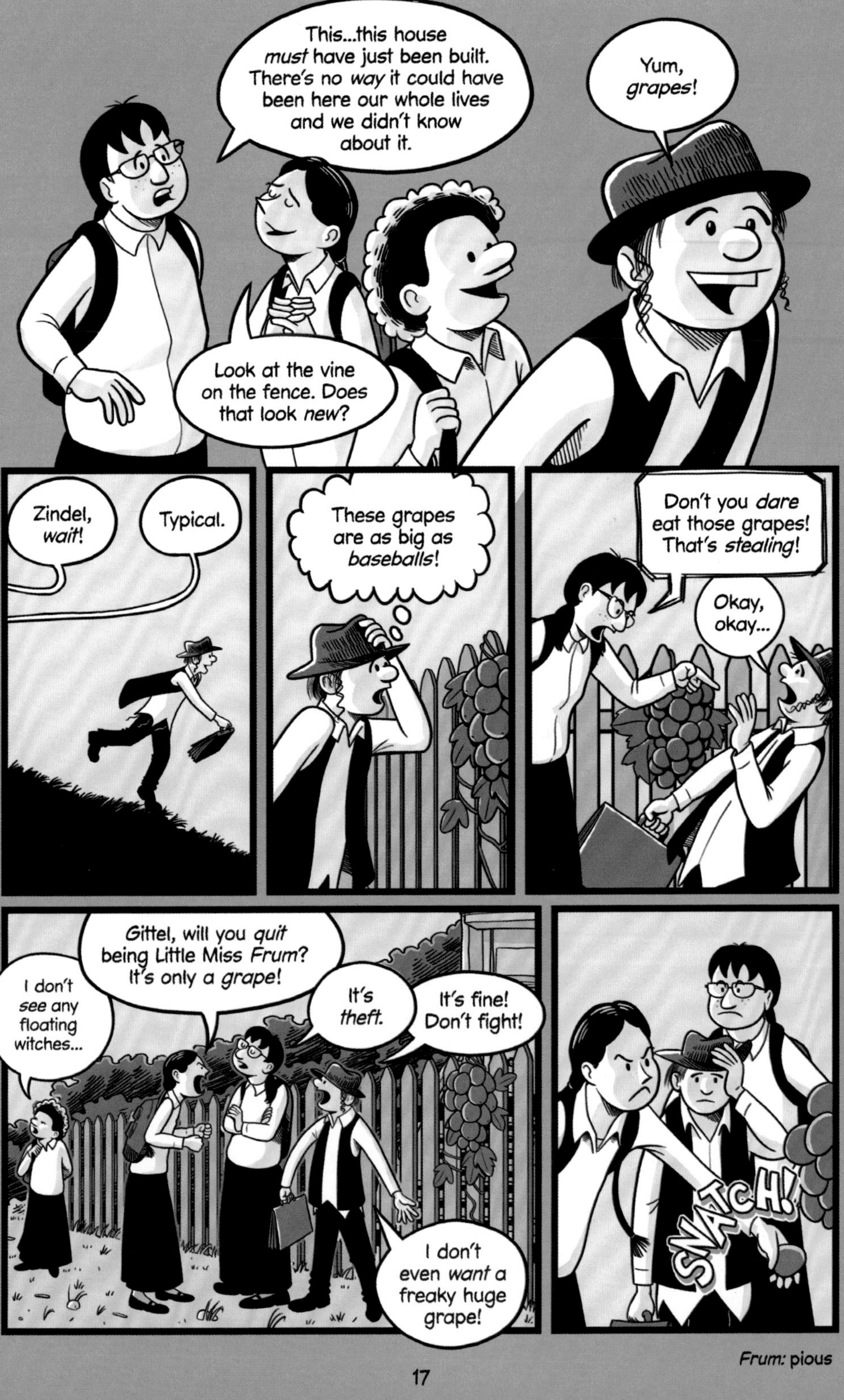
This...this house *must* have just been built. There's no *way* it could have been here our whole lives and we didn't know about it.
Yum, *grapes*!
Look at the vine on the fence. Does that look *new*?
Zindel, *wait*!
Typical.
These grapes are as big as *baseballs*!
Don't you *dare* eat those grapes! That's *stealing*!
Okay, okay...
I don't *see* any floating witches...
Gittel, will you *quit* being Little Miss *Frum*? It's only a *grape*!
It's *theft*.
It's fine! Don't fight!
I don't even *want* a freaky huge grape!
SNATCH!

Frum: pious

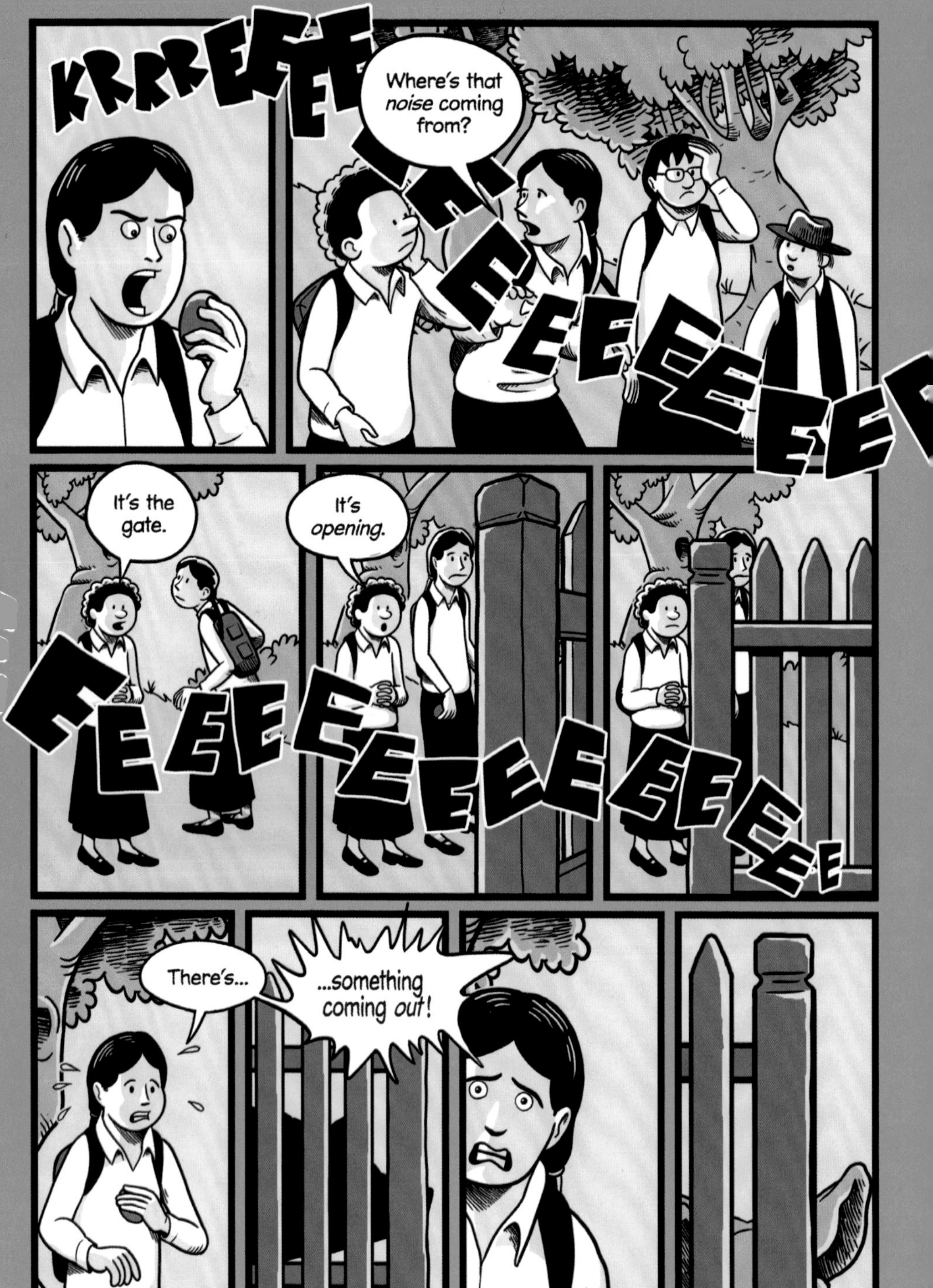
KRRREEEEEEEEEEEEEEEEEEEP
Where's that *noise* coming from?
It's the gate.
It's *opening*.
EEEEEEEEEEEEEEE
There's...
...something coming out!

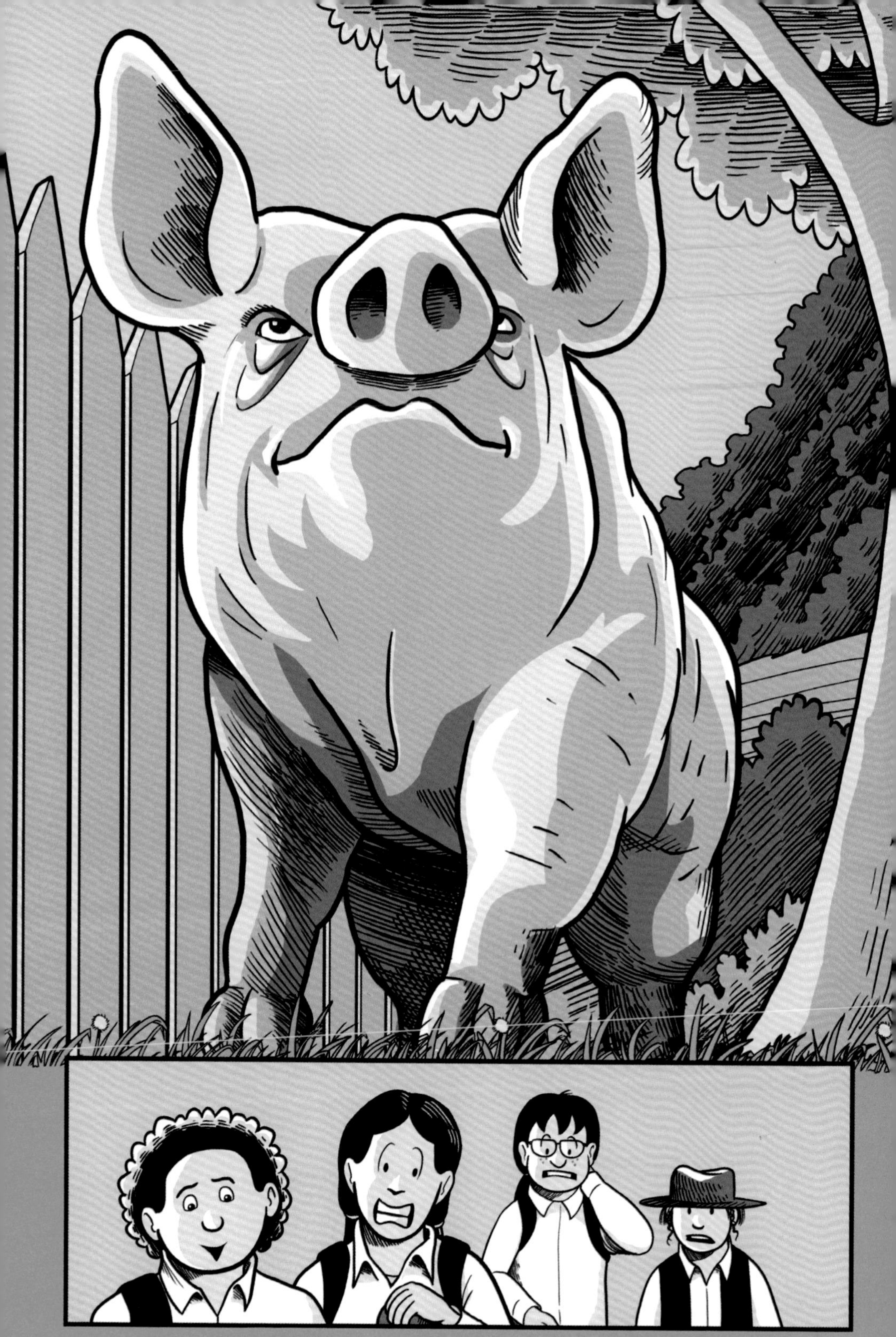

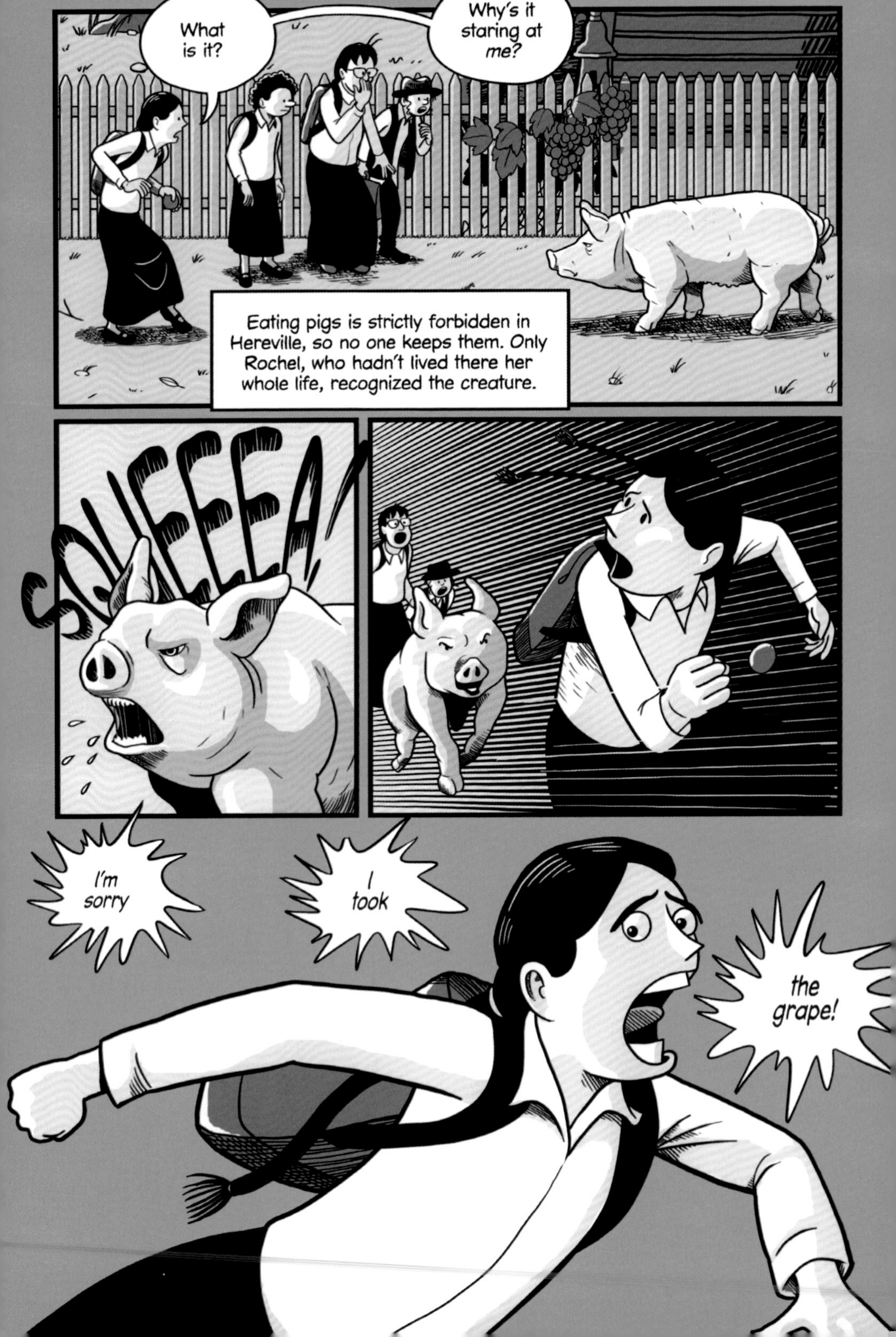
What is it?
Why's it staring at *me?*
Eating pigs is strictly forbidden in Hereville, so no one keeps them. Only Rochel, who hadn't lived there her whole life, recognized the creature.
SQUEEEA!
I'm sorry
I took
the grape!

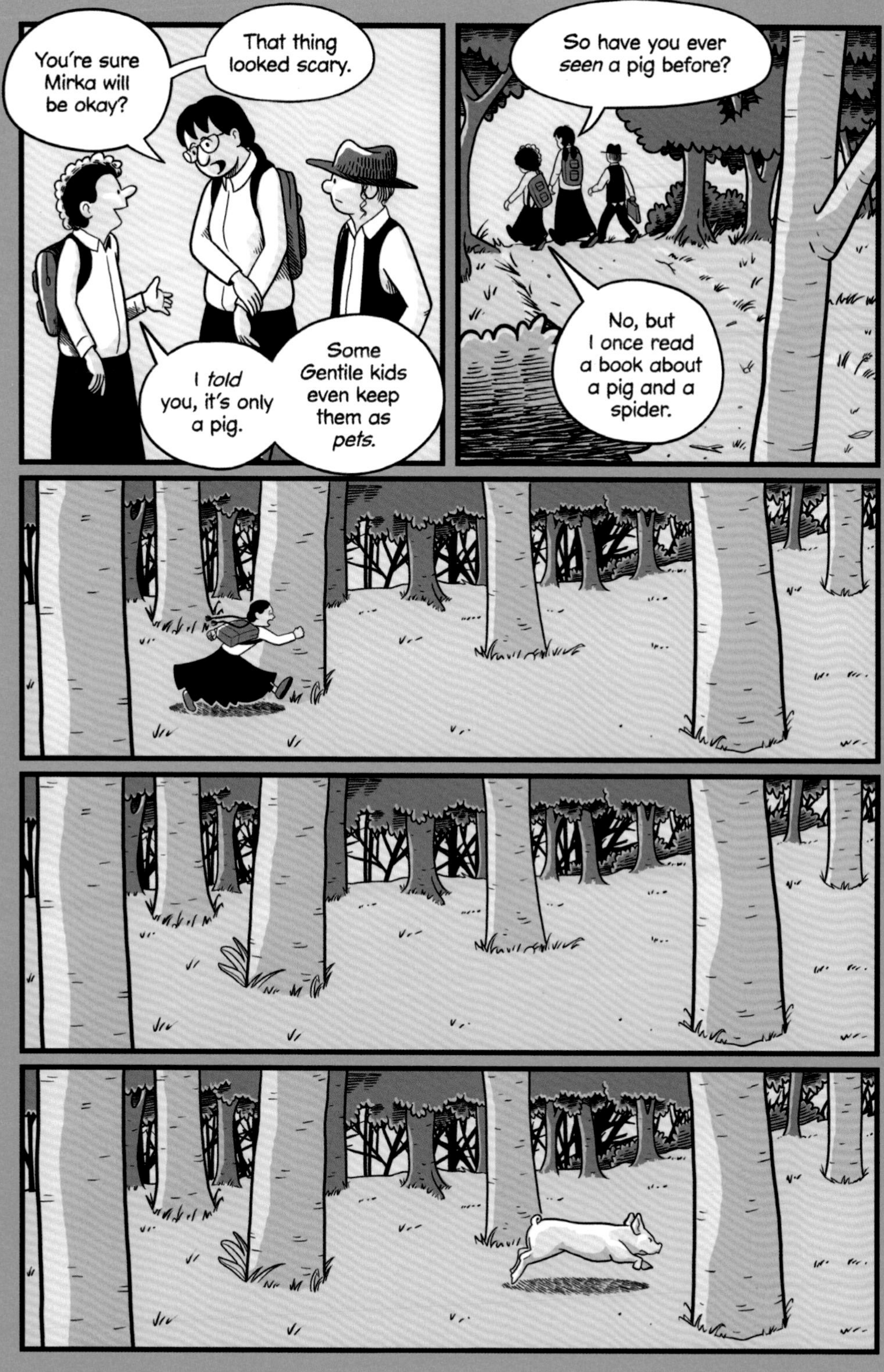
You're sure Mirka will be okay?
That thing looked scary.
I *told* you, it's only a pig.
Some Gentile kids even keep them as *pets.*
So have you ever *seen* a pig before?
No, but I once read a book about a pig and a spider.

Gentile: non-Jewish

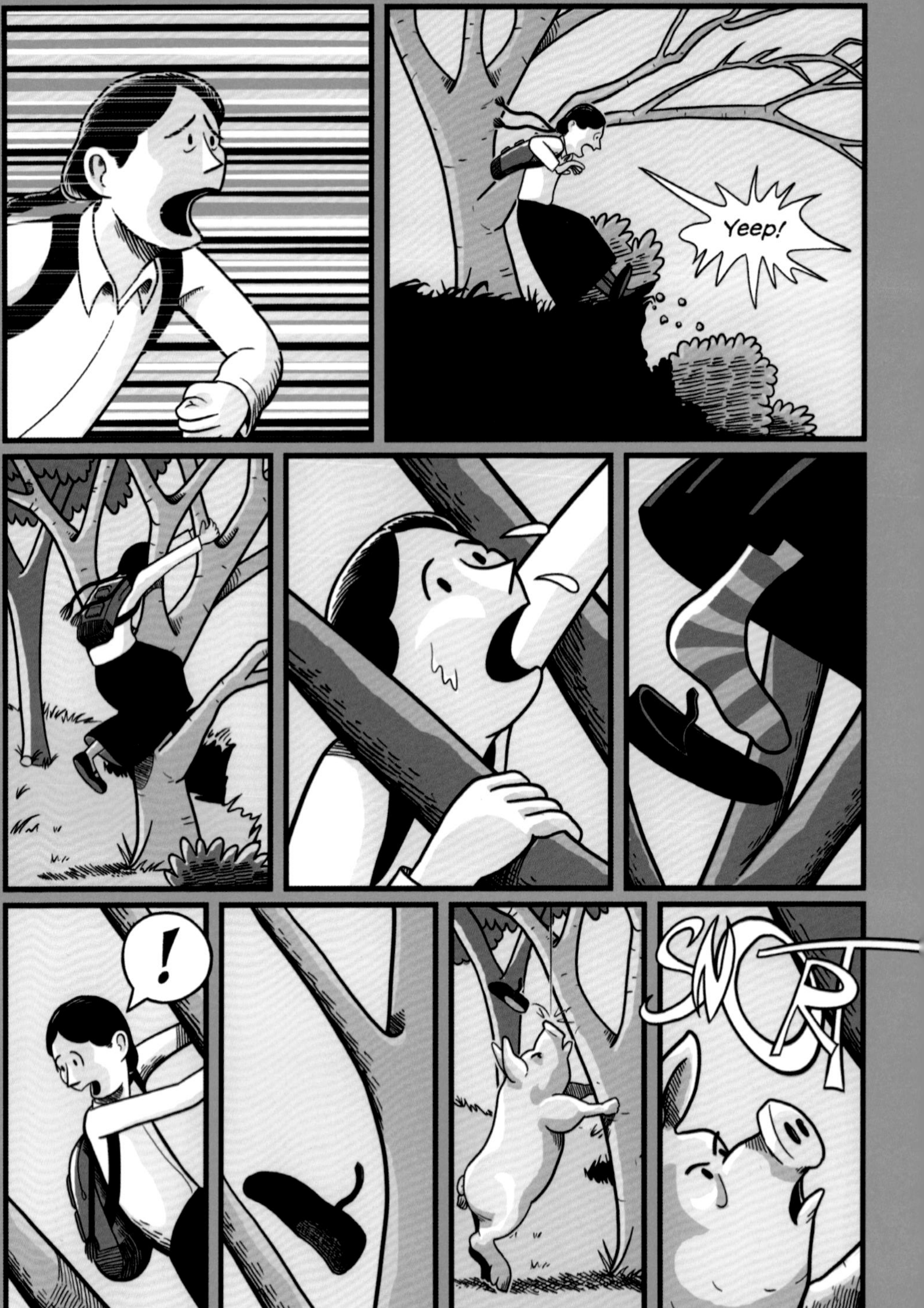
Yeep!
!
SNORT

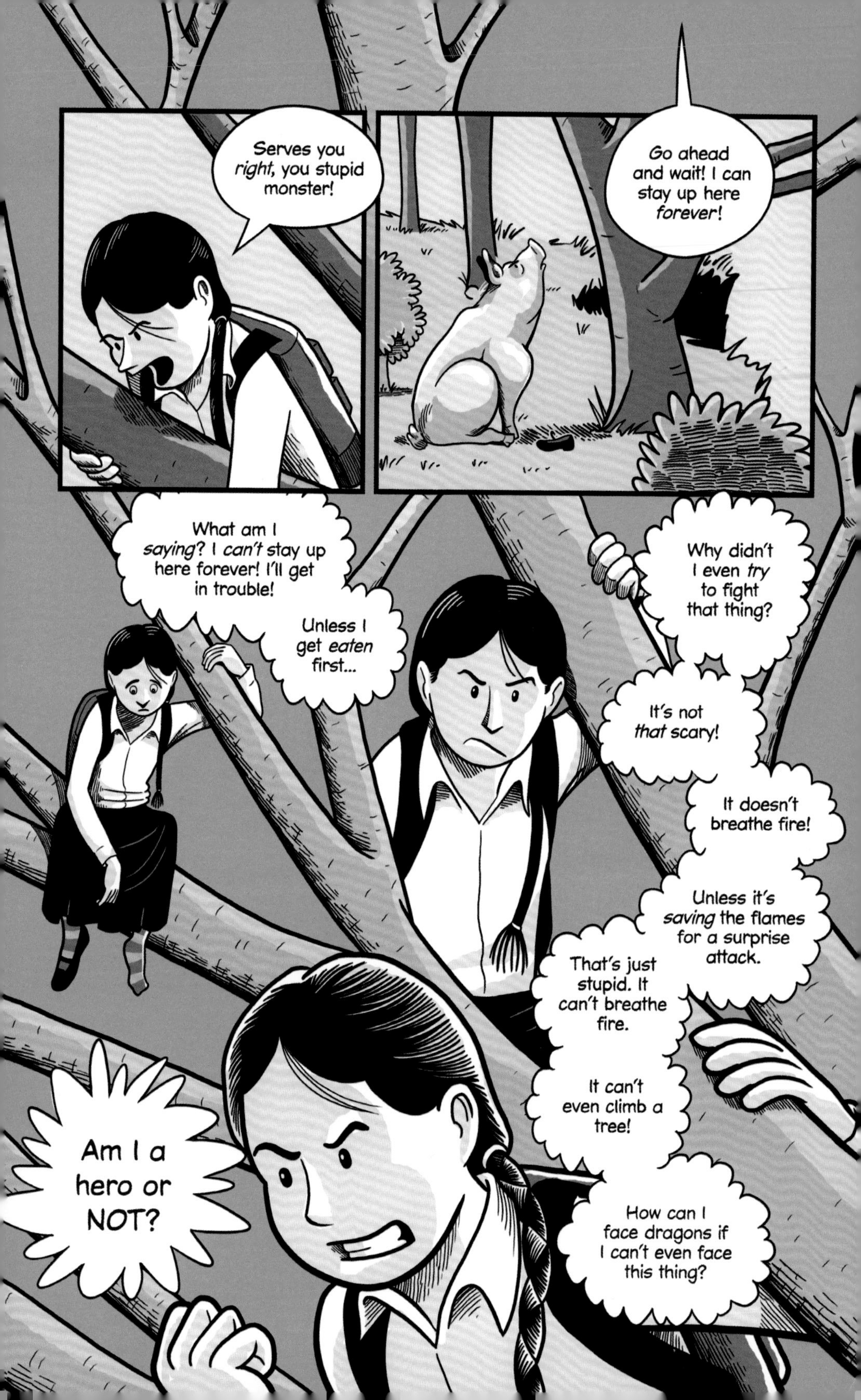

Serves you *right*, you stupid monster!
Go ahead and wait! I can stay up here *forever*!
What am I *saying*? I *can't* stay up here forever! I'll get in trouble!
Unless I get *eaten* first...
Why didn't I even *try* to fight that thing?
It's not *that* scary!
It doesn't breathe fire!
Unless it's *saving* the flames for a surprise attack.
That's just stupid. It can't breathe fire.
It can't even climb a tree!
How can I face dragons if I can't even face this thing?
Am I a hero or NOT?

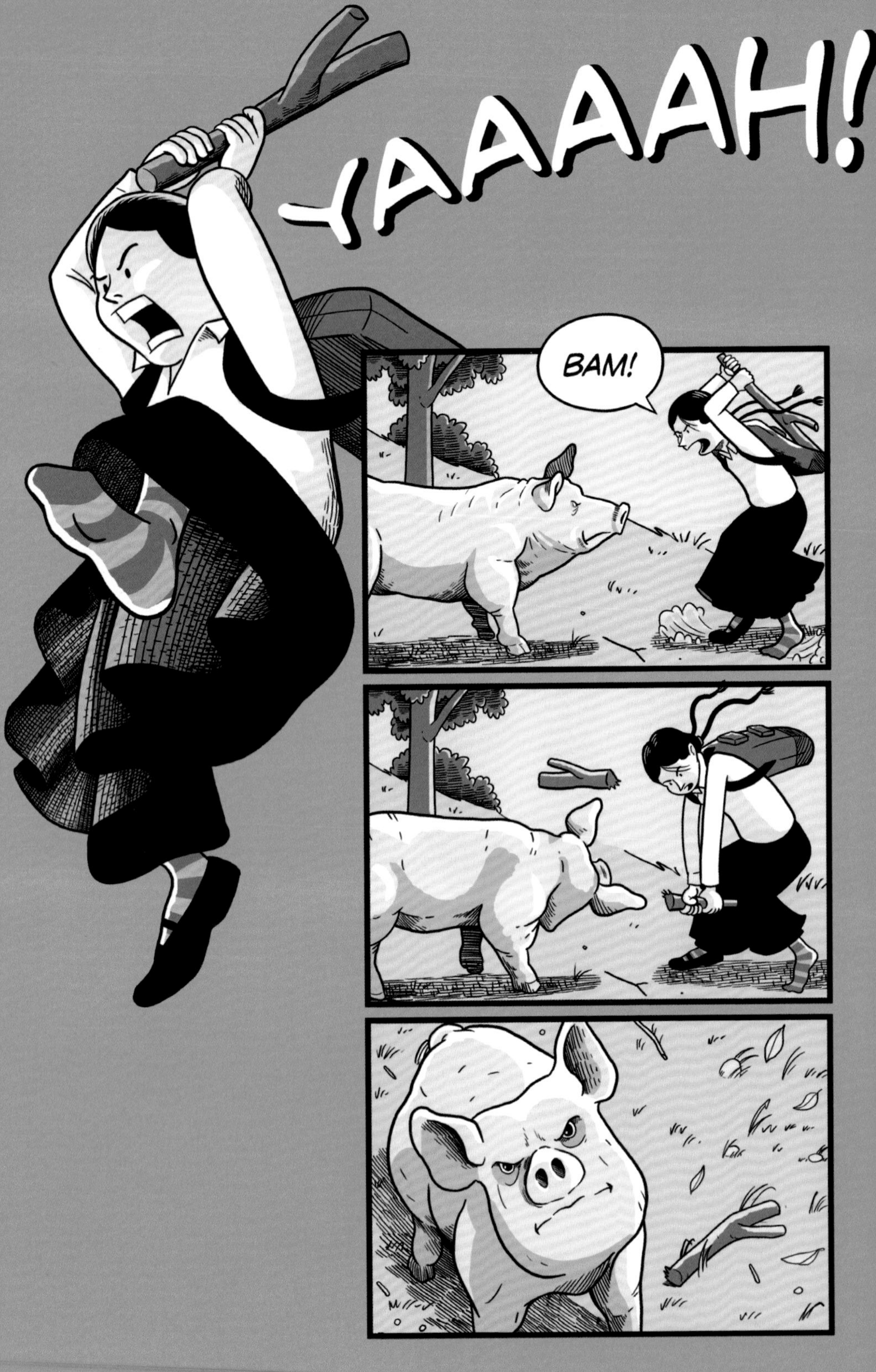
YAAAAAH!
BAM!

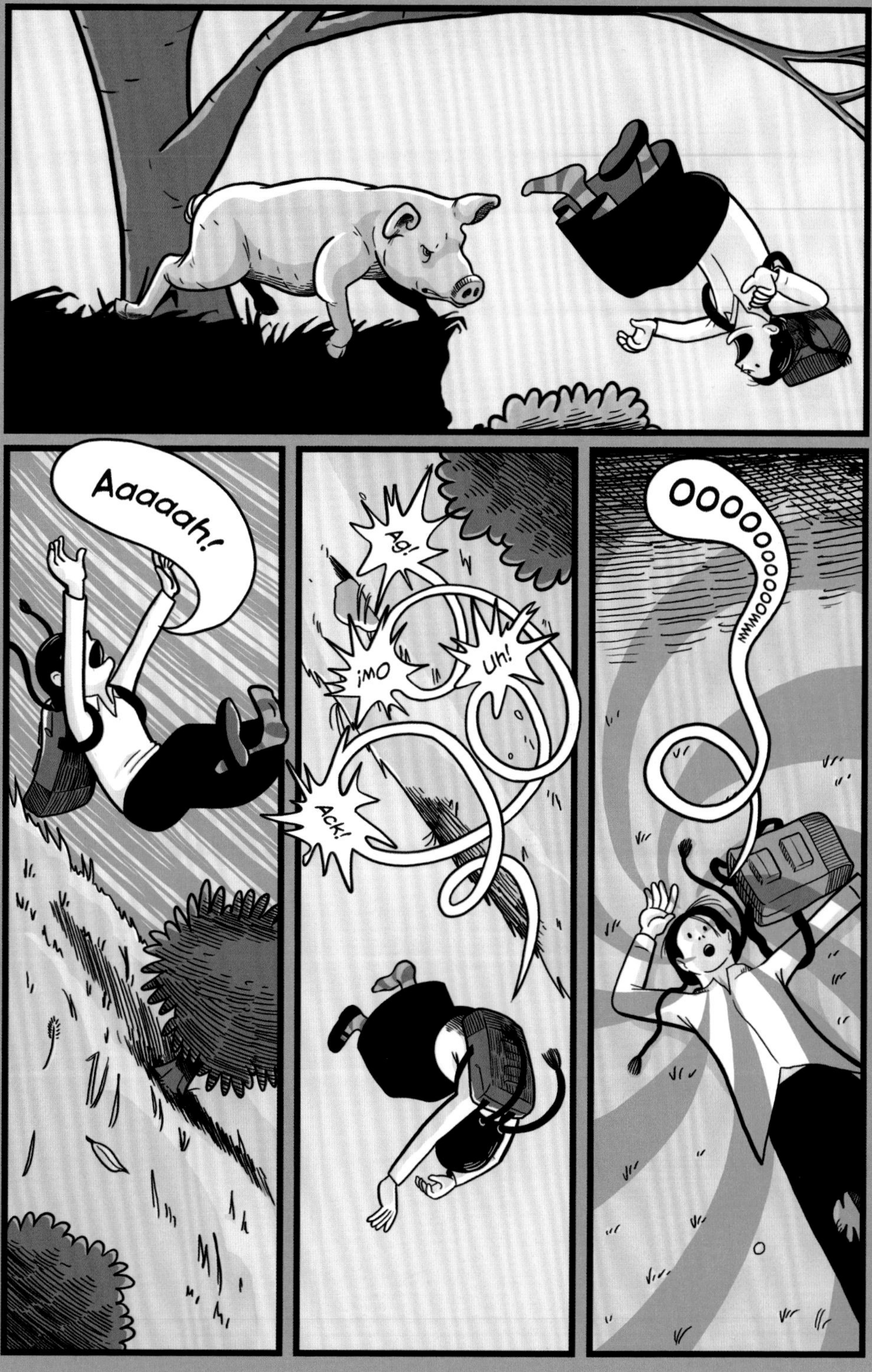
Aaaaah!
¡Ag!
¡MO
Uh!
Ack!
OOOOOOOOOOOMMM

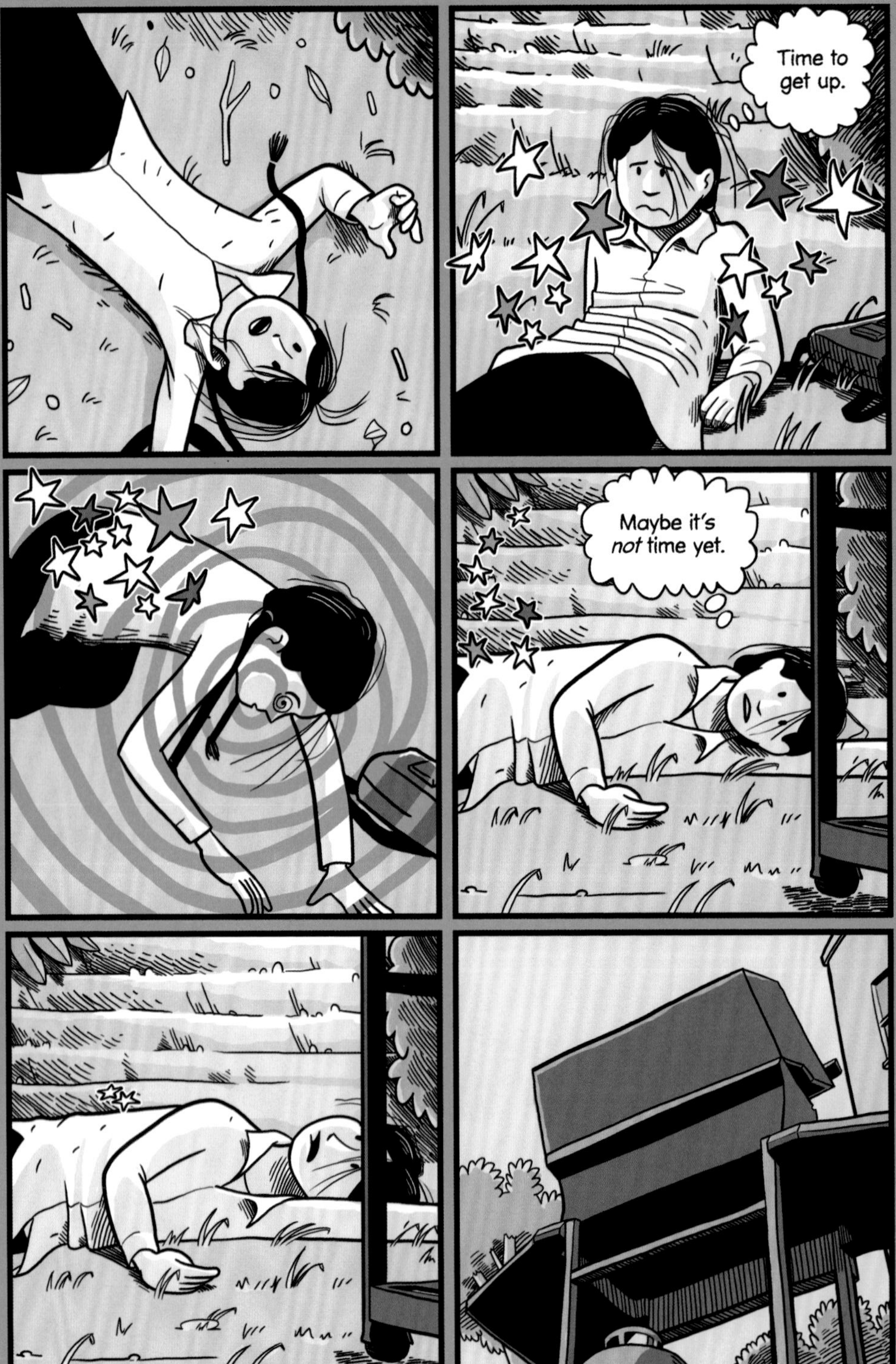
Time to get up.
Maybe it's *not* time yet.

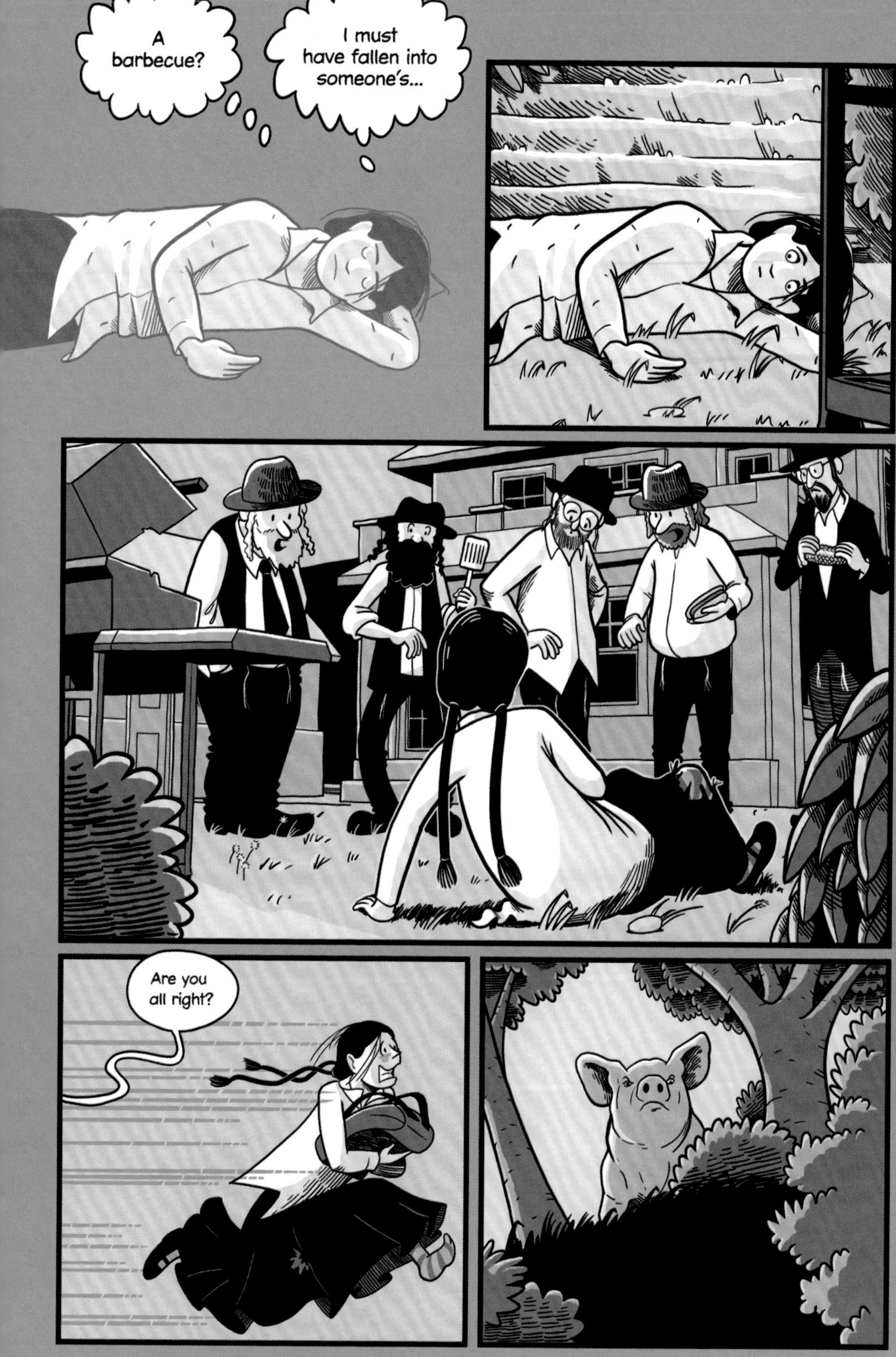
A barbecue?
I must have fallen into someone's...
Are you all right?

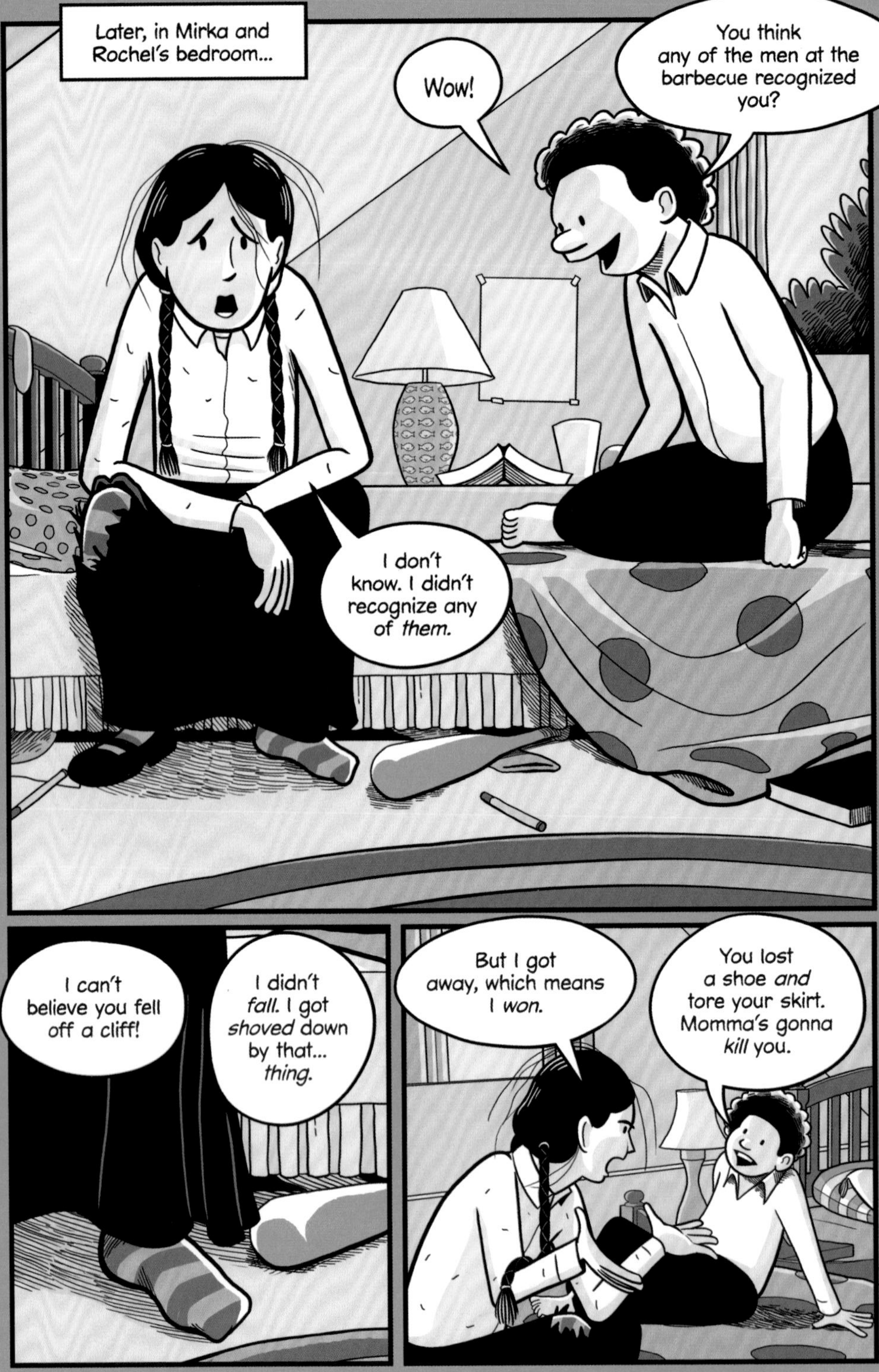
Later, in Mirka and Rochel's bedroom...
Wow!
You think any of the men at the barbecue recognized you?
I don't know. I didn't recognize any of *them.*
I can't believe you fell off a cliff!
I didn't *fall.* I got *shoved* down by that... *thing.*
But I got away, which means I *won.*
You lost a shoe *and* tore your skirt. Momma's gonna *kill* you.

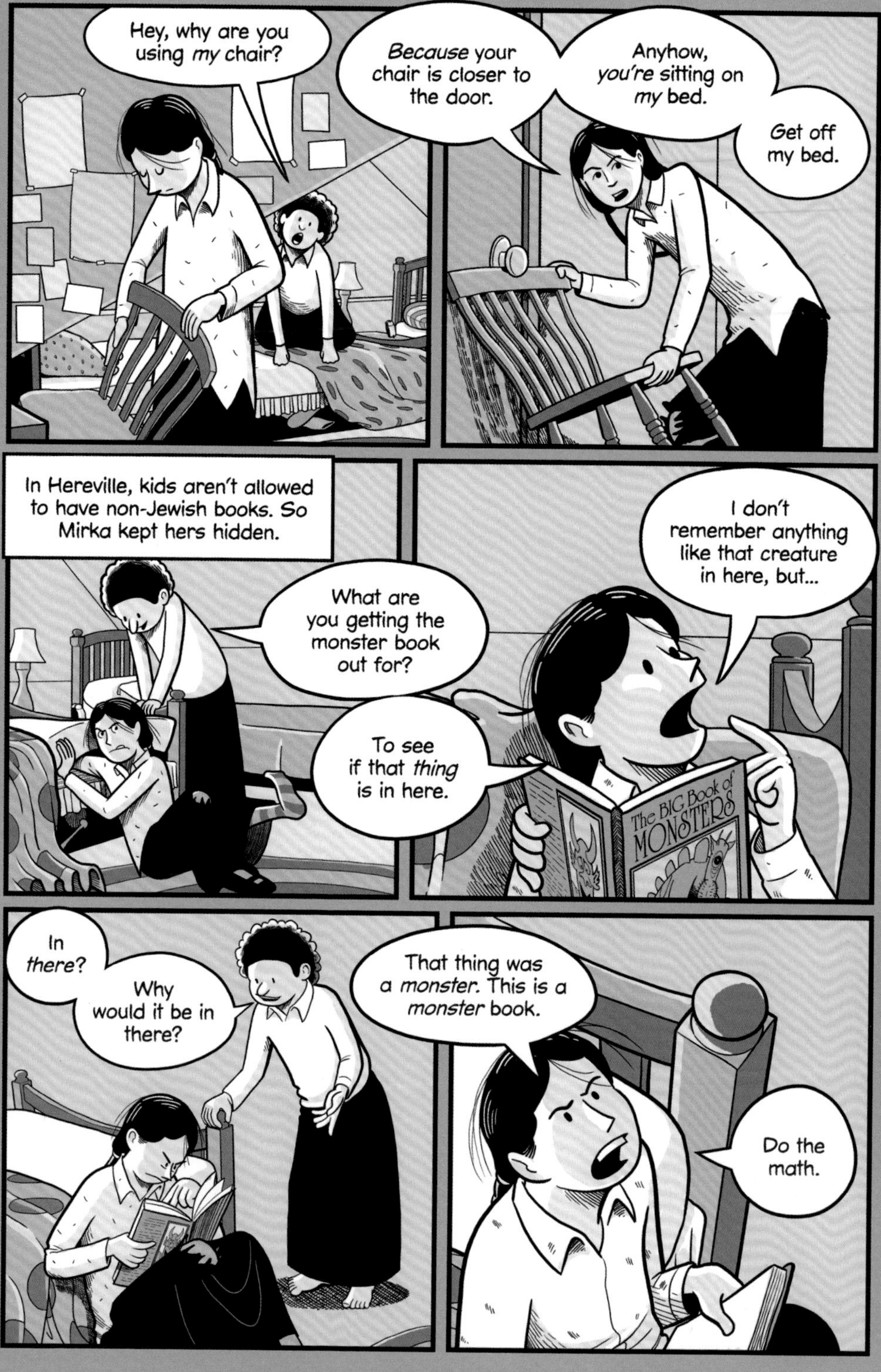
Hey, why are you using *my* chair?
Because your chair is closer to the door.
Anyhow, *you're* sitting on *my* bed.
Get off my bed.
In Hereville, kids aren't allowed to have non-Jewish books. So Mirka kept hers hidden.
What are you getting the monster book out for?
To see if that *thing* is in here.
I don't remember anything like that creature in here, but...
The BIG Book of MONSTERS
In *there*?
Why would it be in there?
That thing was a *monster*. This is a *monster* book.
Do the math.

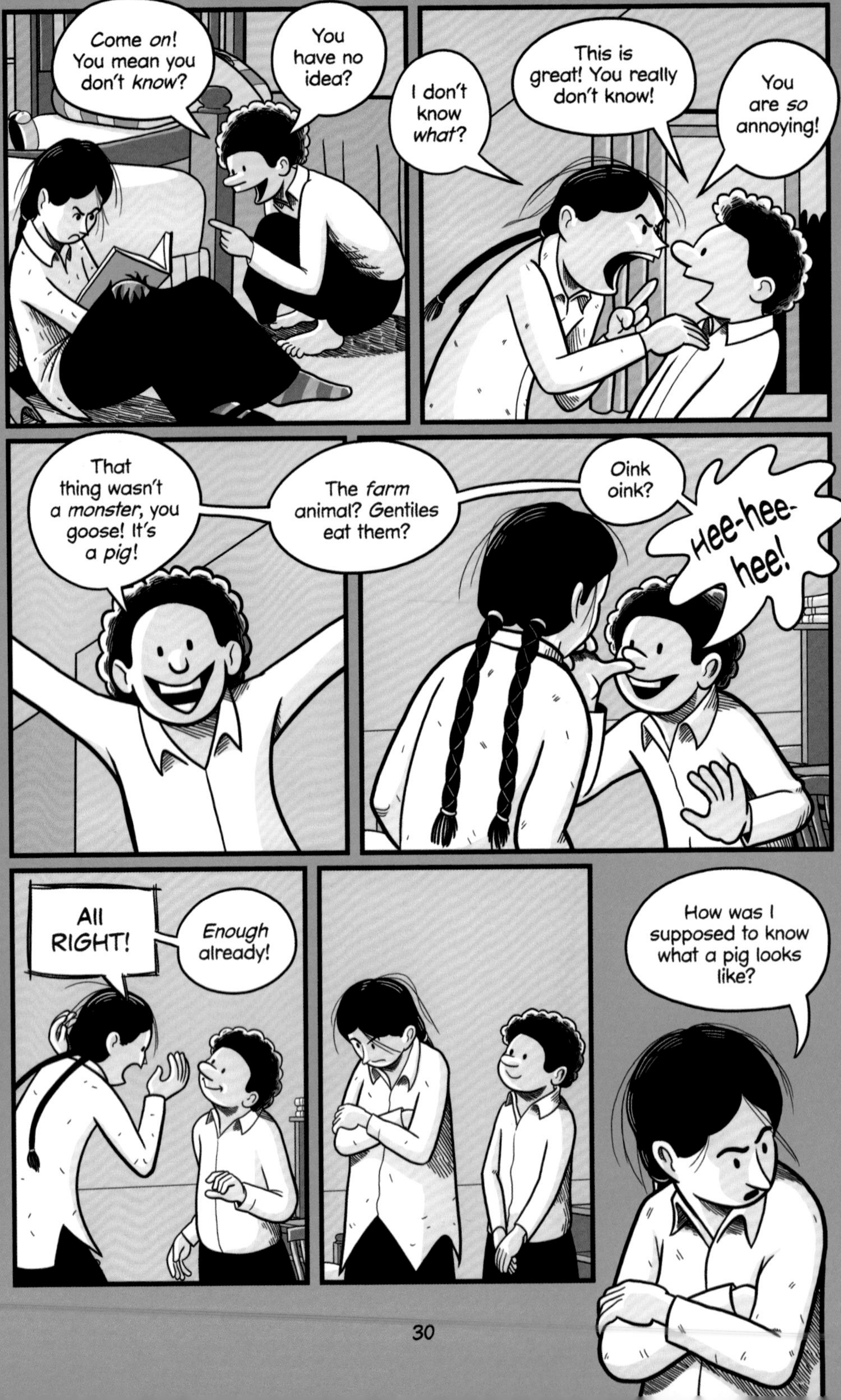
Come *on*! You mean you don't *know*?
You have no idea?
I don't know *what*?
This is great! You really don't know!
You are *so* annoying!
That thing wasn't a *monster*, you goose! It's a *pig*!
The *farm* animal? Gentiles eat them?
Oink oink?
Hee-hee-hee!
All RIGHT!
Enough already!
How was I supposed to know what a pig looks like?

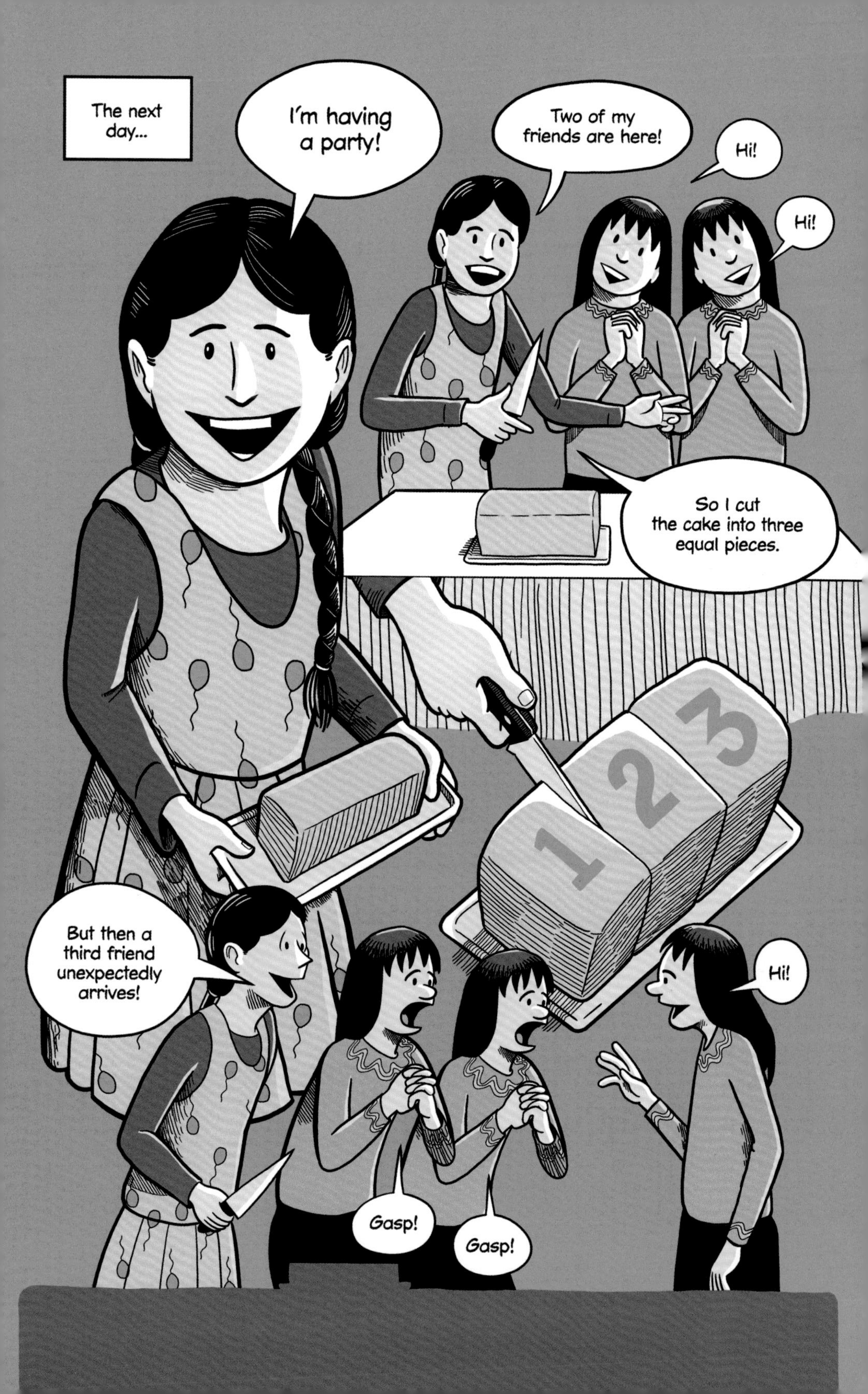
The next day...
I'm having a party!
Two of my friends are here!
Hi!
Hi!
So I cut the cake into three equal pieces.
1
2
3
But then a third friend unexpectedly arrives!
Hi!
Gasp!
Gasp!

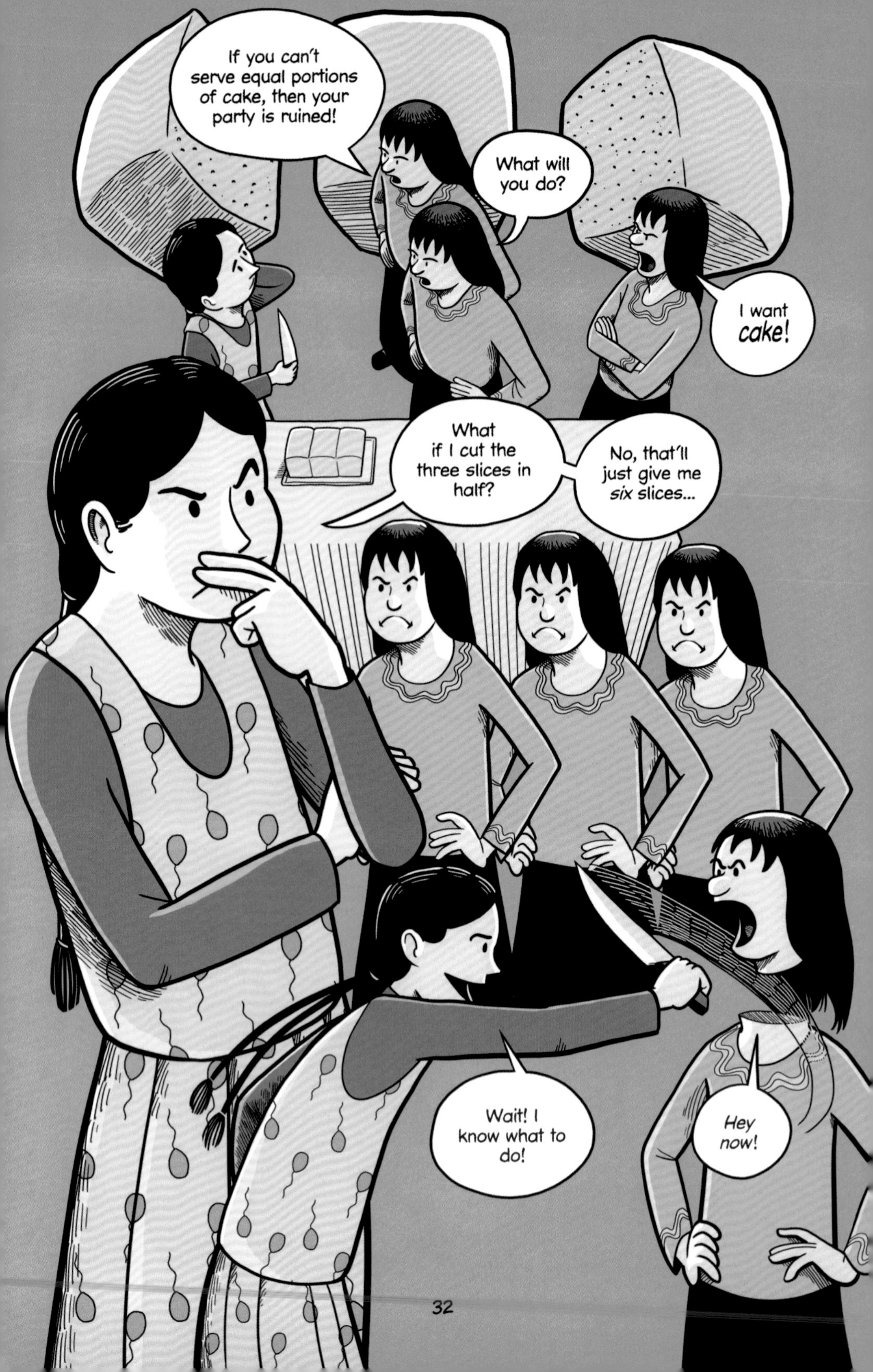
If you can't serve equal portions of cake, then your party is ruined!
What will you do?
I want *cake*!
What if I cut the three slices in half?
No, that'll just give me *six* slices...
Wait! I know what to do!
Hey now!

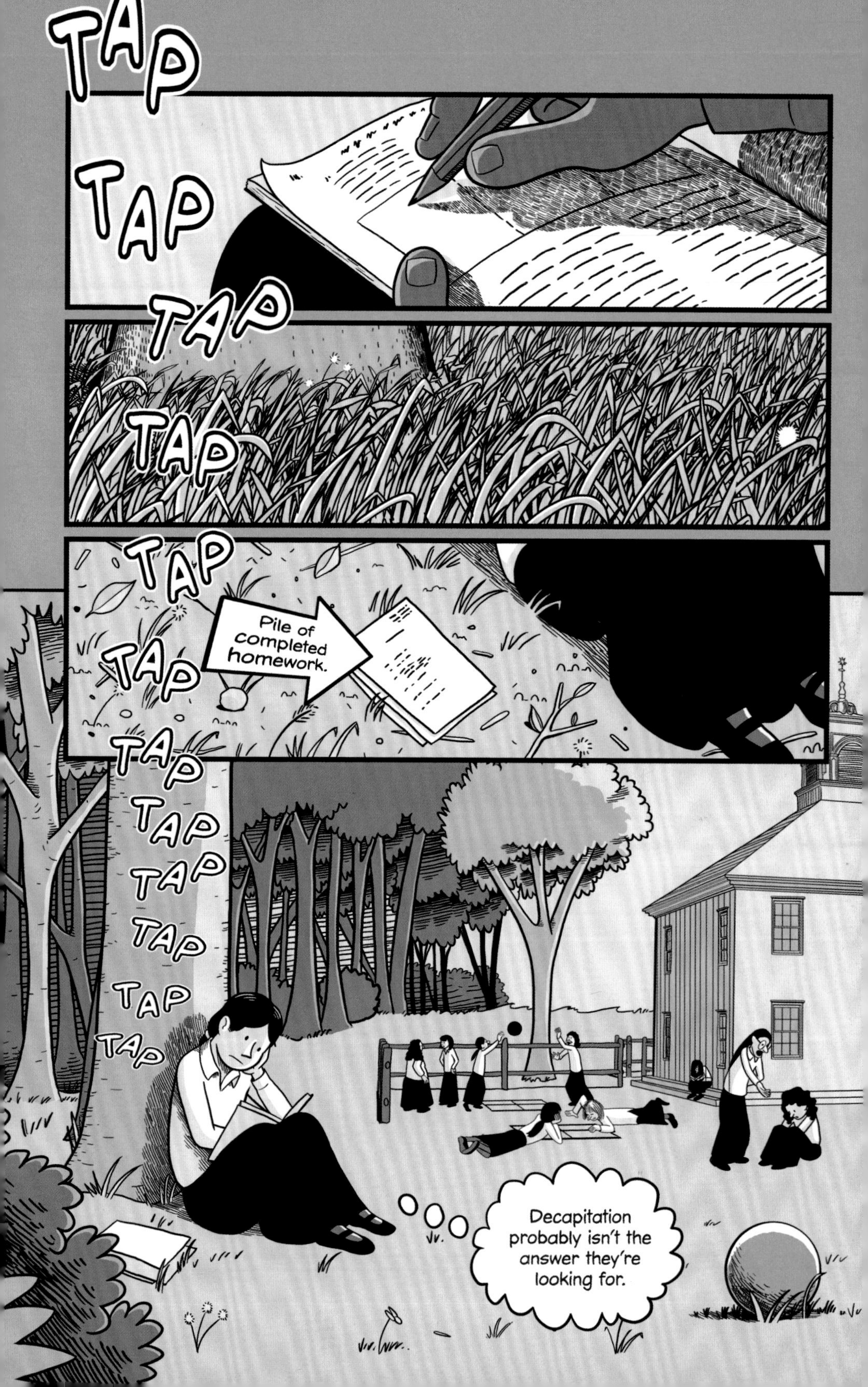
TAP
TAP
TAP
TAP
TAP
Pile of completed homework.
TAP
TAP
TAP
TAP
TAP
TAP
TAP
Decapitation probably isn't the answer they're looking for.

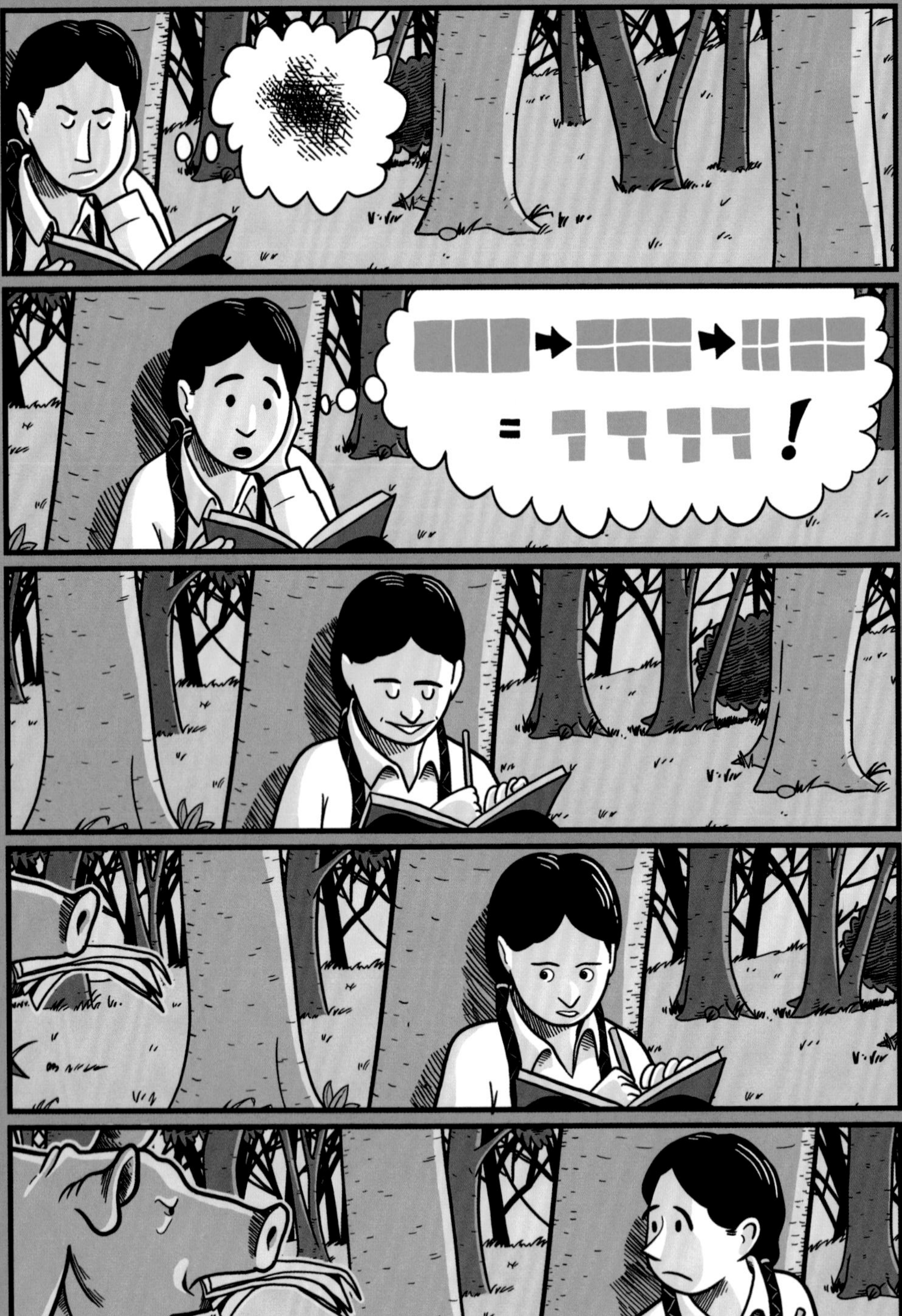

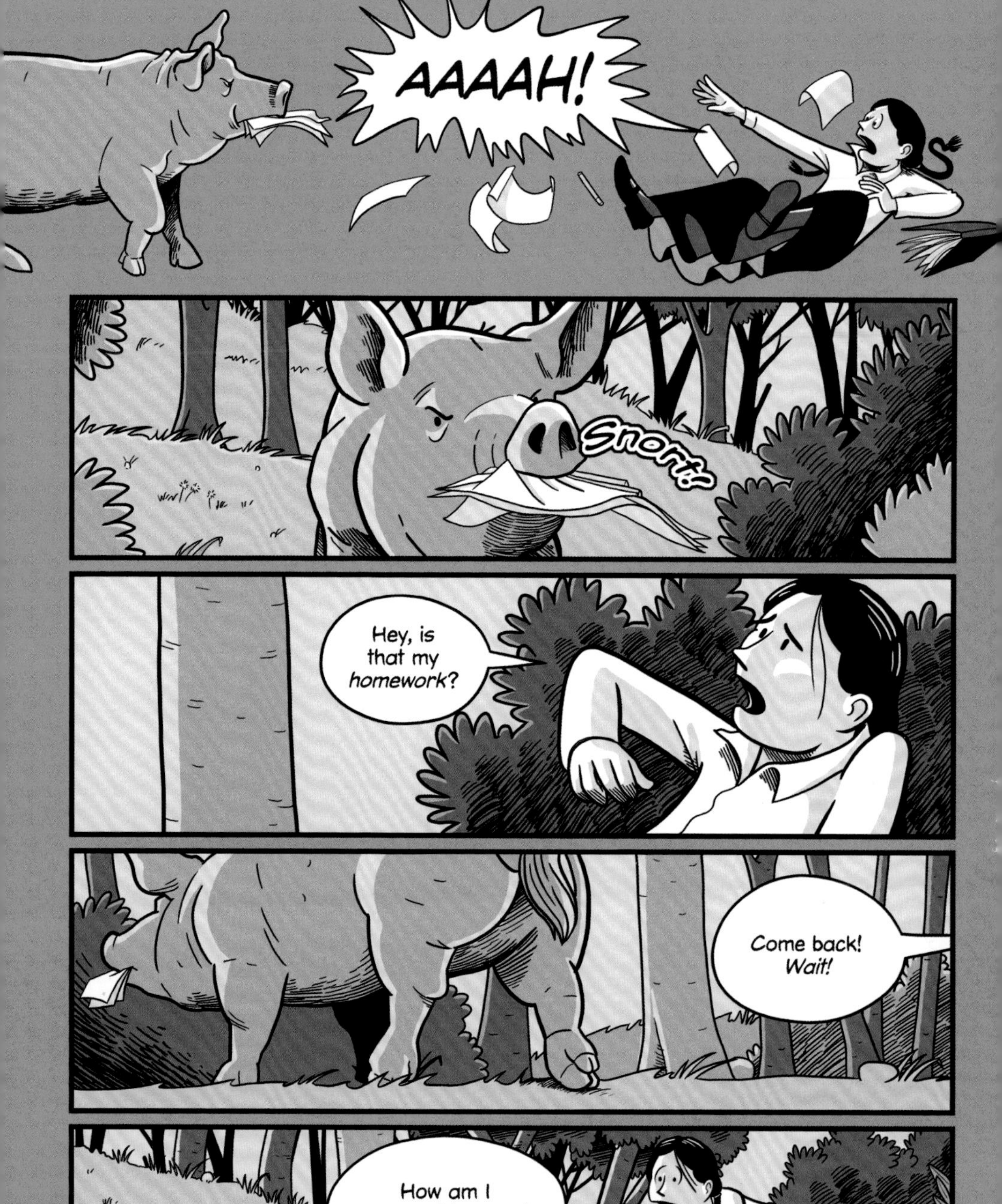
AAAAH!
Snort!
Hey, is that my homework?
Come back! Wait!
How am I supposed to explain this?

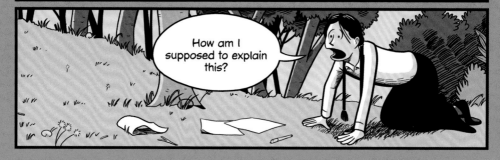

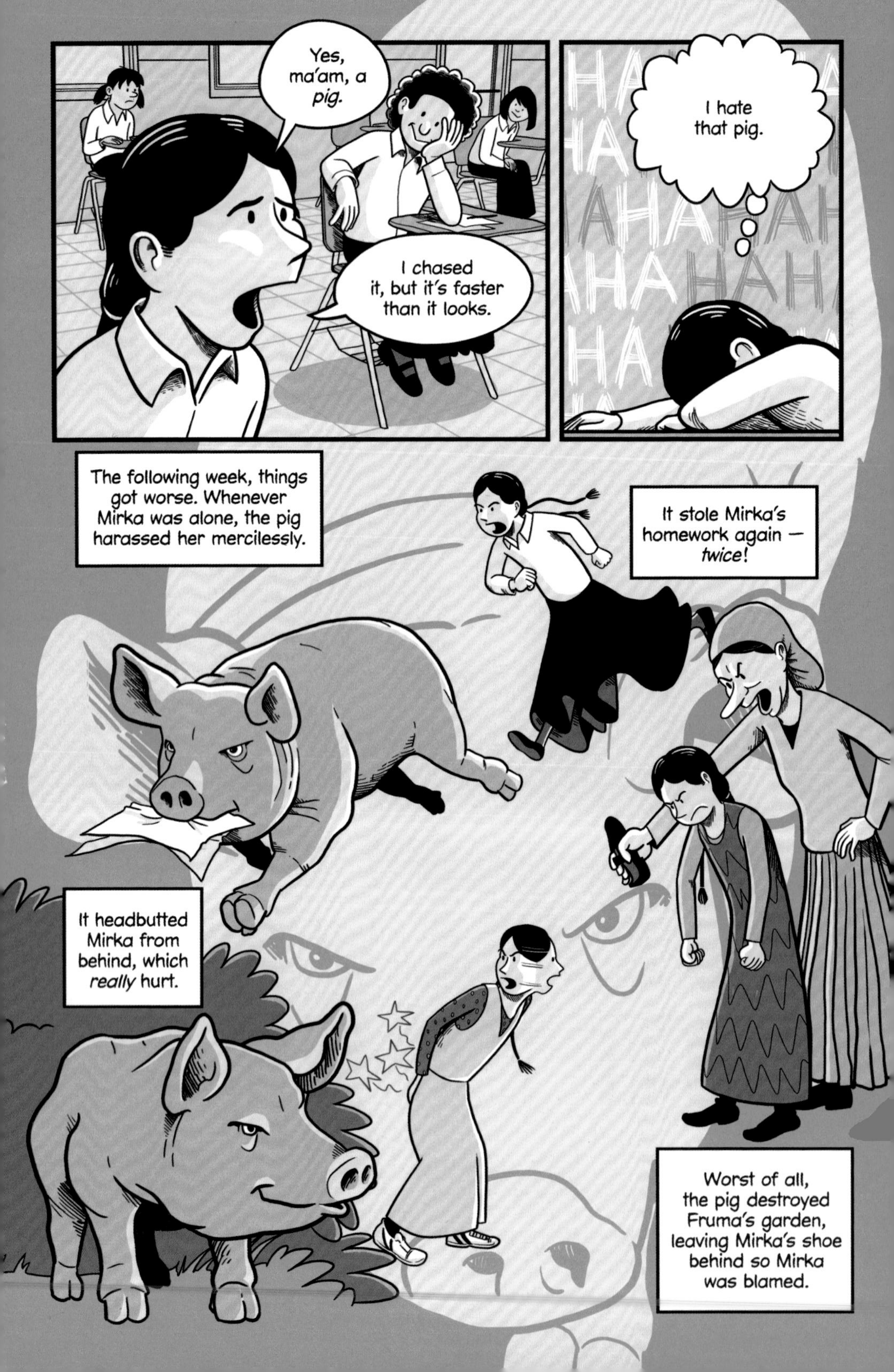
Yes, ma'am, a *pig.*
I chased it, but it's faster than it looks.
I hate that pig.
HAHAHA
The following week, things got worse. Whenever Mirka was alone, the pig harassed her mercilessly.
It stole Mirka's homework again — *twice*!
It headbutted Mirka from behind, which *really* hurt.
Worst of all, the pig destroyed Fruma's garden, leaving Mirka's shoe behind so Mirka was blamed.

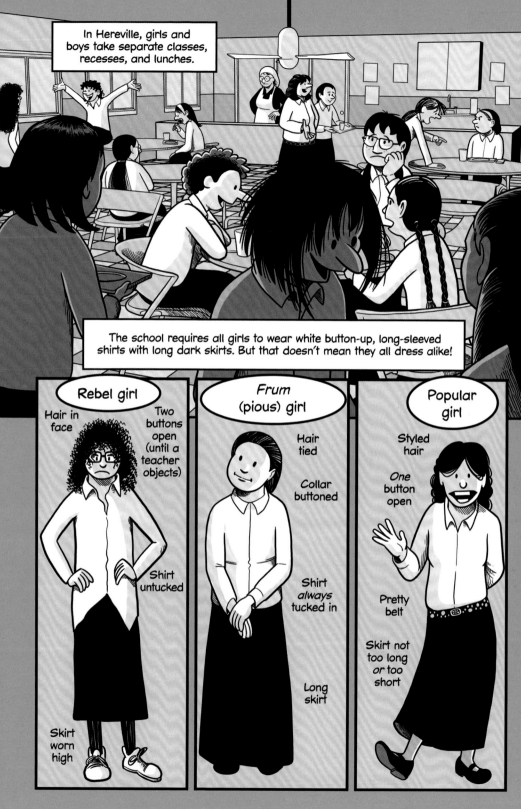

In Hereville, girls and boys take separate classes, recesses, and lunches.

The school requires all girls to wear white button-up, long-sleeved shirts with long dark skirts. But that doesn't mean they all dress alike!

Rebel girl

Hair in face

Two buttons open (until a teacher objects)

Shirt untucked

Skirt worn high

Frum (pious) girl

Hair tied

Collar buttoned

Shirt *always* tucked in

Long skirt

Popular girl

Styled hair

One button open

Pretty belt

Skirt not too long or too short

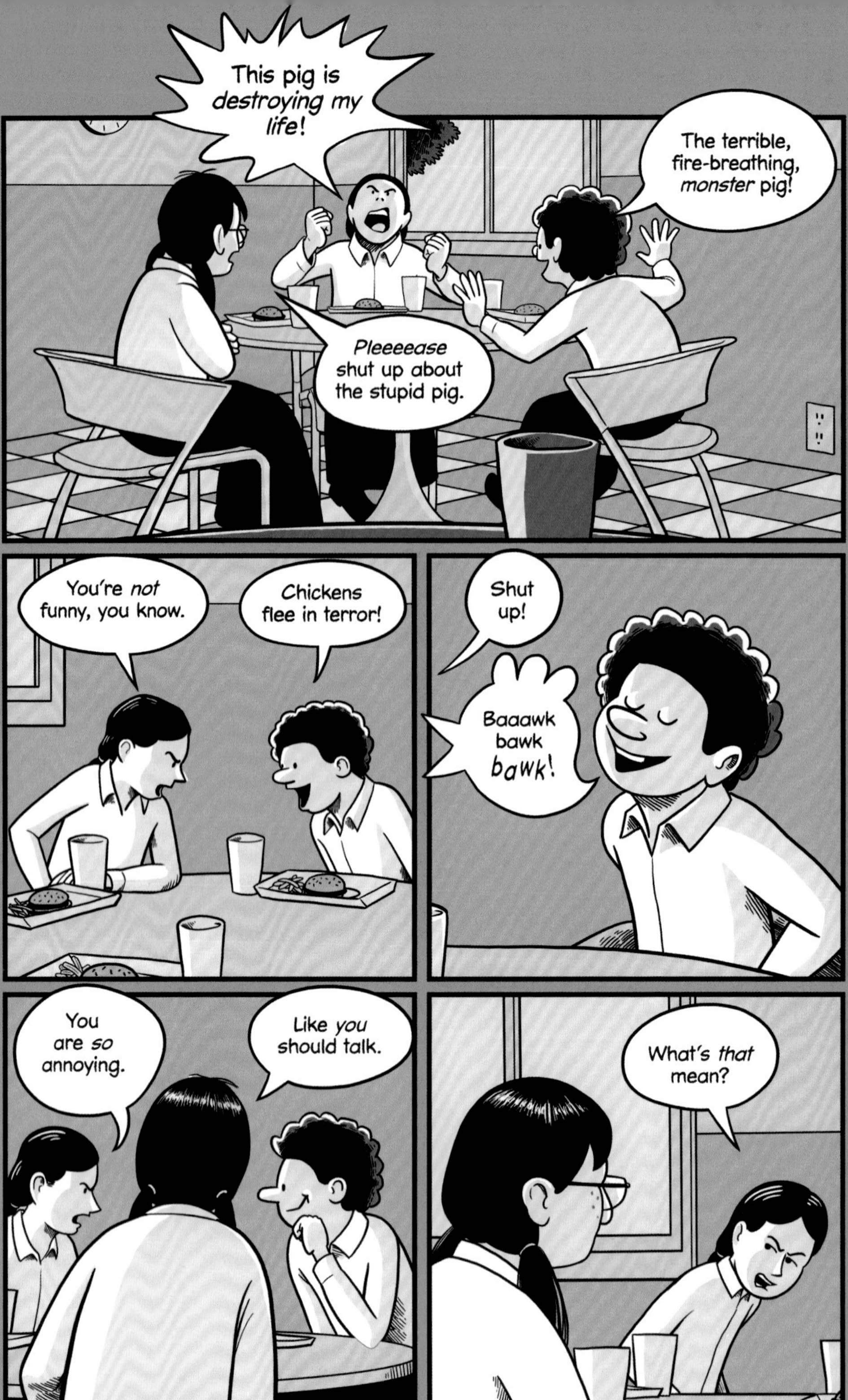
This pig is *destroying* my *life*!
The terrible, fire-breathing, *monster* pig!
Pleeeease shut up about the stupid pig.
You're *not* funny, you know.
Chickens flee in terror!
Shut up!
Baaawk bawk bawk!
You are *so* annoying.
Like *you* should talk.
What's *that* mean?

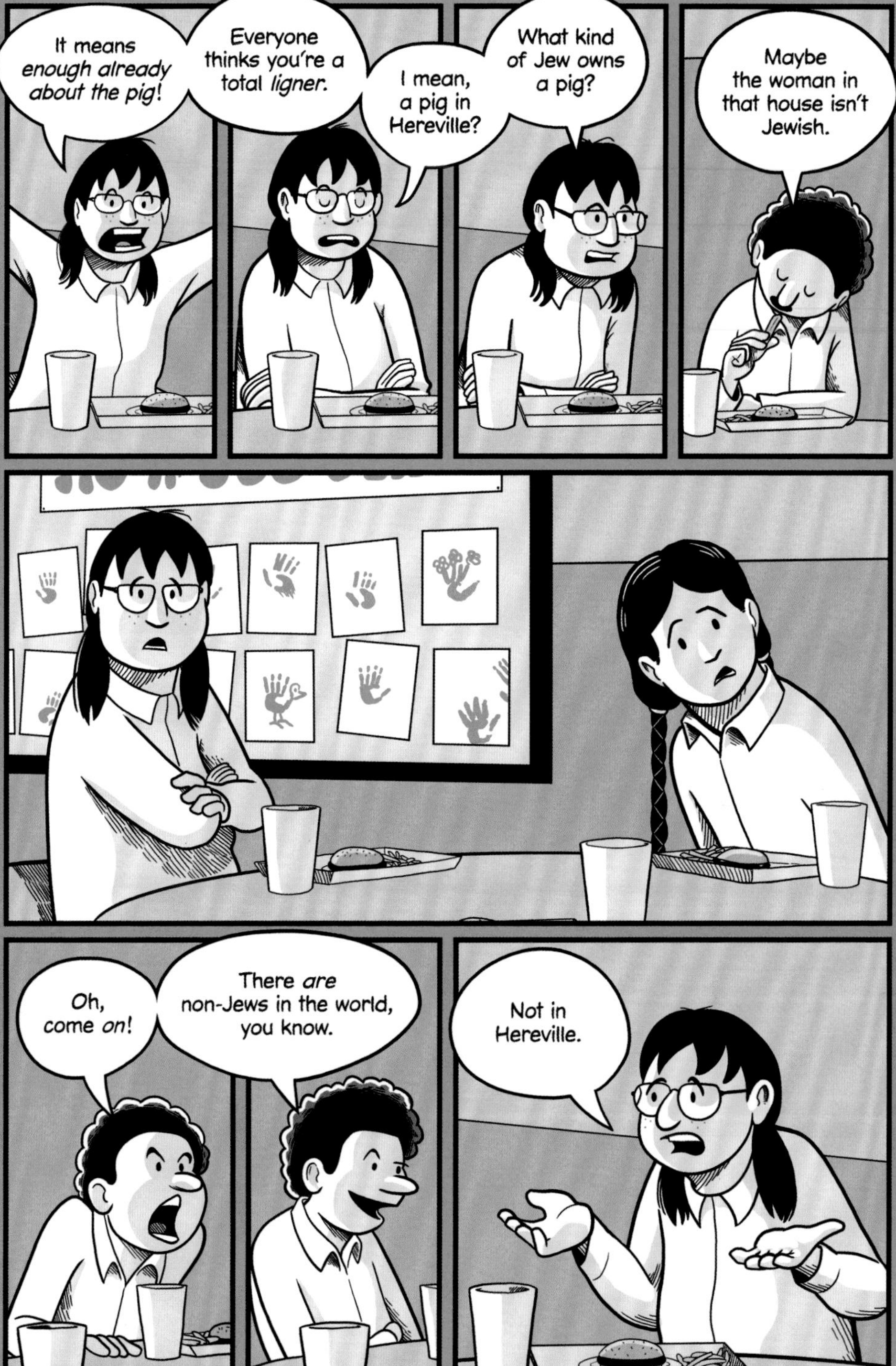
It means *enough already about the pig*!
Everyone thinks you're a total *ligner*.
I mean, a pig in Hereville?
What kind of Jew owns a pig?
Maybe the woman in that house isn't Jewish.
Oh, come *on*!
There *are* non-Jews in the world, you know.
Not in Hereville.

Ligner: liar

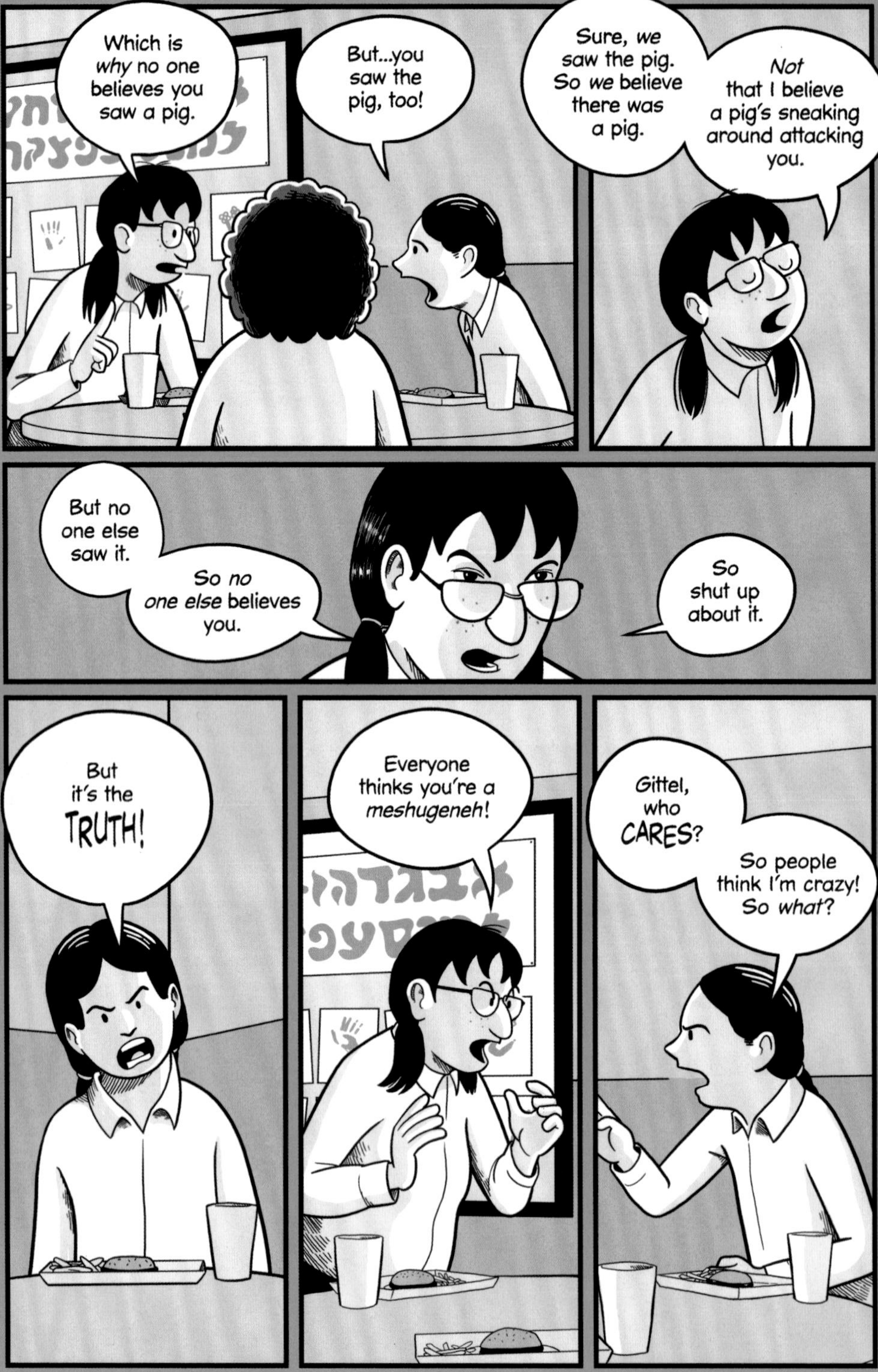
Which is *why* no one believes you saw a pig.
But...you saw the pig, too!
Sure, *we* saw the pig. So *we* believe there was a pig.
Not that I believe a pig's sneaking around attacking you.
But no one else saw it.
So *no one else* believes you.
So shut up about it.
But it's the TRUTH!
Everyone thinks you're a *meshugeneh*!
Gittel, who CARES?
So people think I'm crazy! So *what*?

Meshugeneh: deranged woman

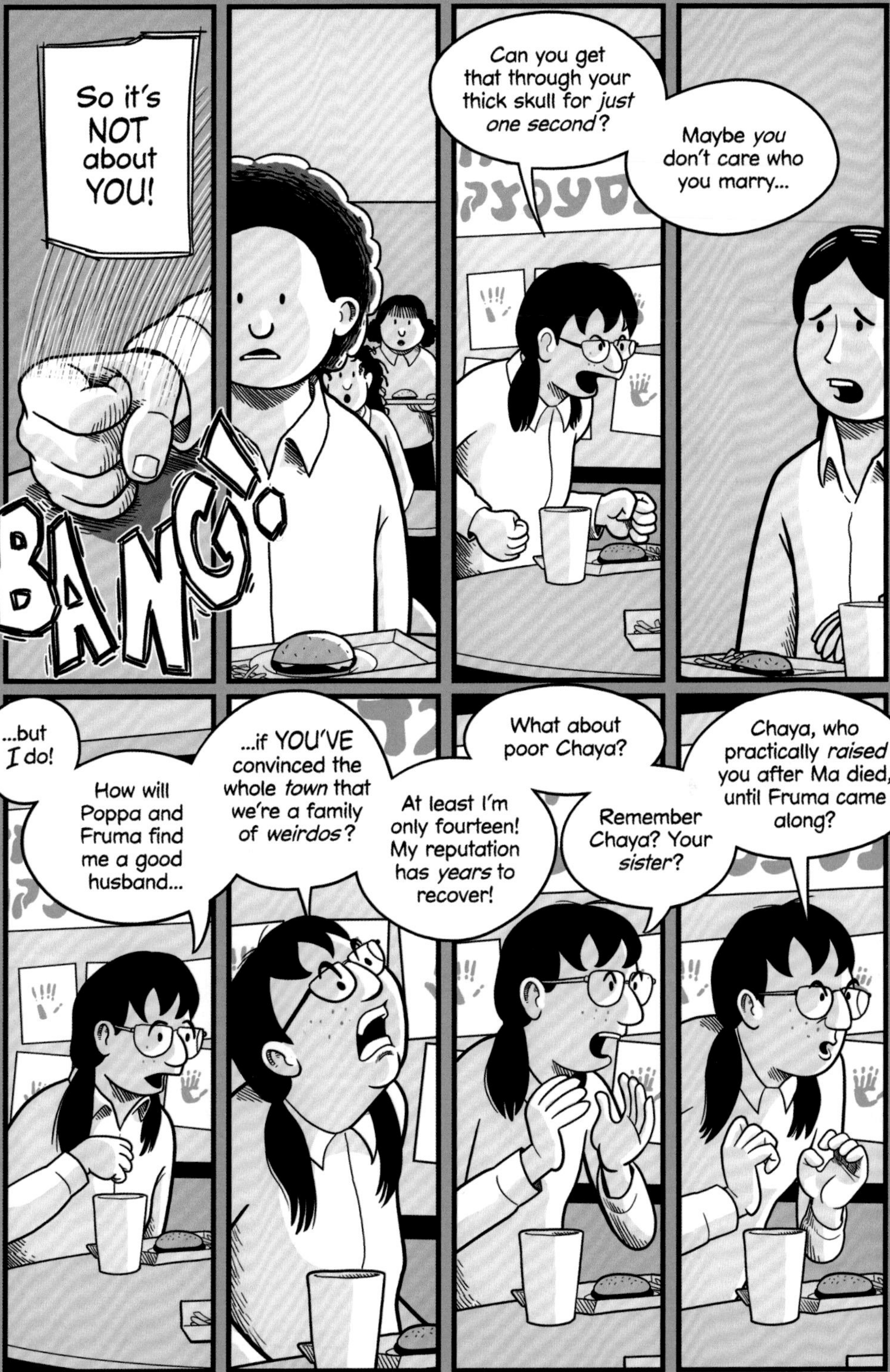
So it's NOT about YOU!
BANG!
Can you get that through your thick skull for *just one second*?
Maybe *you* don't care who you marry...
...but *I* do!
How will Poppa and Fruma find me a good husband...
...if YOU'VE convinced the whole *town* that we're a family of *weirdos*?
At least I'm only fourteen! My reputation has *years* to recover!
What about poor Chaya?
Remember Chaya? Your *sister*?
Chaya, who practically *raised* you after Ma died, until Fruma came along?

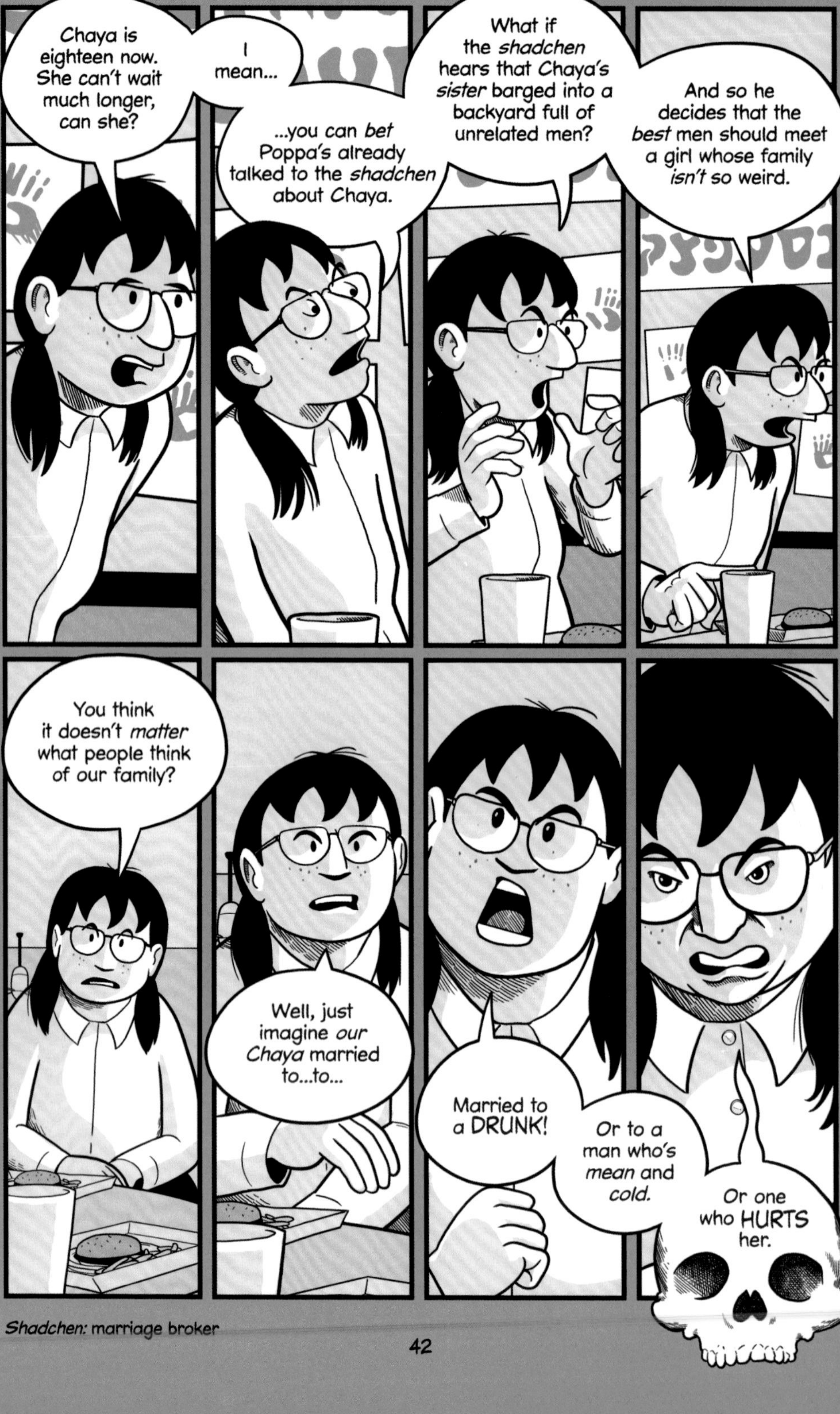
Chaya is eighteen now. She can't wait much longer, can she?
I mean...
...you can *bet* Poppa's already talked to the *shadchen* about Chaya.
What if the *shadchen* hears that Chaya's *sister* barged into a backyard full of unrelated men?
And so he decides that the *best* men should meet a girl whose family *isn't* so weird.
You think it doesn't *matter* what people think of our family?
Well, just imagine *our Chaya* married to...to...
Married to a DRUNK!
Or to a man who's *mean* and *cold.*
Or one who HURTS her.

Shadchen: marriage broker

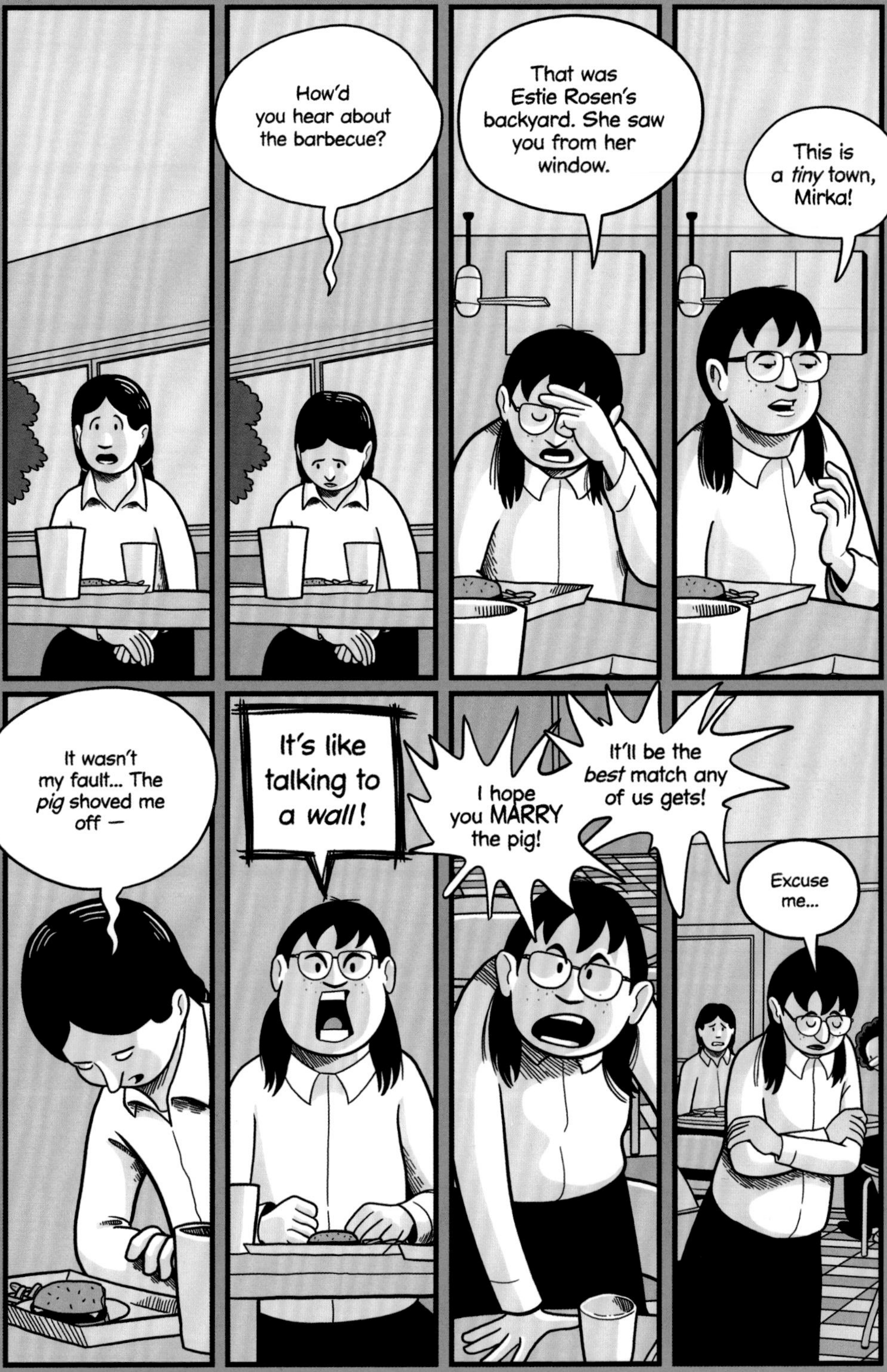
How'd you hear about the barbecue?
That was Estie Rosen's backyard. She saw you from her window.
This is a *tiny* town, Mirka!
It wasn't my fault... The *pig* shoved me off —
It's like talking to a *wall*!
I hope you MARRY the pig!
It'll be the *best* match any of us gets!
Excuse me...

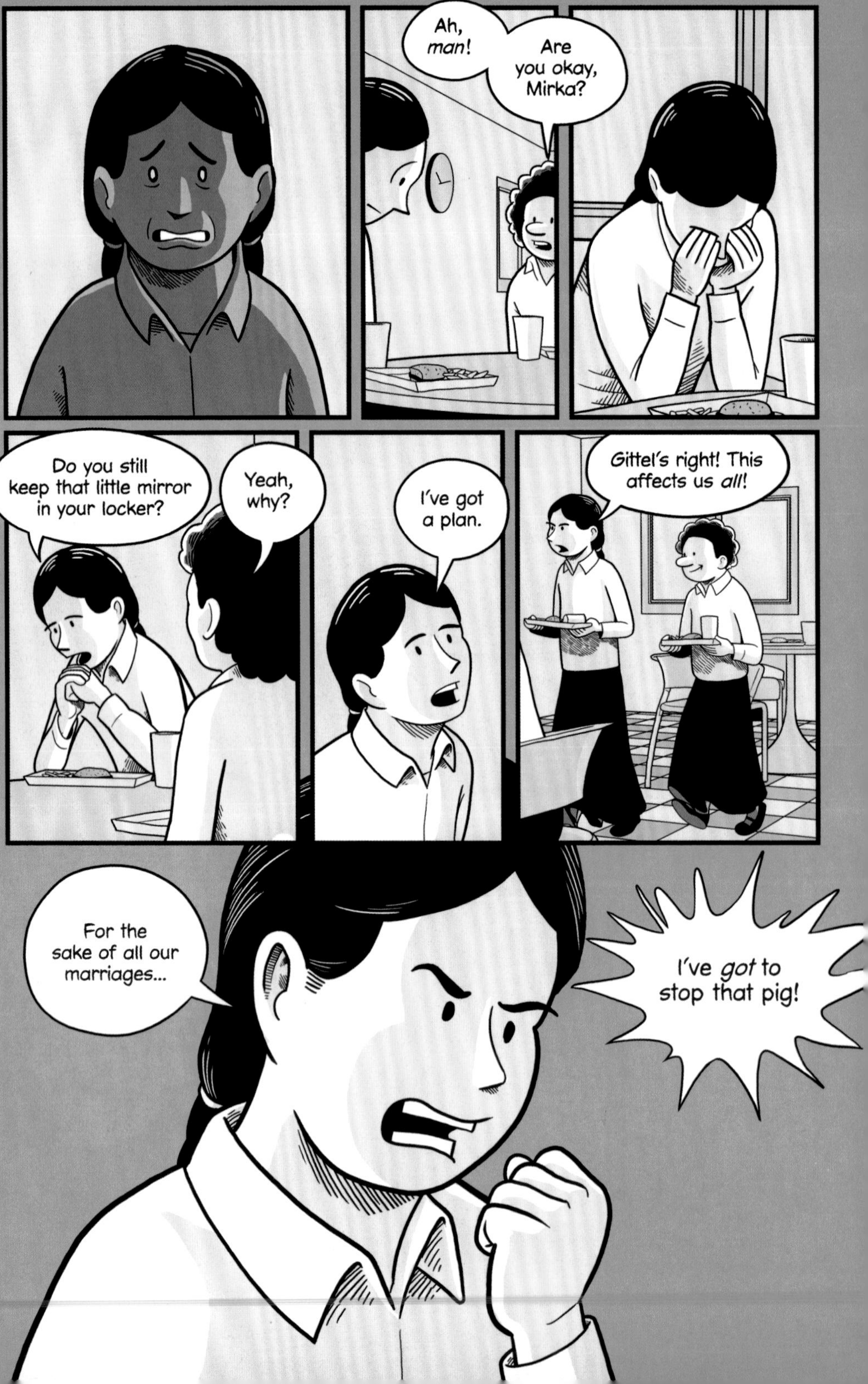
Ah, *man*!
Are you okay, Mirka?
Do you still keep that little mirror in your locker?
Yeah, why?
I've got a plan.
Gittel's right! This affects us *all*!
For the sake of all our marriages...
I've *got* to stop that pig!

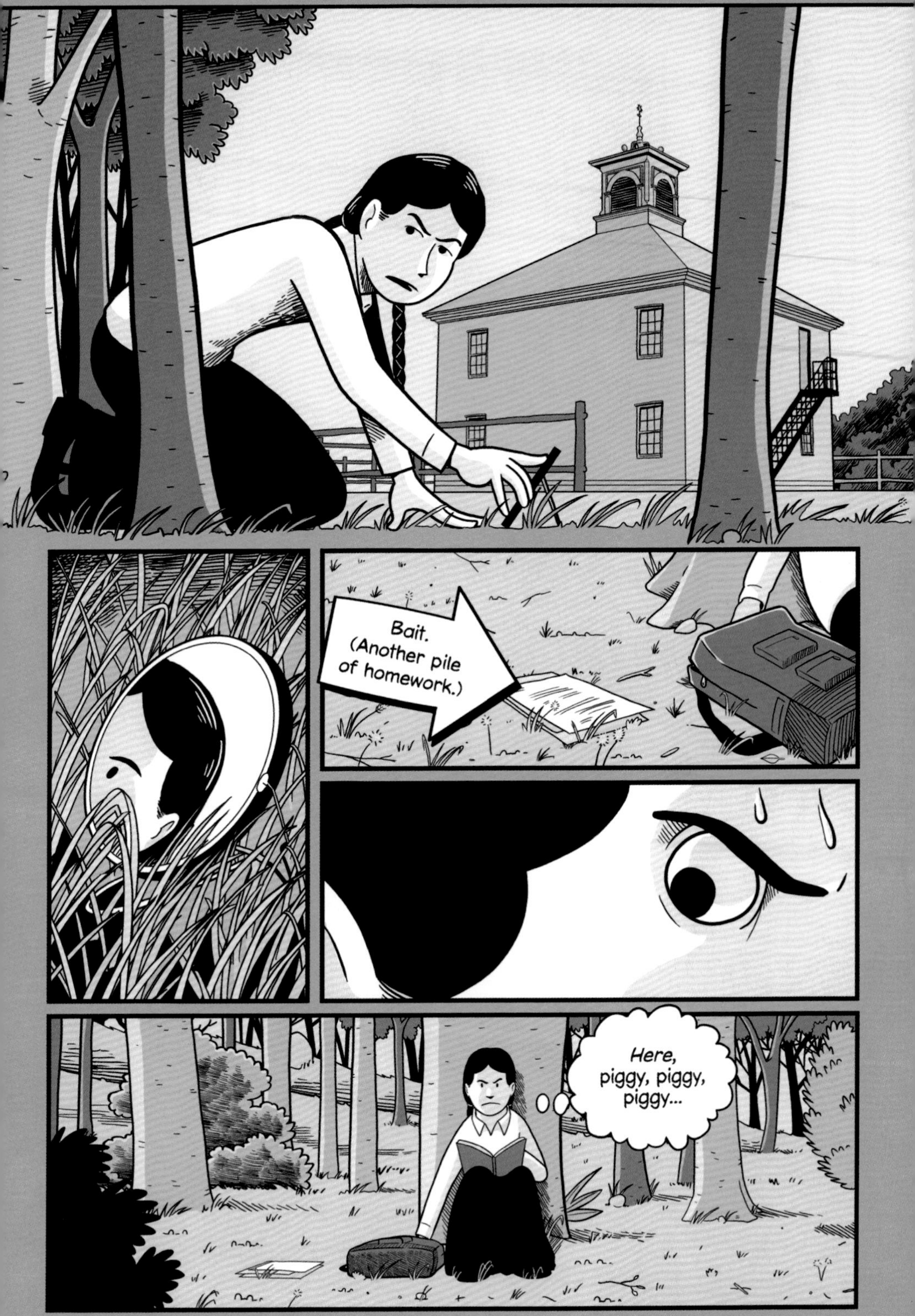
Bait.
(Another pile of homework.)
Here, piggy, piggy, piggy...

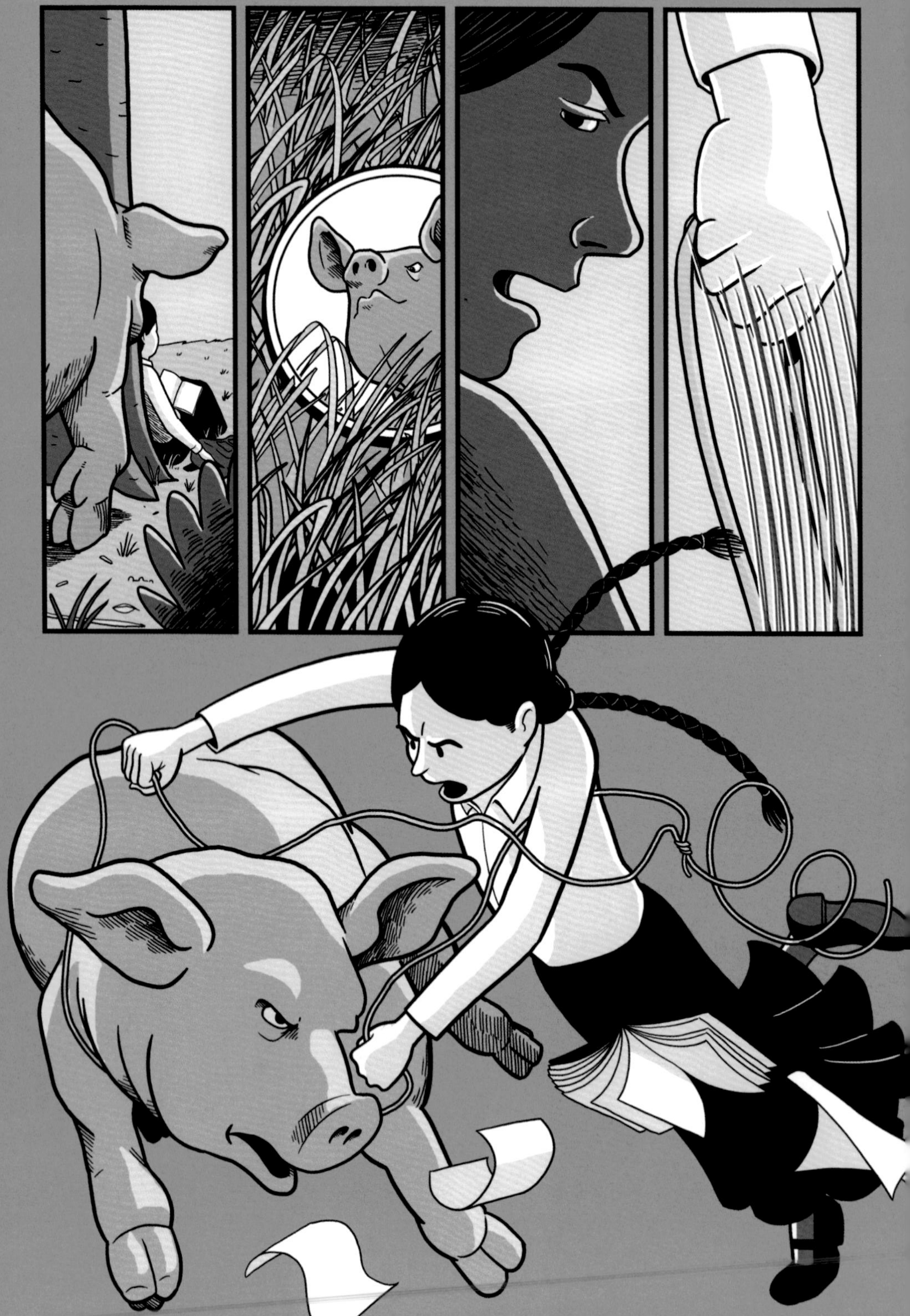

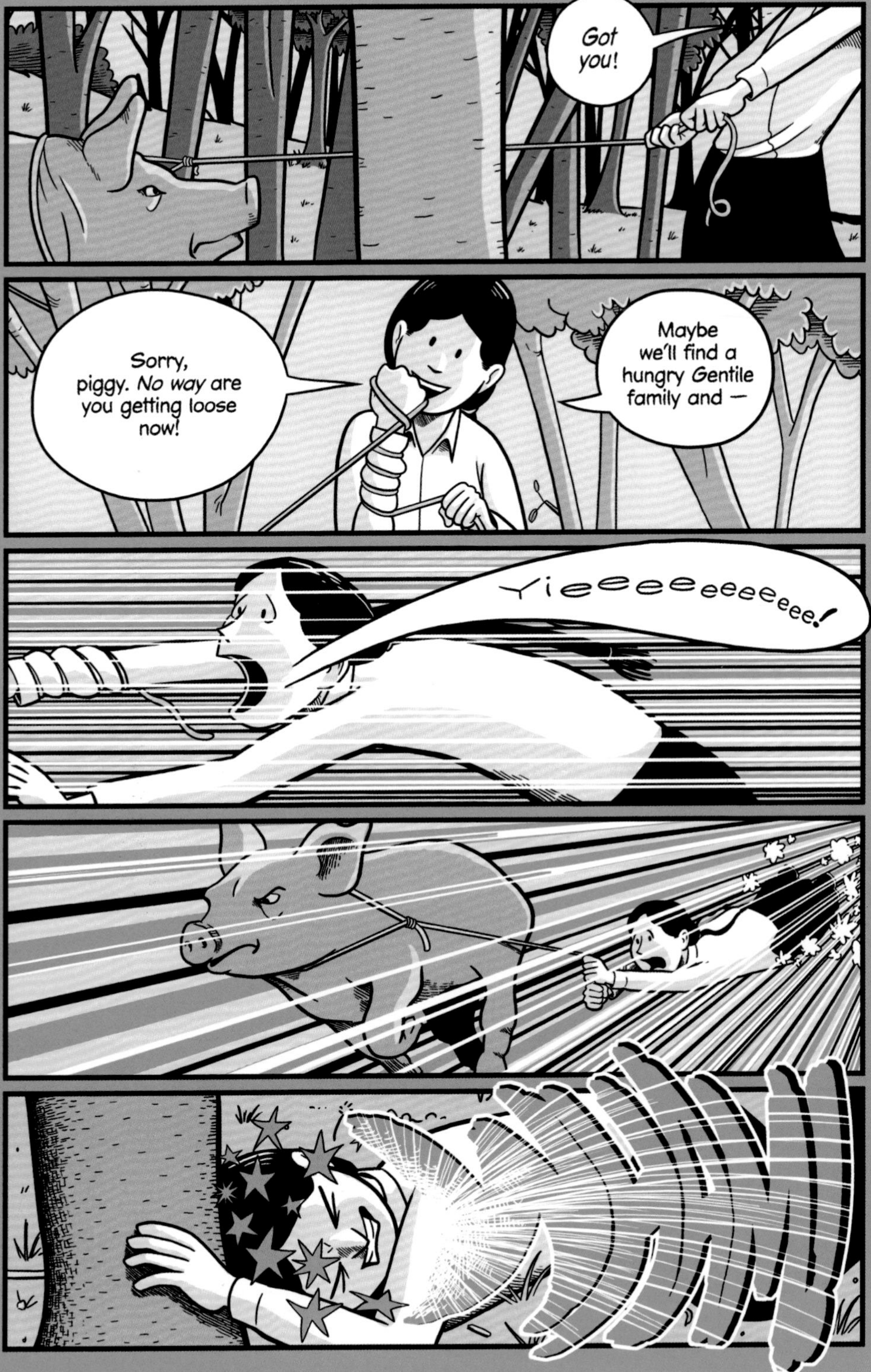
Got you!
Sorry, piggy. *No way* are you getting loose now!
Maybe we'll find a hungry Gentile family and —
Yieeeeeeeeeee!

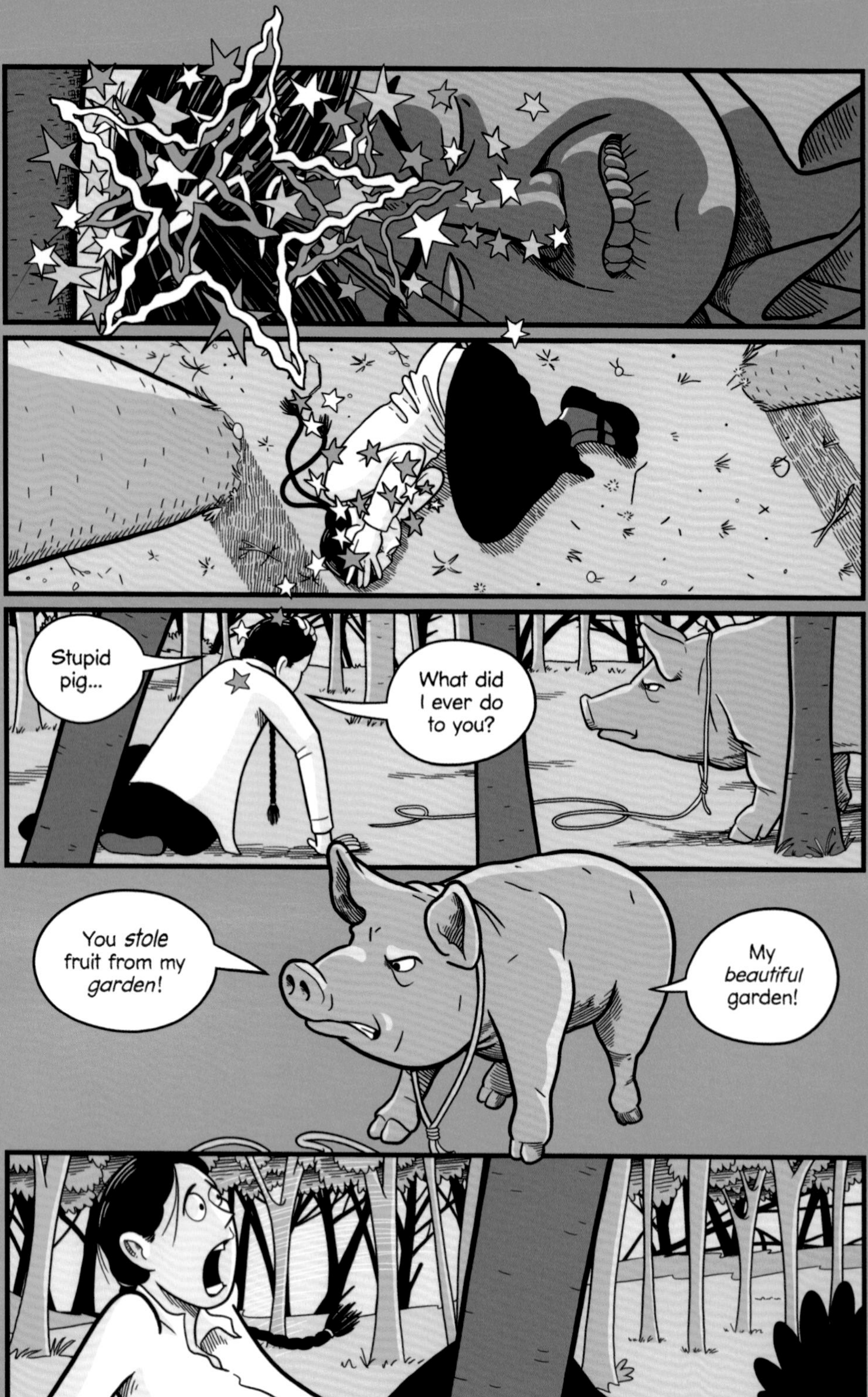
Stupid pig...
What did I ever do to you?
You *stole* fruit from my *garden*!
My *beautiful* garden!

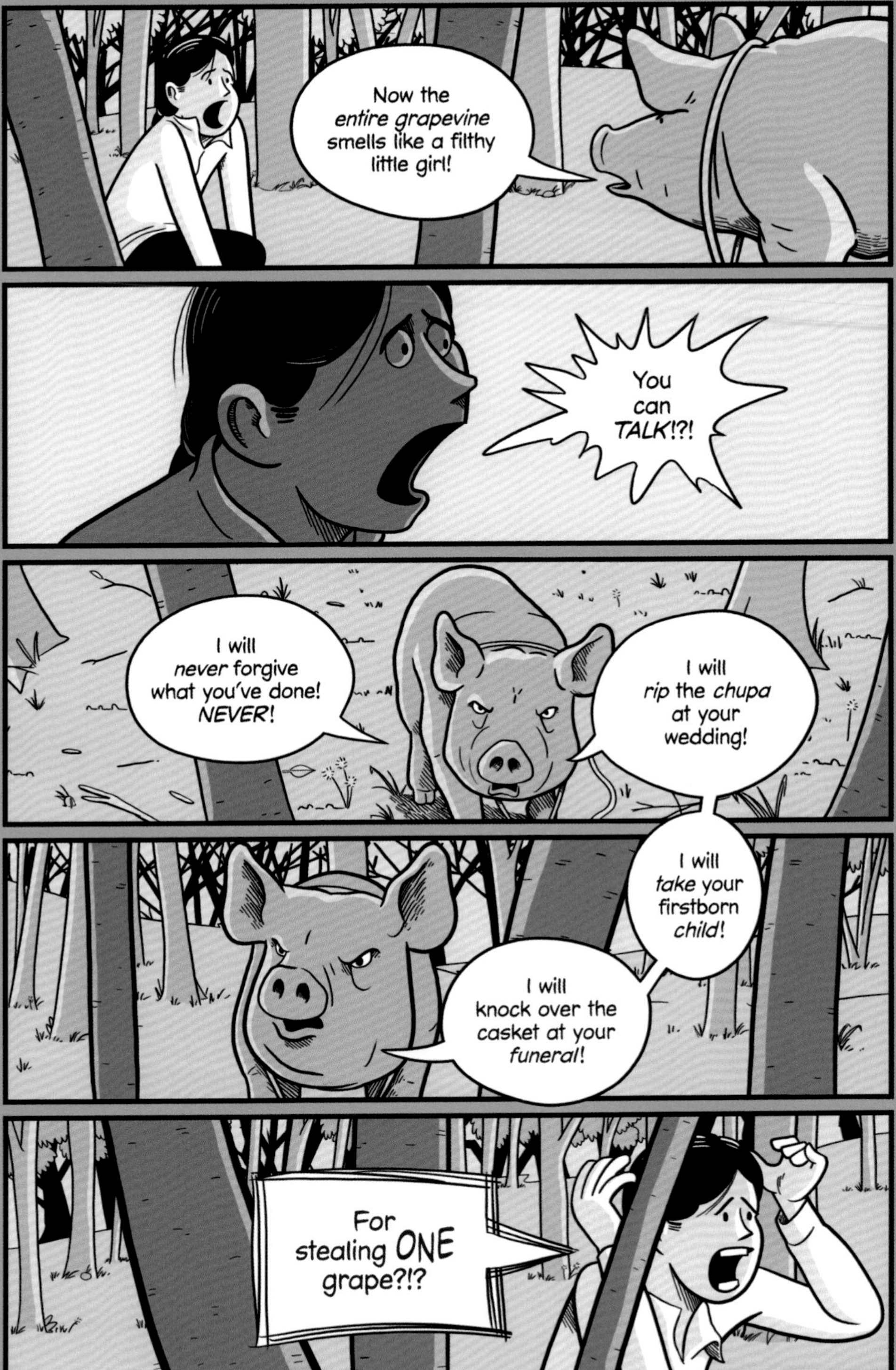
Now the *entire grapevine* smells like a filthy little girl!
You can *TALK*!?!
I will *never* forgive what you've done! *NEVER*!
I will *rip* the *chupa* at your wedding!
I will *take* your firstborn *child*!
I will knock over the casket at your *funeral*!
For stealing ONE grape?!?

Chupa: canopy

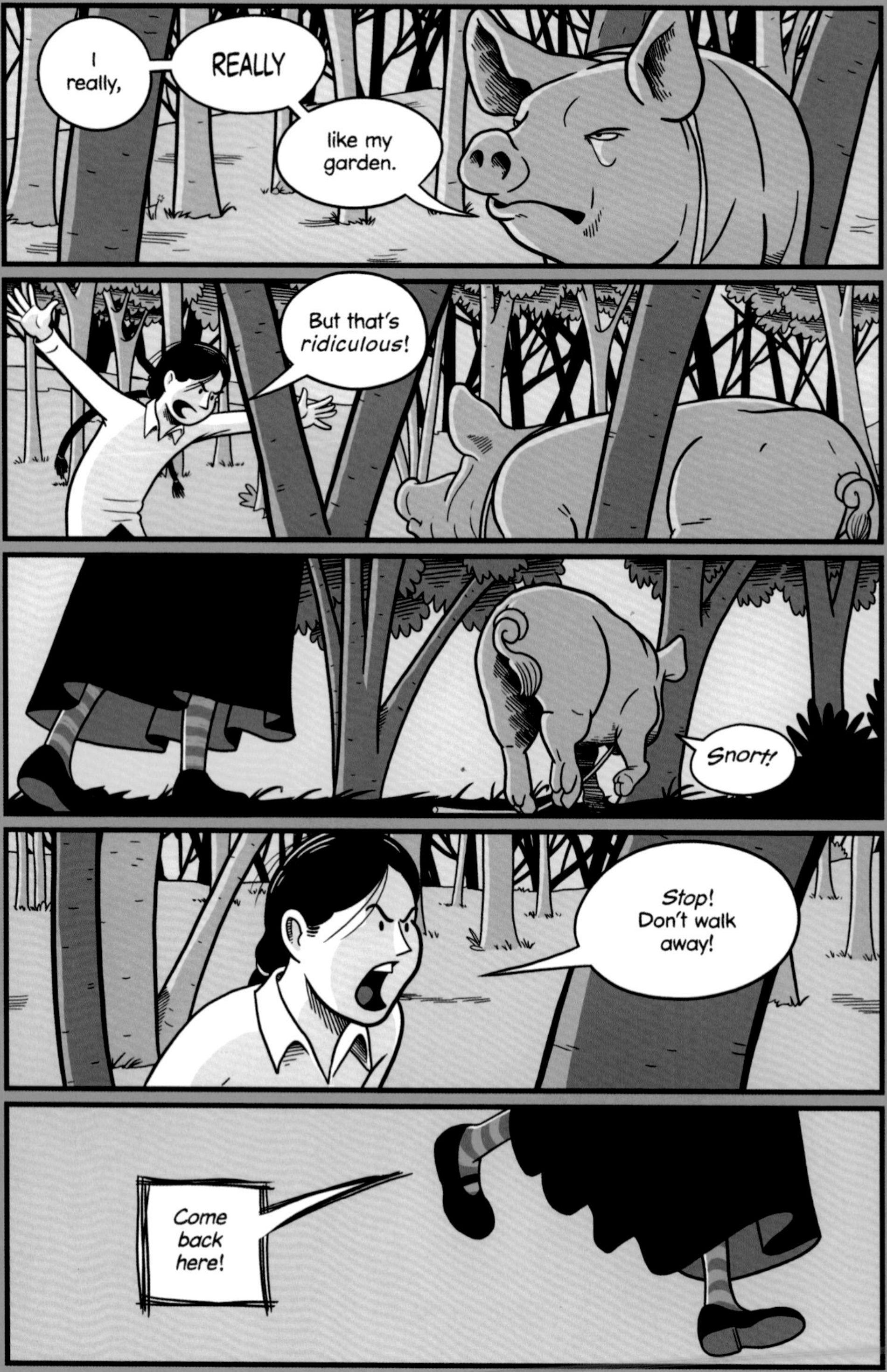
I really,
REALLY
like my garden.
But that's *ridiculous!*
Snort!
Stop! Don't walk away!
Come back here!

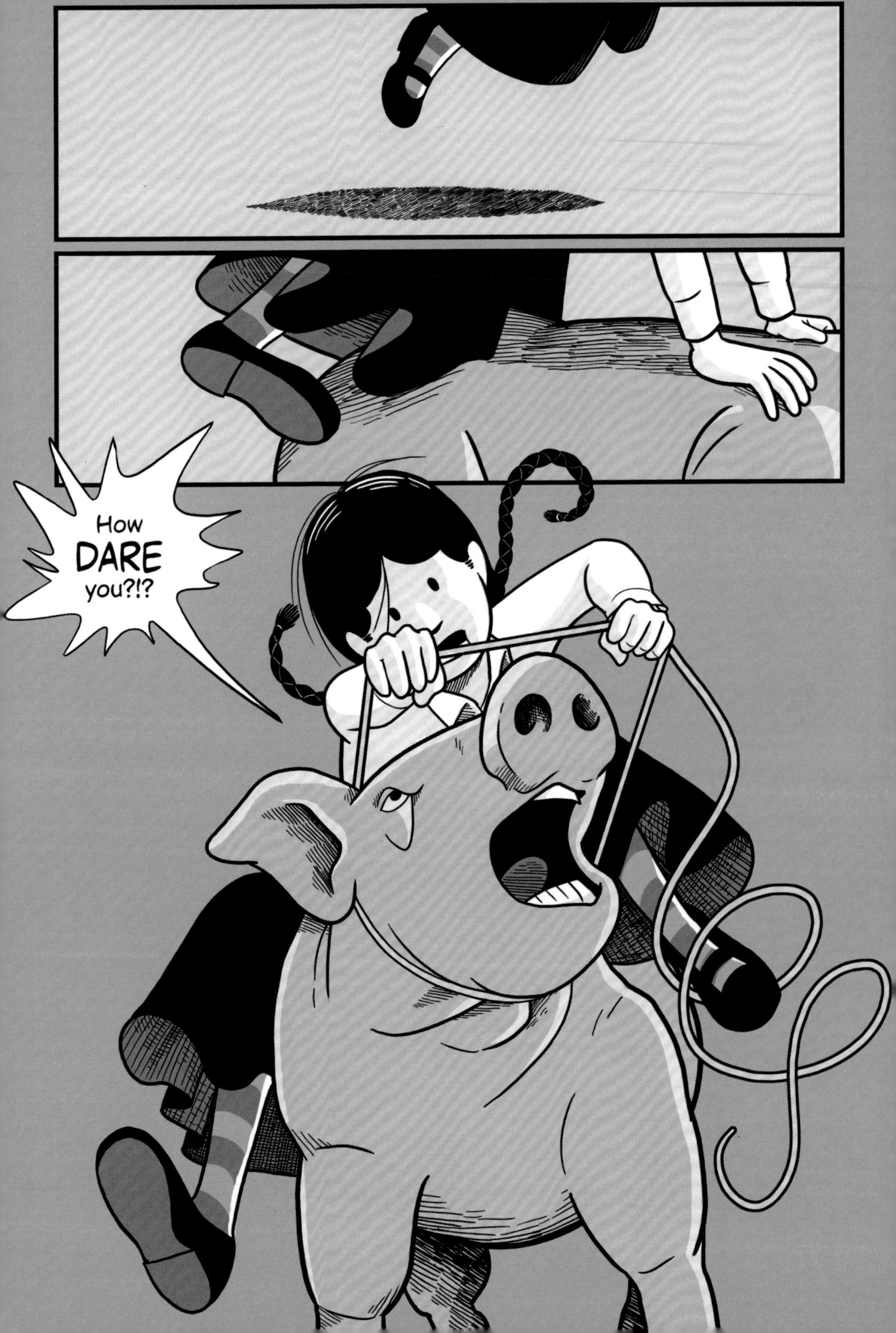
How DARE you?!?

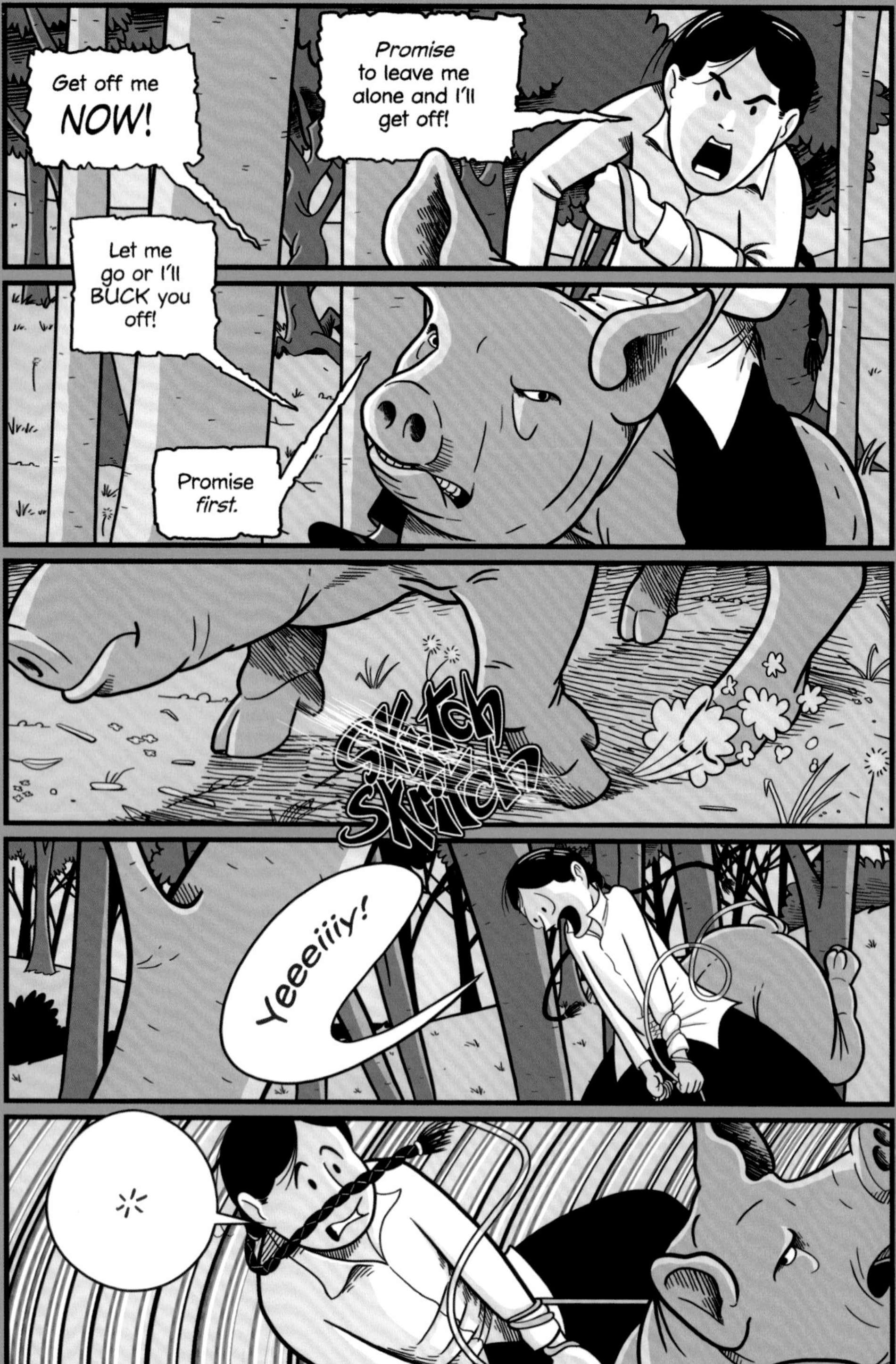
Get off me NOW!
Promise to leave me alone and I'll get off!
Let me go or I'll BUCK you off!
Promise first.
Skrtch Skritch
Yeeeiiiy!

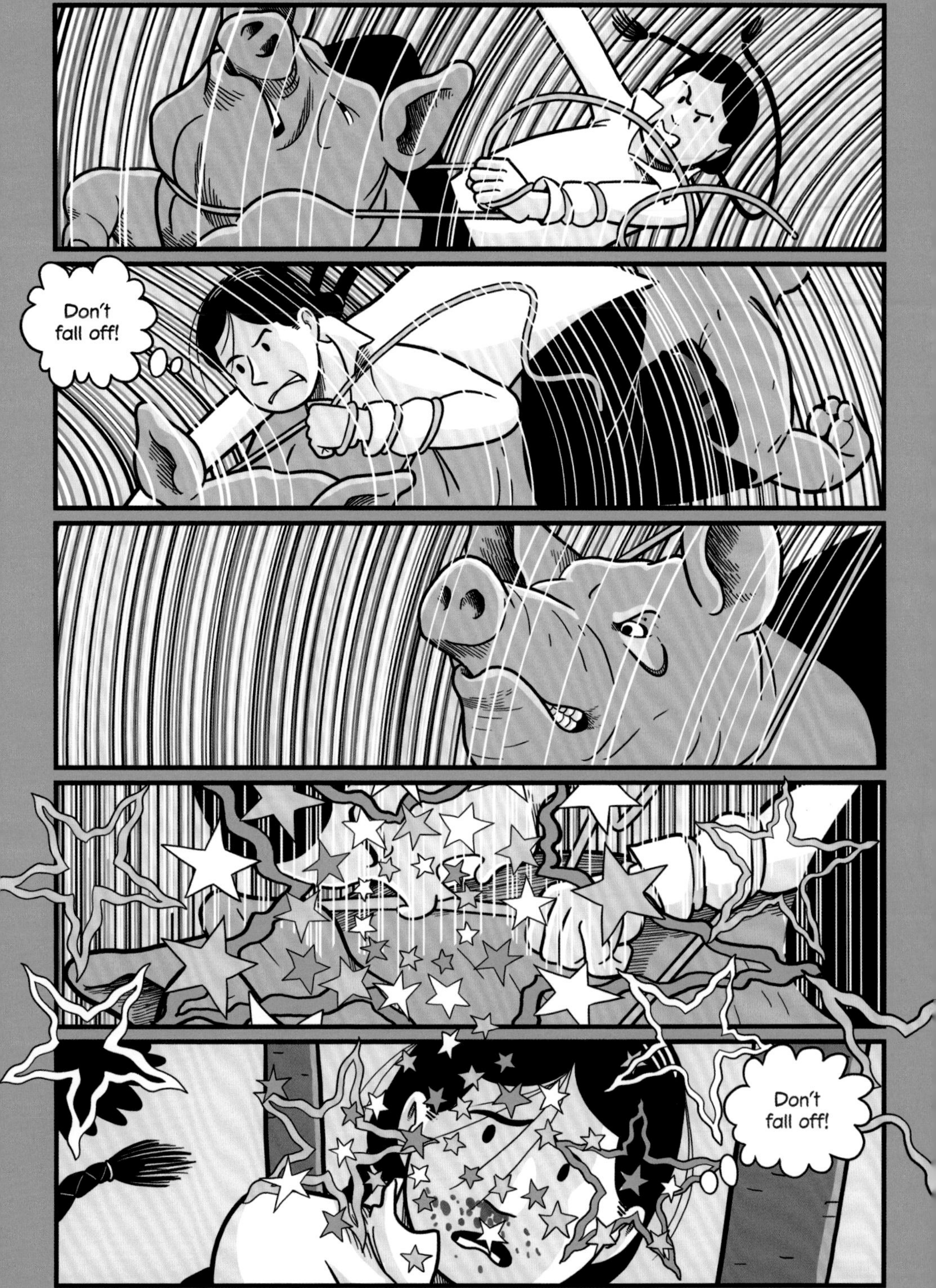
Don't fall off!
Don't fall off!

hork! hork! HORK!
I'LL GET OFF!
Just say you'll leave me alone.
Not if you live a hundred years.
If I can't shake you off, I'll *scrape* you off.

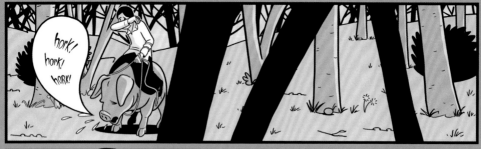

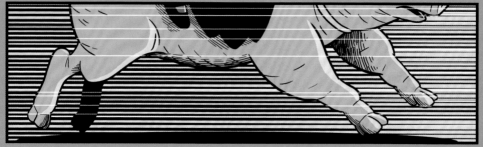

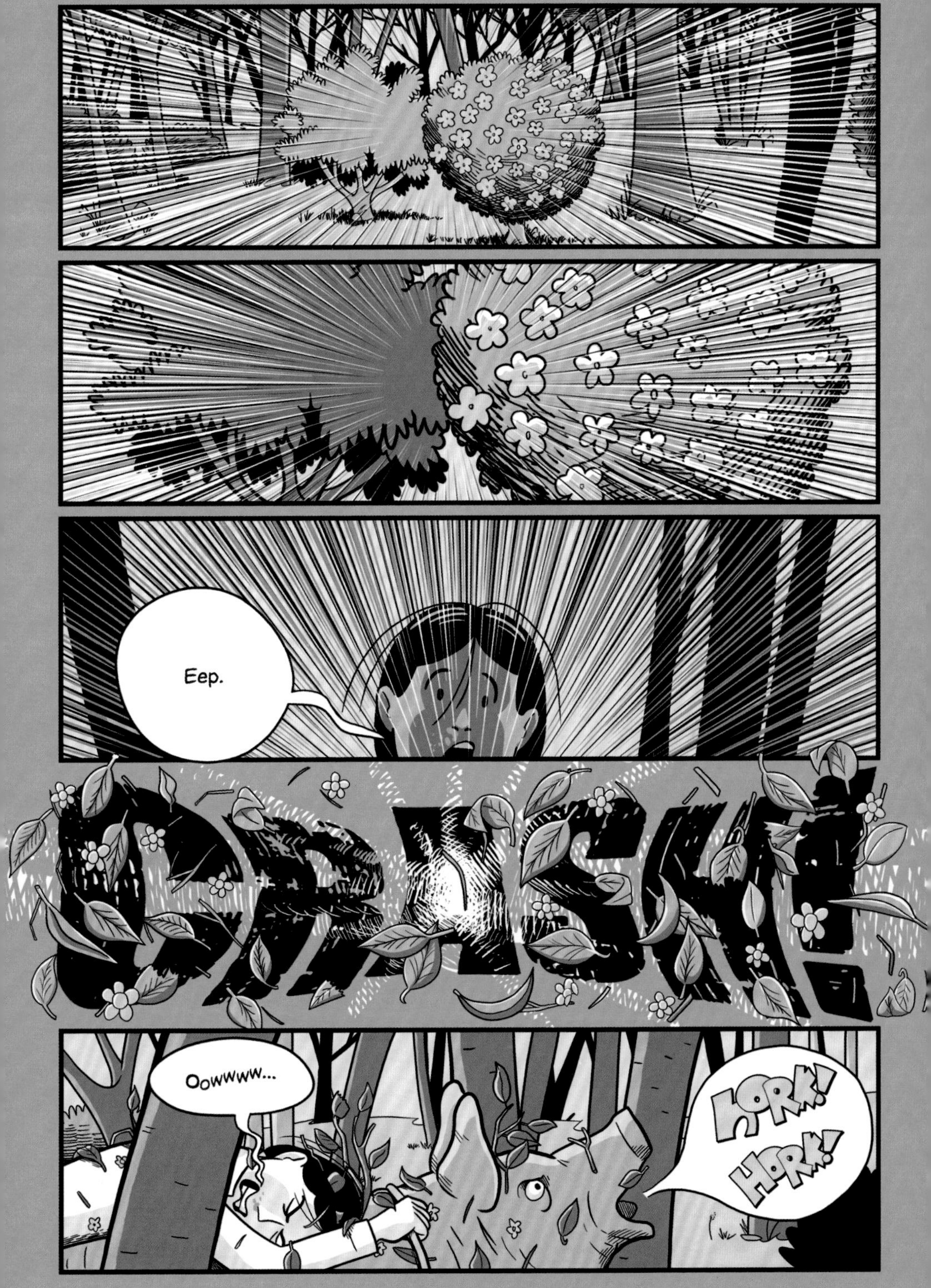
Eep.
CRASH!
Oowwww...
HORK! HORK!

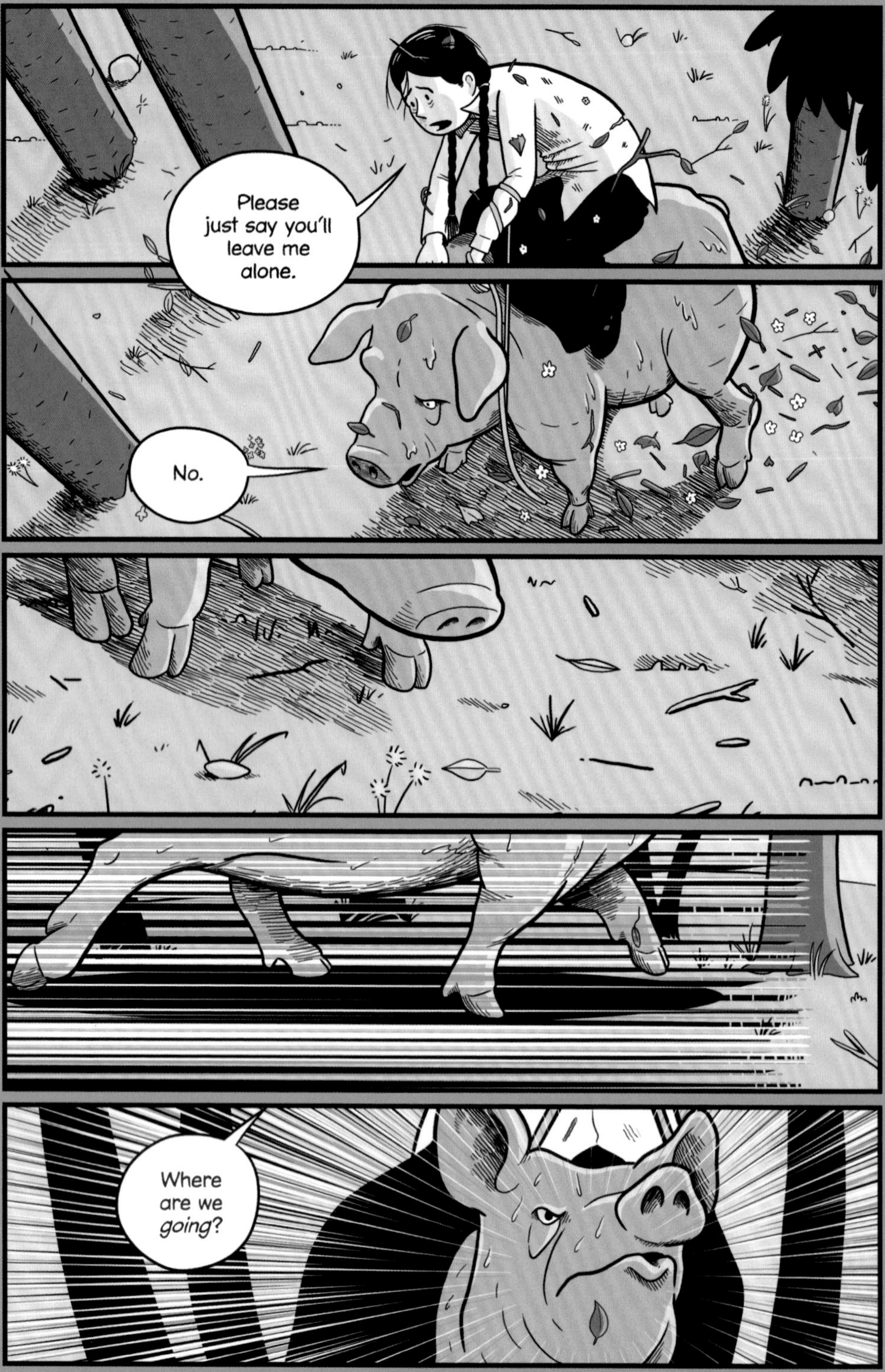
Please just say you'll leave me alone.
No.
Where are we *going*?

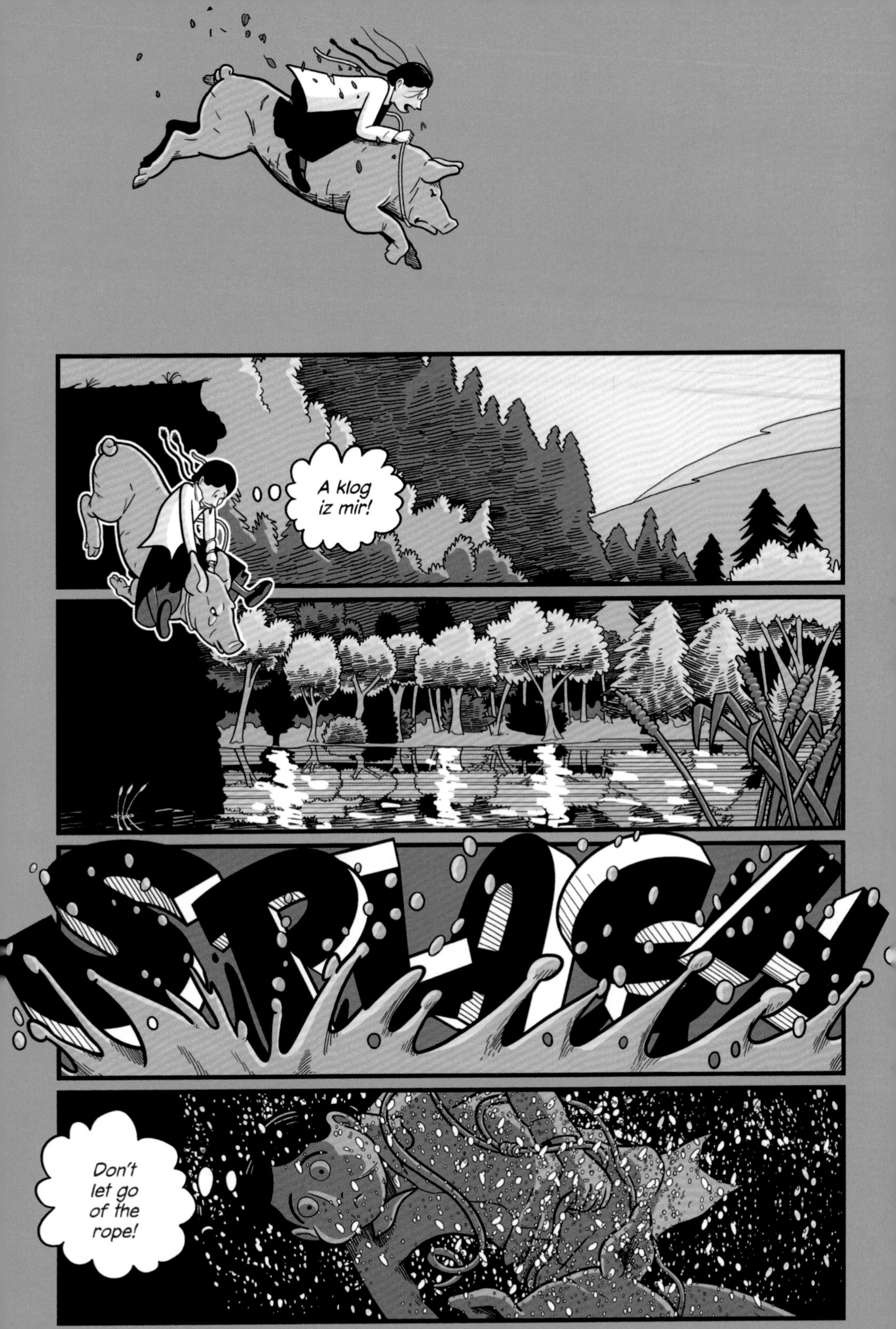
A klog iz mir!
SPLASH
Don't let go of the rope!

A klog iz mir: Woe is me!

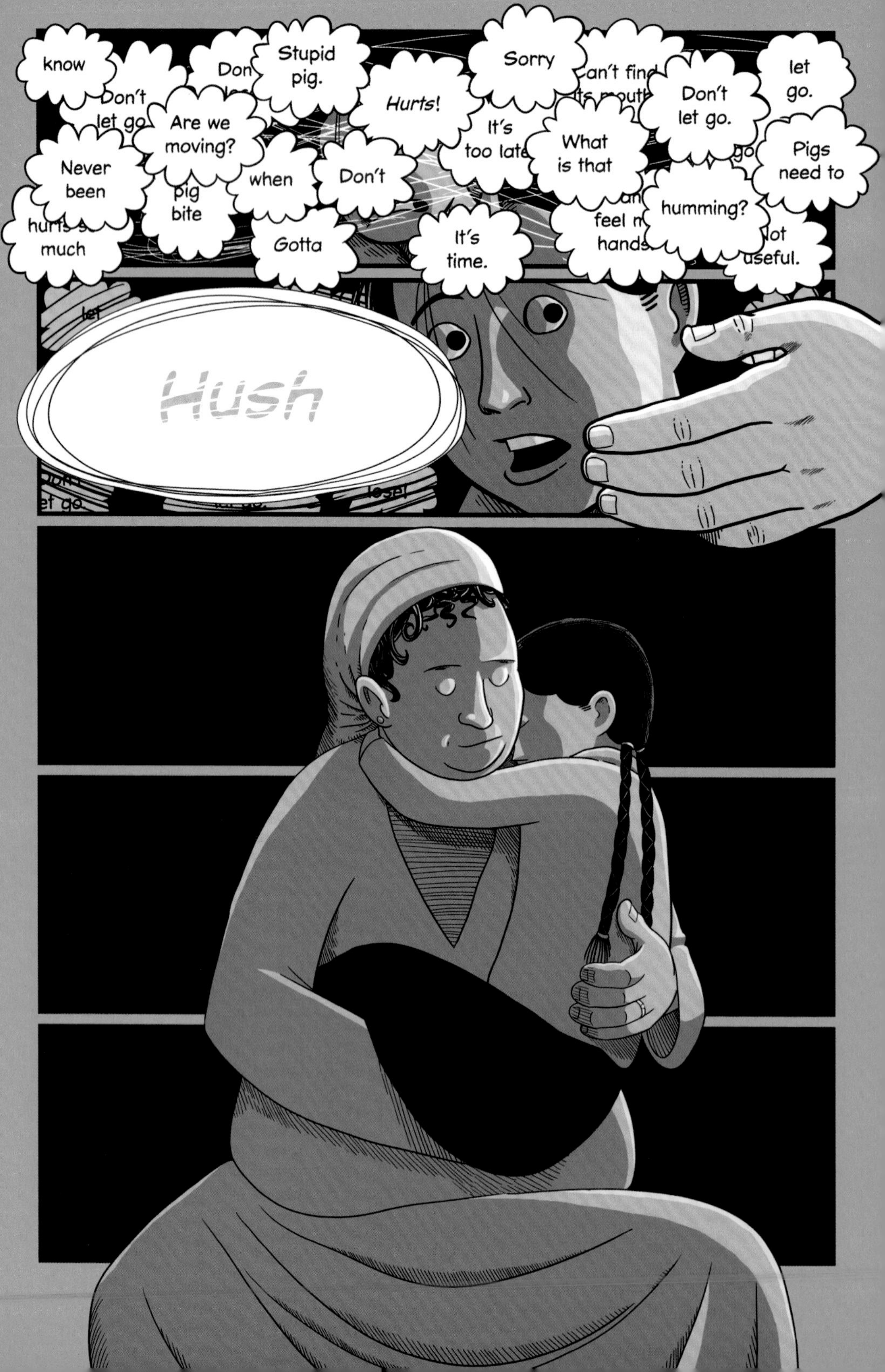
know
Stupid pig.
Sorry
let go.
Are we moving?
Hurts!
What is that
Don't let go.
Pigs need to
Never been
pig bite
when
Don't
humming?
much
Gotta
It's time.
Hush

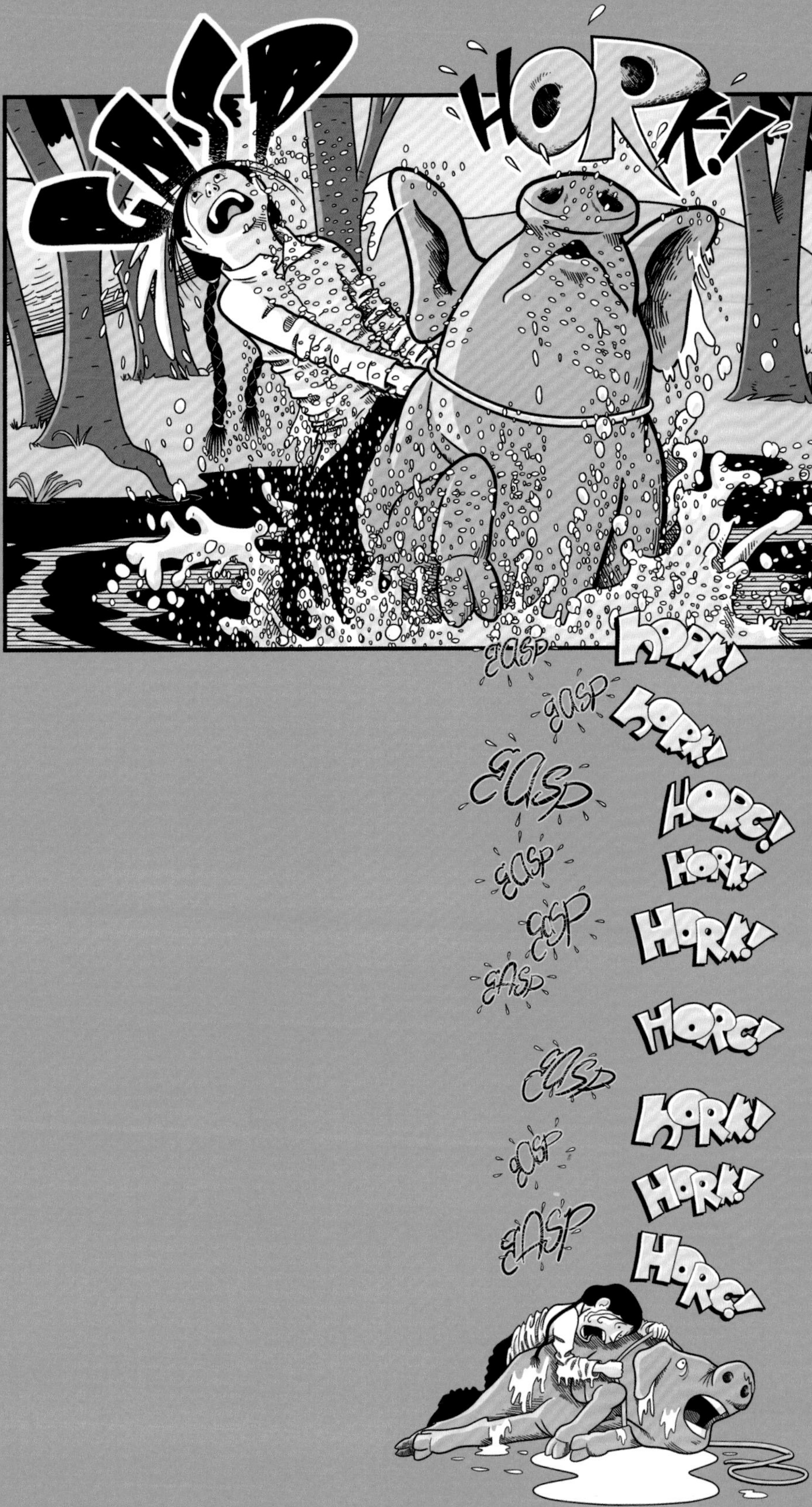
GASP
HORK!
gasp
HORK!
gasp
HORK!
GASP
HORC!
gasp
HORK!
gasp
HORK!
gasp
HORC!
GASP
HORK!
gasp
HORK!
GASP
HORC!

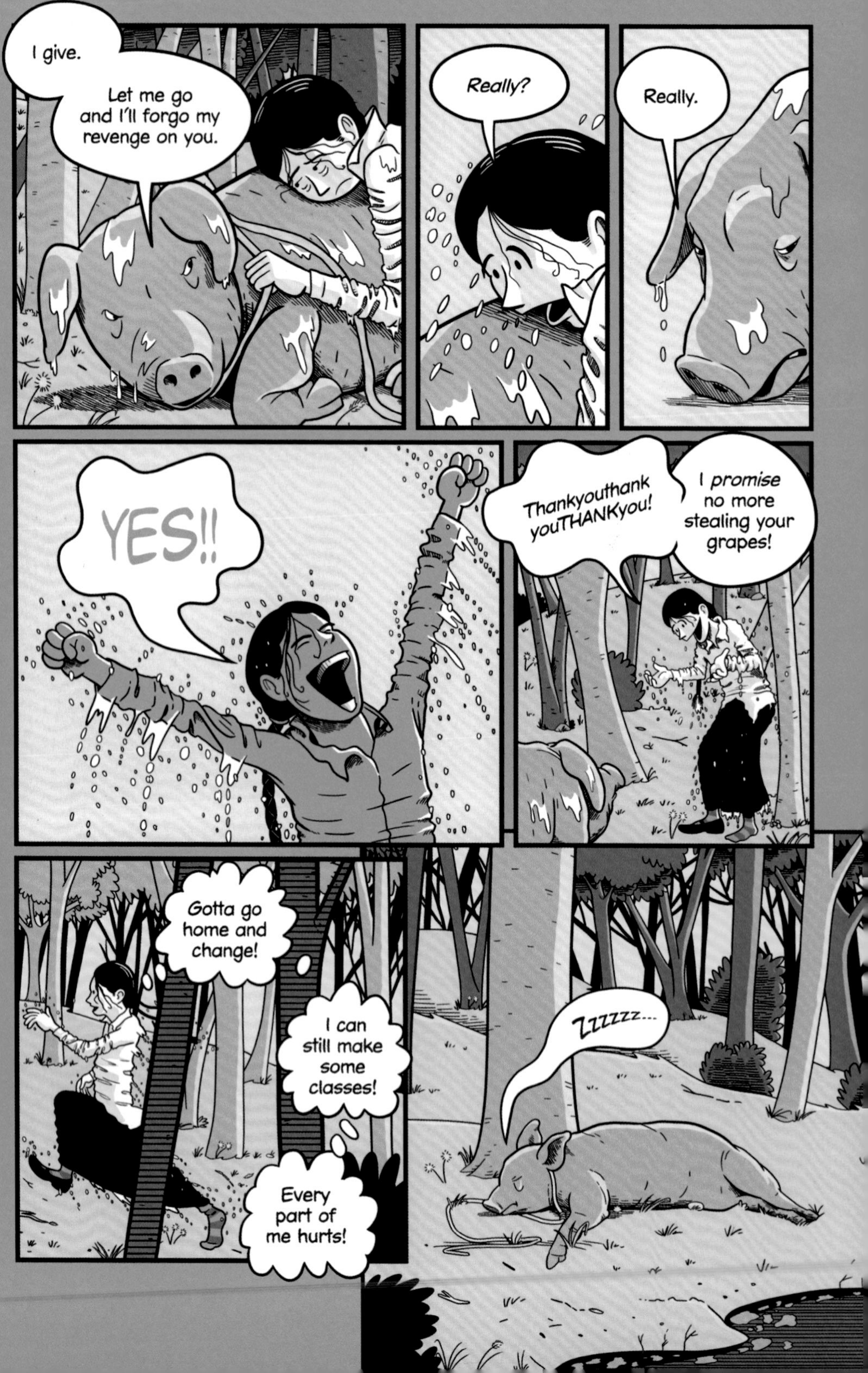
I give.
Let me go and I'll forgo my revenge on you.
Really?
Really.
YES!!
Thankyouthank youTHANKyou!
I promise no more stealing your grapes!
Gotta go home and change!
I can still make some classes!
Every part of me hurts!
Zzzzzz...

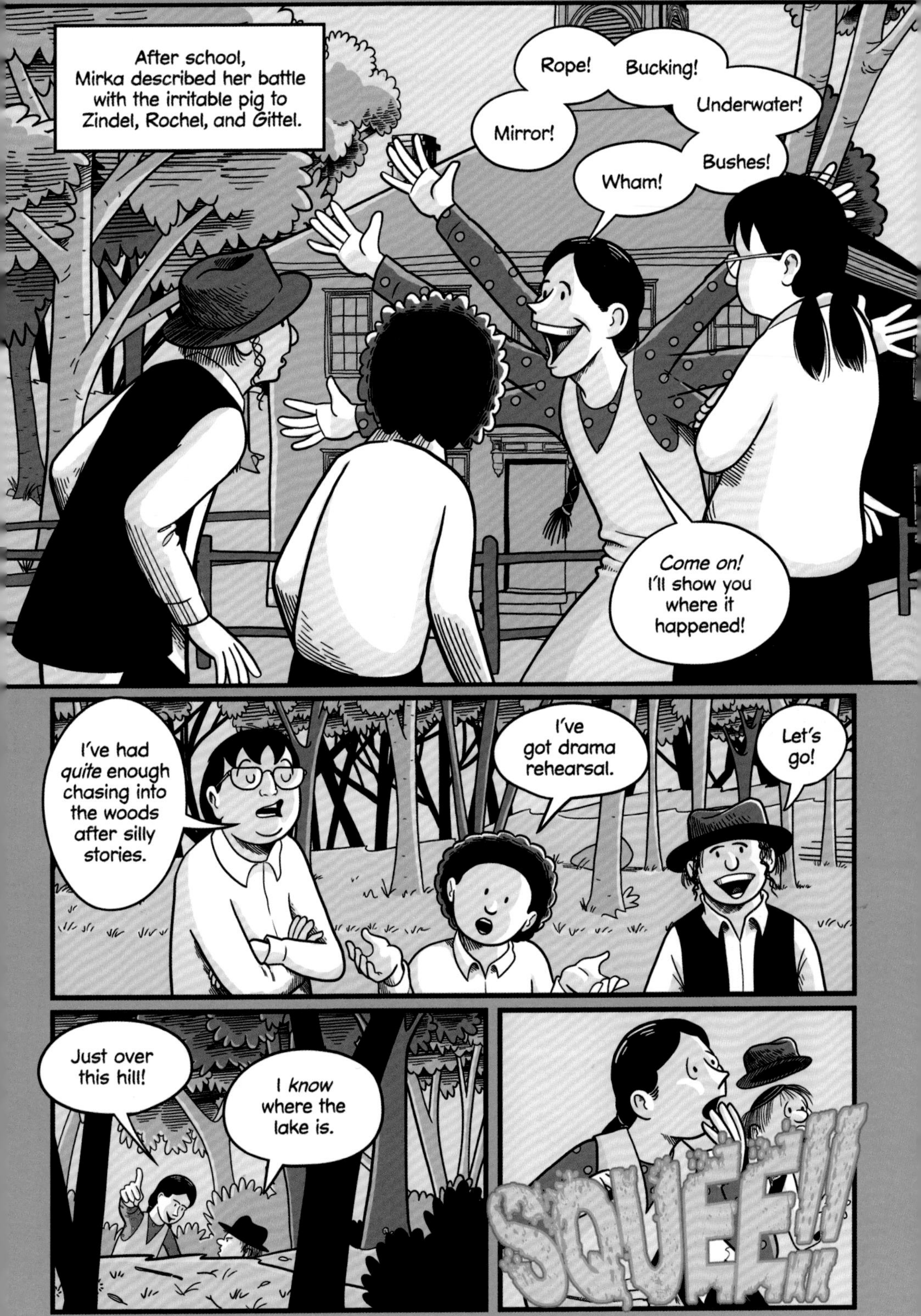
After school, Mirka described her battle with the irritable pig to Zindel, Rochel, and Gittel.
Mirror!
Rope!
Bucking!
Underwater!
Bushes!
Wham!
Come on! I'll show you where it happened!
I've had *quite* enough chasing into the woods after silly stories.
I've got drama rehearsal.
Let's go!
Just over this hill!
I *know* where the lake is.
SQUEE!!

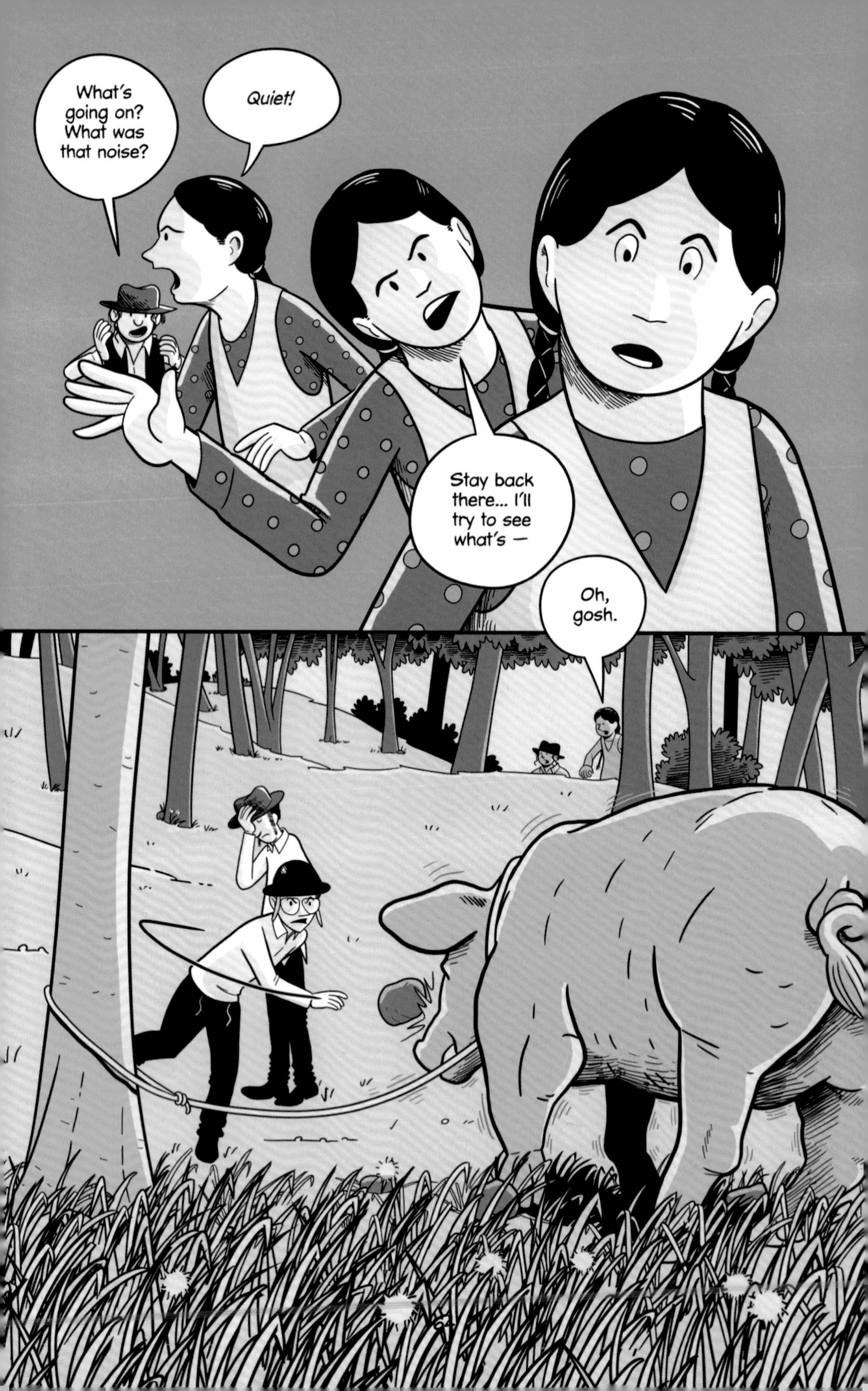
What's going on? What was that noise?
Quiet!
Stay back there... I'll try to see what's —
Oh, gosh.

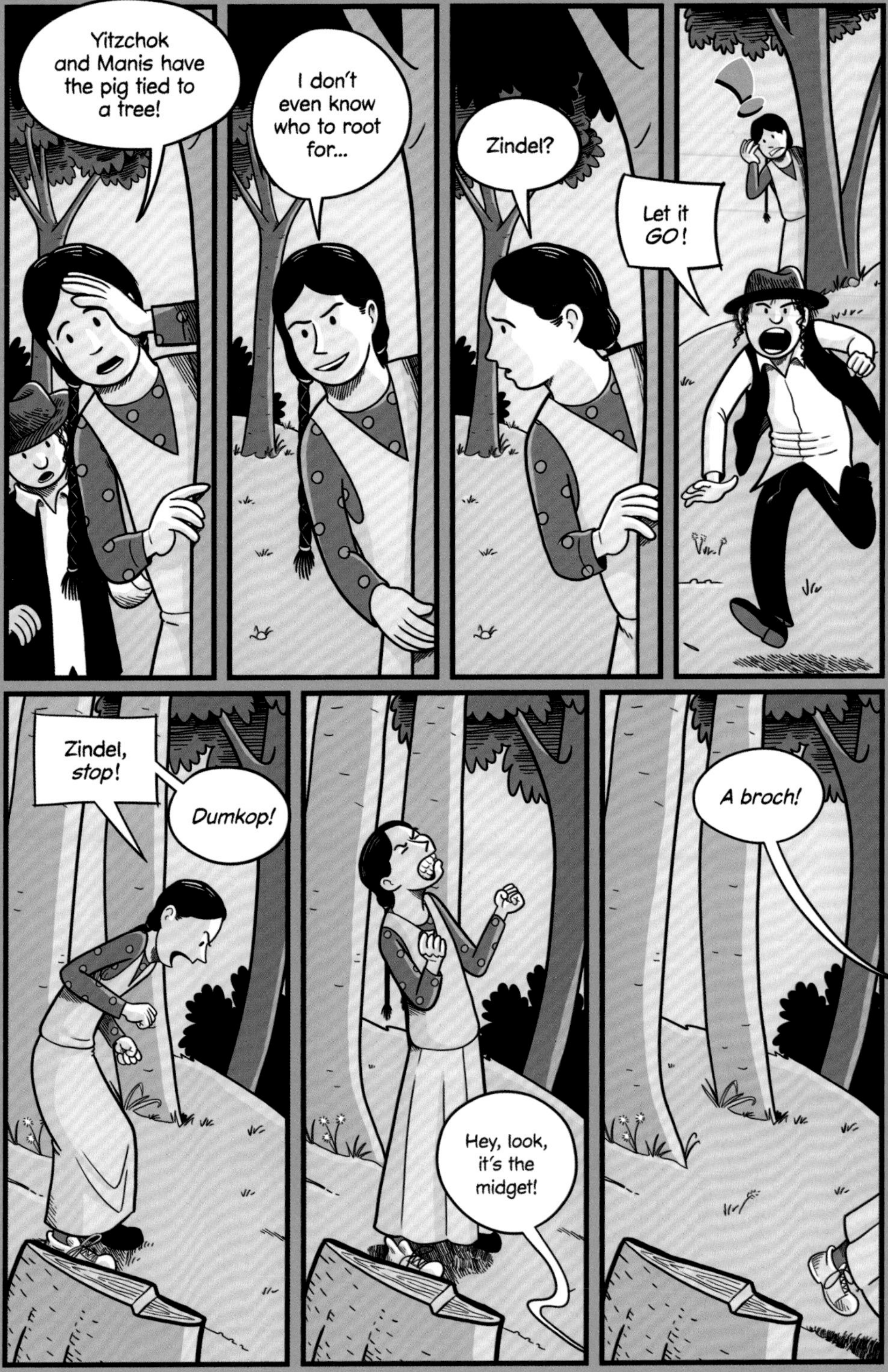
Yitzchok and Manis have the pig tied to a tree!
I don't even know who to root for...
Zindel?
Let it *GO*!
Zindel, *stop*!
Dumkop!
Hey, look, it's the midget!
A broch!

Dumkop: dummy
A broch: ☆@M#!

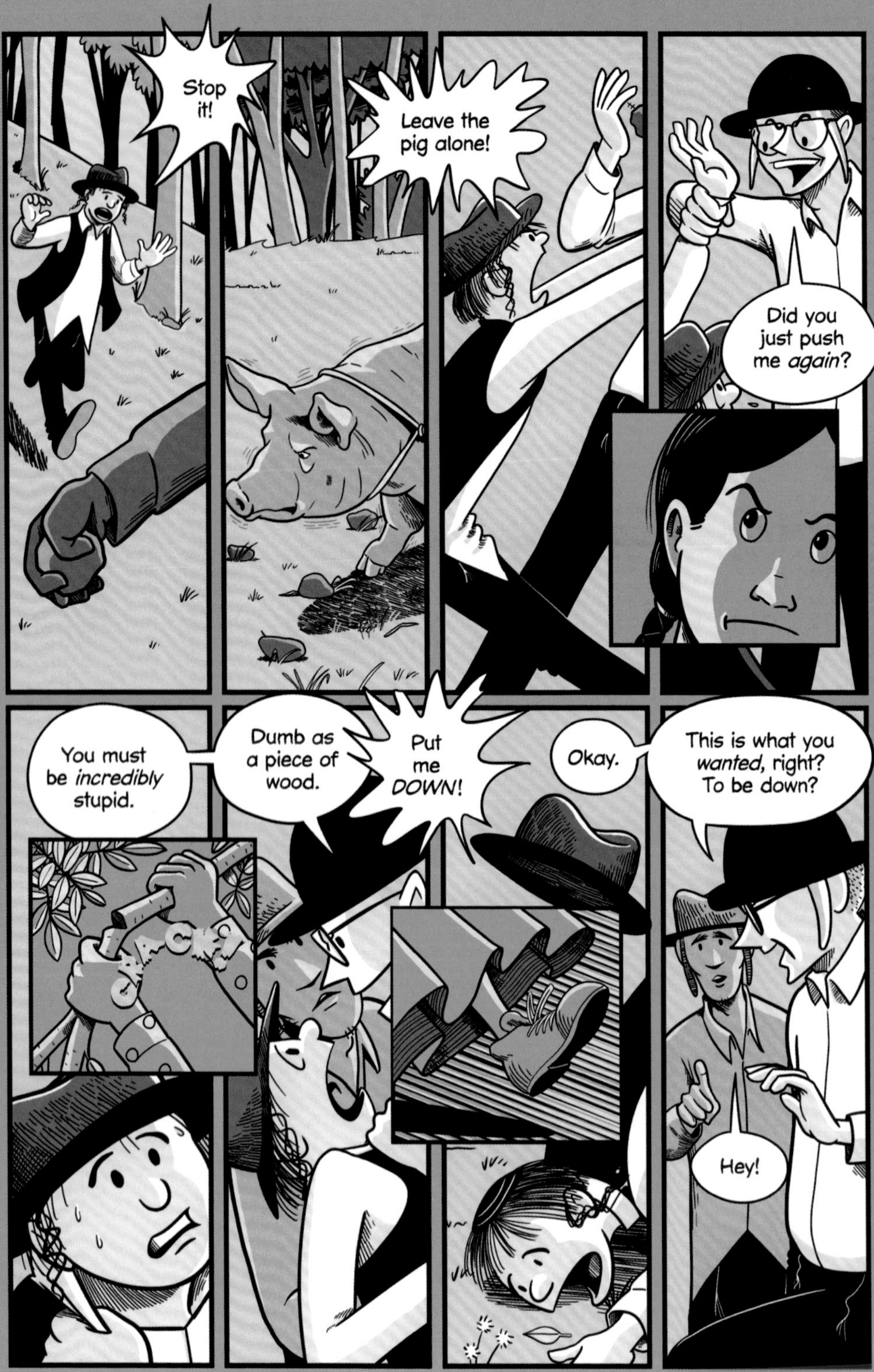
Stop it!
Leave the pig alone!
Did you just push me *again*?
You must be *incredibly* stupid.
Dumb as a piece of wood.
CRACK!
Put me *DOWN*!
Okay.
This is what you *wanted*, right? To be down?
Hey!

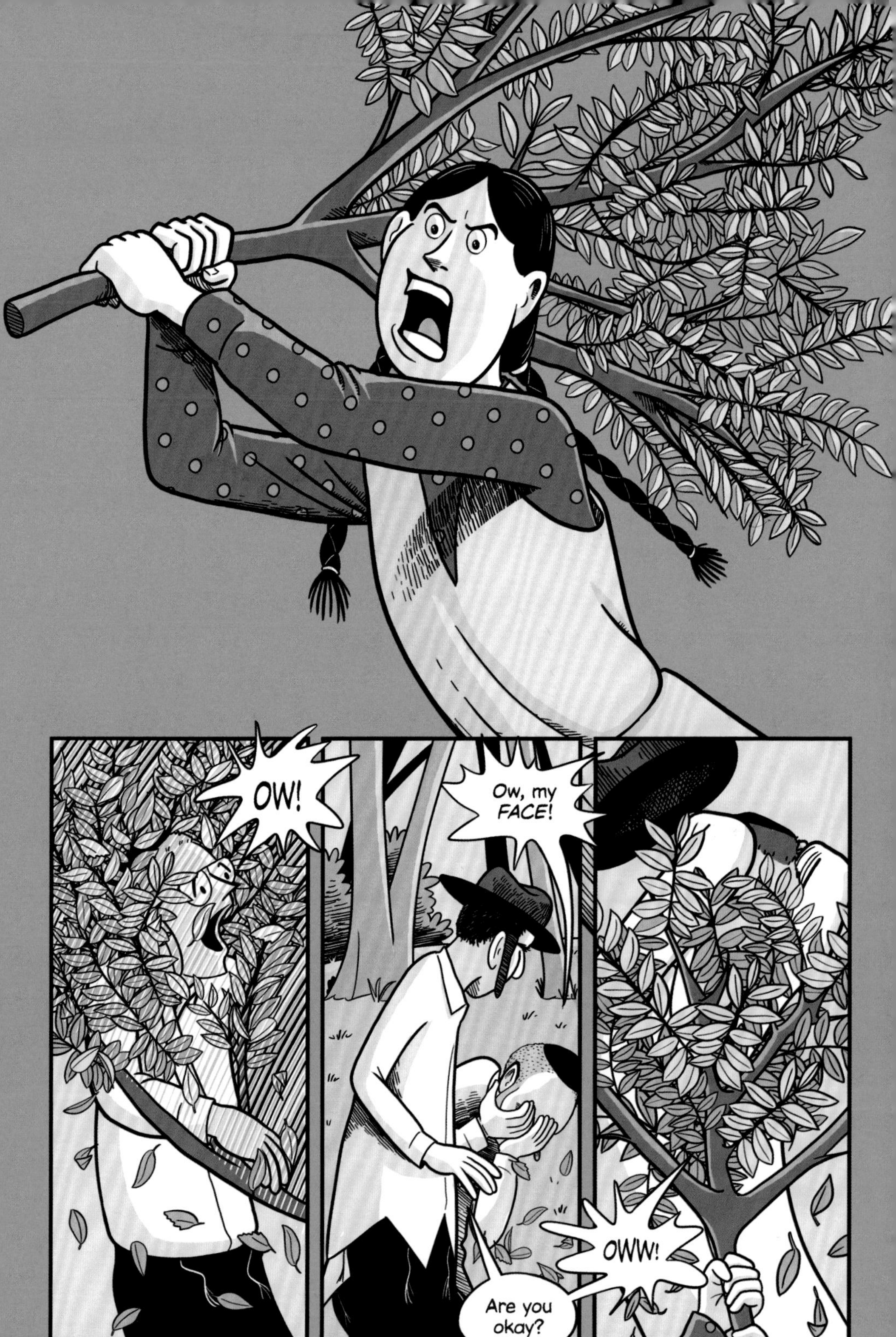

OW!
Ow, my FACE!
Are you okay?
OWW!

Negiah: rules forbidding contact between
unrelated females and males

Nebs: losers

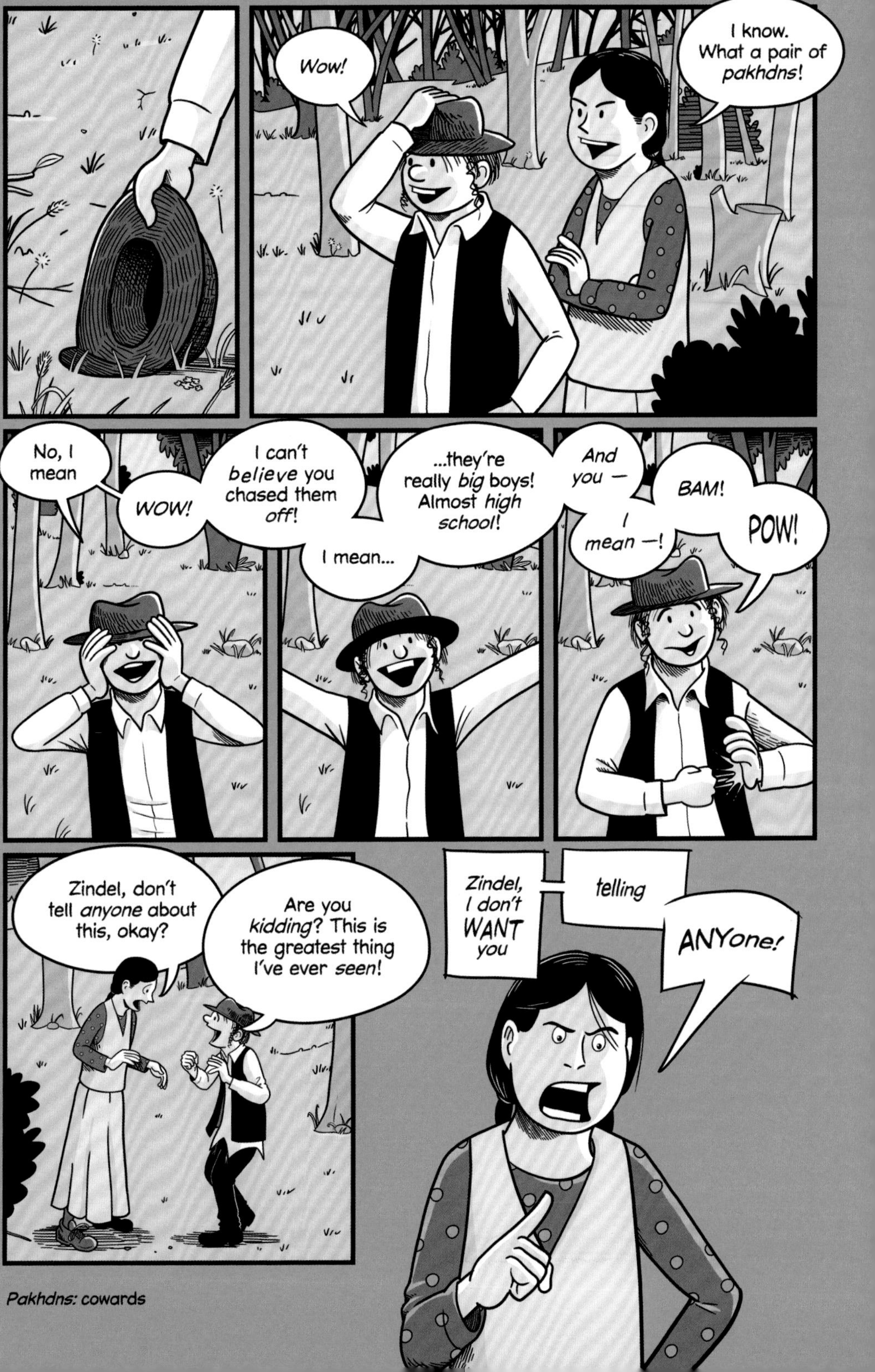
Wow!
I know. What a pair of *pakhdns*!
No, I mean
WOW!
I can't *believe* you chased them *off*!
I mean...
...they're really *big* boys! Almost *high school*!
And you —
I mean —!
BAM!
POW!
Zindel, don't tell *anyone* about this, okay?
Are you *kidding*? This is the greatest thing I've ever *seen*!
Zindel, I don't WANT you
telling
ANYone!

Pakhdns: cowards

70

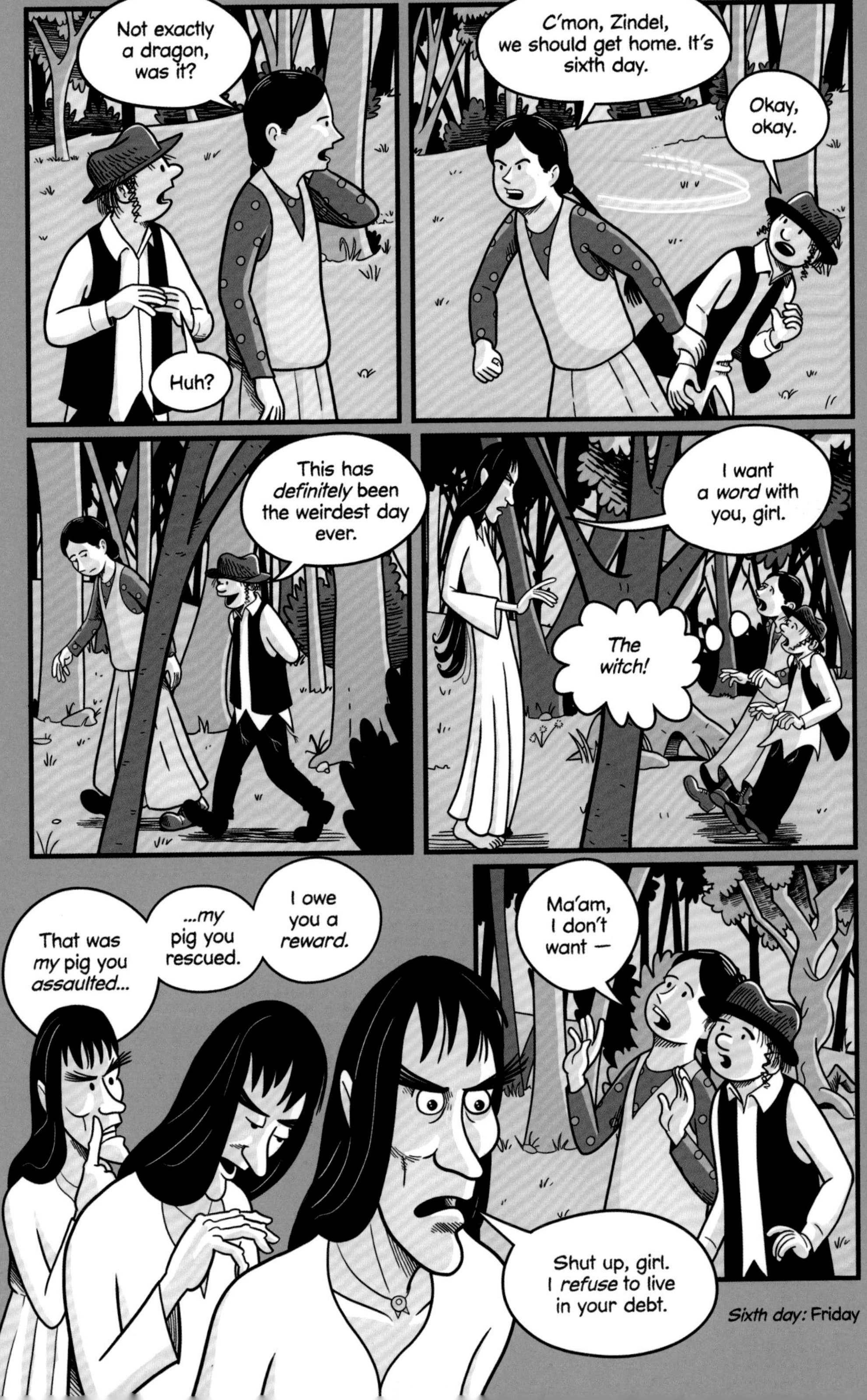
Not exactly a dragon, was it?
Huh?
C'mon, Zindel, we should get home. It's sixth day.
Okay, okay.
This has *definitely* been the weirdest day ever.
I want a *word* with you, girl.
The witch!
That was *my* pig you *assaulted...*
...my pig you rescued.
I owe you a *reward.*
Ma'am, I don't want —
Shut up, girl. I *refuse* to live in your debt.
Sixth day: Friday

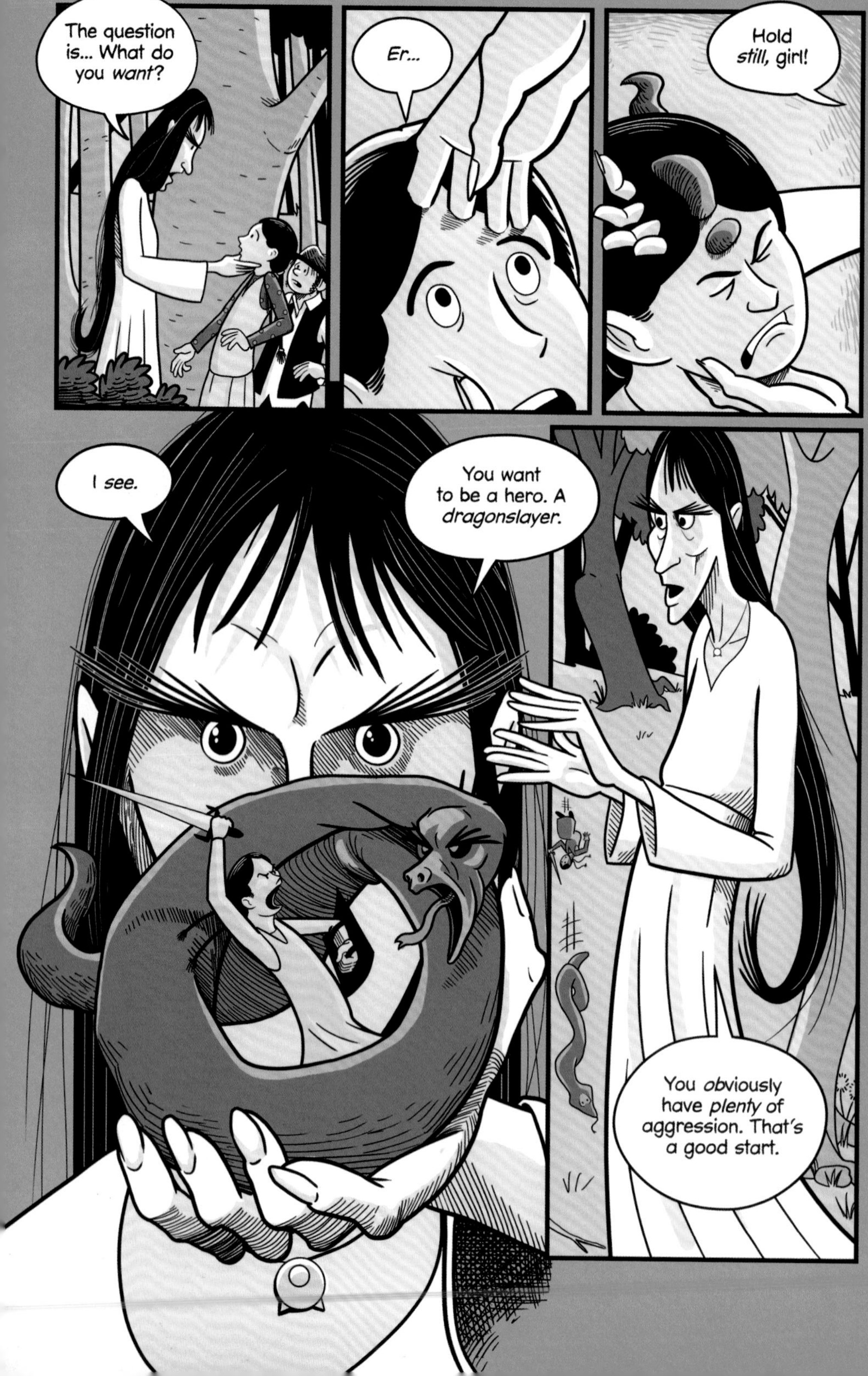
The question is... What do you *want*?
Er...
Hold *still*, girl!
I *see*.
You want to be a hero. A *dragonslayer*.
You *ob*viously have *plenty* of aggression. That's a good start.

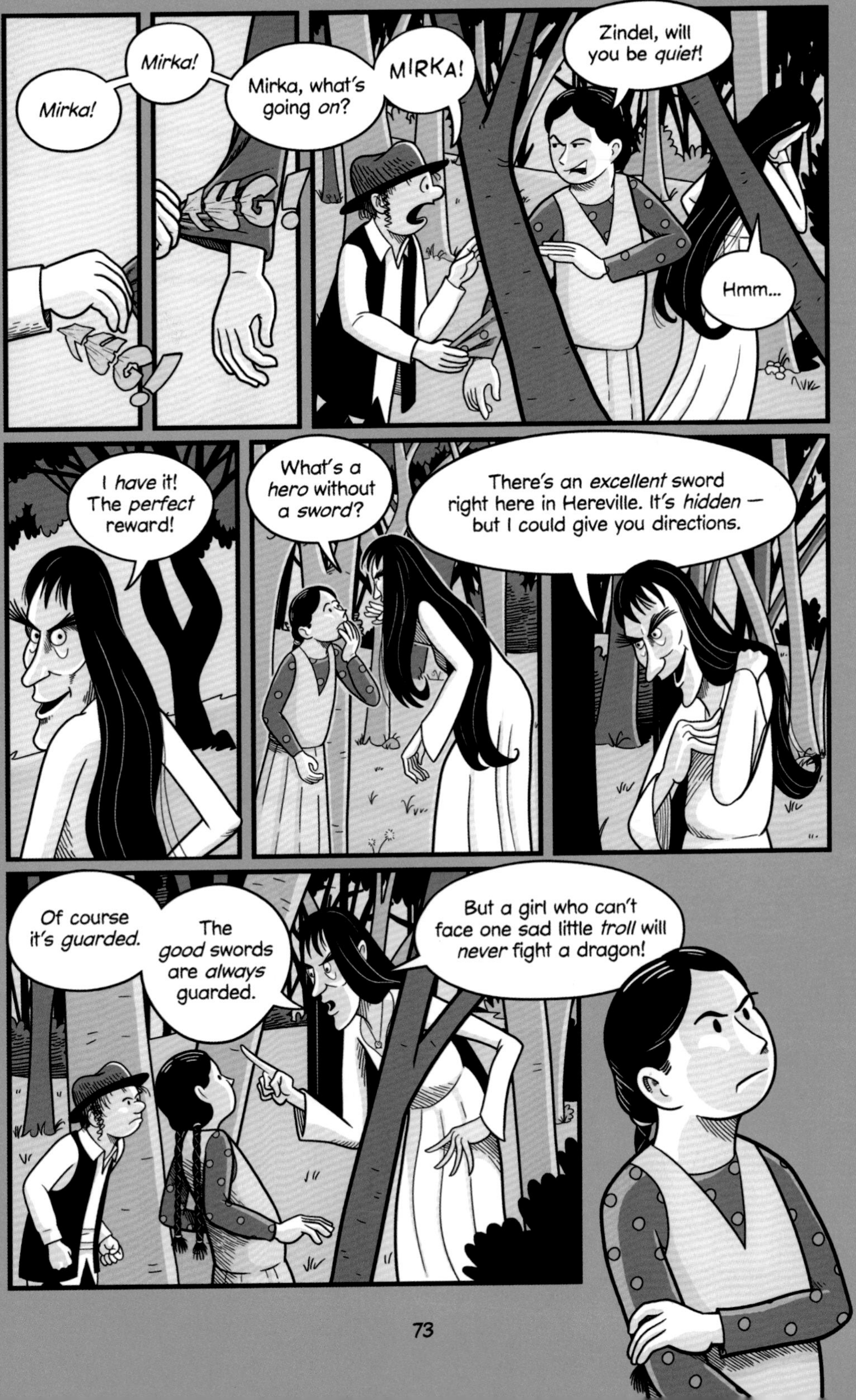
Mirka!
Mirka!
Mirka, what's going *on*?
MIRKA!
Zindel, will you be *quiet*!
Hmm...
I *have* it! The *perfect* reward!
What's a *hero* without a *sword*?
There's an *excellent* sword right here in Hereville. It's *hidden* — but I could give you directions.
Of course it's *guarded*.
The *good* swords are *always* guarded.
But a girl who can't face one sad little *troll* will *never* fight a dragon!

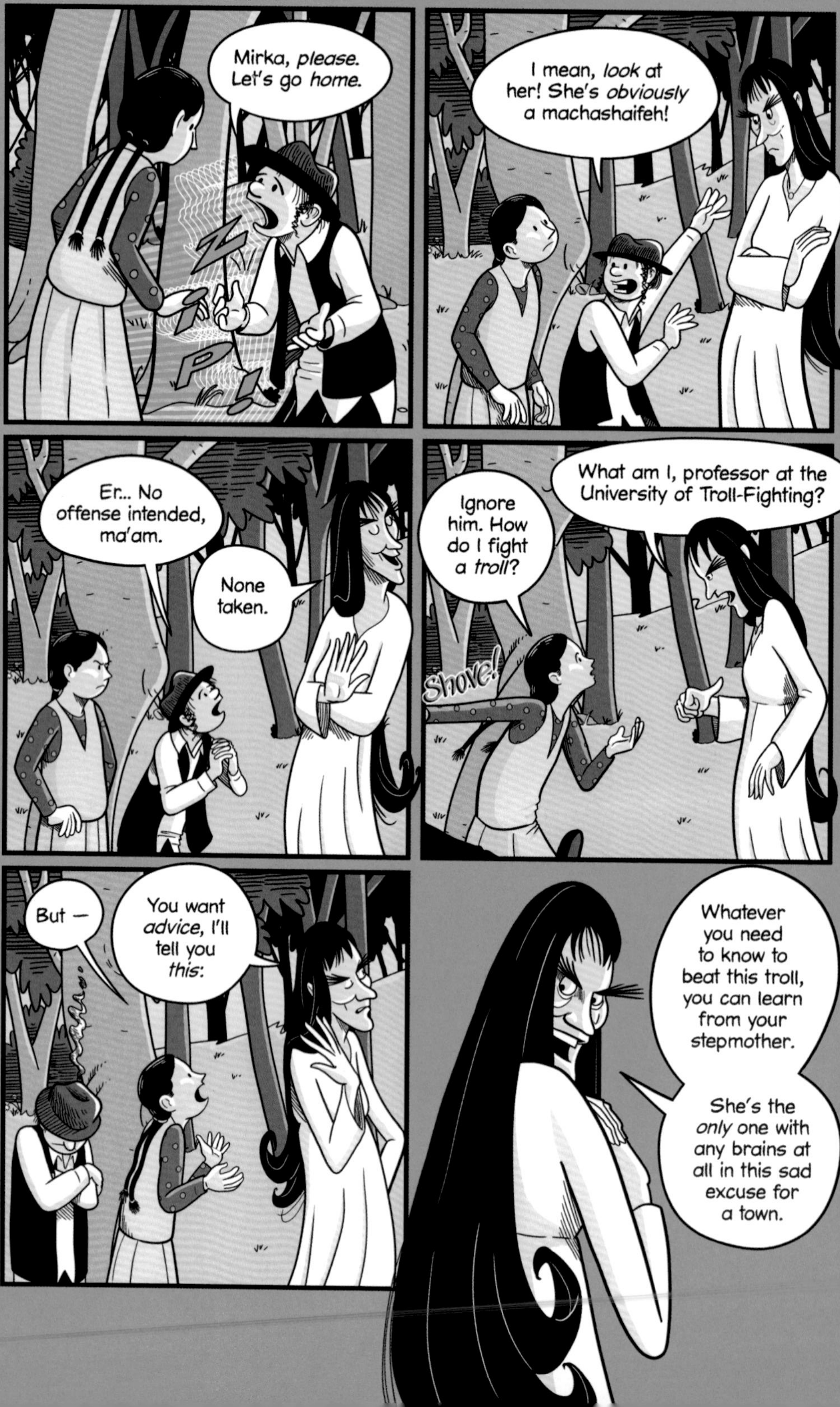
Mirka, please. Let's go home.
ZIP!
I mean, look at her! She's obviously a machashaifeh!
Er... No offense intended, ma'am.
None taken.
Ignore him. How do I fight a troll?
What am I, professor at the University of Troll-Fighting?
Shove!
But —
You want advice, I'll tell you this:
Whatever you need to know to beat this troll, you can learn from your stepmother.
She's the only one with any brains at all in this sad excuse for a town.

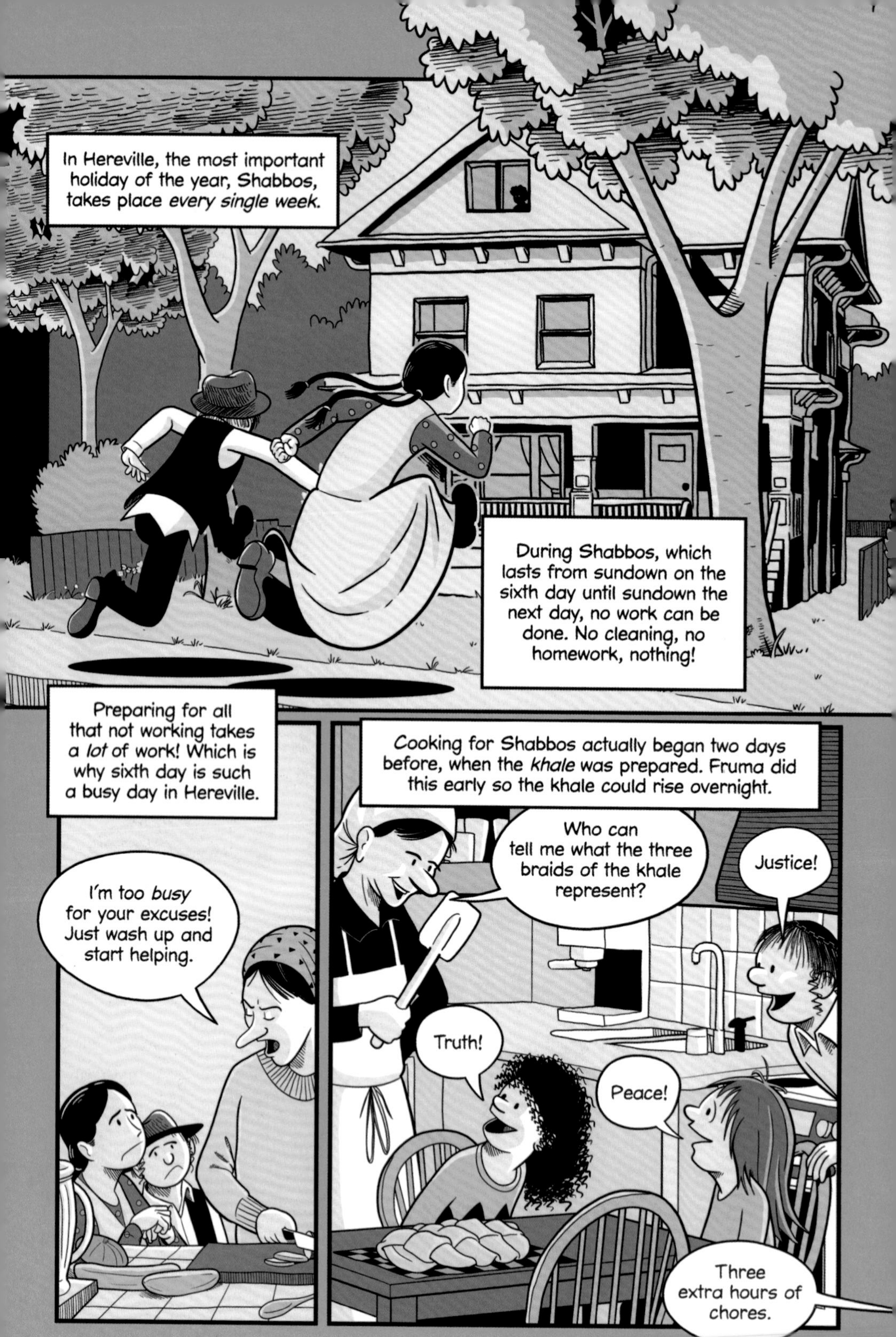
In Hereville, the most important holiday of the year, Shabbos, takes place *every single week.*
During Shabbos, which lasts from sundown on the sixth day until sundown the next day, no work can be done. No cleaning, no homework, nothing!
Preparing for all that not working takes a *lot* of work! Which is why sixth day is such a busy day in Hereville.
I'm too *busy* for your excuses! Just wash up and start helping.
Cooking for Shabbos actually began two days before, when the *khale* was prepared. Fruma did this early so the khale could rise overnight.
Who can tell me what the three braids of the khale represent?
Justice!
Truth!
Peace!
Three extra hours of chores.

Khale: bread

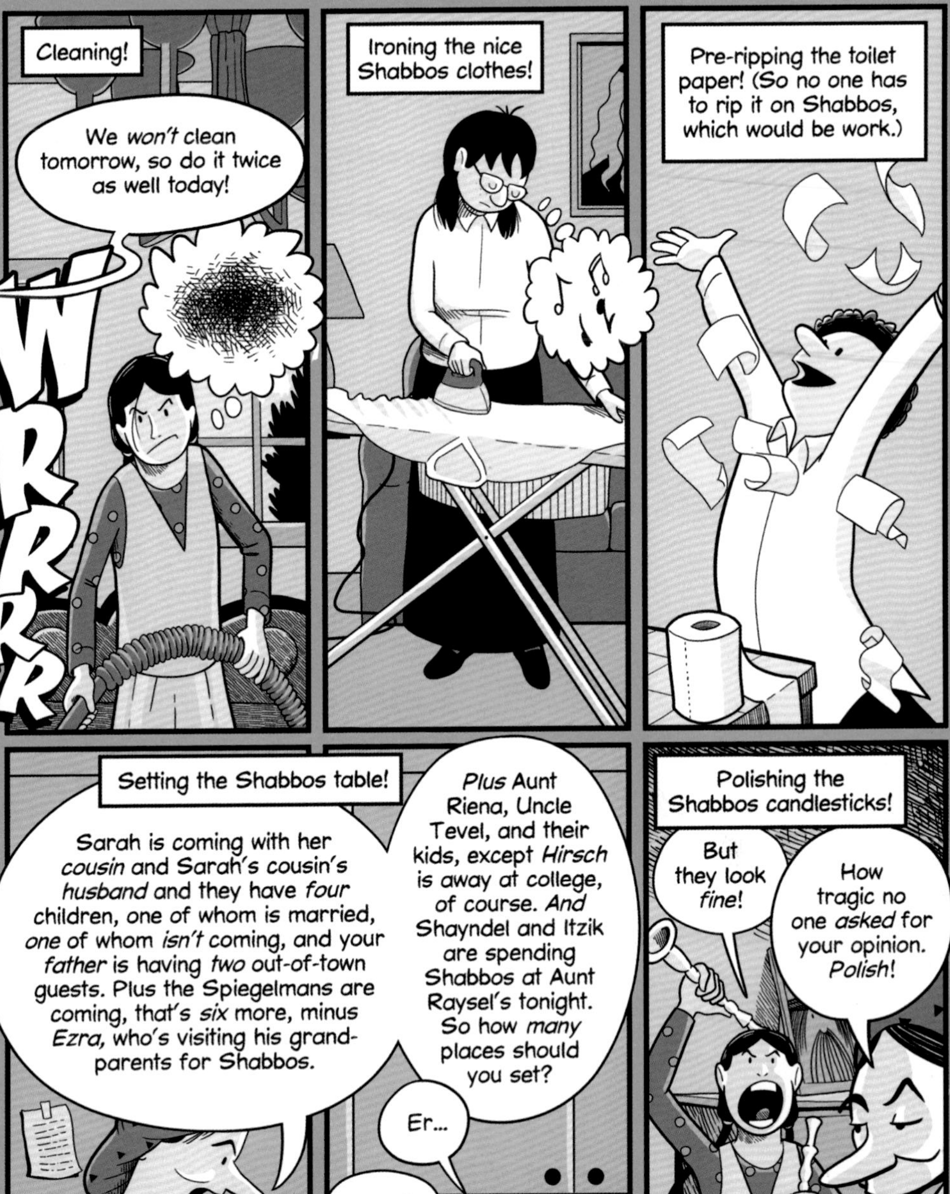

Cleaning!
We *won't* clean tomorrow, so do it twice as well today!
WRRRR
Ironing the nice Shabbos clothes!
Pre-ripping the toilet paper! (So no one has to rip it on Shabbos, which would be work.)
Setting the Shabbos table!
Sarah is coming with her *cousin* and Sarah's cousin's *husband* and they have *four* children, one of whom is married, *one* of whom *isn't* coming, and your *father* is having *two* out-of-town guests. Plus the Spiegelmans are coming, that's *six* more, minus *Ezra,* who's visiting his grand-parents for Shabbos.
Plus Aunt Riena, Uncle Tevel, and their kids, except *Hirsch* is away at college, of course. *And* Shayndel and Itzik are spending Shabbos at Aunt Raysel's tonight. So how *many* places should you set?
Er...
Well?
SNAP! SNAP!
Polishing the Shabbos candlesticks!
But they look *fine*!
How tragic no one *asked* for your opinion. *Polish*!

Pushke: charity box

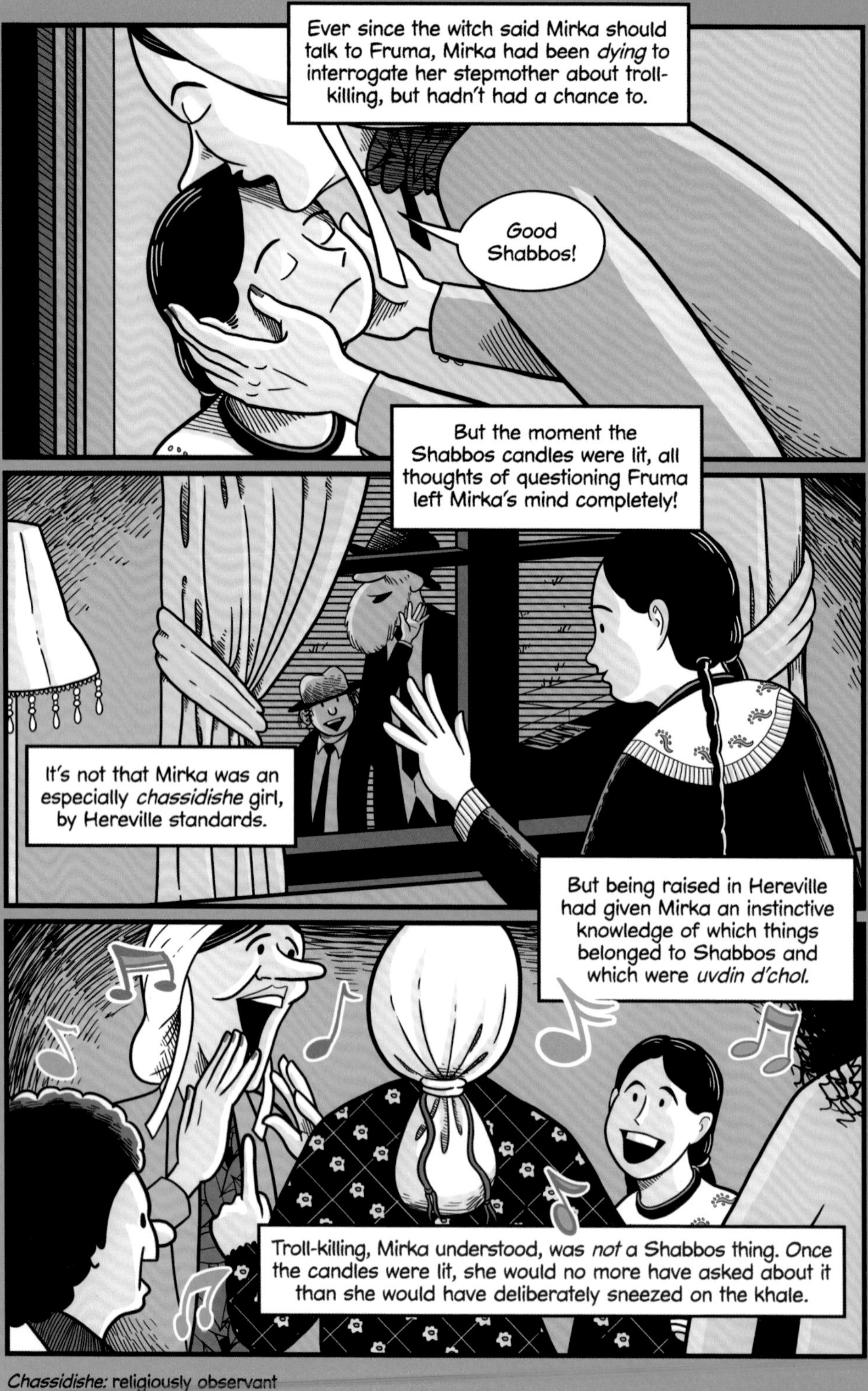
Ever since the witch said Mirka should talk to Fruma, Mirka had been *dying* to interrogate her stepmother about troll-killing, but hadn't had a chance to.
Good Shabbos!
But the moment the Shabbos candles were lit, all thoughts of questioning Fruma left Mirka's mind completely!
It's not that Mirka was an especially *chassidishe* girl, by Hereville standards.
But being raised in Hereville had given Mirka an instinctive knowledge of which things belonged to Shabbos and which were *uvdin d'chol.*
Troll-killing, Mirka understood, was *not* a Shabbos thing. Once the candles were lit, she would no more have asked about it than she would have deliberately sneezed on the khale.

Chassidishe: religiously observant
Uvdin d'chol: weekday things

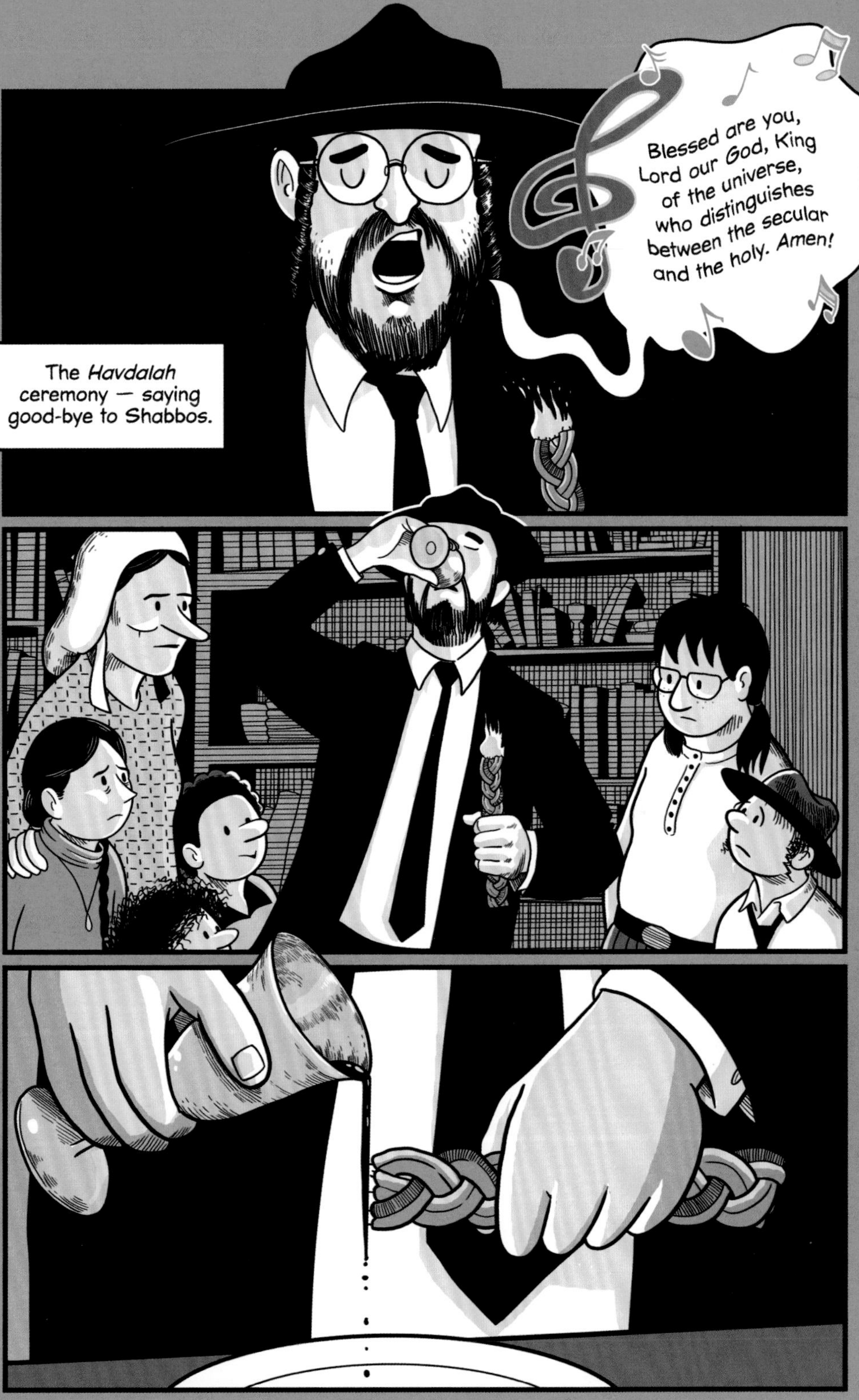
The Havdalah ceremony — saying good-bye to Shabbos.
Blessed are you, Lord our God, King of the universe, who distinguishes between the secular and the holy. Amen!

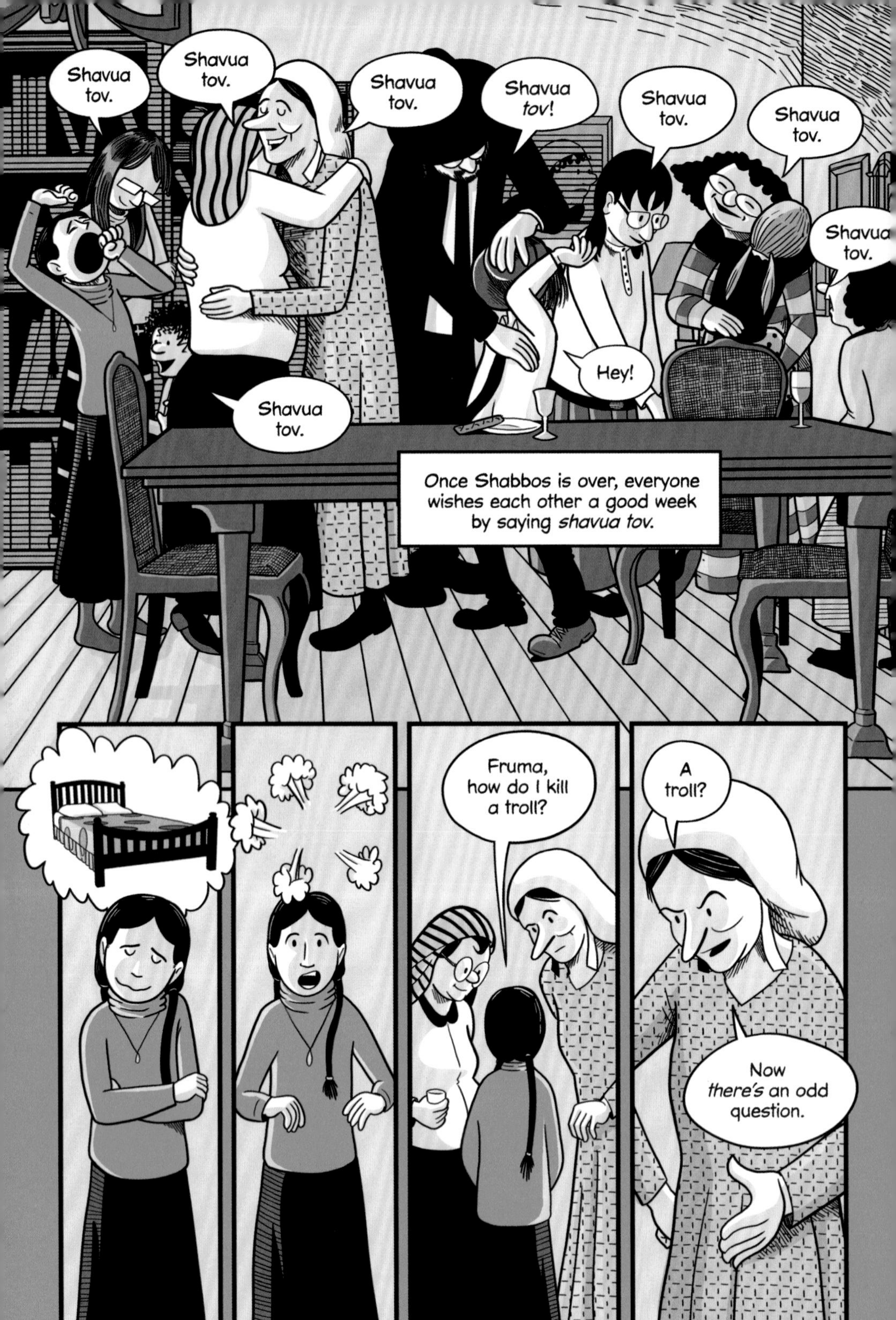

Shavua tov.
Shavua tov.
Shavua tov.
Shavua *tov*!
Shavua tov.
Shavua tov.
Shavua tov.
Hey!
Shavua tov.
Once Shabbos is over, everyone wishes each other a good week by saying shavua tov.
Fruma, how do I kill a troll?
A troll?
Now *there's* an odd question.

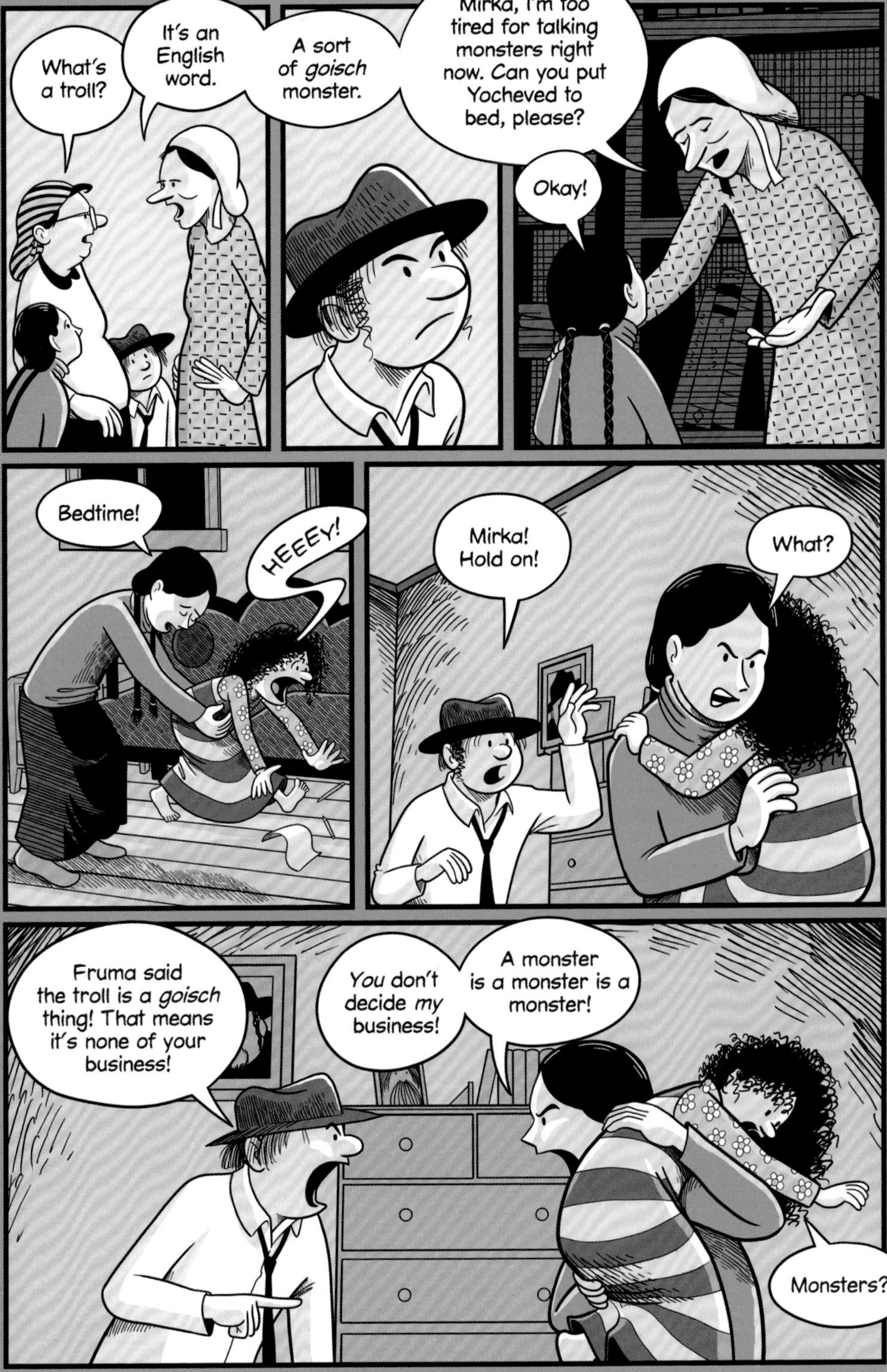
What's a troll?
It's an English word.
A sort of *goisch* monster.
Mirka, I'm too tired for talking monsters right now. Can you put Yocheved to bed, please?
Okay!
Bedtime!
HEEEY!
Mirka! Hold on!
What?
Fruma said the troll is a *goisch* thing! That means it's none of your business!
You don't decide *my* business!
A monster is a monster is a monster!
Monsters?

Goisch: non-Jewish

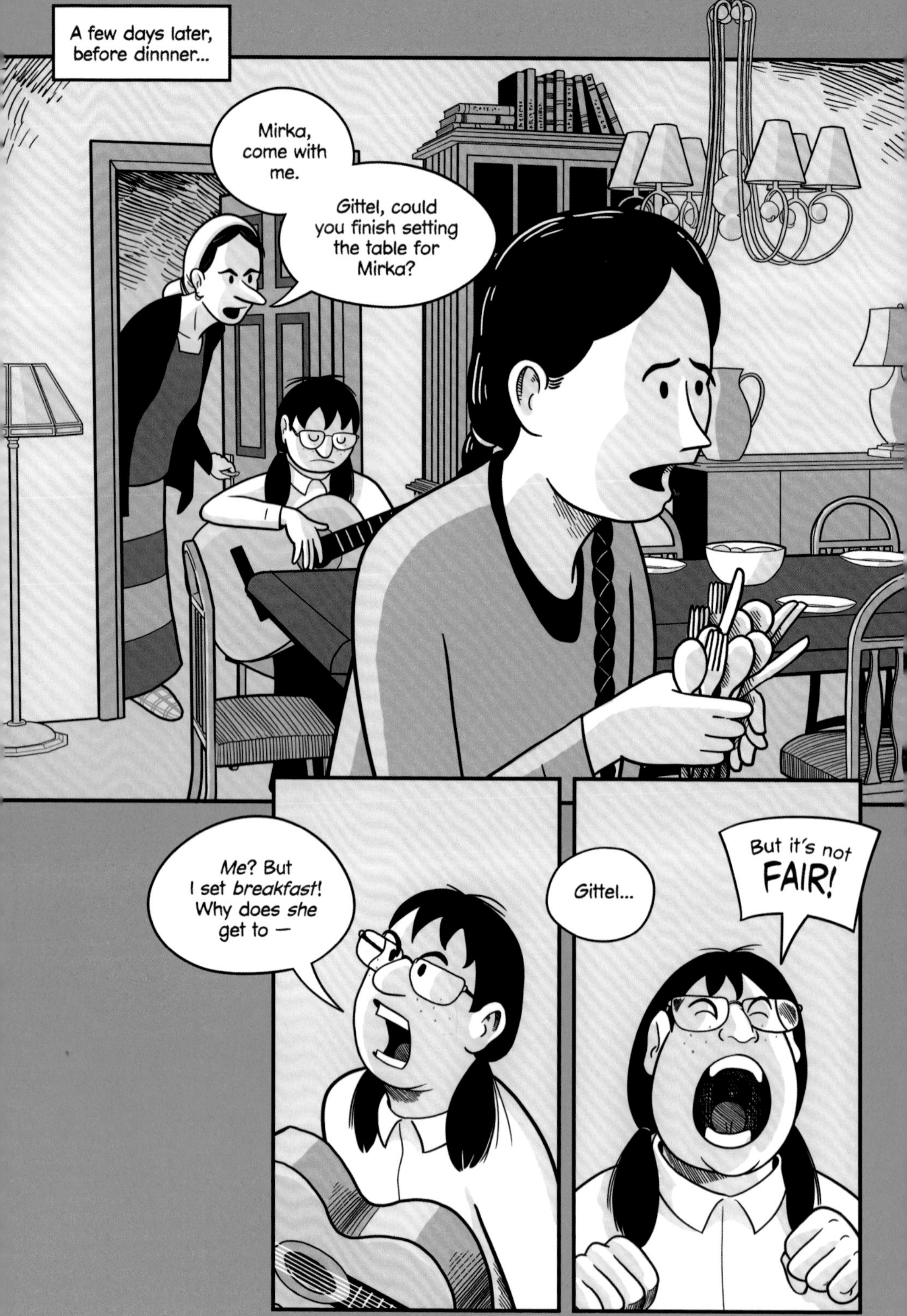
A few days later, before dinnner...
Mirka, come with me.
Gittel, could you finish setting the table for Mirka?
Me? But I set *breakfast*! Why does *she* get to —
Gittel...
But it's not FAIR!

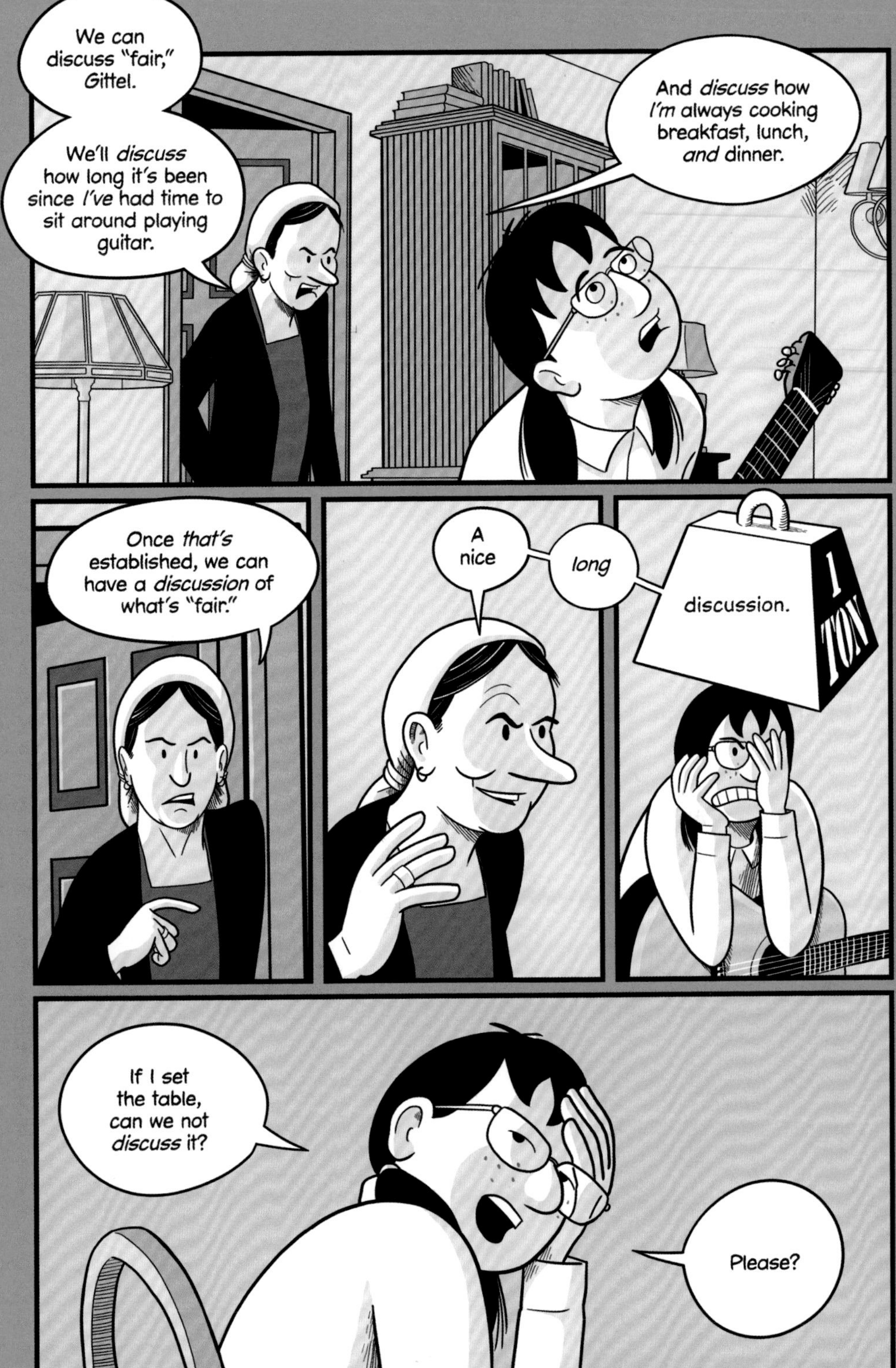
We can discuss "fair," Gittel.
We'll *discuss* how long it's been since *I've* had time to sit around playing guitar.
And *discuss* how *I'm* always cooking breakfast, lunch, *and* dinner.
Once *that's* established, we can have a *discussion* of what's "fair."
A nice
long
discussion.
1 TON
If I set the table, can we not *discuss* it?
Please?

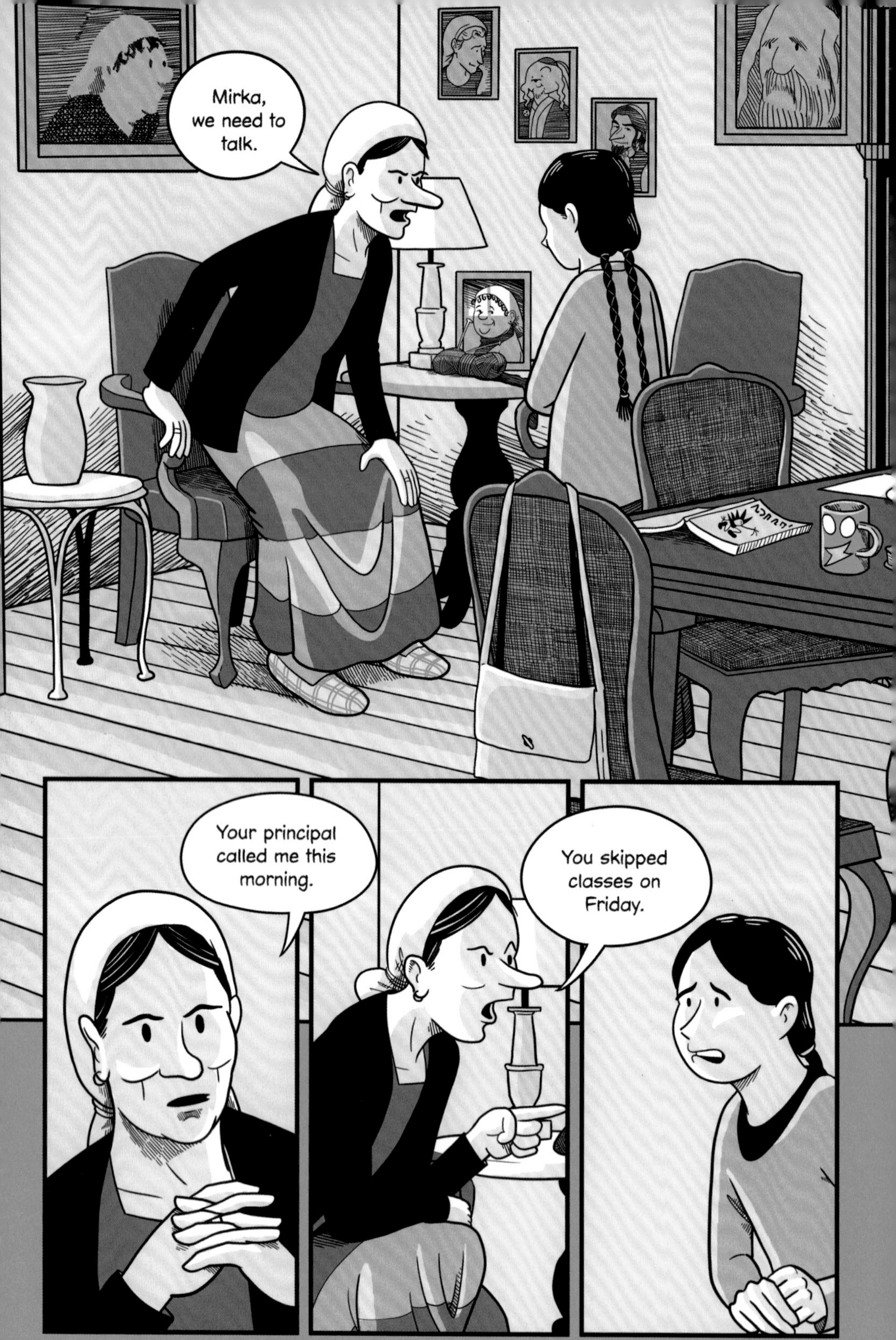
Mirka, we need to talk.
Your principal called me this morning.
You skipped classes on Friday.

The story of Jacob and Esau is in the Torah, which is one of the founding texts of Judaism.

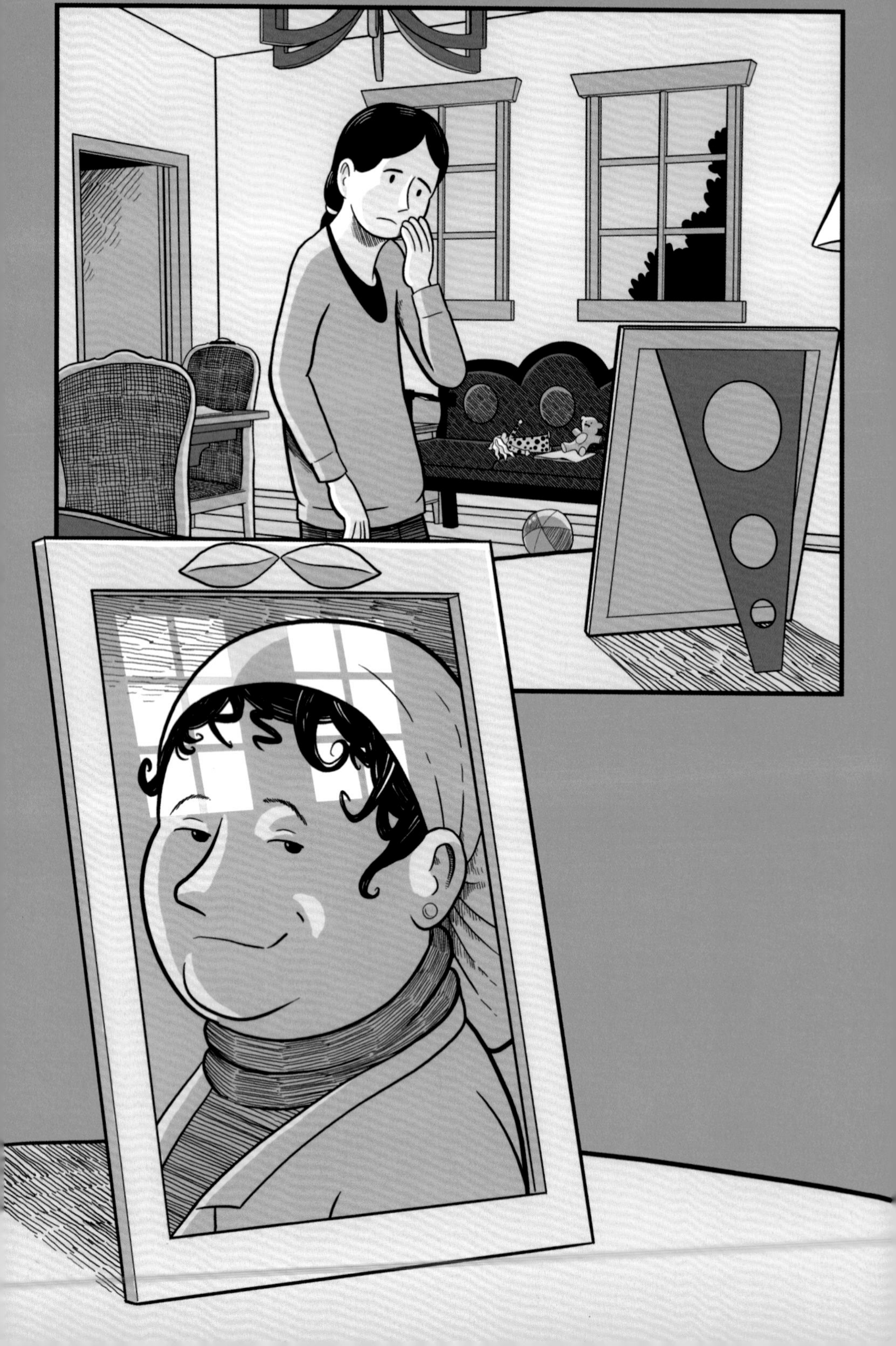

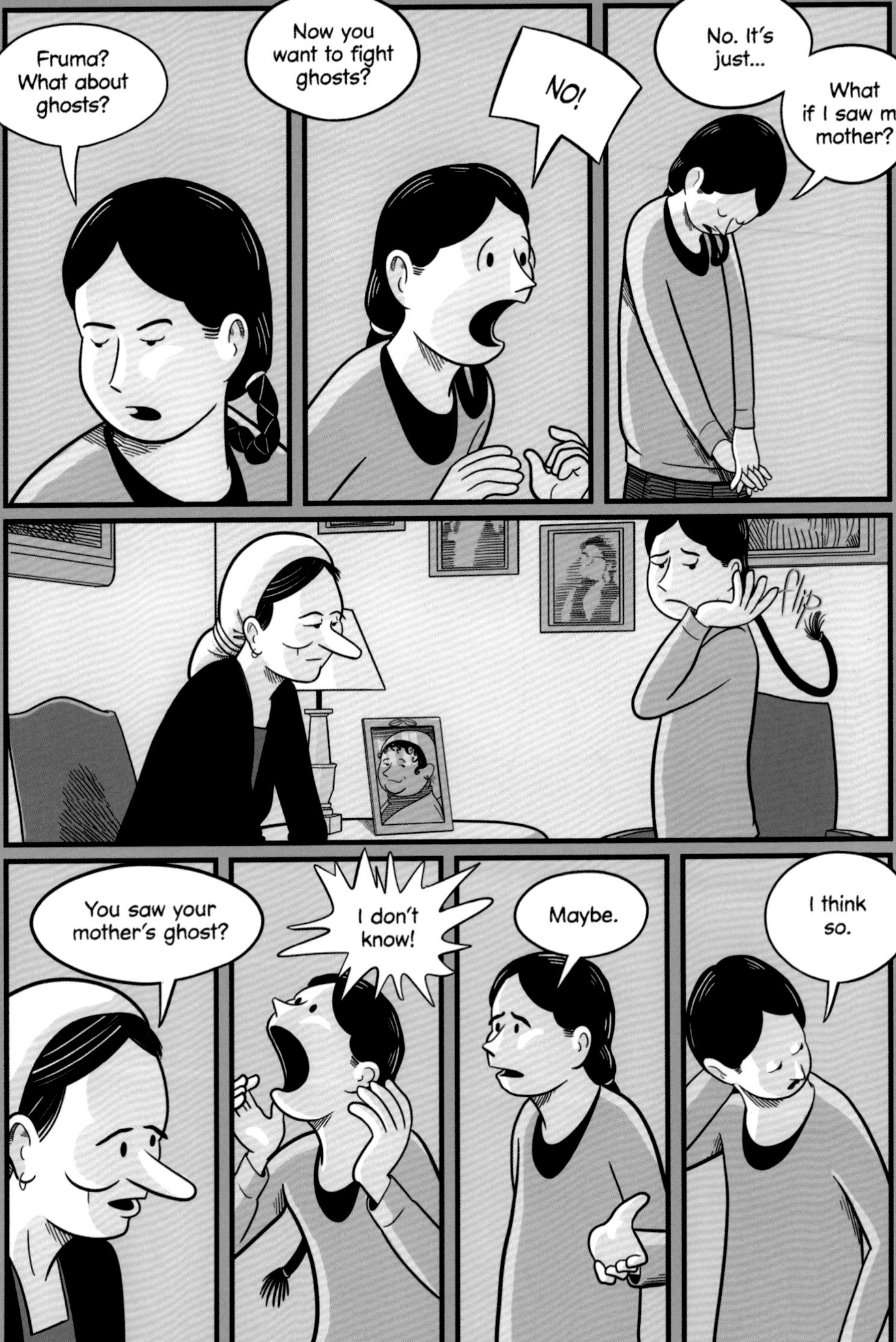
Fruma? What about ghosts?
Now you want to fight ghosts?
NO!
No. It's just...
What if I saw my mother?
flip
You saw your mother's ghost?
I don't know!
Maybe.
I think so.

Dybbuk: ghost

94

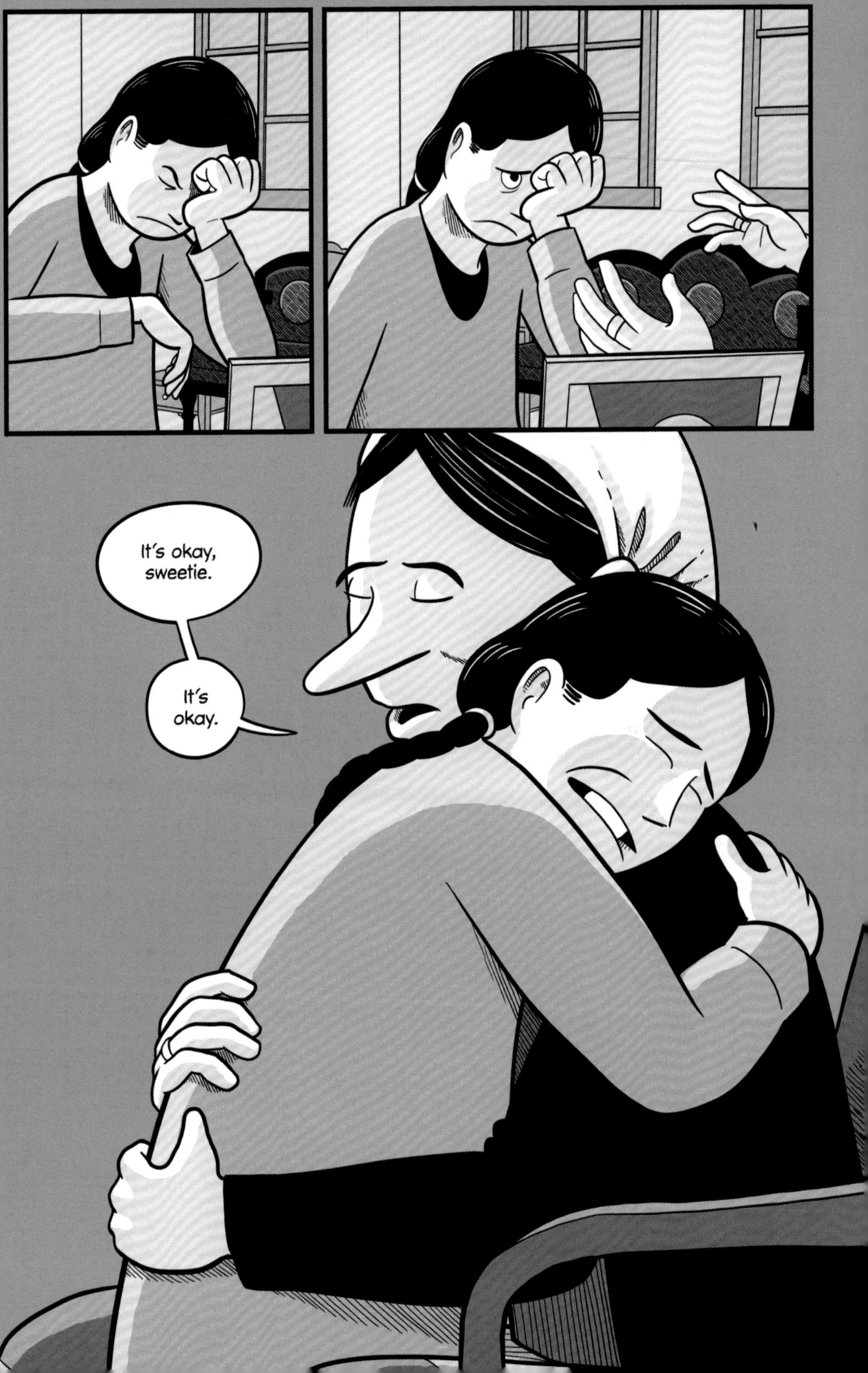
It's okay, sweetie.
It's okay.

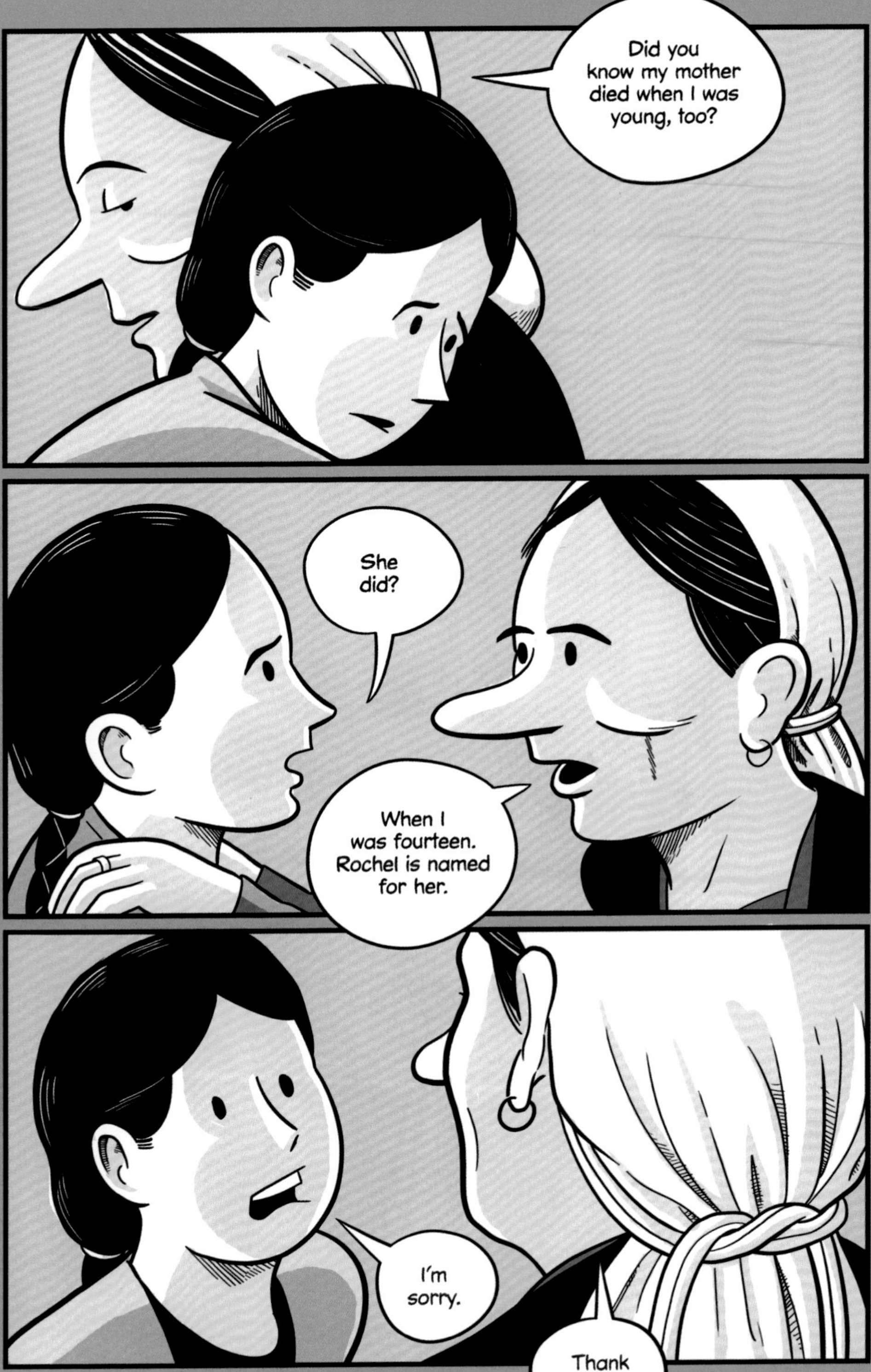
Did you know my mother died when I was young, too?
She did?
When I was fourteen. Rochel is named for her.
I'm sorry.
Thank you.

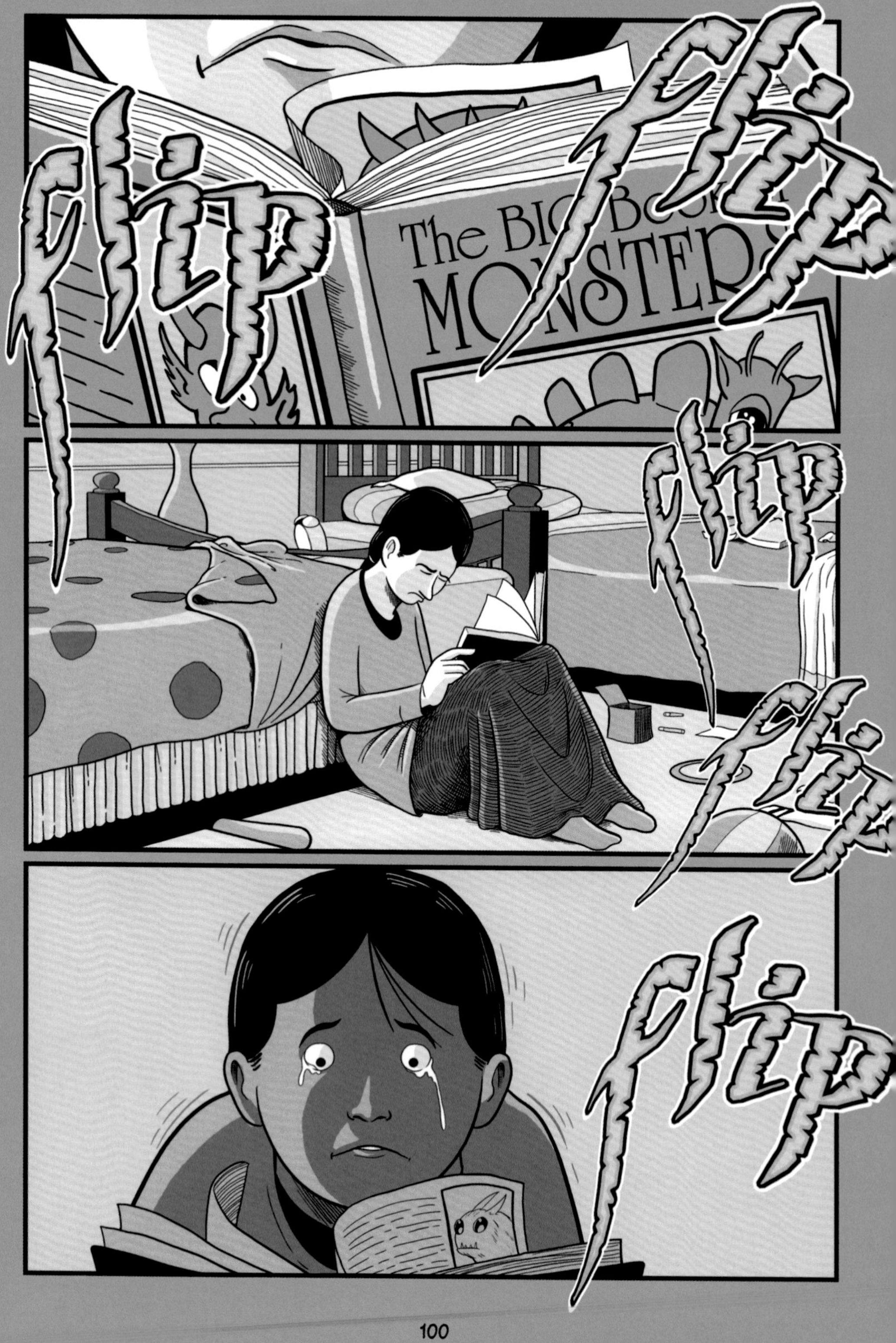
flip
The Big Book of Monsters
flip
flip
flip
flip

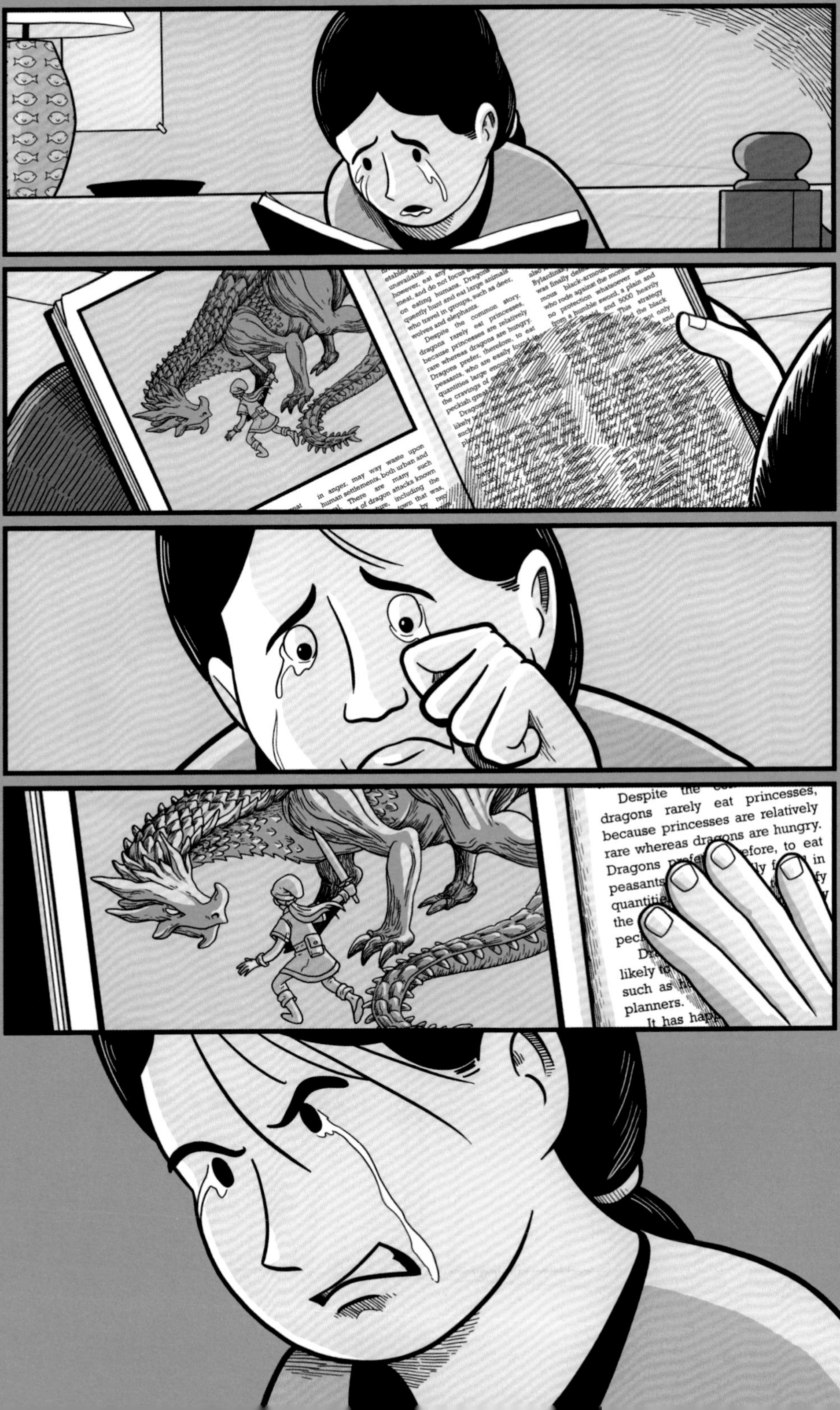
Despite the
dragons rarely eat princesses,
because princesses are relatively
rare whereas dragons are hungry.
planners.

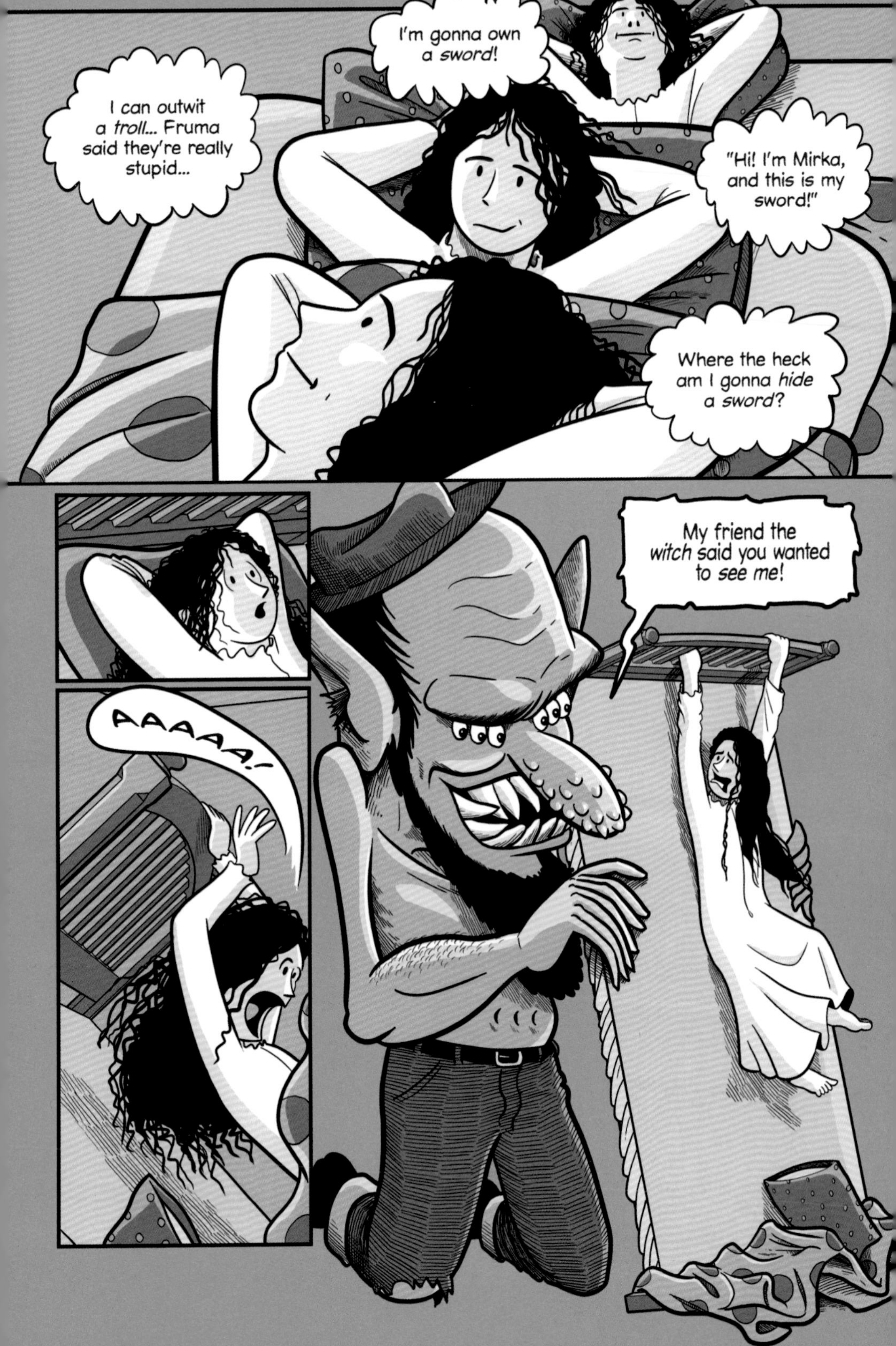
I can outwit a *troll*... Fruma said they're really stupid...
I'm gonna own a *sword*!
"Hi! I'm Mirka, and this is my sword!"
Where the heck am I gonna *hide* a *sword*?
My friend the *witch* said you wanted to *see me*!
AAAAA!

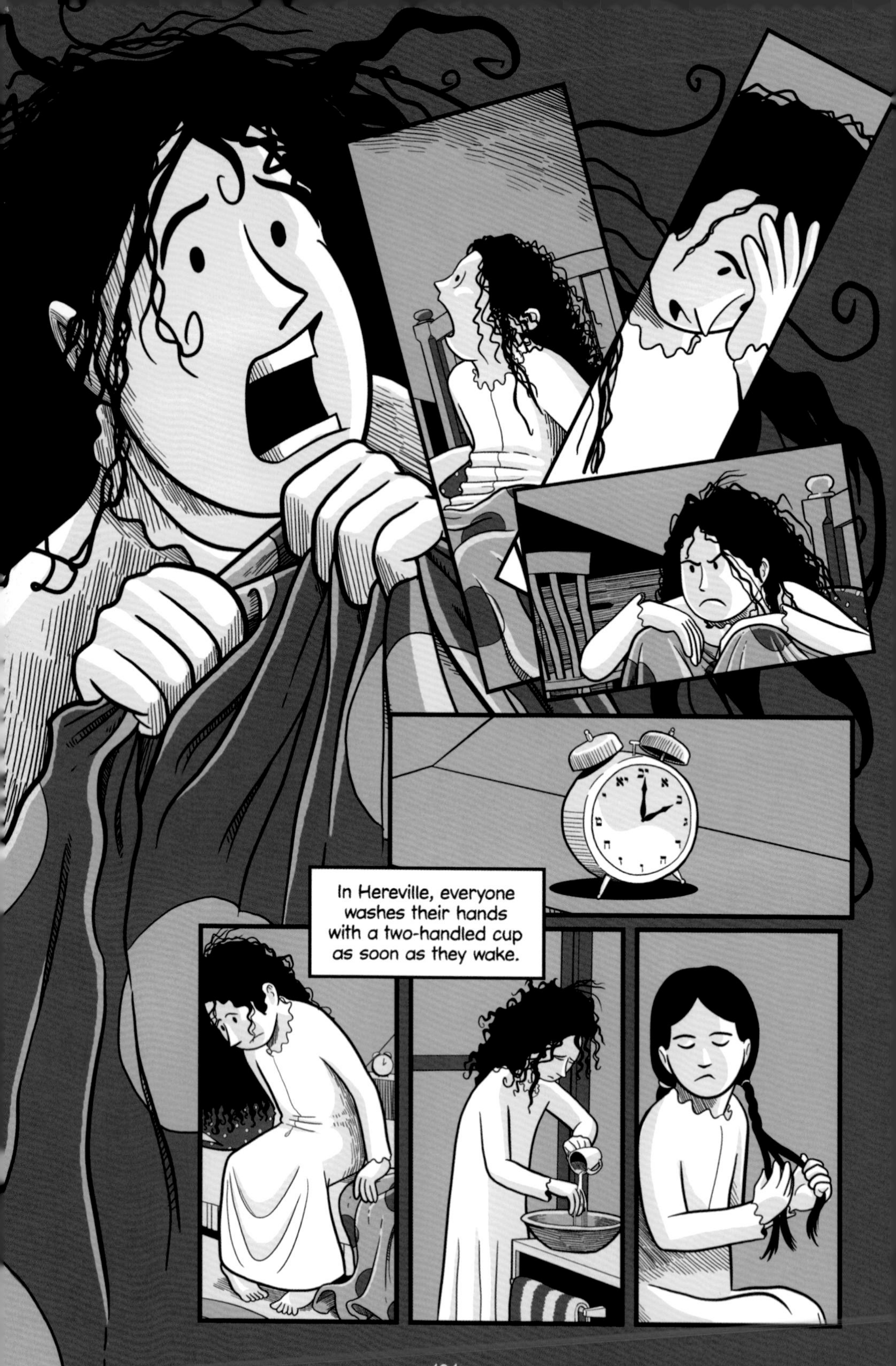
In Hereville, everyone washes their hands with a two-handled cup as soon as they wake.

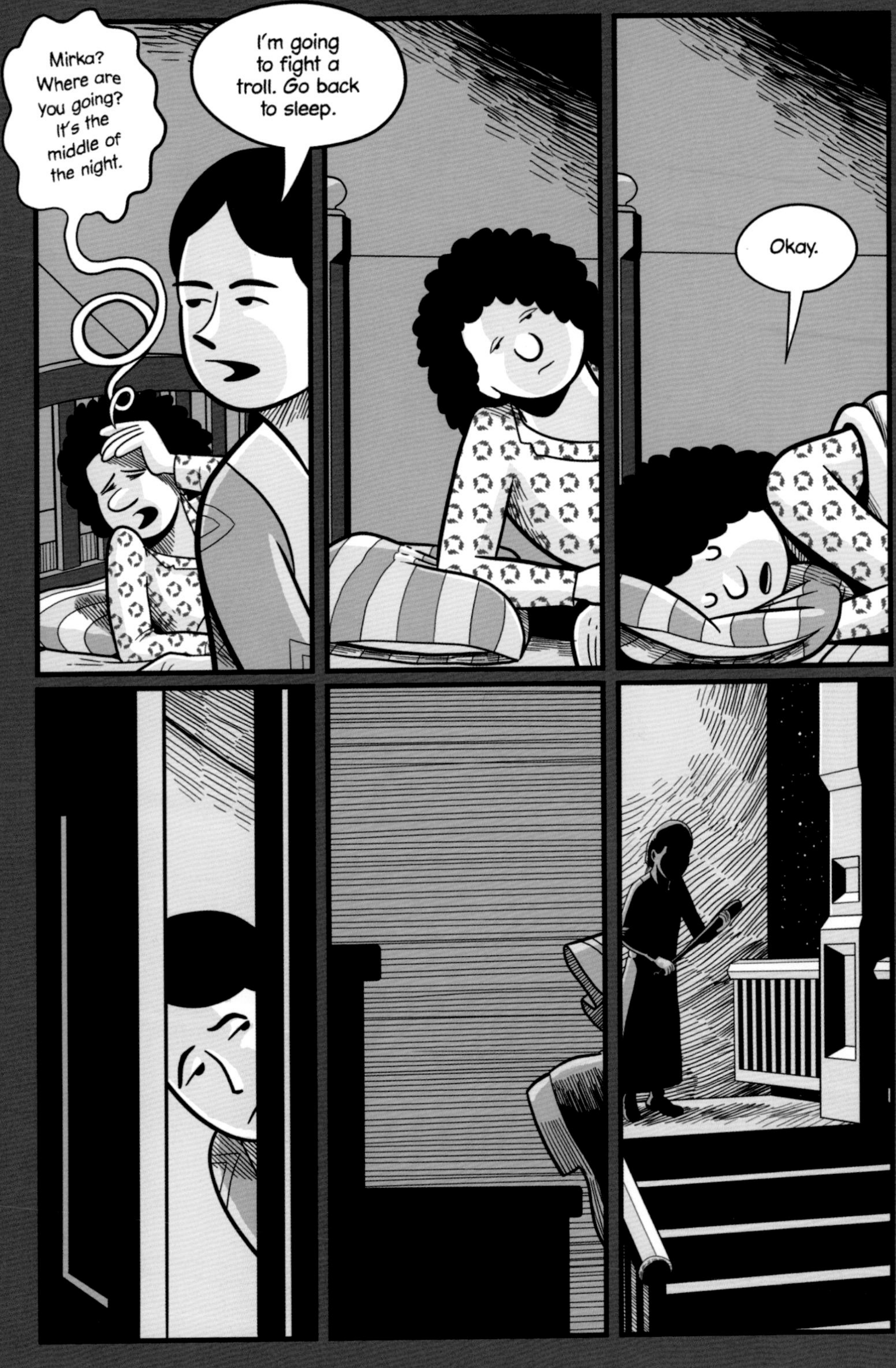
Mirka? Where are you going? It's the middle of the night.
I'm going to fight a troll. Go back to sleep.
Okay.

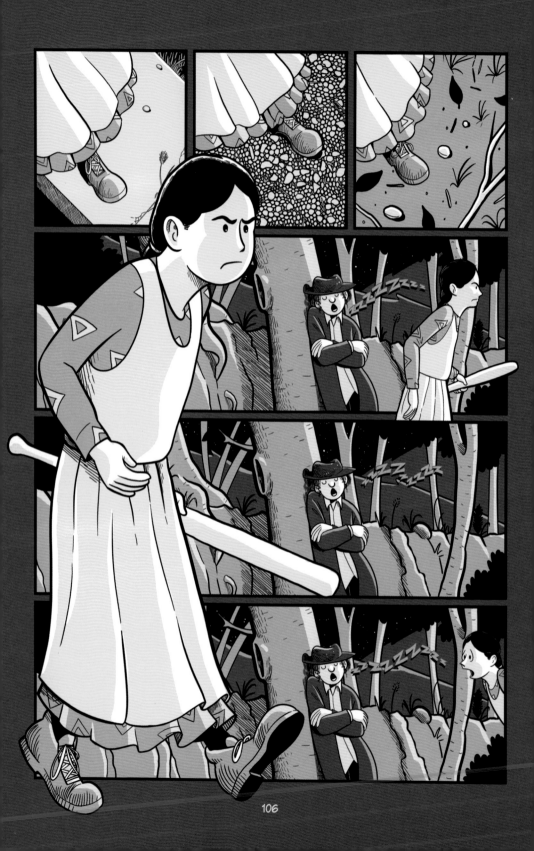

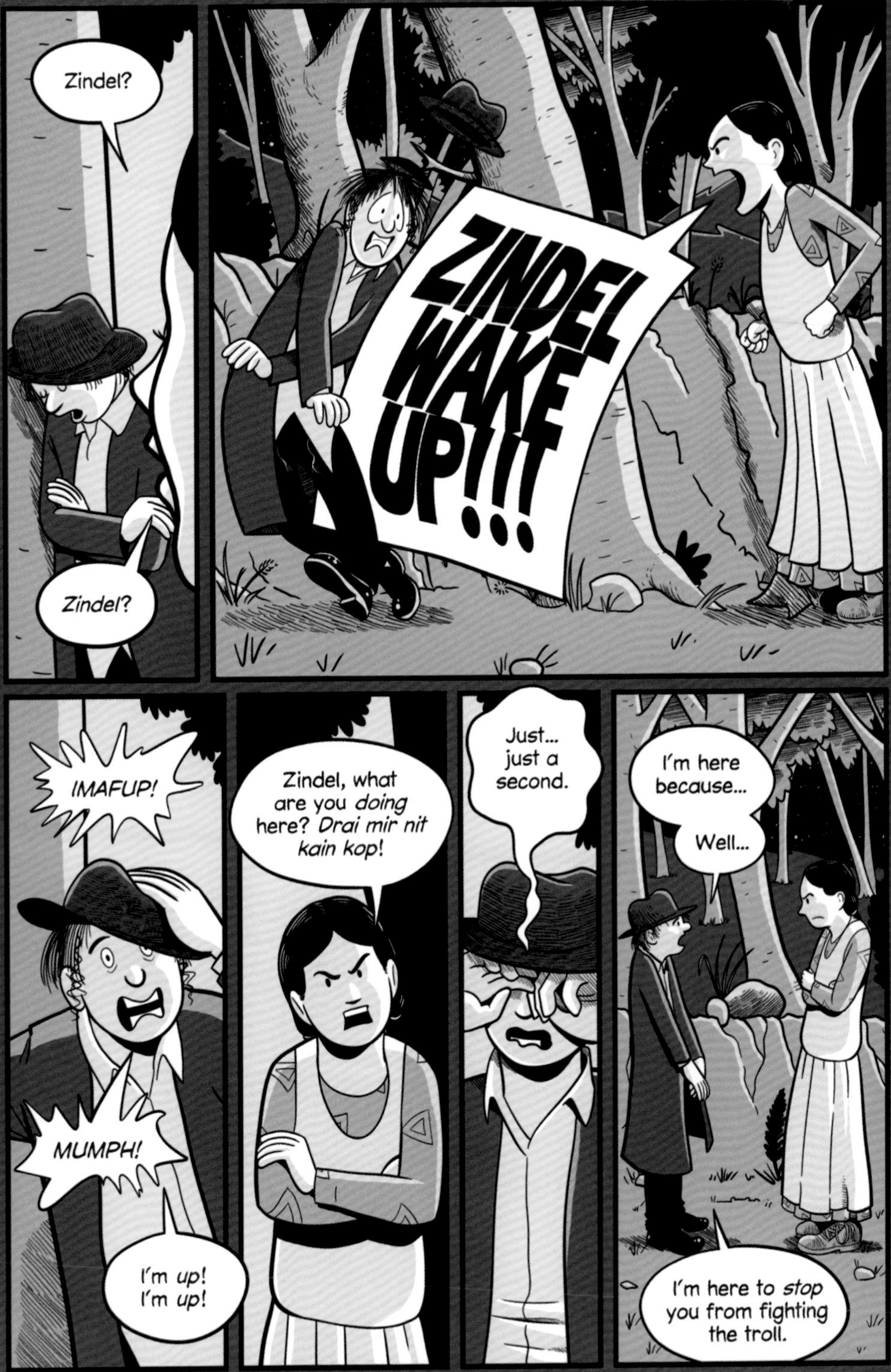
Zindel?
Zindel?
ZINDEL WAKE UP!!!
IMAFUP!
MUMPH!
I'm up! I'm up!
Zindel, what are you *doing* here? *Drai mir nit kain kop!*
Just... just a second.
I'm here because...
Well...
I'm here to *stop* you from fighting the troll.

Drai mir nit kain kop! Don't twist my head! (Less literal: Stop bothering me!)

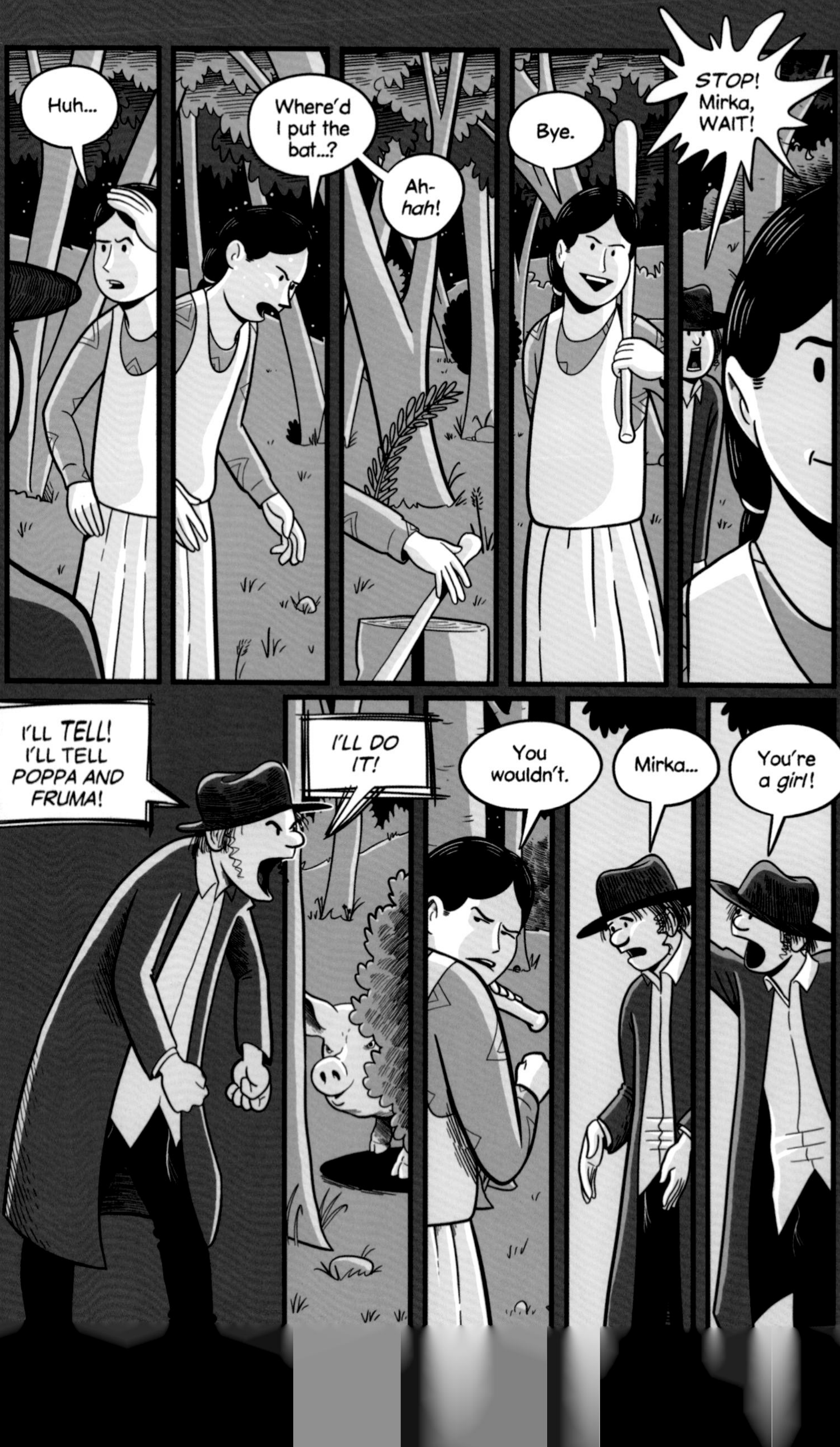
Huh...
Where'd I put the bat...?
Ah-hah!
Bye.
STOP! Mirka, WAIT!
I'LL TELL! I'LL TELL POPPA AND FRUMA!
I'LL DO IT!
You wouldn't.
Mirka...
You're a girl!

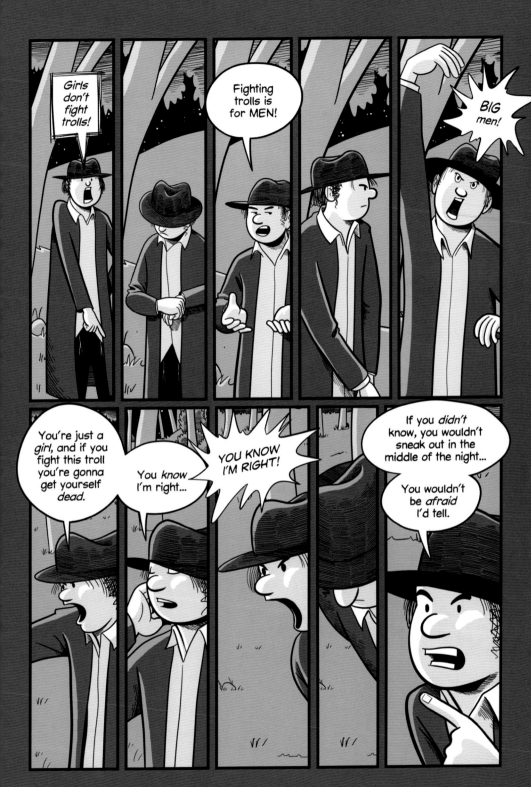

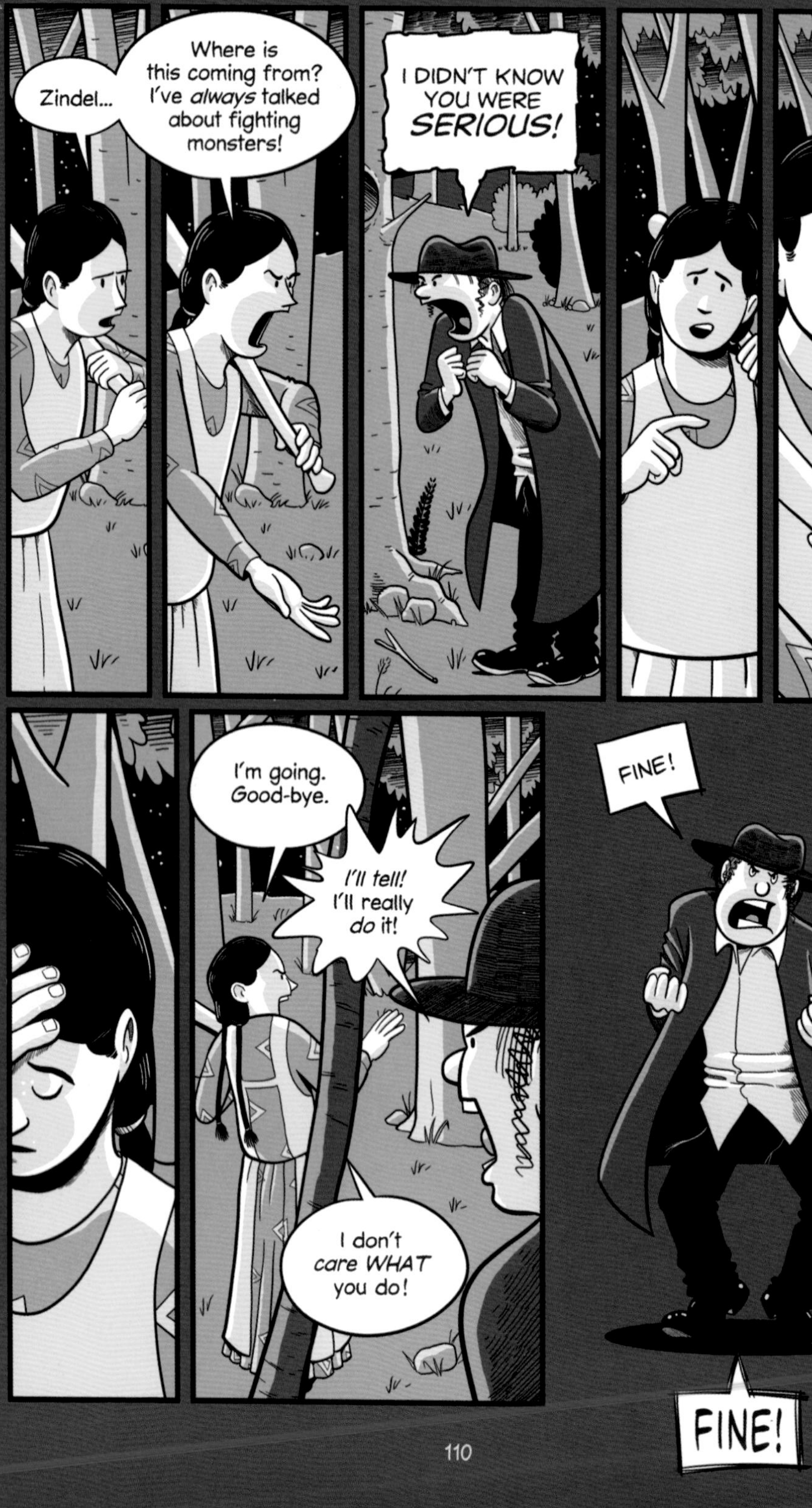
Zindel...
Where is this coming from? I've *always* talked about fighting monsters!
I DIDN'T KNOW YOU WERE *SERIOUS!*
I'm going. Good-bye.
I'll tell! I'll really *do* it!
I don't *care WHAT* you do!
FINE!
FINE!

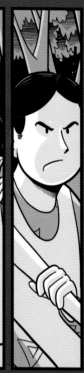

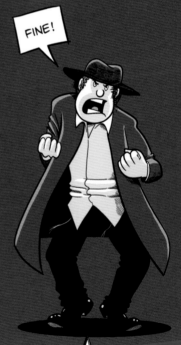

STOMP!
STOMP!
STOMP!
So *let* her get killed by a troll! I tried my best!
She *never* listens! Might as well *red tsu der vant*!
Fine! It's off *my* head now!

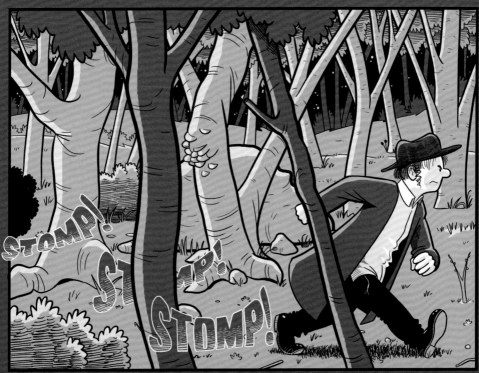

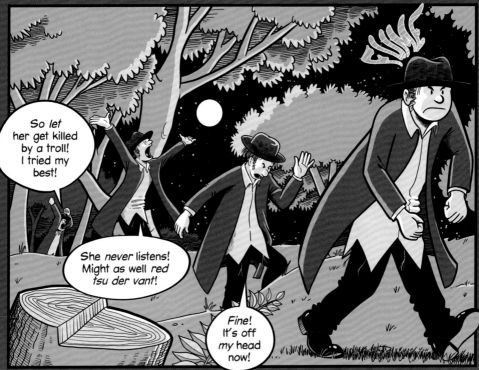

Red tsu der vant: talk to the wall

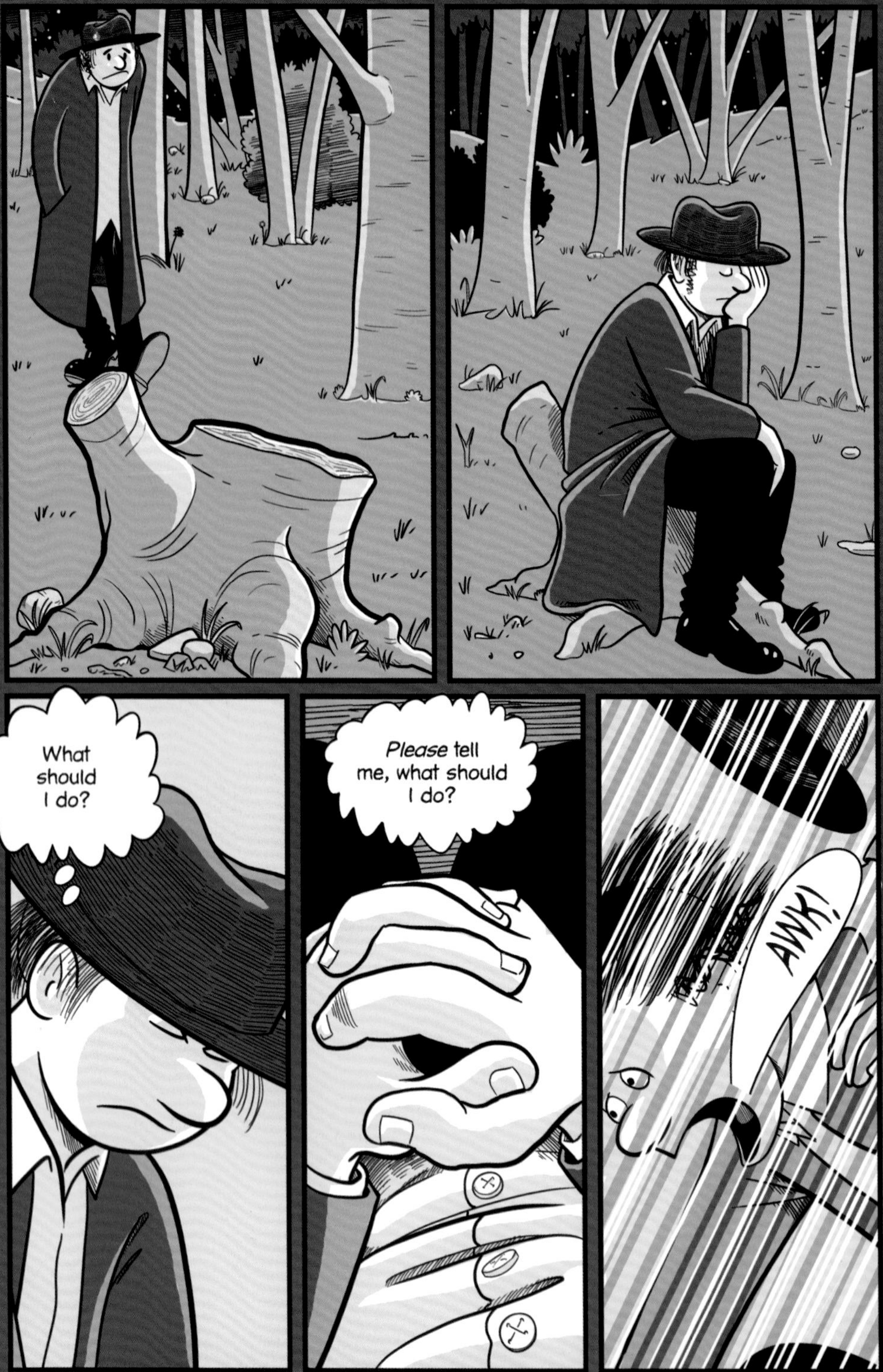
What should I do?
Please tell me, what should I do?
AWK!

113

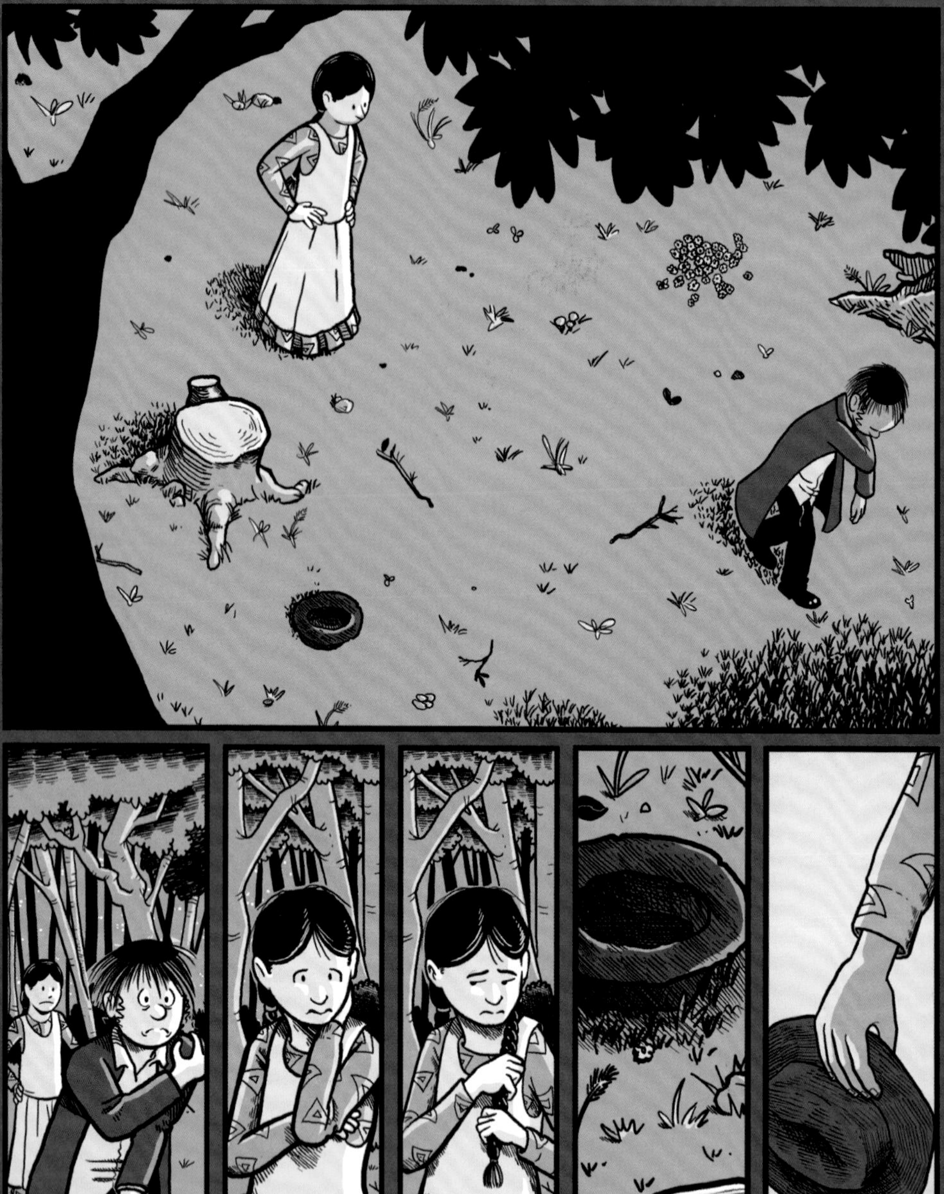

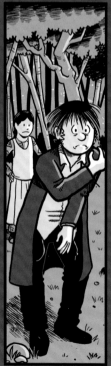

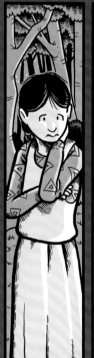

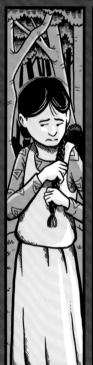

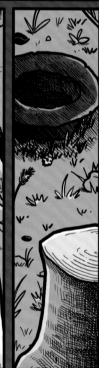

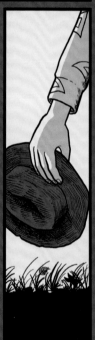

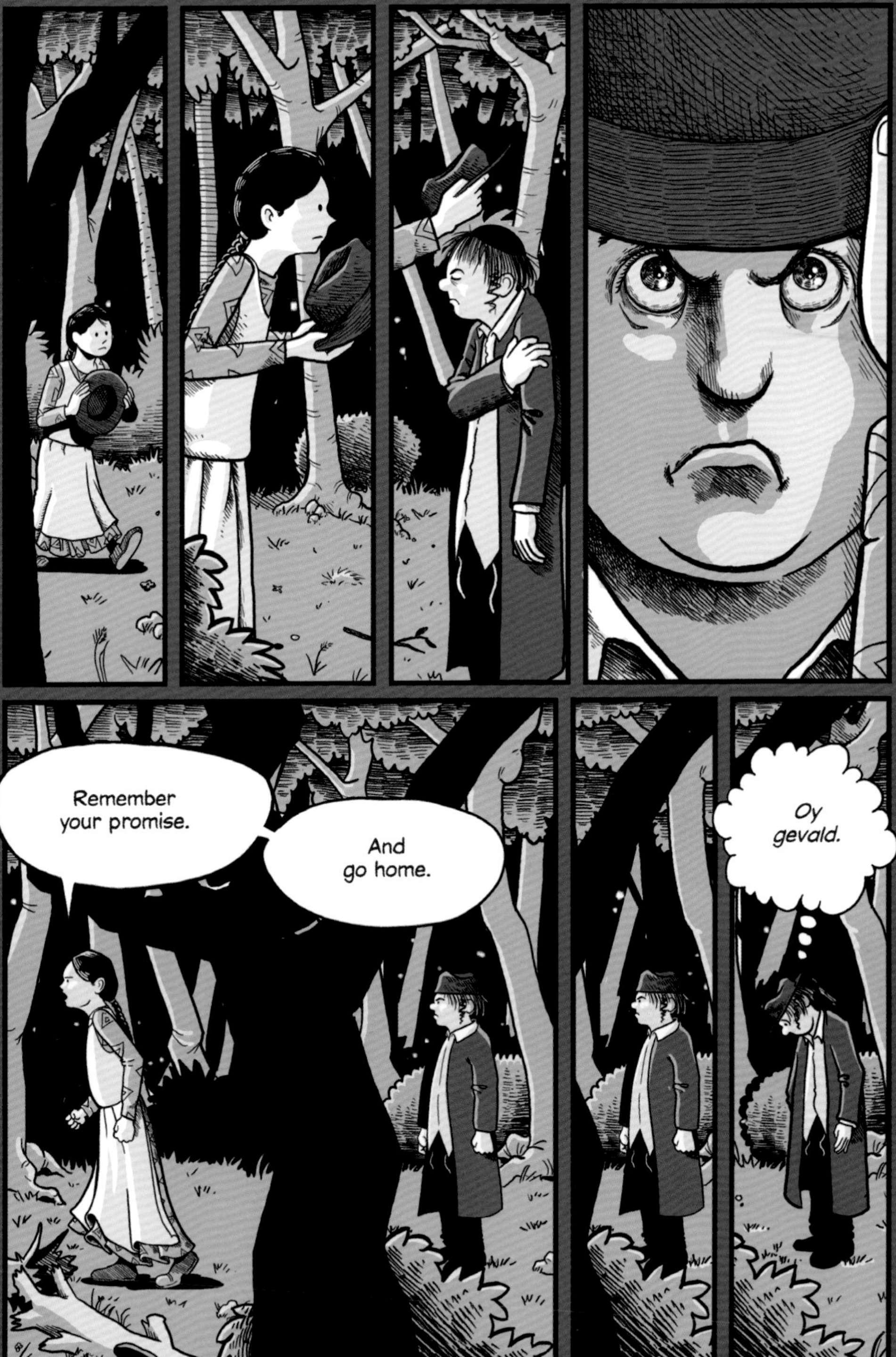
Remember your promise.
And go home.
Oy gevald.

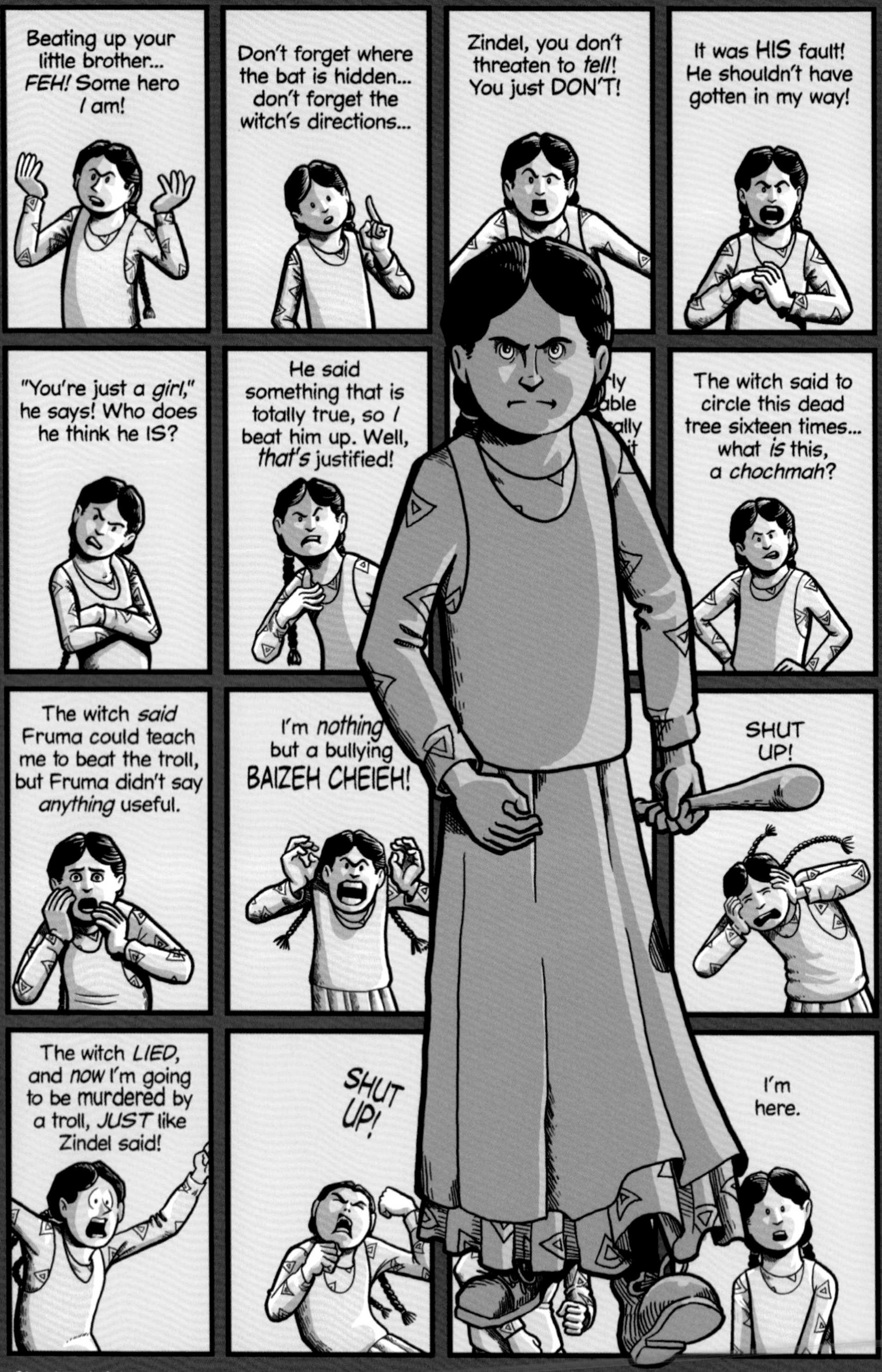

Chochmah: joke
Baizeh cheieh: vicious animal

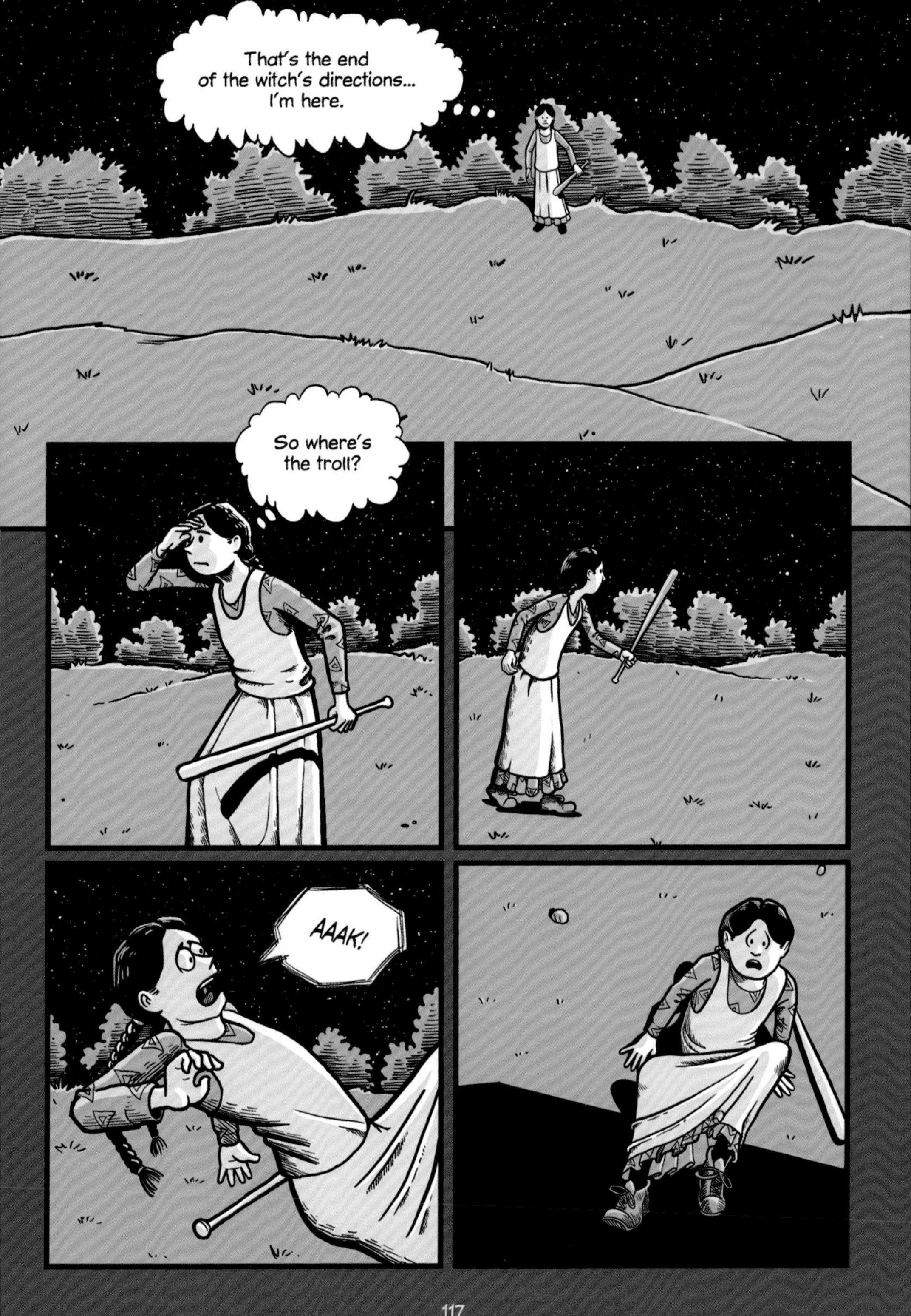
That's the end of the witch's directions... I'm here.
So where's the troll?
AAAK!

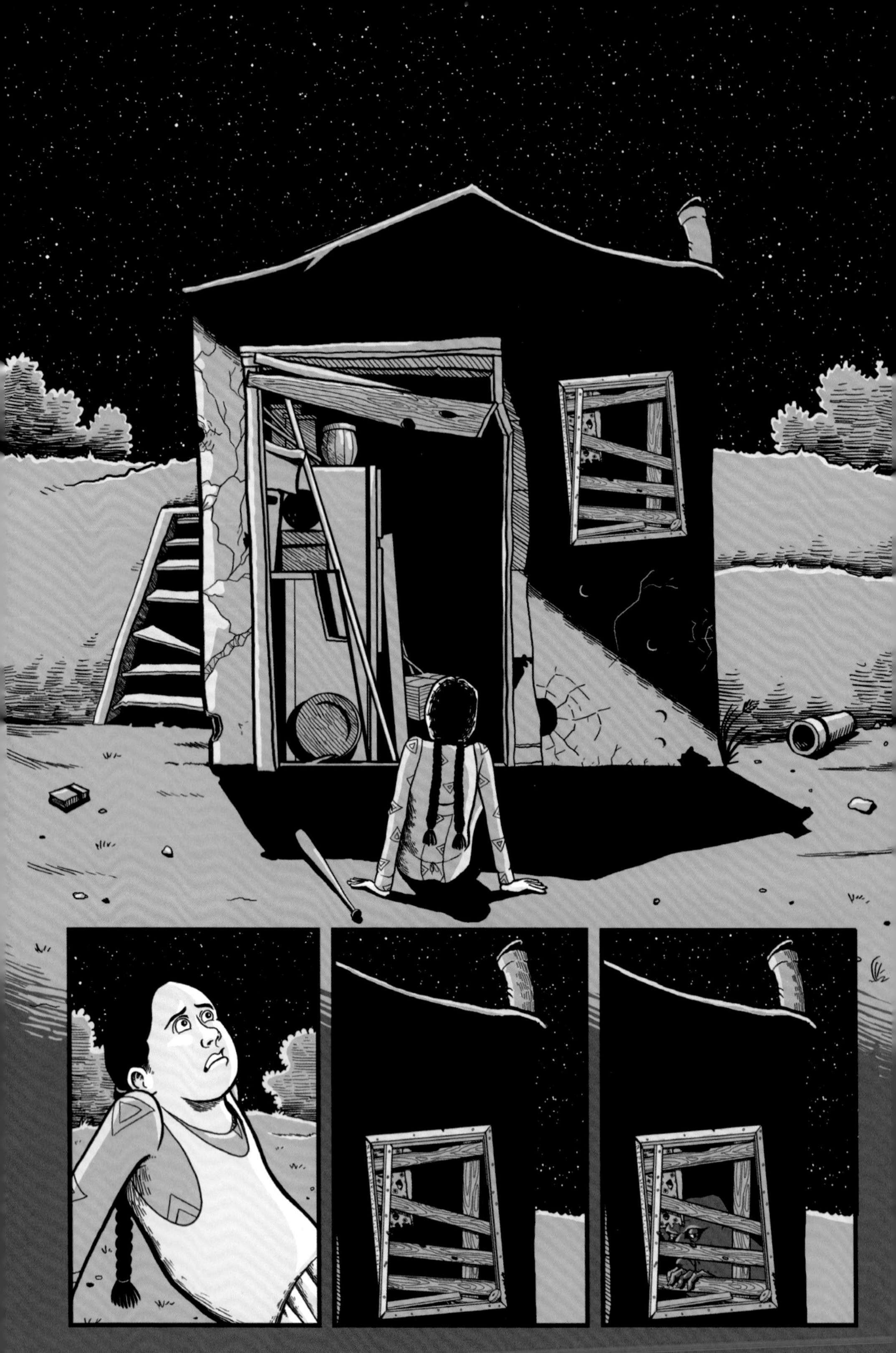

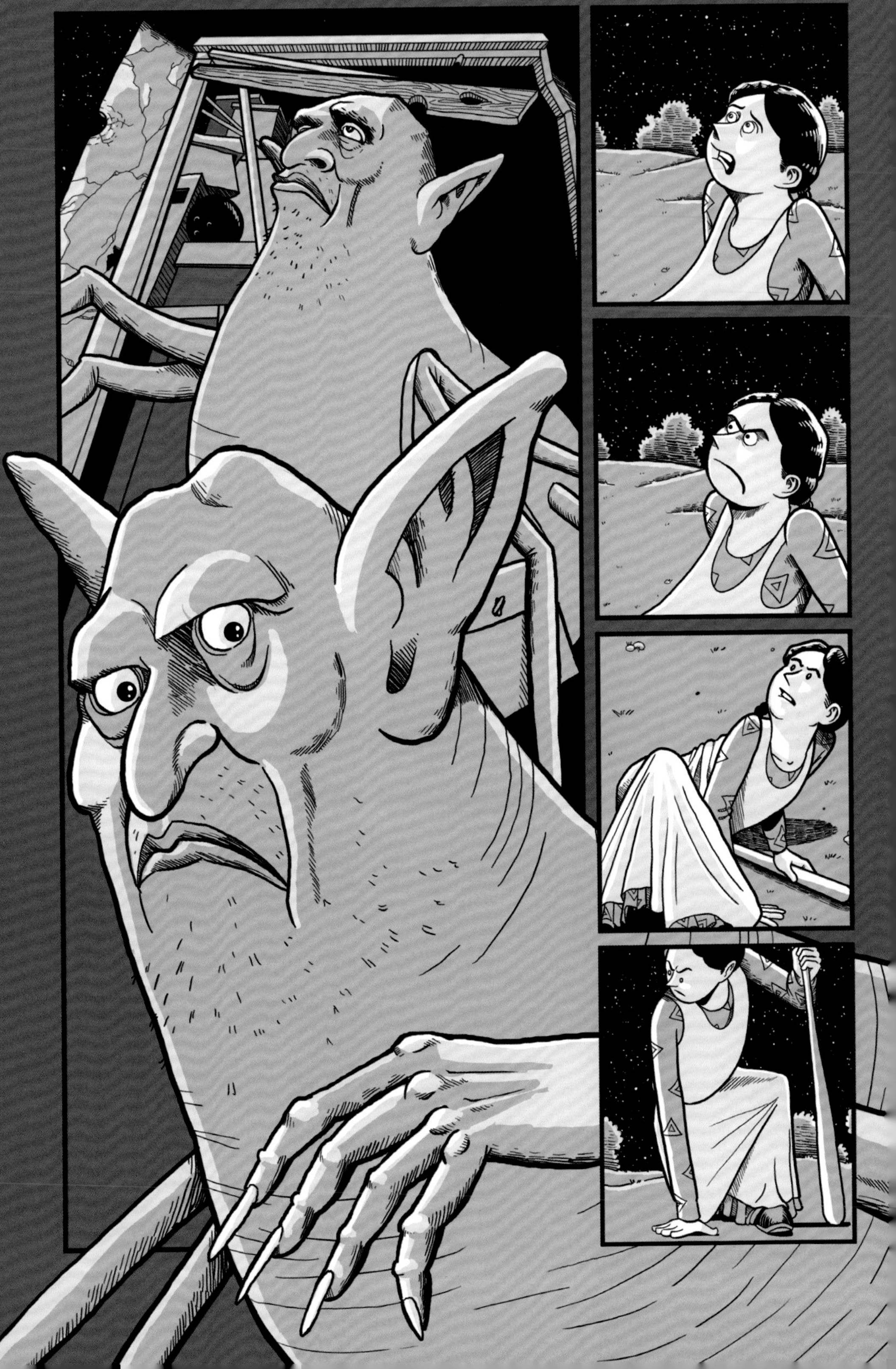

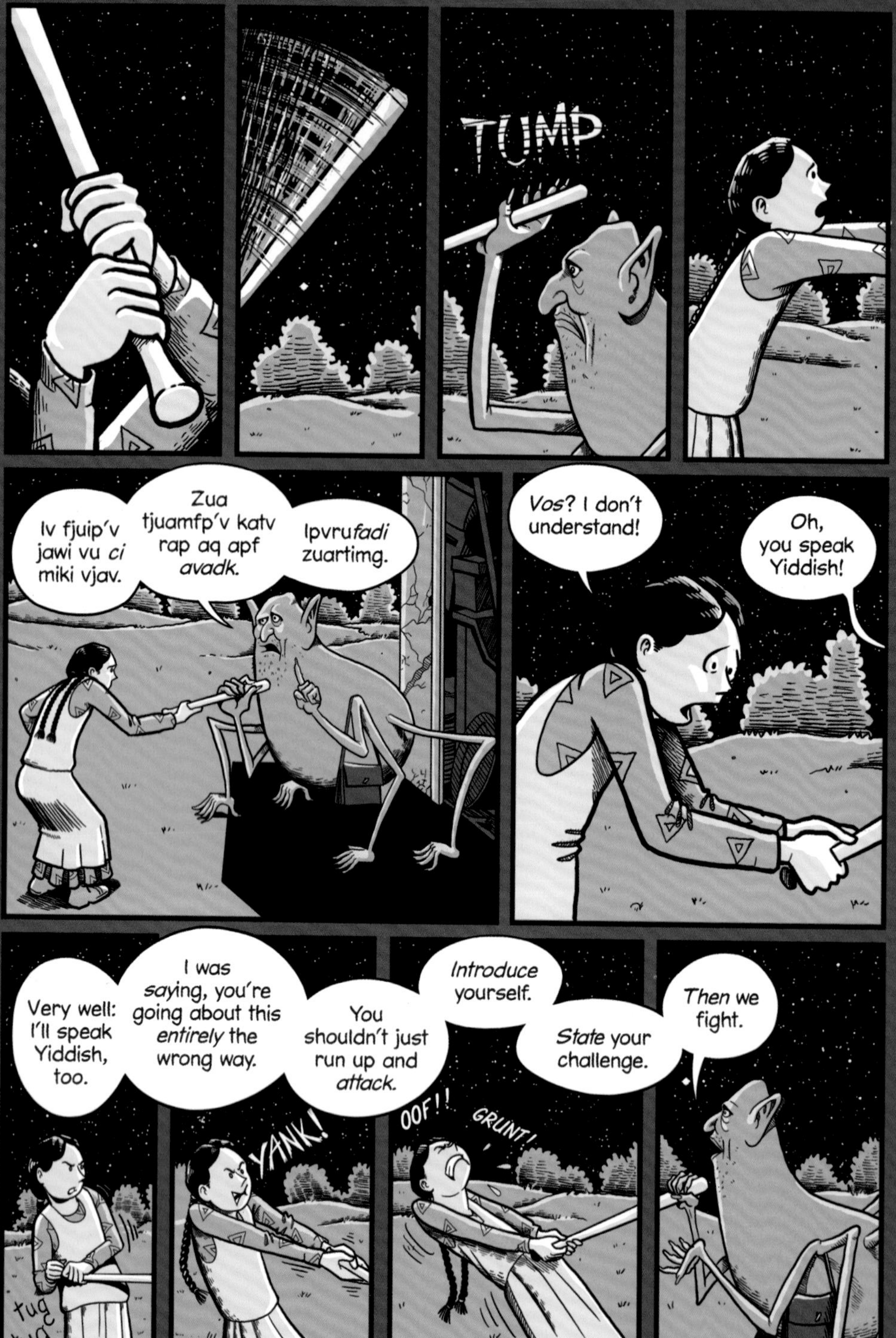
TUMP
Iv fjuip'v jawi vu *ci* miki vjav.
Zua tjuamfp'v katv rap aq apf *avadk*.
Ipvru*fadi* zuartimg.
Vos? I don't understand!
Oh, you speak Yiddish!
Very well: I'll speak Yiddish, too.
I was *saying*, you're going about this *entirely* the wrong way.
tug tug
YANK!
You shouldn't just run up and *attack*.
OOF!!
GRUNT!
Introduce yourself.
State your challenge.
Then we fight.

Vos: what

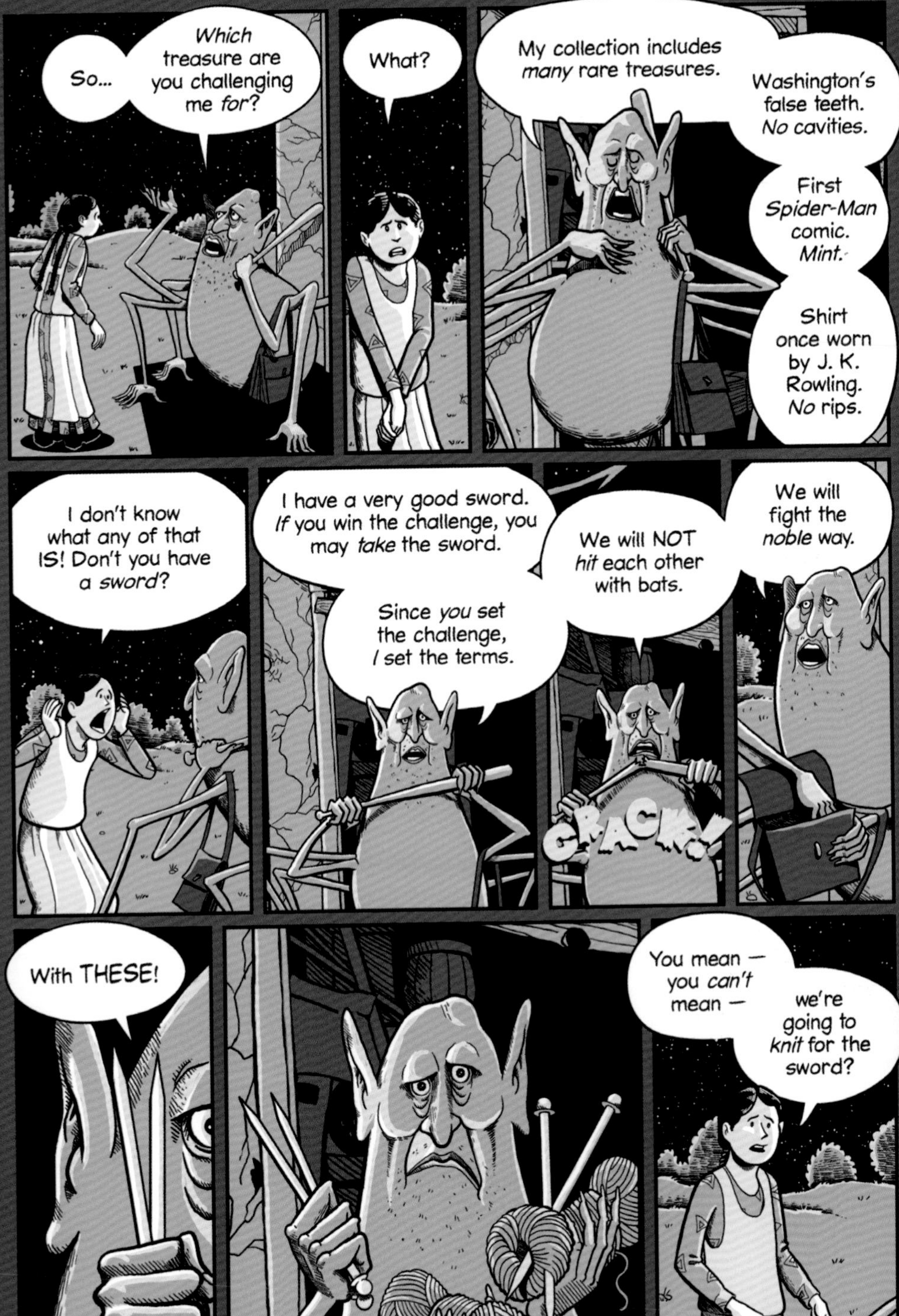
So...
Which treasure are you challenging me *for*?
What?
My collection includes *many* rare treasures.
Washington's false teeth. *No* cavities.
First *Spider-Man* comic. *Mint.*
Shirt once worn by J. K. Rowling. *No* rips.
I don't know what any of that IS! Don't you have a *sword*?
I have a very good sword. *If* you win the challenge, you may *take* the sword.
Since *you* set the challenge, *I* set the terms.
We will NOT *hit* each other with bats.
CRACK!
We will fight the *noble* way.
With THESE!
You mean — you *can't* mean —
we're going to *knit* for the sword?

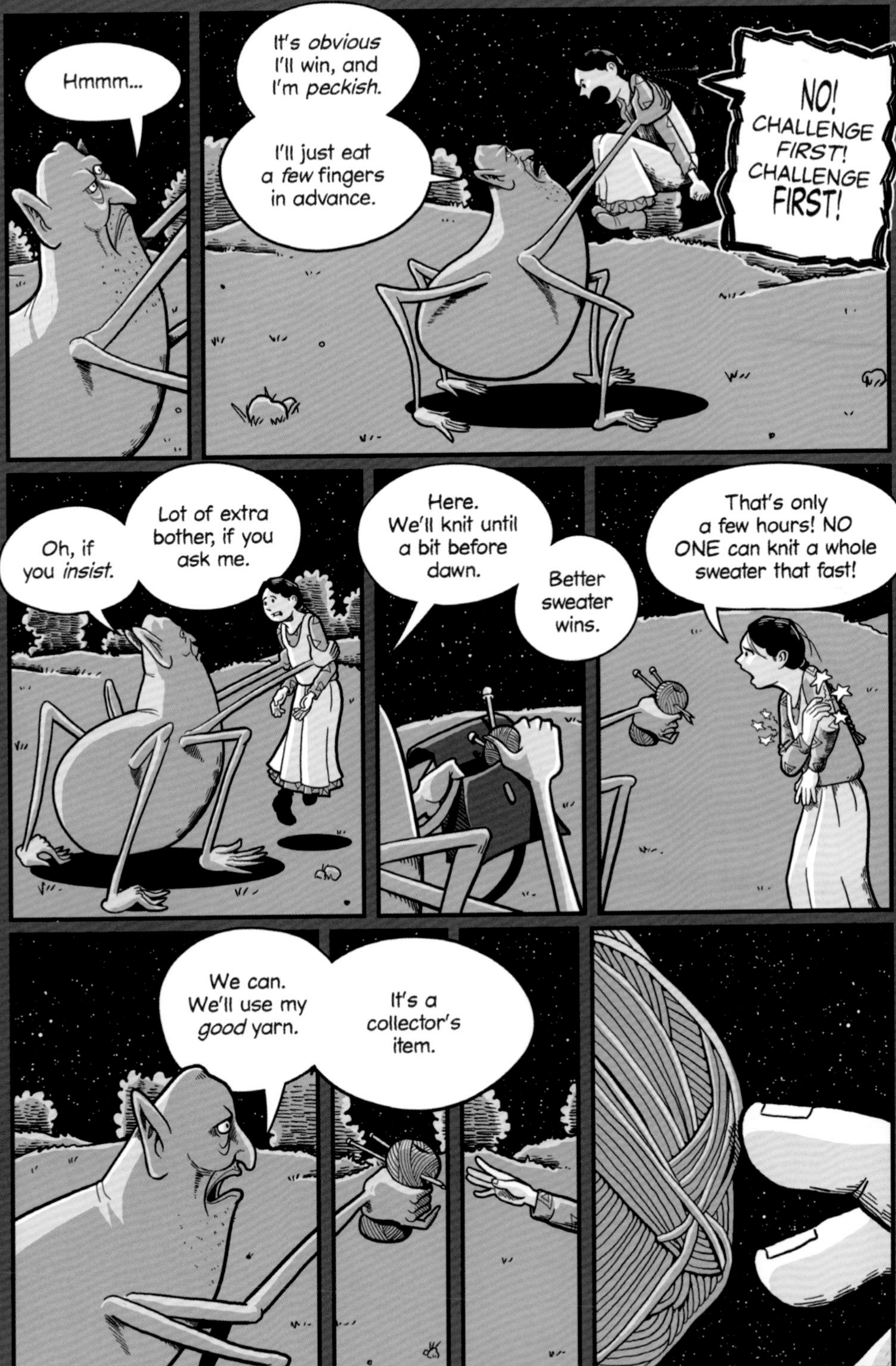

Hmmm...
It's *obvious* I'll win, and I'm *peckish.*
I'll just eat a *few* fingers in advance.
NO! CHALLENGE *FIRST!* CHALLENGE FIRST!
Oh, if you *insist.*
Lot of extra bother, if you ask me.
Here. We'll knit until a bit before dawn.
Better sweater wins.
That's only a few hours! NO ONE can knit a whole sweater that fast!
We can. We'll use my *good* yarn.
It's a collector's item.

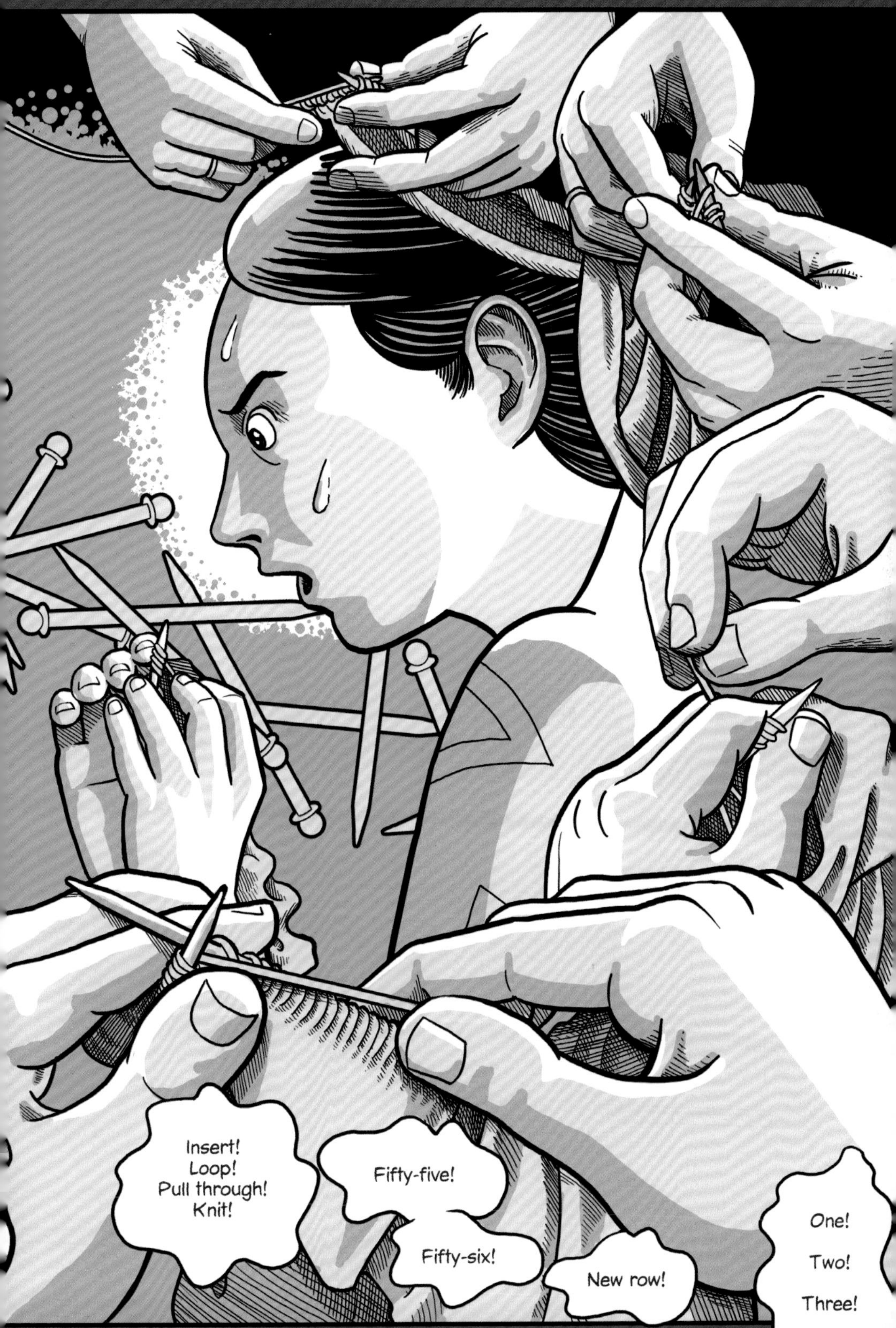
Insert!
Loop!
Pull through!
Knit!
Fifty-five!
Fifty-six!
New row!
One!
Two!
Three!

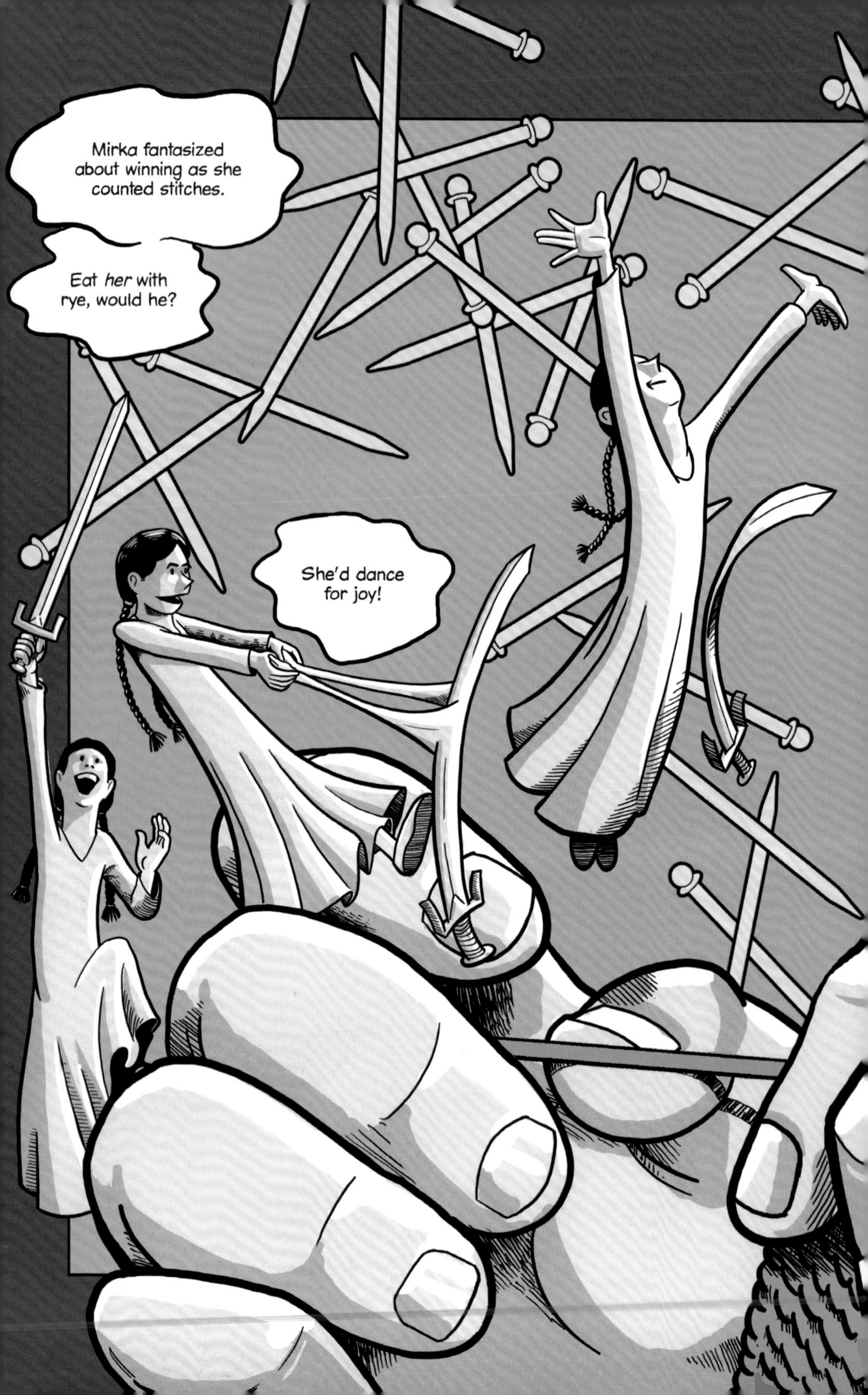
Mirka fantasized about winning as she counted stitches.
Eat *her* with rye, would he?
She'd dance for joy!

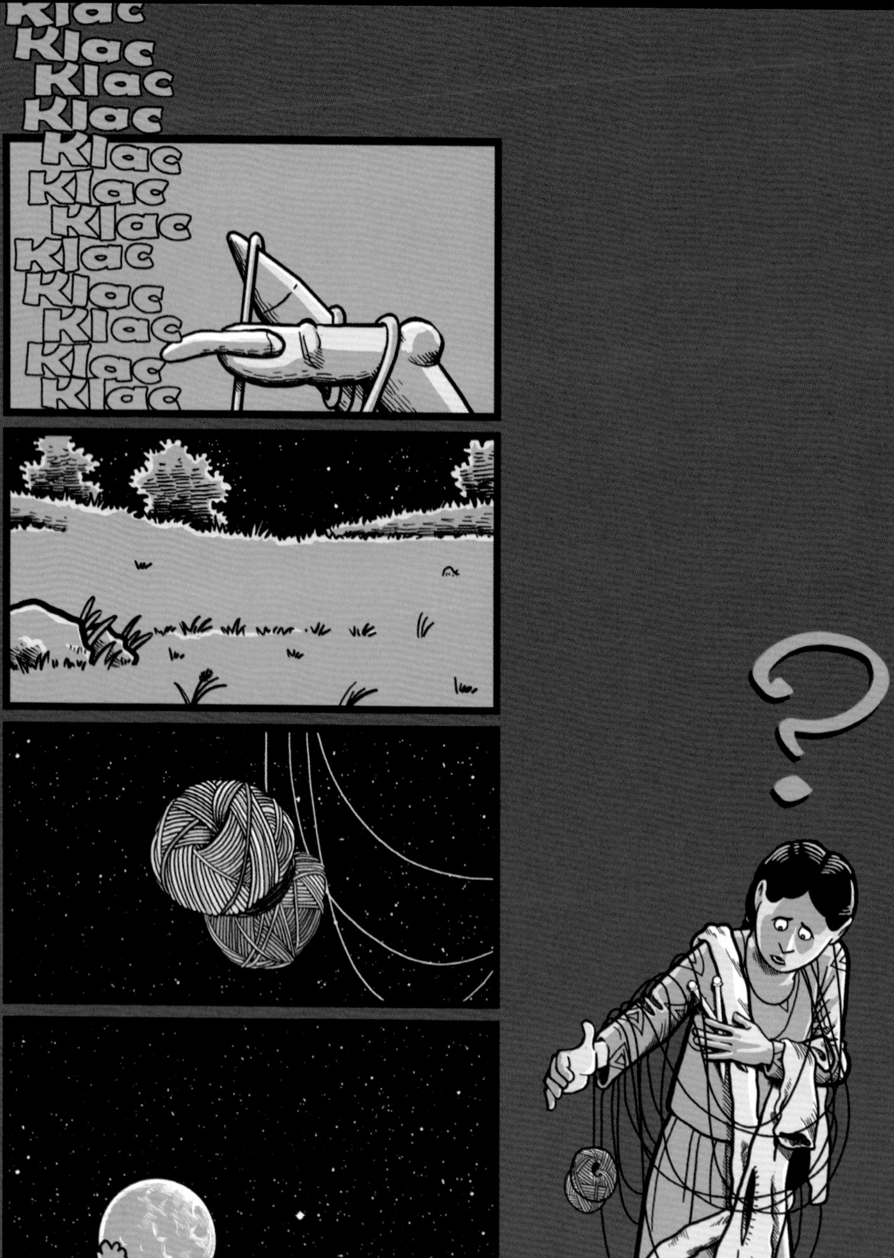
Klac
Klac
Klac
Klac
Klac
Klac
Klac
Klac
Klac
Klac
Klac
Klac

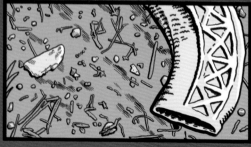

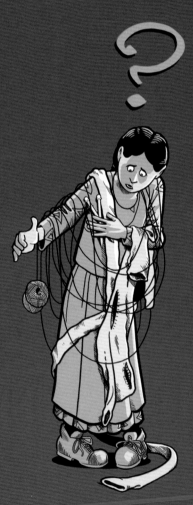

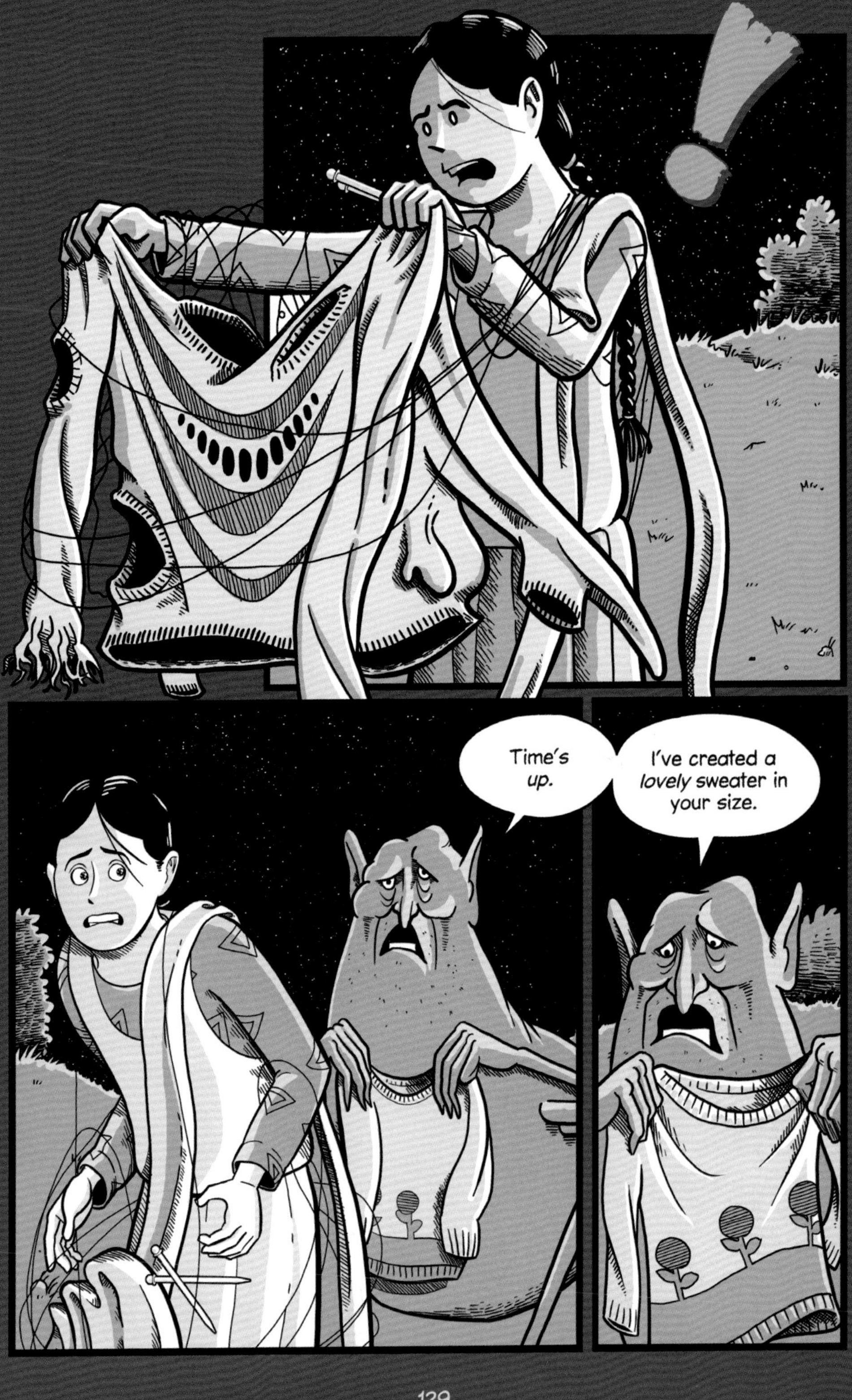
Time's up.
I've created a *lovely* sweater in your size.

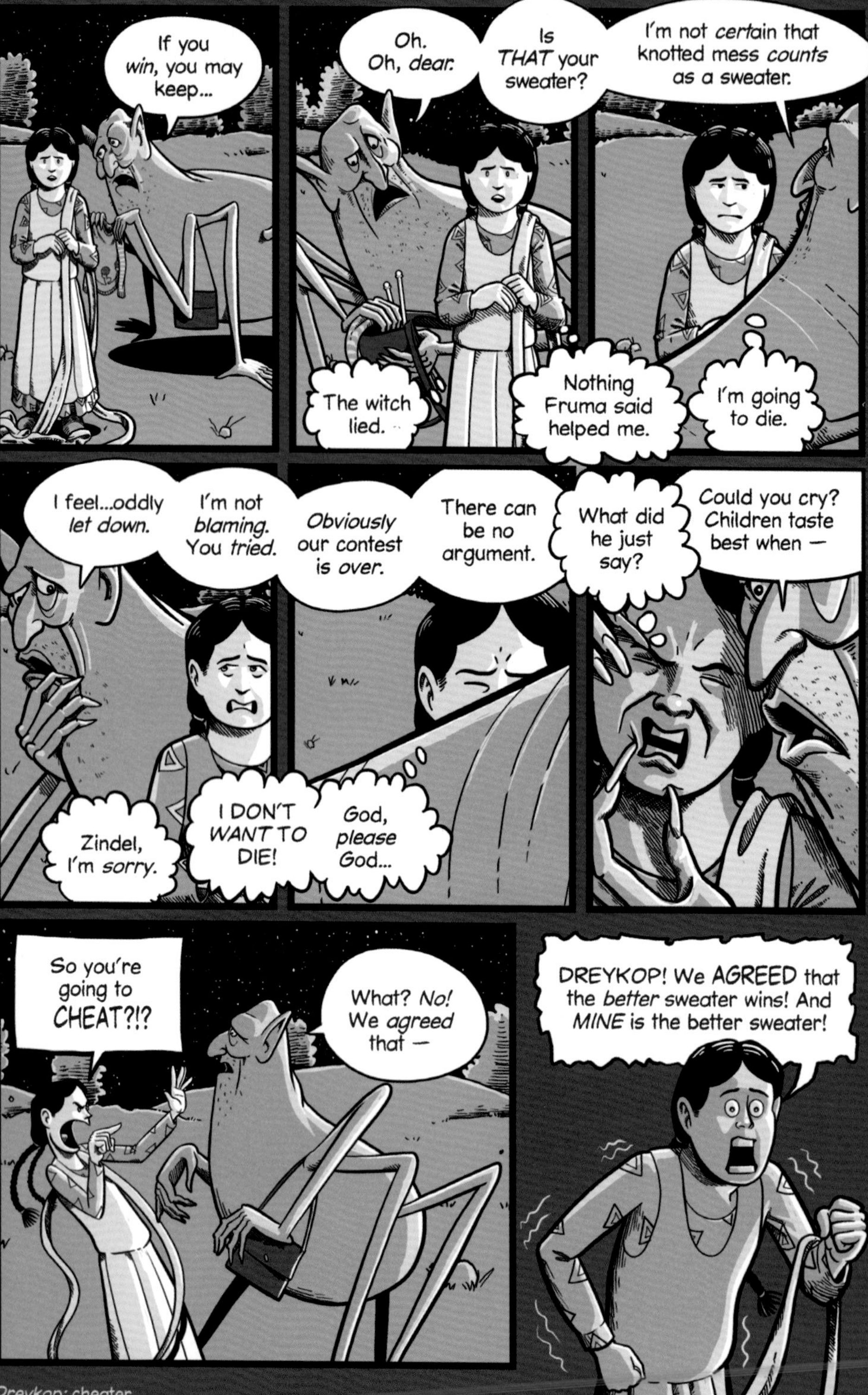
If you win, you may keep...
Oh. Oh, dear.
Is THAT your sweater?
I'm not certain that knotted mess counts as a sweater.
The witch lied.
Nothing Fruma said helped me.
I'm going to die.
I feel...oddly let down.
I'm not blaming. You tried.
Zindel, I'm sorry.
I DON'T WANT TO DIE!
Obviously our contest is over.
There can be no argument.
God, please God...
What did he just say?
Could you cry? Children taste best when —
So you're going to CHEAT?!?
What? No! We agreed that —
DREYKOP! We AGREED that the better sweater wins! And MINE is the better sweater!

Dreykop: cheater

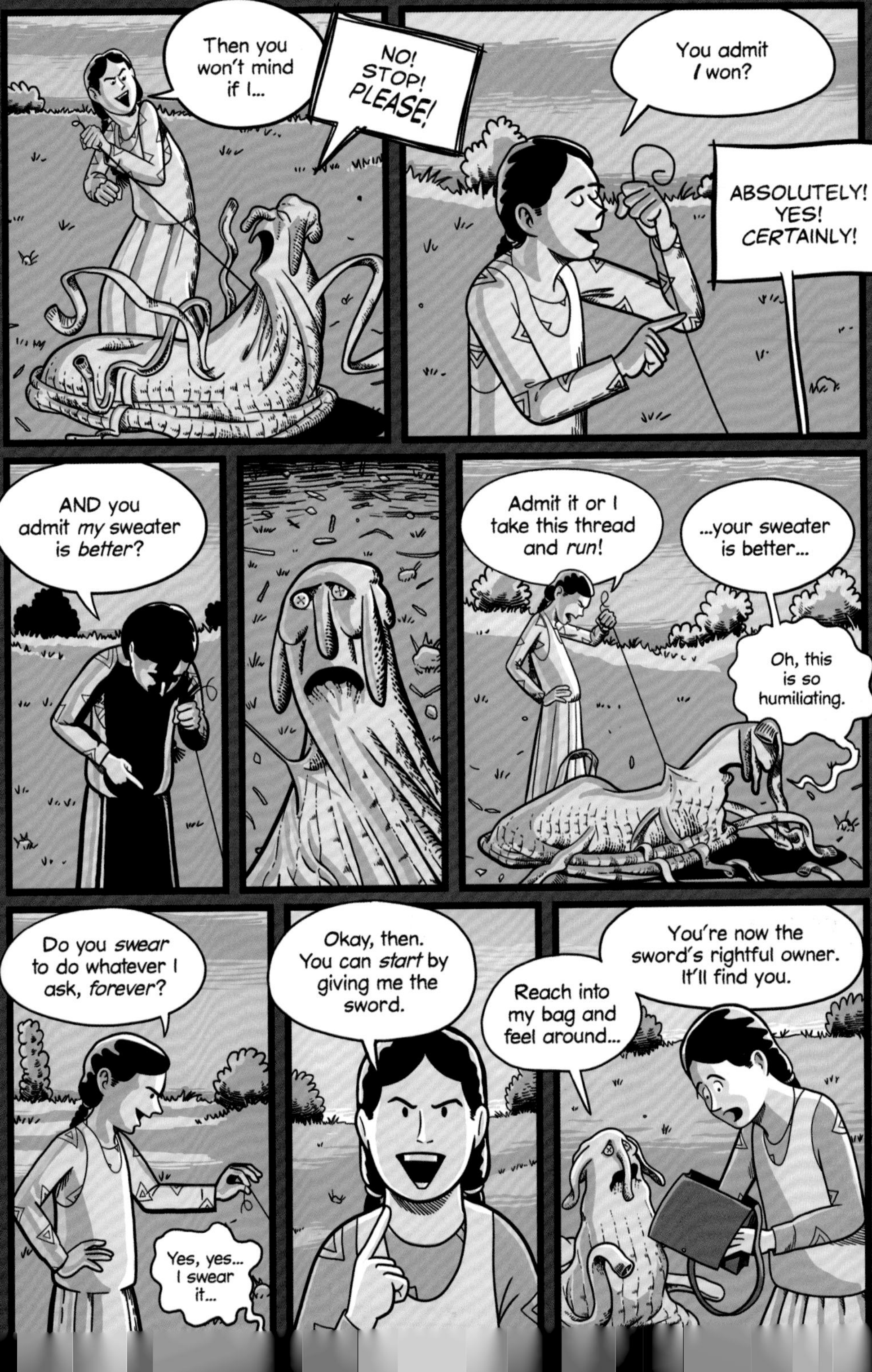
Then you won't mind if I...
NO! STOP! PLEASE!
You admit I won?
ABSOLUTELY! YES! CERTAINLY!
AND you admit my sweater is better?
Admit it or I take this thread and run!
...your sweater is better...
Oh, this is so humiliating.
Do you swear to do whatever I ask, forever?
Yes, yes... I swear it...
Okay, then. You can start by giving me the sword.
Reach into my bag and feel around...
You're now the sword's rightful owner. It'll find you.

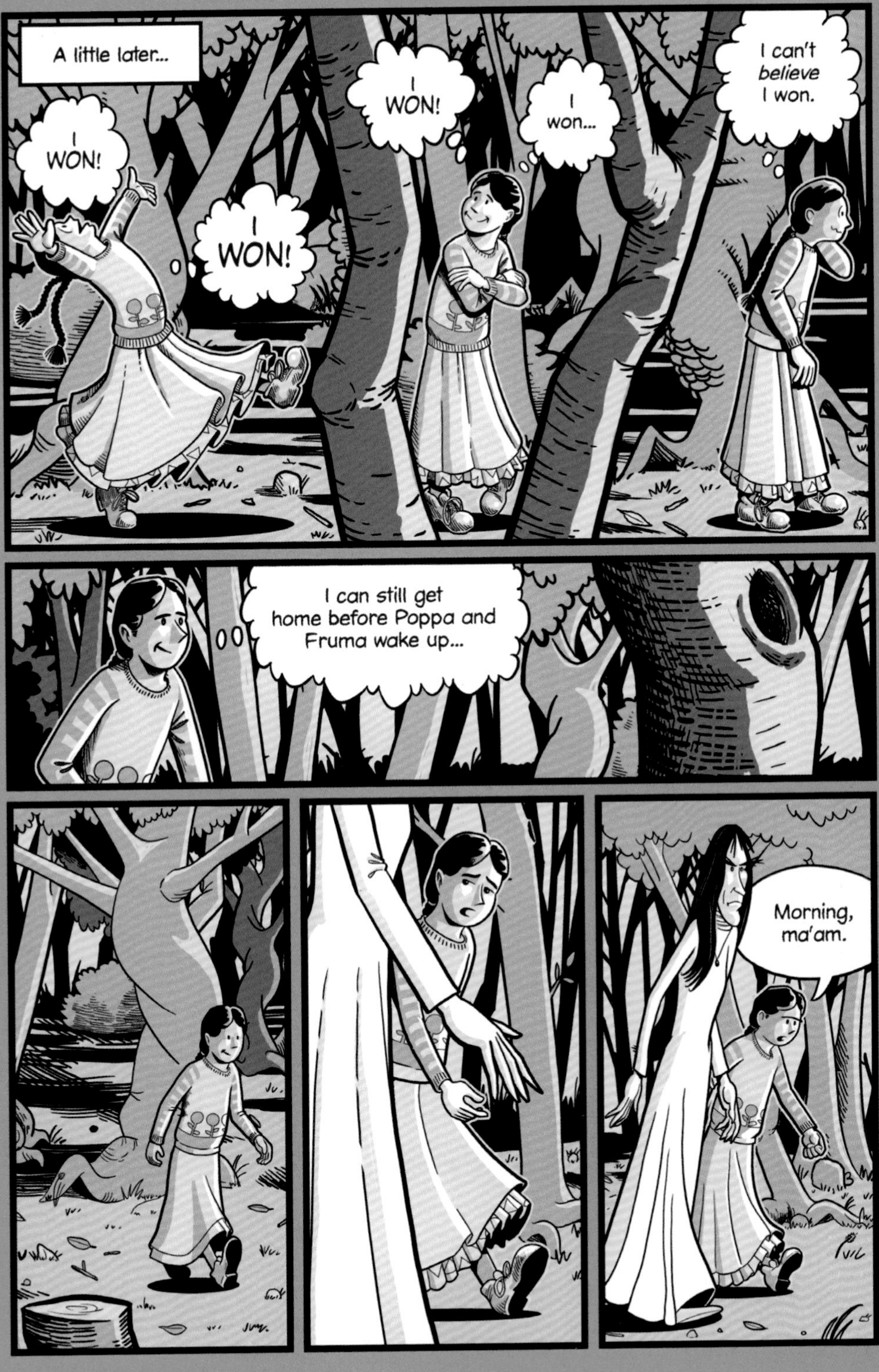
A little later...
I WON!
I WON!
I WON!
I won...
I can't *believe* I won.
I can still get home before Poppa and Fruma wake up...
Morning, ma'am.

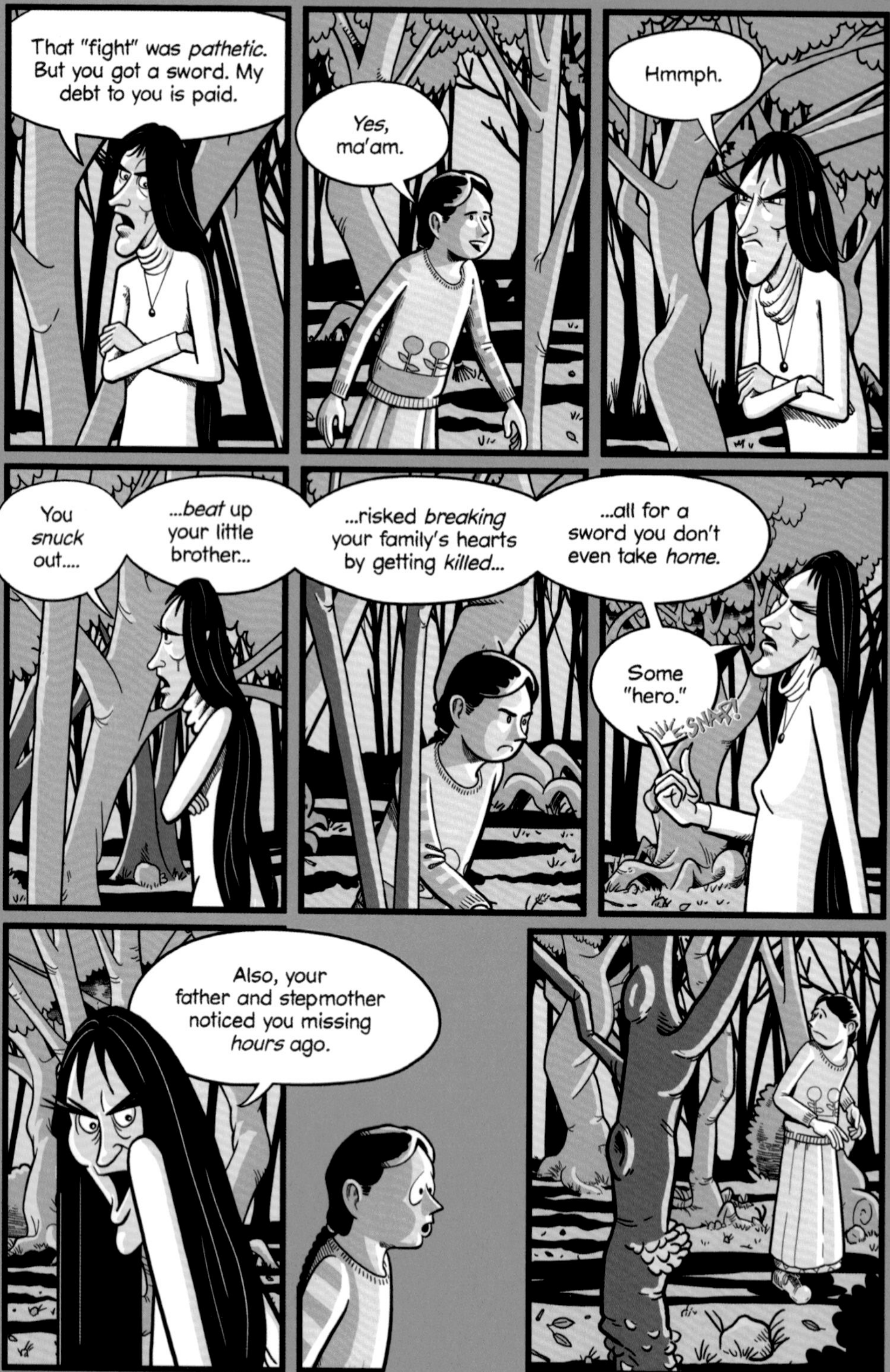
That "fight" was *pathetic.* But you got a sword. My debt to you is paid.
Yes, ma'am.
Hmmph.
You *snuck* out....
...*beat* up your little brother...
...risked *breaking* your family's hearts by getting *killed*...
...all for a sword you don't even take *home.*
Some "hero."
SNAP!
Also, your father and stepmother noticed you missing *hours* ago.

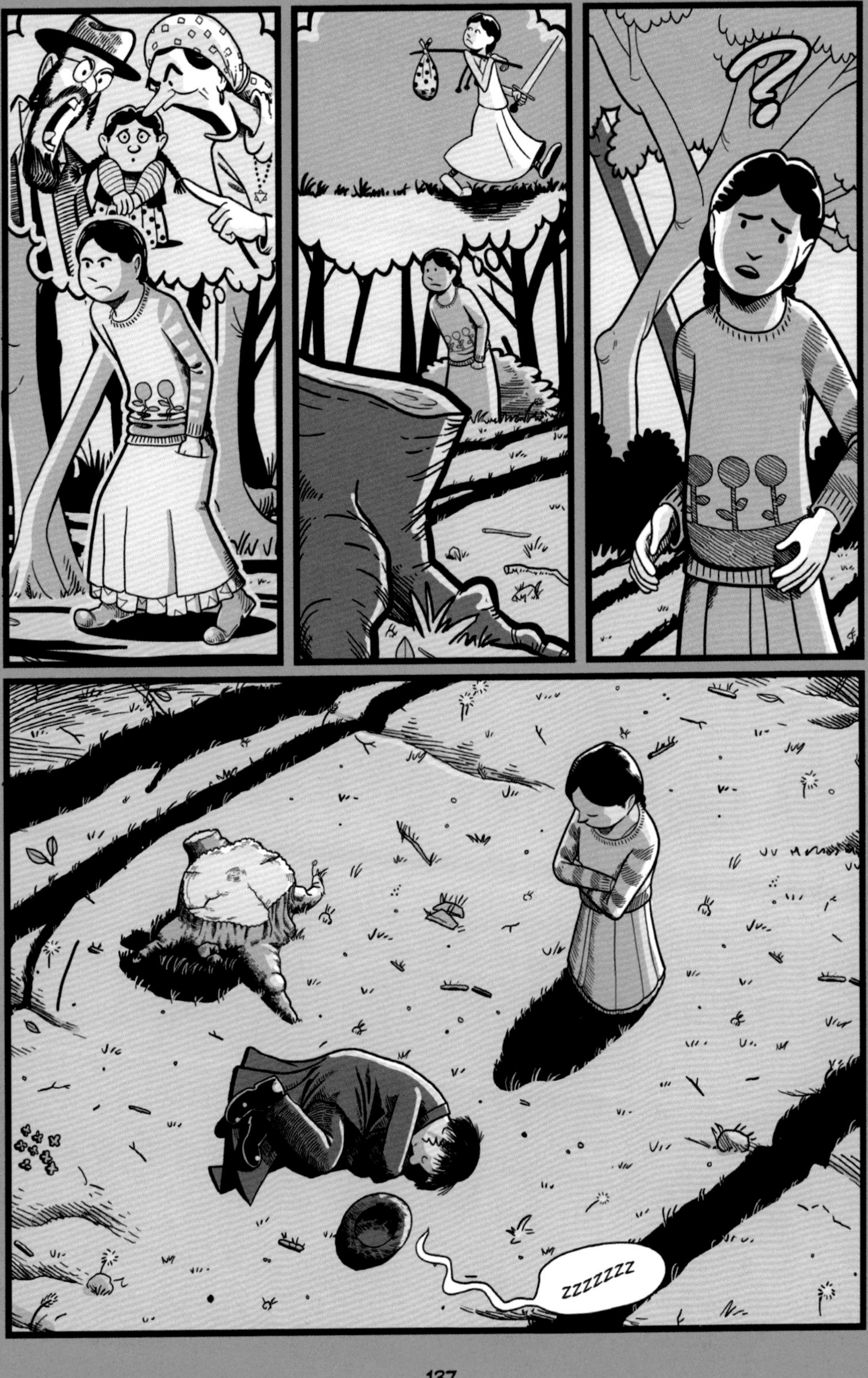
ZZZZZZZ

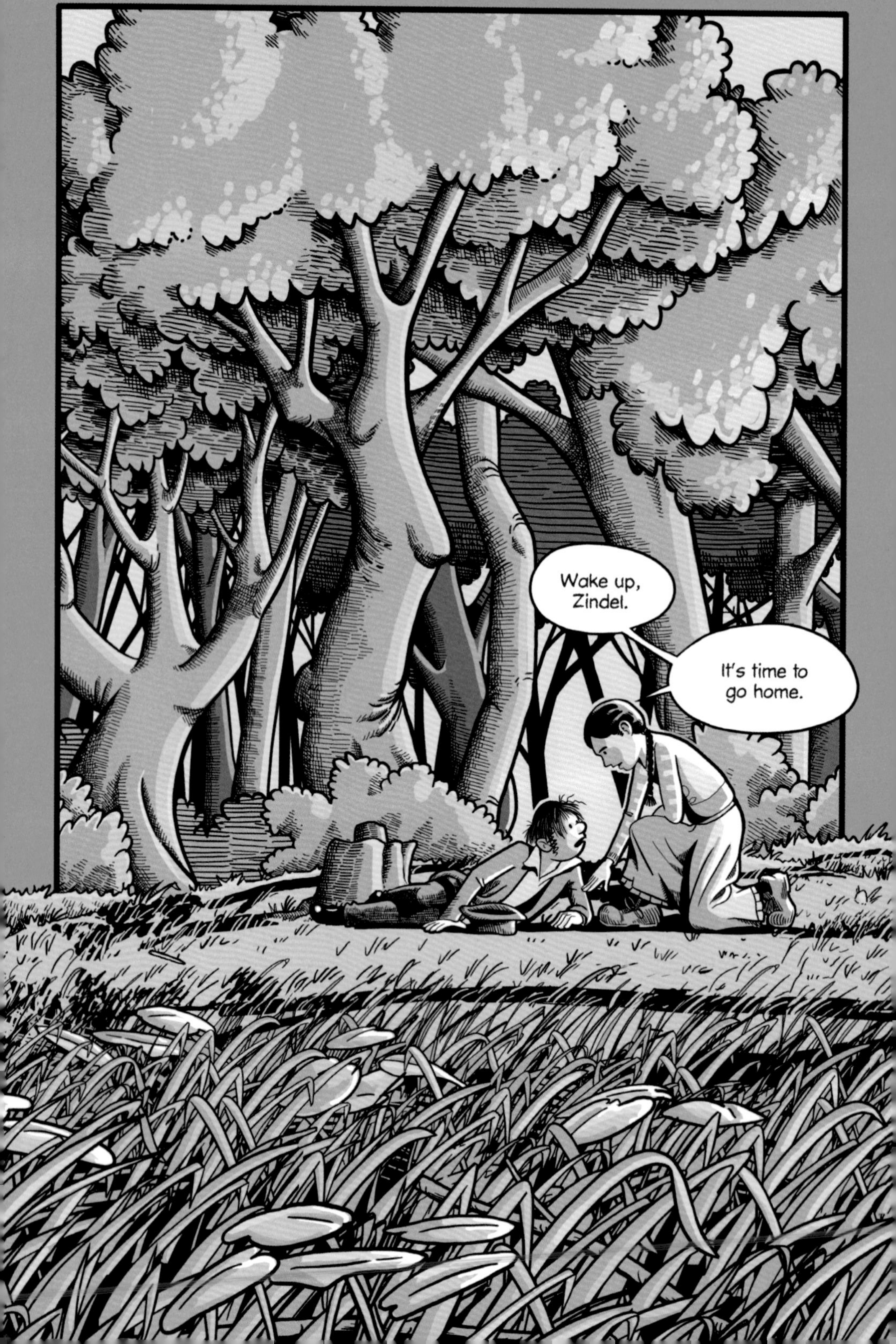
Wake up, Zindel.
It's time to go home.

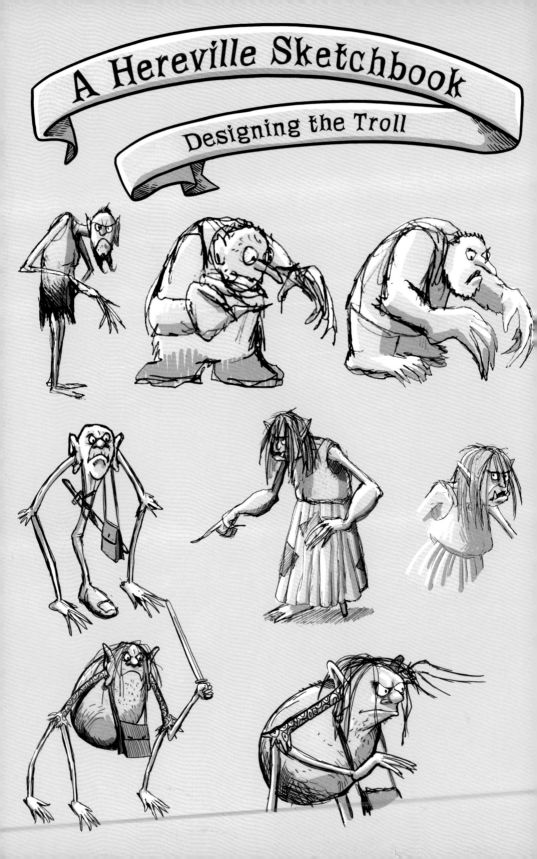

A Hereville Sketchbook

Designing the Troll

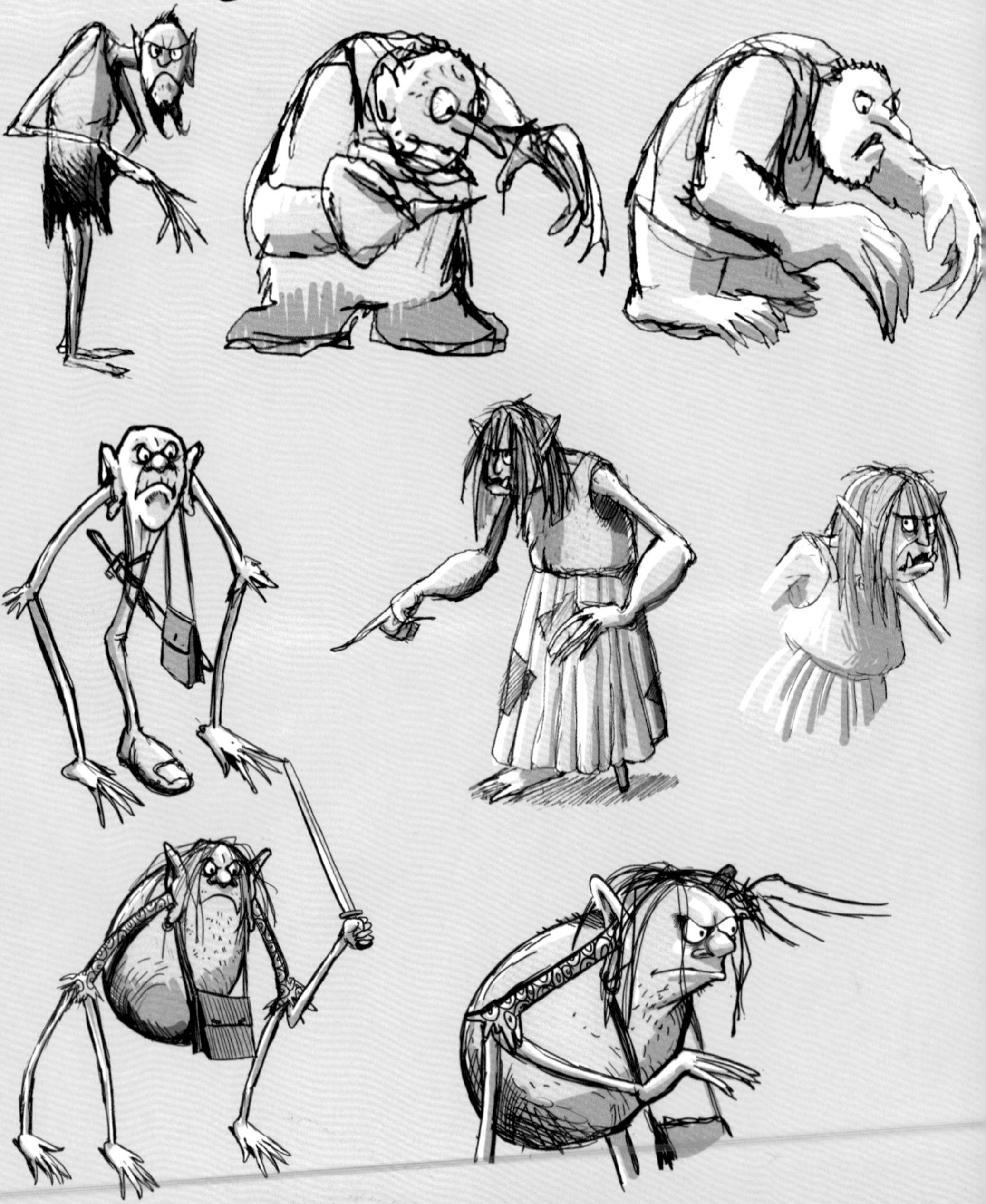

Before I could start drawing *Hereville*, I had to create my characters, which meant thinking about who they are, what they do, and most important, what they look like. That last step meant a lot of drawing and redrawing until a character finally looked "right" to my eyes. Check out these sketches of the troll to see how the process works. For more on how *Hereville* was created, visit me at www.hereville.com.

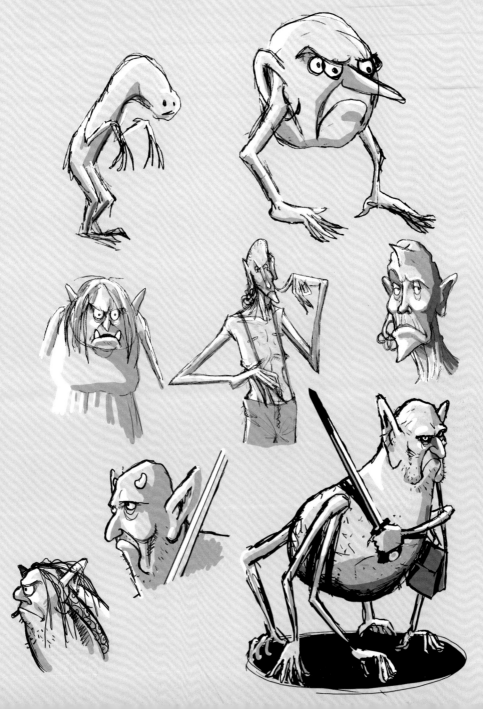

ACKNOWLEDGMENTS

A *sheynem dank* (thank you very much) to Jake Richmond for amazing colors, advice, and calm; Rachel Swirsky, whose contributions are immeasurable; my wonderful agent Judith Hansen; Sheila Keenan, Chad W. Beckerman, Charles Kochman, and the entire Abrams crew; Kim Baker, Toby and Larry Deutsch, Jenn Frederick, Sarah Kahn, Jenn Manley Lee, Kip Manley, Ivy and Scott McCloud, Dylan Meconis, Kevin Moore, Matt Schlotte, and Charles Seaton; girlamatic.com; The Old Church Society; Slate Technologies; and the many more who have helped *Hereville* along the way.

ABOUT THE AUTHOR

Barry Deutsch won the 2010 Sydney Taylor Award and was nominated for Eisner, Harvey, Ignatz, and Nebula awards that year. In 2008, he was nominated for Comic-Con's Russ Manning Award for Promising Newcomer. He lives in Portland, Oregon.

PUBLISHER'S NOTE

Library of Congress Control Number: 2010924236

ISBN (hardcover): 978-0-8109-8422-6
ISBN (paperback): 978-1-4197-0619-6

Printed and bound in China
10 9 8 7 6 5 4 3

ABRAMS
THE ART OF BOOKS SINCE 1949
115 West 18th Street
New York, NY 10011
www.abramsbooks.com